STONE REVIVAL

Peggy Dover

BY PEGGY DOVER

For Alan--He loved well, kept us laughing,
and never refused blueberry pie.

You took the last train home. Meet us at the station, brother.

Prologue

June 12, 1945
Dalemain House—British Intelligence,
Special Operations headquarters
Penrith, UK
Major Edward Bettencourt on staff

Mavis Cartwright sat at a desk going over final paperwork. Upon war's end, she'd returned home to Penrith following a three-year stint decrypting German codes at Bletchley Park. She plans to report for the Diplomatic Service after a brief respite. Because of her fluency in German and high level of success with code breaking, she's working briefly with authorities in a British Army office at Dalemain House, temporary headquarters for Special Operations. Officer in command, Major Bettencourt, has intercepted a strange series of wire messages sent from nearby Rakefoot Station to Peel, a seaside village on Isle of Man.

"Mrs. Cartwright, have a look. Ever see anything like this?"

"It's Miss, Major."

"Oh. My mistake."

Mavis reads the usual information about train times, loads, and destinations, until a line appears with strange letter formations.

"Could be a machine glitch, I suppose," the major suggests.

"Huh." Mavis stares at the odd configuration. "Wait a minute. This looks familiar. John and Axel."

"Oh, yes? Who?"

"Yes. But not at Bletchley. It was a long time back, at school. They were chaps I attended classes with, John Stone and Axel Biggs. John and I dated for a time. The two of them were always competing with one another and cutting up. When studying the life of Julius Caesar, we learned about a cipher used for military messages. John and Axel got it in their heads to make up a modified code of their own using the same type but added memorized words spelled differently using a specific number of the same letter repeated. The rest of us were forever trying to figure it out and got fed up. Never did, but I recall these as the same repeated letter formations." Mavis took another look. "But why? Whatever could it mean?"

Major Bettencourt clipped the end off of a fresh cigar. "I'm not sure. Axel Biggs is the stationmaster at Rakefoot. He oversees the teletype among his other duties."

"Wonder where John Stone is these days?" Mavis said, thinking back. "He was a handsome boy, smart too."

"I don't know the whereabouts of Mr. Stone. But in light of these odd messages and what you just told me, I think we best do a bit of digging. And, Miss Cartwright, let's do keep this to ourselves, right?"

-1-

GLORY

Two months back they said war was over; yet I sat there, shell-shocked on our green kitchen chair. The chair was one of a set John's mum had freshened up nearly twenty-five years ago. The table and six had come with him, along with two leghorn hens, one rooster and a Guernsey cow. I'd married a man with a dowry and counted it a good thing.

Collins, the young assistant from Rakefoot Station, had left the telegram and run off before I could ask questions. 'Dear Mrs. John R. Stone,' it began. Someone I didn't know from the British War Office regretted to inform me that John was dead. My husband had been on his way home to a party and the girls and me.

It was odd, but I couldn't move to save the celebration cake. Now, smoke delivered sweet news gone wrong out my window. *Such waste.* I wondered should I bake another, in case.

The day christened with the letters VE had officially ended six years of chaos and bloodshed, for the time being. We'd done our part, though some of us still waited. Tucked away in the northwest reaches of England, we'd felt some safer than folks in larger cities, especially coastal towns. But recently, a scudder lying snugged in weeds next Knowley's barn exploded, sending the barn and Knowley's bullock splinter over hoof and tines from his baler through Bronson and Aggie Halls' bedroom window. They had been asleep, but did live to tell about the racket many times over.

It would be a time before we trusted our legs under us. No one could determine how long this might take, even though the confident Mr. Churchill had commanded Britannia to, 'Advance!'

The hollyhocks were mockers looking in on me. Reliable companions through years of cooking and washing up—now their carnival nodding and bobbing felt rude and out of place, like a merry-go-round in a war zone. In fact, everything turned ugly and of no account. The momentum of our homecoming fest had thrown me full tilt into casualty like the trains at Cockermouth that time; there was no chance to brace for impact.

Reggie worked for a normal response, barking and raking my legs, and Jingles, our Springer, trotted room to room. Poor dog was looking for the girls to help.

"Mum?" The screen door banged. Claire was home. "Is there fire? Smoke's pouring out the window!" She found the source and turned off the Aga. Claire used a couple dish towels to heave out the smoldering char, pans and all. I watched as she began to air the house. She grabbed a paper from the table and waved it, conjuring apparitions.

I sat. Claire's voice became faint, and the walls went fuzzy from the outside in.

ꞷ

I woke to ringing ears and the cool comfort of our soil stretched under me, with Claire and blue sky overhead. I had no strength. The smoke smell from my shirtwaist drew the horror fresh to mind and made me sick.

"What happened?" Claire asked, smoothing my hair. "The dogs were going crackers. Should I ring up Doctor Farnaham?" Claire knelt and placed her hand under my head. I had her attention. After a day in the field, she smelled of sweat and lavender talc, but she didn't know what to do for me. I felt as though my blood had turned to lead. Pushing against a powerful weakness, I rested on my elbow.

"We don't need Doc. I'll be all right presently. How did you drag me so far from the house?" I looked toward the door.

"It's only a few meters. Can you stand?"

"I think so." Claire gave me her arm, helping me up and we returned as victims to the familiar. It had been such a promising afternoon in our corner of battered England. How I wanted to rewind the day and have the promise back.

Smoke refused to be rushed, causing mayhem throughout the cottage like a sprite. Claire lifted a couple more windows and joined me on the edge of our divan, where she engaged me like I was the child.

"Now what is it? What's wrong?" she pressed.

"Not sure why I didn't save that silly cake. I'm..."

My eyes rested on the August 1945 copy of *Veterinary Record*. I told her, "Claire, there's no good way to tell you. This telegram came. It says your dad is dead." I held it out to her as if I needed proof. She took it, and I watched her face go pale as the words found their target. It was my habit to try and soften life's disappointments for our girls. Trouble was, pain sneaked under doors and around through cracks. It found its way in, and like smoke, you couldn't rush it.

"I don't know details. They could be wrong. Wartime, they could mix up soldiers' identities in the confusion." I tried to believe it.

Claire and I cried and held to one another, avoiding eyes. She would have questions and so did I.

❧

Claire moved to her room as the phone rang. I wasn't up to condolence calls. Do you thank people for being sorry your husband's dead? The ringing persisted. Since John reported for Army duty, our phone had continued to ring for his services on occasion, since he was the only veterinarian available in our surrounds. But I'd given Barbara, our operator at station, instructions to check first before putting a call through. *It could be Syd.*

"Stone's." My voice sounded husky and unfamiliar.

"Dear God, Glory." My Christian name was Gloria but I answered to Glory in Rakefoot Crossing. "It's Axel. I can't tell you how devastated I was when the news came over wire about John. I don't know what to say I'm just…so sorry." Axel Biggs' voice was consoling as our old family friend and Rakefoot station master. "I realize the news is fresh just now, but I felt it my duty to make sure you and the girls were all right, I mean, as far as that may be possible."

I heard steam releasing in frantic gasps. A train had stopped. I gave a try at polite conversation.

"Thank you, Biggs. Claire knows. I haven't told Sydney. She's staying the night at a chum's." I hesitated. "When did the news come? The telegram didn't say what happened, and I'm having trouble letting this sink in." I found the chair.

"Of course you are. It's a shock to us all. Are you sure you're up to details?"

"No, but can't stomach the wondering."

"I took the report from Carlisle Station early this morning. According to authorities, there were no eyewitnesses so they pieced together a scenario based on what was there when they…when he was discovered. John was changing trains for the final leg of his journey home. They found a burlap bag of mongrel pups lying next to him just off tracks. Are you with me, Glory?"

Carlisle. "Yes, go on."

"They think some rotter was trying to dispose of them. John must have seen their movement. It would be like John to try and save the little whelps, wouldn't it now? He evidently tried laying the bag clear of a coal train backing up but his foot wedged in the rails. There was no possible way the engineer could have seen him." Through the receiver, the train shrieked two short blasts. The conductor called the final all-aboard. "Glory?"

I worked to process the information but, something didn't sit right. John might try to rescue pups if he saw them. His foot wedged.

"His foot?" I asked, wondering if it was his right or his left.

"You know it happens, Glory, from time to time."

"But, why would he be coming from Carlisle?" I asked.

"I don't know but with all the troop trains running full bore, he likely thought it quicker to take a less traveled line. Maybe. I can't know for sure."

"Do they need me to identify him?" My insides reacted and I shook.

"No, Glory dear. His mustering out papers were legible. You could see the body, but, I would strongly recommend against it. Remember him, rather, as he was. Don't you think that's what John would want?" I heard Biggs try to speak low to someone there.

The subject had never come up. Cold shakes came in waves. "I best let you get on with your work."

Surely, Axel felt the loss. He and John had gone through school together. They were close friends and competitors in class offices and athletics, even going so far as devising a secret cipher known only to them for private communication. They'd taken out a couple of the same girls, in fact there was a time when Axel made clear his interest in me. We double dated briefly with John and a girl named Mavis something. But John was a finer dancer, and the clear choice overall. I set my cap for him, and he won me.

"What can I do?" Biggs asked. "Would you want me to make

arrangements? I'm acquainted with the necessaries since my mother's death last autumn." I became aware of my breathing. John's funeral, not the homecoming we planned.

"Yes. I don't know where to start." I cried deeply without making a sound—so grateful he was willing. "We had a little money put by. No insurance." A country vet didn't make enough for extras.

"There, there. We'll worry about that later. Biggs is a step ahead of you. Try to get some rest and leave everything to me. I'll talk with you soon."

I rang off, ragged after hearing particulars. He seemed to be taking the news rather in stride. I'm not sure where we'd have been without friends like Biggs.

✑

As painful as telling Claire had been, facing Syd, our twelve-year-old, was a greater dread. She was Sydney with an 's' after John's favorite uncle. Since the time she burst three balloons in a dart game at county fair, and her pop said 'Good on ye, Syd,' Syd she was and no mistake.

She was a small, female model of John. Everyone knew of their common bond with animals and that one day she would work official-like with her pop in his veterinary practice. She'd already been up to her shoulder in a cow's backside, Syd had.

I was relieved she was at Gillian's for weekend. It gave me a chance to put off the telling and decide the best way. I thought it might be better for Claire to break this news. I would wait and approach Claire with the idea tomorrow after she'd had a little more time to come to grips.

Suppertime came with no takers but I went through the motions. Momentum. Bangers and eggs were available. Their aroma mixed with that of burnt cake; but the evening breezes came up and made quick work of earlier tailings. A shame they didn't blow the nightmare out with the stench.

❧

Next evening when Claire returned from Land Army work, I followed her into the small room she shared with her sister.

"You look tired, come sit." I patted the quilt John's mother had pieced from scraps of his family history.

"I'm completely whacked. My back feels near to breaking after bagging potatoes all day. I shouldn't have gone, but thought it would be easier to work. Mindless motion just makes more time for dwelling on trouble. Syd home? Does she know?" Claire stretched and grimaced.

I massaged the small of her back and took a chance. "Not yet but she should be soon. She's got to be told straight off." I looked round their neatly divided space, not a girly room, really. "You and Syd—you share a special bond, right. I've been thinking it might be easier if you broke the news to her, instead of me." I didn't have long to wait.

"Easier for who? You?" She was off the bed and heading for the door. "No. It's not my job to tell Syd." She grabbed a jar of cold cream off their dresser and slammed it back.

I began to cry again and Claire returned to the bed. Her callused hand felt rough on my arm. "You're our mum. News like that has to come from you." Claire declared it, and I knew no tears would follow to weaken her position.

There would be no tears from Claire and no argument from me. I'd given up wrangling with her after John reported for duty four years hence. At fifteen, she'd stood like a ruling monarch in her ways. At times, John could work diplomatic magic with her, but it wasn't my gift.

"Never mind. I was wrong to ask." I stared out the window. "I'll tell her when she comes. But I'm not convinced." I moved back to the kitchen and the chair. "No, sir." The snakes in my stomach roused as I rehearsed the conversation with our Syd girl.

"I'm sorry, Mum. No good pretending," Claire said. She pushed her door almost closed. "I'm going to try for a lie-down. No sleep last night."

As I waited for our little one, I imagined John—Chicory, as I called him when I felt the flirt, striding up from rounds. The spice of his arrival preceded him from a fresh slice of Old English in his pipe. Sometimes he'd poke his silly head up among the flowers and give me a fright. He knew I'd be getting his supper. He knew I was useless without him.

- 2 -

GLORY

Our home was small and tidy — we fit it comfortably. The four of us had been content. With one missing, nothing worked the same. Memories abiding in the leftover spaces brought me low.

As I looked on the once familiar garden, Syd came into view. She and her best chum had occupied recent days making "Victory" cards and decorations for a gathering that would not happen. I opened the door, held the screen for Syd, and I smiled.

"Hi, Mum! Look at all the streamers we made. Gillian's mum even stopped her preserving and joined in; she was so excited for us. Claire home? I want her to help hang these. Won't be long now, will it?" Syd sang the words and held out the party box. Her eyes shone like the sun's reflection off Blea Tarn. It had been a long time since I'd seen that life in her. I'd rather have been the one dead. I kept the smile on as I removed the box from Syd's arms and placed it on the kitchen table. I took hold of our child's paint-stained hands, held her to me and cried silently against her shoulder. Her soft curls smelled of hay and peach preserves.

"What's wrong?" Syd asked. Claire cried softly behind the door. "Mum?"

"Let's walk, Lamb." With my arm around her compact shoulders, we walked outside and braved that summer afternoon. We sat on the bench under the rose trellis. Syd only needed to look into my swollen eyes.

"Pop's not coming home, is he?" She turned and stared at the stone path leading to the barn.

"No, darling. They say he's not coming home." I needed to hold her and feel her warm skin, but Syd was elsewhere. "It was a train accident. Pop supposedly rescued a bag of pups some monster was trying to destroy." My tears returned with a will.

"Oh." Syd looked at the walk. "Where are they?"

"What?" I reached for the useless handkerchief in my pocket.

"Where are the puppies?"

"Well, I don't know. I didn't think to ask. Biggs might know."

"Yes, do ask. They're our responsibility after all." Syd loved animals like John did.

I'd survived the retelling and Syd took the news in stout fashion. She walked to the barn, her refuge in times of trouble and celebratory chamber on good days. All days fell into one of two categories now she was twelve. I thought to leave her alone. She was an independent child.

☙

I rose early, preferring it to lying awake with a great, long day of grief staring back. I moved like the tide, going in and coming out from one room to next—washing up, cooking, staring out windows. Always in motion. With opportunity for work exhausted, I often walked.

Rain and buckets of it was the price we paid for the green glory of a Lakeland summer. The ancient landscape mated rugged strength with beauty in the wind-scoured pikes and transient forces. Battlements of old stood patient though disrespected at times beneath progress and pavement. How we had loved our corner of England. Rakefoot was a ten-minute stop on the short line between Penrith and Workington. Visitors came if the sun showed up, and their return reminded me that our village was charming. Lakes surrounded us as well as phantom tarns to the brim with salmon and trout. Forces appeared and swelled during heavy rains. In summer, flowers poked from walls and crannies, working a sampler over the town. But beyond the obvious lay reverence—a rich history of battles fought and won that acted on folks like a magnet. The landscape wore a painted but honorable face to hide the scars as a politeness.

The wireless blared away and served to drown what mutinous thoughts broke through. Invariably there was news about demobilization, a long word for packing up a war. It didn't help when the number one song from the States drifted over the waves; it was a silly tune with nonsensical words called *Chickery-Chick*; different from chicory, the herb we used to stretch our precious coffee. Since chicory was my love-name for John, the song reminded me that John was now everywhere.

Friends claimed our love was like sugar and salt—sugar to draw out good humors and salt to preserve our good looks. Maybe they were right. John had me by six inches with wavy, black hair like Ronald Colman and regal forehead. His deep eyes confessed a passion for life and for me. His smile was either heaven or a worrisome thing, as John could be full of the devil certain times. His companion pipe sticking forth made it the worse for smirking. One was rarely without the other; the smile and the smoking bowl worked in tandem.

John sometimes compared my eyes to the color of lichen on pike stones. A scant neck, stone or two of extra flesh and a slight overbite were my personal discouragements. The latter came from sucking my thumb well into childhood, the former I shared with

Aunt Nancy, a rollicksome aunty with whom I endured the short-coming. I'd no one but myself to blame for the spare fat, except maybe John. I ate most when I was happy. I'd kept the fullish figure John had declared in mixed company was 'not too thin and not too thick, but curved in all the right places for dancing and squeezing.' John would always be the best looking man I've known because I knew him well.

The stain of the first war reappeared. John narrowly missed the call because of his age at the onset. Somewhere between Germany trying to starve us out and the Yanks joining the fray, we fell in love. Four years after, John completed his schooling in Edinburgh and we wed. All we wanted was to show off for one another, to make love under a tree somewhere—anywhere. Nothing else mattered, until Claire made us three. Our love was sustenance between two wars. The first had threatened happiness; the second annihilated it. One thing I hated to admit, war was a persistent adversary.

At forty-eight and a family man, John was safe from conscription in this war. But we were all expected to lend a hand some way. The War Department requested his veterinary services in looking after horses and mules in the collieries, since younger vets were off killing the hateful Nazis. His response was predictable. John didn't consider staying on home front sacrificial enough. But he and another vet who practiced in the Yorkshire Dales had disregarded their territorial differences, gotten together over a pint, or several, at Brakeman's Tabby, and agreed to serve for the animals' sake. *To the beasts and to England!* I could hear their mugs clatter.

I wondered yet why John had boarded at Carlisle to the north of us when his last known assignment was Liverpool. I offered this and other questions to Claire but she had little patience with what she'd termed my "denial." I'd have to get a copy of the official report from someone.

Shared loss is a damnable way to discover the truth about

those you love. Then the ordeal of a funeral—having to endure others' good intentions with polite responses.

The service would be closed-casket.

ॐ

Monday afternoons found me on my knees near St. Kentigern's Cross, outside Crosthwaite Church. I'd stopped attending services years before. It was lonely in the pew without John's fine voice next me. Now, pungent moss bearding the stone walls and wind through an oak met my soul. I suppose you could say that's where I worshipped. Maybe I could call it that. Any road, it was peaceful.

A thumping of ladders against the old kirk, and two workers in animated discussion about Knowley's blockbuster surprise chipped at my thoughts that day. They tried to reinforce the stained glass windows as a few cracked with the vibration. The windows fared better than Knowley's bull. Crosthwaite didn't have the coppers to fix them proper right off, and professionals in glass repair would likely have no lack of work in years to come, but the parishioners hoped to buy time with wood veneer and tape.

My devotion was directed towards flowers of all persuasions, but especially old roses. Those at Crosthwaite found me puttering among their bushes by the walkway and in cemetery. Chaste whites and rich reds grew as descendants of the generation that championed our wedding day. John and I walked that aisle in finery nearly twenty-five years ago. Our roses would serve again when John marked this aisle without me.

Standing with care and gathering my gardener's tools in a bucket, I braced my back with grubby hands, stooped to sniff of a fragrant crimson fellow and pierced my finger. With my eyes closed to the blood, and taking in that blessed perfume, I was but twenty and waltzing in white satin. Enduring through tomorrow would be nigh to impossible. And when we sang John's favorite hymn, *Be Thou My Vision*, as we must, I would fix my eyes on the roses.

'Be Thou my breast-plate, my sword for the fight;

Be Thou my armor, and be Thou my might.

Thou my soul's shelter, and Thou my high tower;

Raise Thou me Heavenward, O power of my power.'

❧

For a few days, neighbors brought food and sympathy in casserole dishes and wrapped in brown paper. I spent more time deciding which dishes remained edible than I did eating. I never doubted the sincerity that brought them but during it all, I was alone. I wondered about so many things, like if the Army would ship John's personal articles to me or to station. His veterinarian satchel had his initials in gold above the clasp. Syd would want that.

Claire worked and returned to her room. Everything I said sounded forced because it was. Soon, her job with Land Army would end. They had released most young women involved with this mass work force already. These game lasses had worked the farms like the men they'd replaced. I worried what Claire would do since there was no money for university. She'd likely end up leaving us for the big city like others her age. Nothing and no one to hold her here. How lonely it would be not to have Claire to bake and talk with. I couldn't think on it for long.

Syd was more distant than usual, spending all her spare time with critters. I was there but no one noticed, consumed, as they were with their own thoughts—young too.

Late summer rains came and soaked the gardens and fells that held our village. It soaked inhabitants too, and washed up returning soldiers to decorated homes and tables dressed with the good linen and Dundee cake. I battled hateful thoughts that won out more than not since I gave them their head.

16

I couldn't attend the festivities. Reasonable people understood, but not Eunice Quimby. She and her husband, Roger, were decorating for a nephew who was to arrive the following week. Eunice felt that it was in my best interest to rouse myself and come over for some 'cheer and company, something to divert your brooding ways' was how Eunice had insisted on it.

The Stones and Quimbys had been neighbors ten years. The two of them didn't get out much, but stayed home working jigsaw puzzles in their front room. These were on permanent display in various stages atop a card table splotched with beer and pockmarked by fags left smoldering. Bowls of crisps and piled plates of toffee candy were on hand as reward for each fit. Roger and Eunice grew larger annually, but especially him.

I knew too well that Eunice would go all out for this rare gathering with friends and family and would not take no for an answer, but I dreaded it and sincerely hoped I would fall ill the day it arrived. Not too ill, mind. Just some meek germ. In her exuberance, she failed to notice that her party fell on 15 August.

- 3 -

GLORY

The day that would have been our silver anniversary, V-J Day, and Eunice's party all collided. Bombs with storybook names—Little Boy and Fat Man—made a horrific end of Japan's bold assault on the Yanks. They were the first nuclear bombs ever dropped and I hope the last from daily accounts coming over the wireless. Celebrations throughout Europe and the States would rouse again. The Quimby home was one humble example.

Eunice's enthusiasm jumped out and snatched us in at the Quimby's front stoop. "Welcome, Glory love! Now we can all say good riddance to this bloody war once for all." She gathered me to her bosom. "And Claire, so glad you decided to join us, you poor little thing." Eunice Quimby dropped her jaw, resembling a basset hound. "Enter and join the festivities. Getting out the house, you know, being among people, that'll be just what the doctor ordered for you both. By the by, where's Syd?" Not waiting for an answer, she moved off. "Here's a little sparkplug to get you started." She dipped yellow punch from a crystal bowl she'd inherited from her mum.

Claire pinched my arm. I'd convinced her to join me against her wishes, a rare feat. With most of the guests pushing fifty, I was sure she'd have chosen potato bagging. Eunice shoved the drink into my hand, spilling a little on her sequined slipper. Then she directed us by our elbows into the middle of the room toward a young man in uniform—central grape in a cluster of welcomers.

"Meet my nephew, Albert Rand, just back from RAF. He was in some sort of Special Forces or something. You must let him tell you all about it." Eunice broke a smile that sent her eyes inside black crescents as she gave tooth to the introduction. Sometimes those forthright incisors still held me fast until I caught myself.

"Hello, Albert. So pleased you made it back safely." I offered my hand, slightly self-conscious. My memory of John was so strong I wondered if others saw him.

"Thank you, Mrs. Stone." Albert cleared his throat. "I'm sorry about Mr. Stone."

Evidently, they could. "Yes." The evening belonged to Albert, not me. I took a drink of whatever was in the glass and tried to indulge how John and I might have celebrated the day, and night. Perhaps a dinner at Chesterfield's at the start, and then a stretch of the legs to water's edge and a dip in the altogether.

"Nice to meet you, Miss Stone." He was all politeness as he took Claire's hand and lingered half a tick long.

"Welcome home, Albert. And no Miss Stone nonsense, just Claire."

Her eyes picked up where their hands left off. Claire no longer appeared bored, but he bore a close watch.

"You remind me of someone. In the movies, I think. I'll have it, yes, Ingrid Bergman, the Swedish actress; you're the double of her." I expected him to ask for her autograph next. Claire laughed because she'd heard it before. It was true and she milked it.

"How did you like me in *For Whom the Bell Tolls?* Coop and I became such friends."

Her accent was practiced and subtle enough to be provocative. This foreign flirtation was all the encouragement a lovesick soldier needed. I'd never seen her behave like that. The obvious chemistry made my insides squirm.

"Maybe you'd like to go over your lines with me tomorrow night." He pressed in, glancing at me. "Like over a cold…a, hot Darjeeling and biscuits at the station?"

Sounded safe enough even if he didn't drink a proper tea. Still, the way he eyed her…I wanted to take Claire's arm and break the spell but my intention could backfire. I escaped rather to memories of former gatherings John and I had enjoyed.

We knew practically everyone in the village. There were a few visiting relatives from Workington. Eunice's brother, Finlay, still worked as a clerk in the iron and steel factory there and returned each night to his orange tabby, Rufus. He served as record keeper in "A" Company of the Local Defense Volunteers. I fancied Finlay could have been an attractive man, but for his awkwardness. He reminded me of a marionette in a sort of a constant motion, always at the ready to please.

Axel Biggs was there. It was good he was out again as well. I'd heard he hadn't been to many functions since his mother died October last. They'd been close. When her health began to fail, and just before his wife, Trudy left, she'd come to live with them.

He'd recently visited us with paperwork and details for the funeral all laid out. He insisted on paying for a fine hardwood coffin with polished brass fittings and white sateen lining. He ordered it through a company in Cockermouth and had it delivered to Carlisle. The War Department must have supplied the Union flag. It was striking against mahogany.

Biggs had served as the village Air Raid Patrol. But for years prior to that, he'd been a sort of capable older brother to us all.

He'd divorced or so we assumed, when Trudy remained away, and had never remarried. Other women apparently held no attraction.

Claire was certain he did look at "skirts," as she said it, when he thought he was undetected. She told me he was subtle about the business, using one-way glass in his office in station. Her accusations were appalling. I'd reminded her of the danger of an overactive imagination and that she should show respect to a man who'd done so much for his community. Claire was an observer, but often unduly critical.

Biggs nodded and smiled at me from across the room, lifting a glass of port. I returned the smile if not the gesture. He kept looking so I decided to walk about the house.

The Quimby abode was little changed without the jigsaw focal point. The freckled faces of the Quimby children smiled from frames askew on the walls. There were four offspring, each represented in order from cradle through secondary school. All had moved off and pursued lives elsewhere.

"Roger, would you please get off tha' bum and put a song on the player." This was no mere request from his loving spouse.

"Yes, Euny." He roused his overstuffed blue serge and lumbered to the record cabinet. "What would you want to hear?" Roger's voice was like air making slow release from a balloon.

"Oh, something patriotic to make us cry. And don't be sticking none a tha' bagpipe noise on. Last time I had to hear that droning I got an awful pain in my head." Eunice shot Roger her familiar *I'm only just putting up with you* look then shook her wobbling pile of yam-colored hair.

The dulcet voice of Vera Lynn began to "Bless 'Em All" from the Victrola in the corner.

I was ready to conjure my own headache as an excuse to leave early, when I noticed Roger's subtle but promising sway. I'd shared the privilege of being present twice before when Roger felt rompish, and if this was to be one of those, it was worth the wait and discomfort of eating Eunice's beetroot and courgette salad. Roger's seat was vacant so I sat among its worn cabbage roses.

Along with the side-to-side movement, a mischievous smile appeared on his rather nice lips. Say what you will of Roger Quimby, he had Cary Grant's mouth, though planted in a Captain Bligh face. With eyes downcast in a world of his own, the muse whispered his name. When he'd broken out at Brakeman's Tabby, John said he'd missed his calling, sure. Now the smile, the sway. Yes, it was forthcoming.

I watched as heads turned. Some present had seen or heard tell of this quirk in his nature. The knowing ones scooted back to give freedom of movement. Eunice groaned and I enjoyed watching my high strung friend. She resigned to moving vases and other breakables to the kitchen sideboard, but she didn't stop him, thank God. Likely she reckoned it as free entertainment.

Finlay manned the Victrola, assuring there would be no breaking the spell. We could all count on him for that. The drink Eunice had given me made its presence known and helped ward off anxiety, a recent cloud with the rest of the business. Not that any of it was gone, just floating invisible.

As the music reached a crescendo, I stood to witness Roger snatch up frail Mrs. Cavendish, the vicar's wife, and carry her off, a giggling princess down the hall and back, corsage bobbing as she went. It could have been anybody.

I was drowning in the memory of John's arms around me at the last dance we'd shared. It was for the dedication of a new music hall over Darrowby way. John was masterful on the floor.

After the dance—Roger's, and John's and mine, I wished I could rush home and continue the fantasy alone. I bowed to Roger, gesturing toward his throne where he fell, not to stir for the remainder of my time there, though an adoring audience plied him with conversation and black currant tarts.

Eunice began replacing ashtrays and clocks to their rightful positions and reassumed command now that the world had returned to normal. She'd grown fidgety since the kiddies had flown and with Roger having gone placid long ago, except for these infrequent departures. Her solution was to try on other people's lives like overcoats. Eunice ferreted out information and shared it over tea into any willing conduit. Sometimes I had no stomach for the offal, but listened for the same reasons Eunice clucked on, as a diversion from the ordinary, even though it was all quite ordinary only under a different roof.

I realized my situation had opened up new vistas of opportunity in her field. Eunice helped people. As best friend she felt it only right to invest most of her supposed wisdom and insight into helping me get on. Eunice called a meeting as she claimed my elbow rudder. I was looking for Claire to make an exit as Eunice made a pronouncement.

"Glory, love, I haven't had a moment to catch breath what with Roger's waggishness and seeing to the party. Let's hop the train tomorrow or next and visit the cinema at Penrith." Eunice wasn't asking. It was the plan. "I think tomorrow would be best. Sooner the better."

"Sounds lovely I admit; though I am a bit short these days. Not sure I should spend the one and nine. What little we'd put by is most gone. I don't know where we'd be without a garden, Greta's milk, and the pigs." Through the front room curtains, I saw gauzy images on the porch swing. Claire and Albert, too close.

I looked past the two in the direction of our beloved pikes as if they held buried treasure, enough for the girls and me to survive. I saw trails scoring the fells as dusk crept in blurring the lines. John and I had walked them with and without need for conversation, in good times and during a row. Endless summer afternoons had hosted picnics with boiled eggs, cheese and bacon biscuits, and homemade jam. John once told me he was only marrying me for my strawberry preserves. I smashed a fruit-laden biscuit in his mug, but he forced a sticky kiss on me in return.

After our food settled and talk faded, we rolled ourselves down haunches of warmed earth. Our revolving laughter sounded like someone monkeying with the volume on the wireless. Then we'd pick grass stubble off one another until desire won out. Two became one. Let no man put asunder. "Happy anniversary, Chicory," I whispered.

"Huh? Now that's just what I'm meaning to talk with you about." Eunice was talking to me as from a hole.

"I'm sorry, what?"

"We need a plan. You might not take a fancy to what I'm going to say, but it's for your good and all. I'll come by your place at 1:45 tomorrow, our treat. Now don't fret, love. After the pictures we'll have a nice cuppa tea, and I'll tell what's been brewing in my head."

It was more than tea and a movie, sure.

- 4 -

CLAIRE

"**I** saw Mum's face as we left. She'll be wondering what we're about." I looked toward the dusky horizon as a nightjar darted. Albert swiped twigs and leaves off a neglected porch swing that squawked when we tried it.

I hadn't been out with any boys, unless you counted poor Paul Beachum. Beach and I were solid chums, like girlfriends really. Now here sat Albert, a different species altogether from Paul, himself done up in shiny glory with a will to recklessness.

"What's she afraid of?" Albert asked. "You're a big girl, old enough to know what you want out of life; and it's more than poking the fire in the folks' cottage, I'll wager. Fine looking girl like you is bound to hook a permanent glance one of these days." Albert smiled a lot. He was good at it, and he'd drawn closer without my noticing.

I felt kittenish, like when I used to play it cute with Dad for a licorice sweet. Albert was a soldier, likely bound to some military code of conduct. Flirting came naturally, but I answered his question.

"She's needed me more since Dad left us. Syd's always off with her animals. I think Mum might be afraid of being alone."

"She's been without him for what, three or four years now?" Albert asked.

"Yeah. I guess it's different. She saw an end to it. I mean, men don't survive a whole war just to die twenty miles from home, do they?" I smoothed back a few loose hairs.

"What a rotten bit of luck." Albert looked uncomfortable.

"Her questions about Dad's death are becoming blasted irritating. I wish she and Syd would face that he's gone and move forward." Albert just nodded. I thought to change the subject.

Field work was miserable, but at least it had left me toned and brown. I wasn't a marshmallow, and I'd earned the pleasure of observing that fact. Albert sometimes glanced toward the house and the room full of guests who'd gathered in his name, but he was observing me, too. I'd seen that look before, only now it wasn't from a wrinkled, married farmer.

"Tell me about your special mission. Isn't that what Eunice called it?" I plucked at the buttons on my new dress. He looked at me as if I were a plum pudding about to slip away. "Or are you tired of telling your adventure?"

Albert straightened himself. "Are you sure you want to hear it? You're taking an awful chance you know. Once a soldier commences war talk, there may be no stopping him."

That smile. He was frightfully handsome with his pomaded hair and simmering eyes, plus his mischief was contagious and he smelled good. There was no one in Rakefoot like Albert. He'd been places, exciting places at his young age, and lived to tell about it. He seemed so free; he likely wouldn't let that liberty go anytime soon. I wasn't sure I wanted to either. It's just that women didn't have many choices about a future if marriage wasn't in it. And I did want marriage and babies.

"Of course I want to hear. I'm sure you were brave as can be." Those words with a flip of hair found the bull's eye of what drove him. Just then, the screen door squeaked and Mum came through. She stood on the porch in front of us smiling pitifully.

"Let's go home, Claire. I need to check on Syd." There was that look again. It was the same one directed toward Albert inside. Mum was overly protective these days. I wasn't a suckling calf, but nearly twenty.

"I'm not ready to go just yet, Mother." Albert seemed impressed. "Albert was just set to tell me about his special mission and it would be rude of me not to listen. I'll be along presently, I promise." I hoped mum wouldn't make an embarrassing scene. I'd stated it firmly enough.

Mum looked at Albert, then down to the scuffed wood planking, hand on her tum. "All right. Make it soon."

I endured a wave of guilt as Mum made her way down the steps toward our darkened home. As she passed beneath it, a shaft of dim yard light stroked her auburn hair. She clutched that old jacket to her chest as poor protection against the evening breezes. I could have been watching myself walk away—a diminishing shadow. I almost ran after her, but the hypnotic motion of the porch swing and Albert powering it was too much.

I hadn't lived at all—not like some girls in the Land Army group. Mum had no right to try to hold me back.

The nightjar buzzed high against the deep blue. I looked, but couldn't pick it out. Cricket chirp surrounded us; the racketing insect's work was at an end and so their lives would be soon. Though summer ran a close second, autumn was my favorite season. The promissory hints of its coming moved me through the finish of a cruel summer. Smoldering leaf piles and wood smoke were imminent pleasures—and just maybe, a romance. I'd trade despair for them any day now. For the first time since Dad left, I realized there were choices.

"All right now, where were we? I believe you were about to tell me how many German planes you shot down over Turkey or something like that." I sipped a cold tea and settled back into a cushion as the partiers bobbed to *Mood Indigo* through lace curtains.

Albert chuckled though his eyes rarely retreated. "Oh. It was nothing like that, no. This was a secret mission. We didn't know what sort of muddle we were getting ourselves into when we volunteered. They had no trouble rounding up the dozen of us they needed, though. Most of us were eighteen and ready to die for England, while never imagining we actually would. Britain had aircraft called Bristol Blenheim bombers they wanted delivered to our Finnish friends. Finland needed them to ward off the invading Russians at the time and we were no longer using them, as they were already outdated. But I guess the higher brass thought it would be an affordable show of support for our struggling ally." Albert cleared his throat, sipped from his glass, and watched me.

He was brave, too. Not a braggart, just stating facts made more impressive by way of humble delivery.

Albert continued, "Trouble was, we had to go undercover. They swore us to secrecy and took back our uniforms. They put us in civilian clothes and as far as everyone else was concerned, we were no longer in the service. Our folks were devastated, thinking us deserters and we couldn't say a thing to comfort them. Mother had a good cry." He brushed a damsel fly from my shoulder and I felt the touch of his hand.

"They stripped our aircraft of any armament so there would be no way to defend ourselves in case of an attack. To worsen matters, they removed our RAF roundels and replaced them with the blue swastika of the Finnish Air Force. The emblem was whitewashed but still showed through making us a target for either side." The memory was a painful one, evidently.

"To make short work of the story, we delivered all twelve of the beasts safely on February 26, 1940 to a frozen airstrip on Lake Juva in Finland. I won't soon forget that day. Afterward, we returned to the fray as regular RAF. There, now you've heard it. Are you duly impressed?"

Albert caught eyes with me. Had he asked something?

"Yes. But that's an amazing story. Um, now that you're home, what will you do?" My normally glib tongue floundered.

"I'm going to thank the guests for their warm welcome, excuse myself from the festivities and walk you along the water, that is, with your permission, Miss Stone." He actually lifted my hand and softly kissed it. My cheeks warmed, and I was grateful for the dark. An awkward blush now would utterly give the game away.

"I told you, no Miss Stone, just plain Claire. And I'd be delighted to walk with you."

As far as you wish to go.

"You may be just Claire, but you're anything but plain." Albert rose and extended his hand.

Eunice greeted us with a highball in one hand and a green smeared spatula in the other. "Where have you young people been hiding? Naughty, naughty. I'm glad you're having a grand time with Claire, Albert love, but you are the guest of honor. Most of my guests haven't heard of your heroic adventure. And I simply won't allow them out the door until they know what a brave blighter you are!" There were Mrs. Quimby's teeth. This was their night to shine too.

"Well, actually, Aunt Eunice, Claire and I were just preparing to walk about the garden and down by the lake. Thought it might clear my head, so full of military protocol and...mustering out rubbish you know. A dose of night air might restore a bit of the old Albert." He smiled eagerly at me. I doubted the old Albert had strayed far.

"Oh, Albert." There was that droopy jaw move of Mrs. Q.'s

that signaled unfulfilled expectations. "I'd so hoped you would regale us with your frightening feats of heroism. Please." She handed the spatula to Roger, laid claim to Albert's elbow, and that was it.

We looked at one another knowing further protest was useless, so I enjoyed the telling again, only this time with a dash more pepper for the larger audience. He was what Mum used to call Dad—plucky. I imagined him in the cockpit of that bomber, smiling all the way to Finland.

After he finished, he grabbed his flight jacket from the hall tree, draped it over my shoulders, and ushered me out the door into a promising summer night.

"I thought I'd never get through it. All I could think about was a chance to be alone with you." Albert reached for my hand. Yes, he was moving fast. The momentum of my plan of redemption through this soldier carried me full tilt into a dream. No time to brace for impact.

We walked down the road about a quarter mile until we reached the turn toward Scafell Pike, the path Mother and Dad called theirs. Albert asked how I was handling life with Dad gone and added how tough it must be on the three of us. I'd needed to talk and was glad to oblige.

"It is hard. I think about him every day and things I wish I'd said. He didn't have to go, you know; he chose to help in the collieries. I worry about money, but I think it's harder on Syd. Not sure, since we never discuss it. Dad and I never spent much time together. He was busy with his work." I looked toward the house. "Mum never showed favoritism with us girls. I understood why Dad did though. He and Syd were so alike. She went with him on rounds and told everyone how she'd be working with him someday in his practice. I had no right to resent it." I tried to be honest without sounding small. The result was a diluted truth, but I didn't have to model my threadbare emotions before we reached the water.

Albert replied, "I think we all believe our parents show favoritism, whether or not it's warranted. It's a child's way of rationalizing the love they lack. I was an only child and still found rivals for my dad's affection; his job, the time he spent polishing the auto instead of my ego. But we have to make our own love, Love." He reached for my hand again. His was warm.

We locked eyes, and he melted me like an early snow. We stopped beneath a tree on the water's edge. His arms were around my waist, and he pulled me close. He took my breath, but I didn't fight him. I'd corralled him, sure. I saw that.

When his face came so near I could feel his warm breath, there was no time to resist if I'd wanted to. And I didn't want to. He grazed my cheek, nuzzling the length of my neck and up until his lips were full and warm on mine. In twenty years of life in Rakefoot Crossing, I'd nary a clue that a kiss could feel like that. My head floated, and I felt weak. Afterward he knelt heavily to the grass and lifted his arm for me to join him. As I did, he laid me down, leaning over me, smoothing my hair and kissing me again, this time more passionately. His breath came heavier and I wanted more than anything to fall in with his rhythm.

"What are you doing?" A light blinded us, but I knew Syd's voice.

Albert and I stood so fast we knocked heads.

"Are you alright?" Albert asked.

"Yes. Um, what are you doing out here in the middle of the night?" I tried sounding angry, hoping to dismantle Syd's resolve.

"Excuse me, but I believe I asked you first." Syd wasn't quick to back down like Mum.

"I don't owe you any explanations, missy, but if it'll satisfy your curiosity, Albert and I were just admiring the night sky and remarking how many stars you can see out there." I randomly pointed out to space. "It's so clear. We thought we saw Mars on the horizon, didn't we, Albert? It glowed red." So did I. I felt it.

"I don't think you could see anything with him over top of you," she replied.

"See here, we've not met. You must be Syd, Claire's little sis she's been bragging about." Albert to the rescue. "I do see what you mean about her eyes. They are rather more beautiful than most girls' her age. Ravishing really." He paused, expectant while Syd stared at him. "I'm Albert Rand by the way, Eunice Quimby's nephew. You were supposed to come to my party tonight, but you snubbed me. No matter, we can make up for it now, shall we?" Albert made a second cast.

"I doubt you would have been available for conversation, Mr. Rand." she looked from him to me and back again. "I'm going home to tell Mum." Syd turned to run, but I clapped a hand on her shoulder.

"Just one minute. It seems we both have a story to tell. What do you think Mum would say if she knew you were out romping about like a fairy in the dark without so much as a sweater? Did you sneak out the window again?" I recognized the blue plaid dress she was wearing. Grandmum, Goby sewed it for my graduation from primary school. Seeing little sis in it made me ache for old family times.

"I was looking for Cassidy. I had all the cats in except him. With his crippled leg, it's a danger for him to be out all night." Syd wrapped her arms around herself.

"We're all getting chilled here. Let's head for the house and we'll spread out and hunt the stinker along the way. What say?" Albert took a deep breath and exhaled loudly. "Here, puss, puss, puss."

Maybe it was a good thing Syd happened along when she did, the brat. But I looked forward to a follow-up with Albert. I plunged cold hands deep into my dress pockets and the three of us turned toward home. Anyway, we'd have to face Mum together. Though not all that fearsome in deed, I never let her know that I dreaded Mum's tears like everything.

- 5 -

GLORY

I noticed the barn light on before entering the empty house. Syd must have been tucking away the animals. I hung my old jacket next John's slicker on the coat peg by the door and ran my fingers down his sleeve, into his pocket. I felt something like a dried stalk and pulled it out — a rose, I thought. Then I remembered this was the rose he'd offered me the day he enlisted. When I refused the flower, he tucked it away. Wish I'd been strong instead.

I walked to the breakfront with the dead thing, pulling open our drawer of important papers. The brown envelope under the girls' birth certificates held our wedding certificate, which I'd labeled along with the date—15 August 1920. My thought was to place the rose inside and mark the envelope with our expiration date as a couple, but once I opened the flap and caught a glimpse of yellowed edge, I had to look it over—the form that sealed our love in the county registry. I had to look and allow the tears to blur the vicar's signature and ours. It was an official document, one that stated we were legally married. But they needed certificates to record deaths too. To declare people officially dead. This I had not seen for John. After three weeks, there was no death certificate. I wondered how long it normally took. Maybe longer during these times of extravagant loss. I would wait a short while longer.

Walking back to the door, I tried to see through the blackness outside. If Claire wasn't home within the hour, I'd go looking, whether or not I embarrassed her. Albert looked like he'd pounce on the first naïve female to come his way. Claire had more sense, though she certainly hadn't discouraged him with that foreign accent and lolling about on the porch swing all hours.

It was late but a stout cup of tea would go down good to chase the fog left from whatever was in the punch. Being among familiar faces was a comfort, even though I did feel a bit like an outsider with my nose pressed against the shop glass. I couldn't say if every couple was happy, but they were a twosome.

I was relieved there were no tiresome questions put to me about John. I did fine for a first outing, really. And maybe Eunice would forget about the town visit for awhile. I didn't feel up to gadding away from home just yet. Syd might need me and I wondered about being away from home should I have another of those strange bouts with nowhere to get off to.

After tea, I drowsed on the divan. Teasing dreams came, frivolous and fragmented with strange characters playing John and the girls. Joining them was a tall, shadowy figure, a grim reaper sort. I woke to a determined darkness that settled in and returned me to my proper place.

The clock clanged, demanding twelve times that the girls weren't in the house. I jumped and grabbed my jacket and a torch from the kitchen drawer. Stepping outside, a chill penetrated my coat even though the night was mild. I started for the barn and shook from some dread—a sidekick to the dark; they had paired up.

Coming toward me from up road, I saw an occasional beam

of light and could make out shoes crunching through gravel and a rippling of voices talking over one another. As the sound drew closer I could make out three figures, then one called to me.

"Hallo, Mrs. Stone. It's Albert escorting your wayward girls back home."

Why was Syd with them? What did we know about this soldier boy except that he's Eunice's nephew? So what? Don't all miscreants have a nice aunty somewhere? The shakes found their home in my stomach.

"What were you about, young lady?" I steadied myself with the porch railing and looked at Syd.

"I was looking for Cassidy. And…" She looked at Claire.

"Girls, go to bed. I will talk with you tomorrow." There was obviously more to this evening than I knew or wanted to know then. My boldness may have been as obvious as Albert's intentions but I forced myself to stand and look at them until they left.

Claire couldn't leave without a disclaimer. "I'm not a child, Mother. I shouldn't be treated like Syd. I'll go for now because I'm tired." She offered Albert a simpery smile. "I look forward to seeing you again, Albert." She turned her back on her audience.

"See here, I am sorry about what happened, Mrs. Stone. It shan't happen again." Albert played the contrite Boy Scout.

"What did happen?" I looked at the flyboy.

"Well, I just mean having her out so long when we just met and all. I understand how much she must mean to you at a time… at this time." He looked past me.

I watched him struggle. *You haven't the faintest notion.*

"Yes, she does indeed. Well, good night, Albert. And I do hope you take the time to visit your aunt and uncle before you head back. I'm sure I can speak for Claire when I say we had a lovely time at their place tonight."

"Good night, Mrs. Stone." He shuffled off like a scolded pup.

I didn't need further excuses for missed sleep, but up popped this one.

ભ

After the party, I was ready to hole up again. The next afternoon found me in garden regretting my compliance to go with Eunice to pictures. Tomatoes and beans wanted preserving and weeds were making a final stand. The flowers needed dead-heading too. I'd no business trotting off.

I'd read a story once about a woman in Appleby who sang to her sweetmeat squash and credited the love songs she crooned for growing the biggest orbs in Cumbria. Her pies were prizewinners too. So, I thought 'why not' and tried poetry on my flowers, and though I was doubtful it had anything to do with the results, they did appear to thank me by giving it their all. Show-offs, they incited envy in older generations of gardeners, which was never my intent. These weathered villagers took their gardens as seriously as any dairyman his herd. Such a one was Mary Thompkins who always came by whistling.

The tune was a stew of "Don't Sit under the Apple Tree" and "Melancholy Baby" as far as anyone could guess. But when Mary puckered up, it came out more like "Don't Sit under a Melancholy Baby Eating Apples." I heard the strains of it now, with my knees in the dirt and zinnias hanging on to the season.

Mary had tried various ways to obtain some secret she imagined made our garden superior to others in The Crossing. She tried bullying a confession out of me by laying on guilt about her being an old woman, nearing 'her eternal threshold.' I assured her I was not holding out, but the belief in some hidden elixir seemed to motivate her to keep plugging. Mary would need to play through quickly today so I could clean up in time to meet Eunice.

"Hello, Mrs. Thompkins. Lovely day, eh? What's that tune you're whistling?" I kept attention to dried petals.

A large, black shape floated near. "Dalemain. Cawk!" Natty the raven greeted me, alighted on my shoulder and clamped beak to my sunbonnet. I dipped, but held my balance.

"It sounded like that bird said Dalemain," Mary commented.

"Yes, it did. Syd's been teaching him some new phrases evidently. Isn't that something? Birds can talk?"

"Such an odd thing to teach a bird to say." Thompkins continued her critique. "Why not Polly want a cracker or some'at?"

"He's not a parrot, Mrs. Thompkins. He's a raven."

"What's that on bird's leg?"

"I don't know. Must be something Syd rigged up." I finished quickly and glanced at Natty's leg. "Looks something like what they use on carrier pigeons for delivering messages."

He was a hulking bird even for a raven and was the lone feathered member in the Stone menagerie ever since Ira Erickson, hired man next farm but one, took aim at his mate. Syd nursed his misses to no avail. Even after that, Natty didn't know better than to align himself with us—his new flock. He craved fresh fruit, company and shiny things. Somehow, John and Syd had trained him to mimic words and phrases. I found it unnerving at times but most of the locals loved him.

"Och, crazy bird." She waved her cane Natty's way. It was an effort for Mary to remain silent as she helped herself to a lung full of sweet issue from the phlox. But I heard sniffing. "I see thee workin' awful hard at marigolds yet, and getting late in season. Aye? I woulda thought with mister gone and all, thee mightn't have time for flower gardening. Psh. Thee might be off for a job to keep t' lasses in shoe leather. And there's feed thee'll be needing for t' livestock." Mary nodded in agreement with herself, took her cane, carried mostly for earning a better seat on the train, and broke up clods along the fencerow.

The verbal assault caught me off balance. I needed no reminding. I'd never learned a trade—only keeping a home and raising the brids. Laying down my spade, I set Natty on the ground next to a grub snack.

"Can't you just enjoy the flowers, Mrs. Thompkins? Any road, I wouldn't give up gardening particularly in hard times. Now if you'll excuse me, I must be off."

Mary went whistling on her way as if she'd fired no shot and wasn't it a lovely day, but not before I heard her say over her shoulder, "Maybe thee could put that bird to work in circus."

"Mm, yes." I spanked at my apron and removed my hat for the big excursion.

Next door, Eunice charged outside barking orders. "And don't forget to clean the cooker like I told you! I'll be back in time for late supper." Turning her attention to Finlay awaiting directions, she said, "C'mon then. We'll have to get a move on if we want to catch the two fourteen." He matched her steps as they joined me.

"Hello, Love. I saw you with Mary Thompkins. What did that old biddy want, your secret formula?" Eunice laughed as she searched through her bag to make sure she had everything. "Let's see, change purse, lip rouge, hanky, spike." She seemed satisfied.

"Well, hello, Finlay." I looked at Eunice. He lifted a hand up and down. "Spike?" I questioned her. "Who's Spike and why is he in your handbag?" Finlay laughed heartier than I deserved.

"Don't tell me!" Eunice's stage presence emerged. "Didn't you hear of the woman in Liverpool attacked last month? She was just walking along minding her own p-s and q-s. Jumped her from behind, he did. So, I'm carrying this railroad spike for protection." She pulled it out and made thrusting motions towards Finlay and me.

"Well it seems an unwieldy manner of defense." I was sure Eunice wouldn't get the opportunity to put her weapon to use in Penrith or anywhere. Eunice's nature suggested a formidable person. She wore her dominance on her sleeve.

Finlay hadn't uttered a word and I was surprised to see him in tow. "Good you could join us, Finlay." I frowned at Eunice who flashed those incisors like a threatening primate.

"Thank you. I'm not required at work until Wednesday next so Sis said why don't I come along? I don't know when I've been to the cinema. It might have been all of two years ago. Remember, Eunice when you and Roger came to visit Rufus and me and we made the trip to Carlisle?" He was oblivious of the grenade he'd just thrown by mentioning that town.

Eunice took my arm. "Um, maybe so. What are we going to see today? Something nice and cheery? I hope it's got that lovely Grant gent. What I wouldn't give to find him tucked in my Christmas sock, eh?" Her elbow prodded at me.

I hadn't been to Carlisle since John's accident. Any jog in that direction could spin me down a hole. I'd barely moved from the house the past three weeks. If we hadn't already bought train tickets, I'd have turned back.

"I think they're showing *King Richard the Fifth*, Shakespeare's tale, with Laurence Olivier. Should be a rouser." Finlay said.

"Oh no!" Eunice croaked. "Not a ruddy war movie. That's nothing we women want to see. Well, maybe Glory and I can window-shop while you enjoy your jousting or whatever they did. Then we can stop off for some tea and have a nice, long chat. Finlay just adores history, don't you, little brother? Smart chap, Finlay."

Now I did pine for my home, my kitchen. I began to feel queasy about Eunice's motives for bringing Finlay. I was quite sure I didn't want to enter into a conversation with Eunice about my uncertain future. And window-shopping was about as satisfying as standing outside a dinner house to catch a sniff of T-bone steak.

"I'd rather skip the shopping. But I could do with a cup of tea. I'd like to hear more about your nephew, Albert. He and Claire seem taken with one another."

"Albert and Claire, I should have thought of it before. They do make a smashing pair." Eunice boarded the train with Finlay and me behind. "He's such a love—an only child but an enterprising person that's for sure."

I thought opportunistic a better word.

It was a short jaunt to Penrith, but it would be a long day. Syd had concerned me lately and I was uncomfortable leaving her alone. She spent nearly all her time in the barn with the animals. That wasn't abnormal, but she hadn't mentioned her pop once since the news. In fact, she hadn't talked about much of anything except that feed was getting low.

Finlay went on to the theater while Eunice and I remained in the station refreshment room. Claiming a corner booth, Eunice poised to lecture—a well-rehearsed lecture, I was sure. She'd paid my way so this was her due.

I'd been able to deflect Eunice's plans before this. Like the time she'd decided they must open a hat shop in Rakefoot Crossing and specialize in French creations. French hats in The Crossing. Well, I knew Eunice's dream to own a shop had been brewing, but she may as well try selling them to the local sheep. I knew I would never convince Eunice of something she'd fastened her mind to, so I diverted her instead to Gert Fotheringay and how much weight she'd packed around her midsection. Trouble was I had to continue until either Eunice wore out or got hungry. Appetite normally won the day.

"What'll it be?" The pained barmaid wouldn't wait long. When Eunice and I looked at one another, she was off to wipe the counter.

Eunice bristled. "A couple a cupsa tea, if it's not a burden. And a plate of biscuits."

"A'right."

Eunice smoothed her feathers and took aim with that big sister look. "I know this hasn't been easy, and you need to grieve. But sometimes we need others to look to future for us when we're down in shadow. Are you listening?" She scowled at the waitress who'd set down the tea with a slosh.

"Yes, I just don't want to talk about this right now. It's only been three weeks. Vicar says I need a year or two at least before making any big decisions or changes. Anyhow, I've been thinking too. I've decided to look for a job as soon as canning is through." I poured a small drip of cream and passed on sugar. Rationing was still in effect.

"A job, eh? What sort of a job?" Eunice took the sugar and milk in hand. "With all the men folk coming home and you never having worked a day out the house? You're not thinking straight about this. And since when have you listened to advice from the vicar? No, what you need is a husband…"

I looked at my chum while she nodded her hair pile, took a second biscuit and persisted against the odds. "… and father for the girls. Before you get too old."

Eunice's words stung. I wanted to escape. The waitress, though I used the title loosely, slapped our ticket down on the table then added as an afterthought, "Anything else?" Her gum smacked.

"Not a blessed thing. We wouldn't want to put you out." Eunice loved the excuse to wield sarcasm more than she disliked the server's rudeness. In fact, it was sport for her since Roger was a poor challenge.

She drew a bead on me, "You don't have to say aught about it right now, but I want you to think this over." Eunice was about to spout and needed sustenance. She reached for the pot of black-berry jam.

I closed my mind, remained mute and admired my friend's pampered, red fingernails. I looked down at mine. Grubbing in the dirt and cleaning house had stained and stunted them. Eunice and I were different yet we fed one another. She spewed flaky crumbs as she pursued her quest.

"Finlay fancies you." She washed down the remainder of a biscuit with tea.

"What? Don't be ridiculous." I couldn't imagine Finlay bringing up the subject.

"Well, I asked him if didn't he think you were a handsome woman. And his cheeks and the tip of his nose turned all over bright red. Now what would you make of a response like that?"

"I might think he'd drunk one too many glasses of your dandelion wine." I didn't want this silly notion of me with Finlay to develop taproots in Eunice's head so it was diversion time.

"Eunice, did you see how that snobby waitress glared at you just then? She flopped her rag down on the bar and gave you a look. Why I'm surprised you have a red hair left on your head, the way she sneered." I hoped I hadn't oversold it.

"Why that little snip! And me about ready to say how tasty the biscuits was." Eunice's eyes grew dark and purposeful as she dragged herself out of the booth and walked toward the bar where the combatant snip cleaned. "Uh, hello, miss."

"What is it?" The server wasn't easily intimidated. She folded her arms. I dreaded a confrontation I'd facilitated but the alternative was worse.

"Well, I was just thinking I ought to remind you that we are the customers and you are the help. Seems to me you should be a lot more courteous-like with those what help pay your wages." Eunice's chest began to heave.

"Well I like that!" The frazzled employee shot back. "You expect me to treat you and your frowsy friend there like you're the Twin Queens a Sheba. I can't help it if you expect people to bow whenever you scrape up enough coppers to visit town!"

She'd wrangled with the best no doubt. Frowsy? I looked down at myself. I could've stood a new frock.

Eunice's foot sat atop the bar rail and she positioned her hands to hoist herself forward. "Listen, pork pie! Take back what you said about my friend. She just lost her husband in the war!"

I slid out the booth and walked over to Eunice. It was my doing, after all.

"Let's go, Eunice. The movie's likely done and it's time I got back." I tugged gently on her shoulder and forced a smile at the barmaid who had pulled back her fist full of wet rag.

"I'm sorry about your husband, Missus, I am. But your friend here has a whopper of a mouth that needs stuffing!" She let fly. Eunice ducked, Finlay walked through the door, and the rag connected with its hapless victim.

The three of us looked at poor Finlay's face, dripping with bleachy beer water, as the rag settled on his good loafers. "Was I supposed to catch that?" Finlay asked.

The rag flinger, Eunice and I looked at one another and broke loose. "Looks as though you did, Deary," Eunice's eye-crescents precluded a howl. For the first time in quite awhile, I laughed. I had Eunice to thank. That was the thing about her.

- 6 -

SYD

12 September, 1945

Dear Pop,

I can barely stand the waiting! Before, it was just a feeling, but the reason I believe would sound daft to anyone else. Claire and Mum have stopped believing in miracles; but it's sad because Mum keeps trying to find out more information from the Army, like where is the death certificate. I'm trying to give her hope without giving away important secrets.

It's great writing you instead of my diary these days because I miss our talks awfully and this is the next best thing for now. I can see you nodding, taking a pull from your pipe, and I imagine what wise or funny thing you might say.

Before, I didn't do much but care for the critters. Mum made me go to the funeral. It was the hardest thing I've ever done. I felt as though everyone was staring to see if I'd cry, and when I didn't, I wondered at what they thought of me. I do my crying alone, anyway. During service, I stared at my shoe buckles, how they looked too scruffy for your funeral and needed polishing and then I thought about Natty with that capsule fastened to his leg. I'm sorry for not paying attention to Vicar Cavendish and all the nice things he said about you, mostly true. I was busy trying to fit pieces together and figure it all out.

Mr. Biggs has been helping out a lot. I don't know who was inside the beautiful coffin he paid for. The lid was closed, so no one will know unless they dig it up. It sure is funny talking to you about your funeral. Ha. It seems the whole village came, so that should make you happy. Soon we can have a good laugh over a couple mugs of hot cocoa, can't we, Pop?

A few days after the funeral, Biggs took me on a tour of Rakefoot Station and showed me parts that travelers wouldn't see, like his office and living quarters. Did you know he has a secret door in his floor that goes to a basement? Rather creepy down there but also cozy with some books, a little kitchen set-up and a chess game. He said the two of you had played there. There's a crystal radio set where he can listen to the war goings-on. He moved the telegraph operation for Rakefoot Crossing down there. He said it was for safekeeping from Germans. I'm sure it's okay if I tell you here.

It's sad because Biggs' mother died last autumn. He talks about her a lot and calls her Mutti, like moo-tee. That's German for Mum. Did he ever show you his strange collection of black, leather gloves that belonged to her? He has them propped upright over woolen bobbins from Briery so that they look to be clapping. If I didn't know he was your good friend, I would have run screaming! Ha.

School started. I'm in year seven in case you lost track. I wish I didn't have to grow up. My new teacher is Miss Vinson. She's nice and smiles a lot. She has cages in the back with white mice and hamsters. I don't know their names yet. We can earn points to use for different rewards. One of them is taking care of the rodents for a whole semester, so that's what I'm going for now.

Roger and Eunice gave a party the other night for their nephew, Albert. He was in the RAF. Claire is gaga over him. Mum and I don't like him much, especially Mum. I stayed home but I met Albert all right. More later.

Mum is fine I guess. I don't see much of her or Claire. I'm busy with the animals and now school, and she's busy with the garden and I heard her talking about looking for work, but I'm not sure what she can do besides take care of us. I don't like bothering her.

Remember when you told me about the time that you and Uncle Dick got into trouble for stealing eggs? Remember you felt sick to your stomach afterward? I think I understand. Oh, Pop, please don't worry but I got into a little jam at school and it's all done with. By the time you read this, it all may be little more than a dark memory.

Natty is smart but he's getting to be a major thief. You recall his tree stump hiding place. I'm always cleaning it out. I found a set of false teeth the other day. They were scummy so I threw them in the lake. Greta and Ollie are fine and all the cats. Reggie and Jingles send their love. Alas, we are eating Winston. He had fine hams.

Well, this is three pages so I best stop. Please do come home soon as you can. It's not the same without you. Just three girls rooming together.

Love and squeezes,

Syd

- 7 -

GLORY

I looked through the window to John's work shed and saw weeds reflected in its dark panes. I'd avoided that corner of the yard. Now autumn was upon us, I couldn't let grass claim his territory. Some days, I jumped when I heard a fumbling with bottles and instruments from inside. Then I'd remember it was Syd picking up where John left off. Often I pretended I wasn't sure it was her. Evidently, Syd never felt John's ghost, or didn't fear it.

Another school year has begun. I was glad for the time Syd had before heading back to books and social demands. She dreads this time of year and hates being away from the animals all day. Besides Gillian, she has no human chums. She feels different and can't hide her awkwardness in a group. I'd tried, on occasion, having birthday parties and the like for her, but invariably she'd hang back, caressing the dogs and watching other girls be girls. She'd reached the age where the fickle opinions of others mattered. Possibly, it was the worst time to be without her pop.

How could I be more for our girls? John was self-assured,

unlike me, more like Dad. Where did you find strength if you weren't born with it? I had wanted to show Dad and Uncle Dick that I was strong. When I was around the two of them, they treated me as an equal. That's when I felt I was on the edge of growing up, and maybe I fit someplace, beauty aside. Once, they allowed I could go along to deliver a couple of rams to Liverpool. Alan Dover, the engineer was a friend of theirs who allowed we could ride in the engine compartment. I watched his every move as we pitched and rocked our way south through the lakes, and learned the purpose for each lever and switch. I began to dream regular of driving a train. Awake, I knew it was nonsense. Syd though, knew she was to be a vet and no mistake.

Syd was not one for coddling, though it would have been a satisfaction for me to coddle her. She found strength in the dependency of her animals and was most at home in their midst as I was in garden. The phone rang.

"Hallo, Stone's...Yes, this is Mrs. Stone... Oh hello, Miss Vinson." Miss Wanda Vinson was Syd's teacher that year. "Is Syd all right? ... Really, what is it? ... Of course, I'll be down. Today after school, right. Good bye." I found the chair. Miss Vinson wanted to talk about Sydney's behavior of late. Naturally, she couldn't go into details. Her behavior? She'd never caused trouble at school, always did her work and didn't talk out in class. It'd be a long day.

Three o'clock approached like a coal car up Troutbeck grade. It was but a short walk to Braithwaite Primary. The fresh air would do me good, but I wished I were walking for my health alone. Crows, their thieving bellies full of maize, croaked and circled high in pairs, empty nesters again. Crows had further chances at raising a flock. I lifted my chin for a heady breath of plant life calling it a year. Afternoon sun didn't warm as it had, and maple leaves were turning an immature shade of orange. Some leaves didn't quite crunch underfoot; they'd fallen prematurely.

A whistle shrieked from the afternoon arrival. Few would get off and those who did quickly grabbed tea or tobacco and popped back on, bound for Edinburgh or London or some purposeful place. Rakefoot Crossing took strangers as far as it could on charm alone. In summer, it was a show-off for tourists who ventured beyond Windermere. Autumn tagged the romantic. Poets and dreamers came in autumn to dream alone and steep themselves in melancholia—fodder for survival during the workday drudge. Winter was a gray and watery shadow of its former way. And spring was hopeful.

I was a small town girl. I'd been more at home with the gander than a gaggle, and content with others' expectations in the roles of housewife and mother, for the most part. These I could be.

A sympathetic breeze blew hair off my face as I turned up the schoolyard path. Children milled about comparing the severities of their new teachers. With only about one hundred students all told, it was more like a large family with its squabbles and wide open secrets. Seemed like one child's shame was another's ammunition.

I stopped at the office inside double doors. "Hello. Please excuse me, can someone direct me to Miss Vinson's room?" A matronly woman at the front desk was helpful.

"Yes, three doors down and on your left. Her name is on the wall by the door."

"Thank you." As I approached the entrance, I began to sweat. I felt shaky and weak and my stomach reacted. I spied a girls' water closet across the hall and dashed in. A damp towel felt good on my face and the back of my neck. I took a few deep breaths and held fast to the sink. Lifting my head to the mirror, a scared, pale woman looked back. I dabbed a coat of Cock's Comb red to my lips and smoothed my hair.

I came out to the hall and could see a young teacher in Syd's classroom sitting behind an oak desk, head down, grading papers perhaps. What was I about to hear?

I gave the door jamb a light rap. "Miss Vinson?"

"Yes. And you must be Mrs. Stone, Sydney's mum." She held out her hand and offered me a chair next to hers.

I looked round at the usual classroom furnishings: chalkboard, globe, desks, maps. There was the Royal Family and Winston Churchill, after whom Syd had named the largest of the pigs--a fact I was cautious about sharing. There was a timeline on one wall following the recently waged battles, culminating with a large VE with what appeared to be sun bursts marking the triumphant date of 8 May 1945, the official end of war in Europe. In red, she had posted V-J Day on 15 August. The date of the telegram—catastrophe between two victories—wasn't on the timeline, but I saw it just as plain, and I'd have bet Syd saw it too. The dates marking the war's end were parentheses cupping our private grief.

On the chalkboard I noticed Syd's name with a couple others written under the heading OVERDUE ASSIGNMENTS.

"Is that why I'm here? Syd hasn't turned in her assignments? Because I think I can shed some light on that." I loosened the grip on my pocketbook.

Of course, my only explanation was that she'd lost her father two months prior. Would that suffice? I breathed easier until I saw her expression.

Miss Vinson sat straight and cleared her throat. She was young. Poor thing, this was likely her least favorite part of her chosen profession—having to confront defensive mums and dads about their unruly offspring.

"If that were the only problem, I would have handled it with a note home. I'm afraid it's rather more serious." She looked at me and I wished she would speak. "Sydney has been taking things." She referred to a list as she donned a pair of readers.

This I was definitely not expecting. "Syd, stealing. Are you quite sure?"

"I'm sorry, but some of the girls caught her reaching into the pockets of the children's overcoats at the rear of the gymnasium and also dinner pails. They're items of little value: a handkerchief, a couple of marbles, cookies—whatever she found. Apparently, she waited until the rest of the class was at recess. I wanted to have you in so we could talk privately about how Sydney is handling her father's death. I spoke with two of her former teachers, and they assured me she is not a difficult student. Sydney has been through enough humiliation over this; I only wanted you to know we're here to help during this distressing time. Has she shown any other unusual behavior?" She removed her glasses and laid the paper aside.

Her smile seemed so sincere it fed my self pity.

Distressing time—it seemed I'd stepped into a nest of those lately, like landmines. Too much out of the ordinary was happening. Bits of me were blown apart. I hoped my voice didn't betray the extent of the wreckage.

"Well, you see, she and her dad were so very alike." I tried to clear a tightness from my throat. "Syd seemed to handle John's death better than I."

Where had I been?

I shook my head. "I feel like a horrible, neglectful mum, the one thing I've taken most pride in." There I broke and was another humiliated member of the Stone family as I cried openly, shamefully. These days anything put me over the edge, and Wanda Vinson's kind eyes were like an engraved invitation. Once I could speak, I managed, "She'll have to give it all back, of course, the things she took."

"There now, Mrs. Stone. It will work out. She has already returned the objects and the children have been sympathetic for most part." Miss Vinson reached out in an awkward attempt at patting my arm, which nearly brought on a second wave. She gave me her handkerchief. I didn't want to soil it. I hated putting her out like this but the poor woman deserved some explanation.

She continued, "I was going to suggest...if provisions are an issue, the church has a small food closet and I know others would be willing to help if they knew there was a struggle. Folks just don't know."

"Thank you. That is kind. Syd hasn't talked about her pop or much of anything with me for some time now. I thought to let her handle her grief in her own fashion and she'd open up when she was ready. Perhaps I should have drawn her out. She spends all her spare time with the animals." I noticed some cages with mice and hamsters in the rear of the room and tried to recall whether Syd had mentioned them.

"I've been trying to maintain a semblance of normal living—keeping house and garden. The girls and I have become distant, nothing like before. John was our magnet." I looked at my lap. "With him gone, we've flown apart. It's a desolate way to live when you've known such togetherness." I sniffed and searched my pocketbook for my own handkerchief. "And I'm so sorry to be laying all this at your door. I guess I haven't talked it out with anyone either." I sobbed and it felt good because I knew I couldn't control it anyway.

Miss Vinson came over to put her arm around me. "There are a couple of other children in school who've lost family members in this war. Maybe it would do you good to talk with their parents. It's a damnable business, if you'll excuse my language. A good heart to heart with Sydney might do wonders. You know her; meet her on her own terms and be willing to listen without having to explain, because you can't." She stood and looked out the large window overlooking the play area.

"You're wise for your years." I swiped my face with my coat sleeve and rose to go.

She turned. "We lost Dad to influenza when I was seven. I can still remember my dear mum trying to offer all kinds of excuses for why God took him. I only hated God for it. I didn't know any better and neither did she, poor dear. We've grown close over the years, so take heart. The unbearable sting will ease." She offered her hand. "It has been a pleasure. And Sydney is a delight to have in class. She is a bright one even though reserved."

"Thank you. She wants to be a vet like her pop. We're fortunate she has such an understanding teacher. Good bye, Miss Vinson." I gave her hanky back.

She looked at it. "Please call me Wanda." Through the glass behind her, a gust released a cascade of leaves. Winter came next.

The biggest culprit of my preoccupation had been money. There weren't enough jobs for returning men, let alone widows. That's what I was now. Widow Stone. All the villages along the Penrith to Workington line were drying up. No need for rail when so many of the industrials and workers that needed them were going under. And German POWs continued doing farm labor. But first things first, I must talk with our Syd.

☙

I knew where Syd would be. I took down Gran Compton's Damask Rose tea set from its special place and brewed a pot. I needed to fuss over her even if she didn't seem to require it. So I filled the creamer too and put what sweet cubes we had in a small bowl. There was no lemon. I'd splurged and baked a small batch of scones earlier. A bronzed hill of them went along with the tea. All of it on the antique silver tray, one of many elegant pieces my Gran had left to me. We called her Goby.

I picked my way gingerly over bunch grass with the jostling load and headed for the barn. I hadn't been out there in two or three weeks at least. It was a world from which I'd disassociated, since lately it made me yearn for childhood when I struggled to find strength.

"Syd?" I called into the dim, cool space. "Surprise. I've brought a party. Are you here?" The smell of hay and rusting machinery took me back to glorious, carefree days.

"Mummie! I'm here." I couldn't tell at first where the voice came from. As my eyes adjusted from the brightness of day, I saw what looked like a bale staircase, climbing up and curving into the loft. Then she peeked over the top, wiped her face, and said, "It's about time you visited my castle." Her eyes looked red from where I stood.

"I didn't realize you had one. Do you think I can make it up there without spilling hot tea all over myself?" I ached to hold her.

"Just hand me things. It's roomy enough. I haven't shown this place to anyone, not even Gillian." Her voice wavered. She was pleased to share it with me, and I felt ashamed.

I handed the party up piecemeal. "OK, that's it. I'm climbing in now." At the top of the curve was an entrance to a clearing in the middle of several hay turrets. It was reminiscent of a fort of my own making so long ago in a wood shed. "May I enter, Your Highness?" I bowed.

At Syd's familiar giggle, I felt connected, like when she'd hiccupped inside me. The grace of it was honey to my soul.

"Yes, you may." She was quite dramatic about it. And I nestled down in the seat she'd prepared for somebody—maybe her pop, but I was there now.

"Shall I pour out?" I went for the pot.

"Please do." There was that snicker again. I felt reborn and twelve.

"Have a scone, Lady Critterly?" I held up the plate and hoped she didn't think that was too sappy.

"I don't mind if I do, Queen Gloria." I hadn't heard my full name in years—maybe since I'd returned home for Dad's funeral.

"I love you, Precious." I almost broke. "There's nothing I wouldn't do for you and Claire. You know?" She looked embarrassed.

"Yeah, I do." She looked down at the napkin in her lap. "You... Miss Vinson told you, didn't she? I begged her not to." Syd's eyes filled.

"Yes, Lamb, she did." I laid my hand on her shoulder. "And I'm right glad too because I don't want any daughter of mine getting thrown into the lockup!" I laughed and she smiled, but we didn't hold back. We wept together.

"I want you to know you can always come to me. I know I'm not your pop and not as good at making things right the way he did, but I'm not too ignorant to learn." I wiped her cheeks and kissed them. "I'm sorry I failed you. Can you forgive me, Syd girl?" I stroked her downy hair and she reached for me again. "I'm going out to find a job. I'll take care of our family, but I'll need yours and Claire's help."

"Me forgive you? Of course, I can forgive you. I'm sorry too. Really not sure why I did it."

"Once when I was about eight, you won't believe what I did." Syd adjusted into her hay seat. "Just after a paddling for stuffing myself full of chips Mum had fried for supper, I went right out to the barn and began catching and grinding up grasshoppers in the vice press." Syd looked at me as if we were playmates just meeting. "Sometimes we do odd things when we're hurting. From now on, we need to talk when we're in a tight spot or feel rotten. Right?"

"Right," she agreed hesitantly. I hoped she wasn't picturing those grasshoppers' mangled bodies. Then she added, "I don't know about Claire though. She's awful thick with that Rand character. I don't think I like him, even if he did find Cassidy in the wheelbarrow the other night."

I hadn't questioned her about that night, and now wasn't the time. I wanted to remain hidden in a charmed loft, chewing a straw.

"I will talk with Claire. Don't you worry." My stomach hurt.

"Oh, look." I saw the gift John had given her before he left. She'd set it in a hollowed out shelf. "There's the jewelry box Pop gave you." I didn't ask what was in it, but she was eager to show me.

- 8 -

GLORY

"**I** got the idea from Natty." Syd's excitement was contagious.
"Natty?"
"Yeah. Ravens love to pinch bright things like jewelry,
keys, tins—whatever catches their fancy. I watched Natty once a
long time back, after school, and saw him flying with a spoon in
his beak so I followed him to a hollow stump in the field next door
and found his secret stash. He had a garter, a red hair ribbon and
a pearl brooch shaped like a seashell. I kept them." She looked up
at me and continued. "I've no idea whose they were. He'd also
collected silly things like a meat tin and false teeth!" We laughed.
"Those were nasty so I threw them out. I thought if Natty could
have a stash, so might I." She softened. "Pop knows about Natty's
treasure. I like to look at these." She opened the box and revealed
more than a random collection. "I put a little after shave smellim
on Pop's hanky, and so I pretend I'm sniffing his neck."
She wafted the hanky in front of my nose and flushed a vivid

recollection. I closed my eyes. I hadn't laundered his pillow cover or the blue flannel work shirt since his last furlough.

Syd continued her show and tell. "Sometimes I put it on Ollie and when I put my face in his mane, he's...Pop. I hear his voice sometimes." She took a large bite from her scone and

continued with her mouth full. "Here's a lucky penny we found fishing over Keswick way." She held up the ordinary penny, though I imagined any object discovered while they were together would bear magical properties. "He said it was like the one Jesus took from the fish's mouth to pay their taxes, and he sure wished we would catch one that would cough up enough coin to pay ours." She laughed.

She handled each item with reverence. "Here's his Meer-schaum. I'm saving it for him. Still has some tobacco in it. With a good whiff of that and his after shave, he's practically here!"

She inhaled and handed it over for my turn to imagine him, so I did.

Remember this, Mummie? It's the photo you took of me on Ollie with Pop beside of us, holding me from behind so's I wouldn't fall."

"I do remember taking the photo. But, why did you say you're saving his pipe for him, pet?"

"Because he's coming back to you — to us all. I don't believe he's dead." She said it as if it shouldn't surprise. "I've never seen him dead, have you?"

"Well, no. But honey...what makes you think he's alive?" She'd handled the news too well.

"Well." She looked into my eyes for trustworthiness. "I think it was God who told me." She waited. "Or an angel, maybe. It was just after the stuff at school."

Happiness took on a sanguine hue.

"God spoke to you?" I tried to sound nonchalant. I wanted

to believe her and if an angel were going to speak to anyone, Syd would be an obvious choice.

"No. Not like we're talking." She looked self-conscious.

"It's ok. Tell me what you heard. I promise I won't laugh."

"I was lying down, getting ready for sleep and I'd just finished asking after Pop. I asked if he was all right and not in danger or hurting, like a prisoner somewhere. A voice clear as day said, 'Pop's coming home.' I'm not even sure if it was a man or woman's voice. I just know I heard it inside. "'Pop's coming home.' Just like that. Then I wasn't worried about him anymore." Syd appeared to me like she was the angel. A consuming peace reached up through the length of her and shone on her face.

Coming home? Had she misunderstood? She also said she'd heard John's voice, so who knew what kind of tricks her mind may have been playing. It did seem that death and grief brought us nearer spiritual interface of some sort. But I was afraid my poor girl had told herself a lie.

"That's a beautiful story, sweet. But if you're sure, what had you crying earlier when I came inside?"

Syd's lip quivered. "Because I felt bad about the stealing rubbish and didn't want to hurt you. I didn't know you knew." I held her to me and stroked her head.

"You're a special young lady, Syd girl."

"Do you want more tea, Mummie?" Syd lifted the pot. "Is anything wrong?"

This was supposed to be a reunion. Perhaps she just needed more time.

"No, Lamb. Nothing's wrong. I imagine he's coming home too sometimes." I took another cup of tea.

❧

Next morning I was up making certain Syd had a decent dinner — ham on a leftover scone, boiled egg and an apple. I'd prodded a few of the hangers-on from Eunice's tree with a rake. To wash it down, a jar of fresh milk. Making one lunch was easy but a dwindling food supply suggested a future crisis. Though the barn held some hay, winter was but a stone's throw behind. And what if the girls took sick? Doc Farnaham was good like John about taking food for pay, but we had no surplus. I'd given most of our clothing coupons to Eunice since we couldn't afford them anyway. Claire had bought two new frocks with her Land Army pay, but that work was finished. No sense even dreaming about money for Syd's university. I didn't know Claire's plans but I hadn't seen much of her lately. My stomach hurt, but I went to our room.

I opened our closet with a view for impressing a potential employer instead of cleaning house. What did I have that was proper? The plain navy blue dress John loved had fared well since I saved it for special outings. A matching belt cinched me in around the middle but accented my ample curves.

My one pair of brown heels with the peep toes would work if I could scrounge up a pair of stockings without visible holes. What with nylon scarce, some enterprising women I'd heard tell of had stained their legs with tea and drawn lines down the backs of them with an eyebrow pencil to pass for seams. I had no one to draw the lines for me, and if I had to resort to the penciled-on variety, I would at least want them straight. Fortunately, I found the pair John brought me when he came home on leave. He'd teased me about buying them for some French café singer, but when I reminded him he'd never left England, he guessed I could have 'em. What a rotter he could be, but his teasing way made me want him more. I did want him.

I decided to start close to home and move outward if nothing turned up. It wouldn't take long for there weren't but five or six shops in Rakefoot Crossing and most were family run. If it hadn't been for the girls, I never would have left my garden. I would have survived on turnips and greens rather than make a fool of myself on the street. I felt the beggar and that folks would look down their noses at my taking a paying job from some deserving soldier. But we had to eat too, and I wasn't about to resort to matrimony under duress. Not with Finlay. Not anybody. Eunice meant well but she was cut from a different cloth—more like a nubby tweed.

I checked the postal box on my way out. There was a letter from my sis in Chicago—nothing from the Army about the information I'd requested and still none of John's personal effects.

Walking was the norm in our village. Faces I met seemed genuinely pleased to greet me, but how could I just walk into places I'd traded for years and ask for employment?

First stop, the Rakefoot Crossing Market. Myron Shiverson owned and ran the cramped grocery and butcher shop. He was there all the opening hours and some closed, weighing out beans, handing down tonics and cutting yard goods for the folk who didn't want to go the few miles up road to Penrith. There they would find all manner of shops and a grand grocery as well, but Myron did a fair bit of trade with those who 'didn't want no truck with big town dealers.' I was sure it had a lot to do with the fact that Myron allowed credit—a generosity of which I'd taken advantage, to further my shame.

Any road, I doubted Myron would need help since he was an all around do-it-yourselfer and by the look of his threadbare shirt and hard driven shoes, he was only just squeaking by his own self.

The bell above the whitewashed door clanged over my head as it had a thousand market days before; only this time I waited until he was through waiting on the others. I'd never noticed how imposing a counter it was—chocked full of pills and poisons. Myron looked tired and worse for wear. Probably a bad time to ask after a position. I turned to go.

"Hello, Mrs. Stone. It is good to see you again and looking just grand. I was saying to Mrs. Shiverson, 'Junebug,' I calls her Junebug. 'I wonder how Glory Stone and the brids are getting on?'

How are you this fine autumn morn?" His smile was full of gusto. Clearly I'd misread him.

"Well, good morning, Myron. We're doing ok, you know, it's hard. But life goes forward, eh?" I smiled at Mrs. Hornby.

"What can I get for you today? I have some nice, fresh haddock. Just what doctor ordered to put roses back in the family's cheeks." His smile turned serious with sudden remembrance about John. It was good of him to be so cordial what with my credit at bursting.

"No, no haddock today, thank you." My hands sweat and my heart banged like a farrier in my chest. I looked toward the door.

"I was afraid I might have lost your business to the up town grocery. But Junebug said you likely was just busy with preserving and settling your affairs and all." He looked nervous and swiped biscuit crumbs from the counter with a whisk broom. "Now, what'll it be?"

He was tall and thin and every inch of him was full up with kindness. Myron's prizewinning handlebar moustache had always reminded me of pea vines curling and meandering, reaching for his ear lobes.

I relaxed and breathed in a couple helpings of the shop's personality: cinnamon, pickling spices, soap, tobacco—a feast for the nostrils. Soothed by the familiar, I stepped forward, strapping on confidence like a hot water bottle. I hadn't noticed Margaret Hornby's boy, Laverne, playing ball with a sweetmeat squash. When he rolled it my direction, it intersected my course and tripped me up as it scuttled across the plank flooring. The action pitched me forward and up to the counter to meet quizzical Myron and his shirtfront. He couldn't see the lurking squash.

"I say, can I get you a chair?" His concern was gratifying.

"I'm fine." Hefting the vegetable onto the counter, I rushed headlong into my reason for being there. "I don't mean to buy anything. What I'm looking for is…work, a paid position of some sort." I didn't want to hear him say anything disheartening at this point, so I kept talking. "I'm strong for my size and fairly good with sums. Ah…I enjoy people." Few people, but it wasn't an utter lie. "Plus, I'm available any hours you might need. The truth is, the girls and I need help but we don't want a hand out, just a chance to earn our way." I took a deep breath and let it out so that I blew a cardboard advertisement for Camel cigarettes off the counter. It had been teetering anyway.

Myron's frown shot me full of remorse. Then he screwed up his mouth so that it disappeared behind the vines. When it descended for speech again, he replied, "Glory." He paused, screwed mouth, let it down, and continued. "What's your feeling about blood? I mean, you've killed chickens."

I nodded and wondered what was coming next. Few local women wouldn't meet that qualification. But I knew Myron to have a keen wit so I reckoned he was having me on. My bill had tripled over the past few weeks, yet I could be sure he wasn't threatening violence. There went his peek-a-boo mouth again. I knew the routine; he was about to speak.

"Funny thing, I was just thinking about taking someone on to study under Old Pete." He checked me for a reaction. Old Peter had been the town's only butcher for the last forty years. "Normally I wouldn't consider a woman for the position, naturally."

"Naturally," I agreed.

"But you and John have been good customers and your little gals have been sort of the children June and I never had. And I'll take a chance on training you for the job of butcher if you want to give it a go." He smiled wide, but it would never beat out the moustache.

A butcher? It was a position of some import to the community. Perhaps not quite there with station master, but the locals all revered Old Pete's way with a cleaver and he would be a hard fixture to replace, even temporarily.

My first thought was to stride right out the door, never to look back. Then I thought of Syd. After all, I'd been cutting up hens all my life. And I'd watched at hog butchering, though I never made it through the entire operation until recently. Beef might be more of a challenge, but weren't they just a bigger version of a hog? Truth was I had no choice.

"I'll try it, Mr. Shiverson. And I thank you for the opportunity." I rested my left hand against a stomach full of giddy squirrels and extended my right hand toward Myron to thank him and seal the deal, but he just looked at it confused like he'd never shaken a lady's hand before and didn't think it worked the same as a man's.

"Right! Now I'm still Myron to you, Glory Stone. We've been good friends a long while and I'll not be changing that. You can start right in tomorrow with Peter. I'll let him know to expect you." He commenced whistling, looked doubtful at my dress and added, "Oh and I wouldn't be wearing aught as nice as all that." He gestured toward my hat. "It's a messy job. We have a butcher's coat for you, but I'd wear thick shoes and old clothes.

The two qualifications I had.

"Would you be wanting the squash?" He asked, pointing at the sweetmeat.

"Ah, no. Thank you very much, Myron." I backed out, smiling.

లు

I nearly didn't make it out of bed next morning for nerves. Claire was right proud of her mum and said she thought I'd do OK and not to be qualmsy, she called it. Syd wasn't as impressed; considering she'd be saving animals and I'd be gutting them. I hoped she wouldn't think of us as being at cross purposes. Folks had to eat. We had to eat. And she relished her sausages as much as anybody did.

When I told Eunice, she laughed and shook her hair mound, assuring me it couldn't last and that I'd better not let Finlay get on that train for Workington without some encouragement to return. I wished Finlay well from a distance.

Of course it was raining. I stepped into a dress in my closet which was old all right, but no older than the next. It was cream colored with a white collar and buttons down the front. It had been a regular attendee at school meetings. Today it was a butcher's frock. The only thick shoes I had were some I'd bought secondhand for walking the fells. They looked dowdy with the dress. Well, I'd be in the back with the coat over. Life sure flung experiences in one's direction one would have least expected.

As I approached the market, I saw Myron hard at it, dusting the shelves and making straight his world of commerce. I had no choice about this. "Good morning," I greeted him as if I'd come to wield a proper knife.

"Well if it isn't the working gal, good day! Peter is expecting you and he's right glad to be showing someone the ropes. It took a little time, and a couple or three pints for him to come right to the idea of a woman at the helm, but I reminded him of the time off he's been asking for. Go on through the back there." Myron gestured. "You'll find a coat hanging by the door on your right and gloves on the shelf above. Don't go cutting off your fingers now. There's no market for digits!" He roared with laughter. I looked at my fingers and shrank a little.

I pushed through the heavy door and found my smock and gloves. What was that smell?

"Hello, Peter? I'm here to learn the trade." I couldn't see him but I heard shuffling from the meat locker. The door opened and out walked a stiff hog, puffing and grunting as it glided up to table. Then it talked, but not so that I could understand it. Not that I would expect to.

"Pshshd t mmitt yerie."

Wham! The hog slammed down onto the cutting table revealing Old Peter behind, a short but stocky man who'd become strong as a tree stump toting frozen animals. He stuck out a stubby hand covered with a gelatinous material, no doubt a residual from his load. My stomach lurched but I figured this was just the beginning of a day littered with challenges. I took his hand and tried to ignore the squish. As he turned to look at the project ahead of us, I quickly wiped my hand and donned the gloves.

"O ye nlwnt be needlkty glmshshmm." He smiled when he said it.

Old Peter spoke in an older Northern dialect.

"I'm sorry?" I said and bent near to read his lips. It was then I realized that Old Pete had no teeth. He repeated himself, only louder this time.

"O ye nlwnt be needlkty glmshshmm." and again, "O YE WNT BE NEEDN TH GLVSHM!" With that, he yanked my gloves off still smiling but breathing harder. I guessed I didn't need the gloves.

Then he looked up at me earnestly, and I knew he was about to tell me something important, something I needed to know about cutting up that hog because he had a large knife in his left hand. He was left-handed? I began to sweat.

Nwt th frs ting ye b nedn nwt hjfu llhidmsnmhst mshsm msyt." Then he added for emphasis, "Rembr t gut owtwurhty the hind end. Aye? Ye wit meh?" He'd asked a question that much was sure.

I nodded and that seemed to please him, so he continued. I thought perhaps if I watched closely, I'd learn despite not understanding a blinking word he said, but I doubted it.

He came to life as he got into his work. He plunged the knife into the hog's neck sending rivulets of a pinkish fluid cascading down the animal, Pete's hands, and eventually the white table. My stomach understood loud and clear that it was going to turn sick. Old Pete didn't recognize what an ashen face on a person meant so he kept on mumbling mumbo jumbo.

"Awwy they cut down bt ty nblymshms ahatey head cheese. Nowt o th besty a waste. Lassie, Lassie?"

I caught the last word or two but failed to halt my descent. I faded out, ending up on the cutting room floor like so many entrails before me. I was grateful for the generous sprinkling of wood shavings. When I came to, my head was resting on a large cheese and Myron was holding a cup of whiskey to my nose. I felt that was a might high to do any good but sat up, determined not to forsake my post. But kind Myron said for me to go home and rest, and to return tomorrow providing I could stand the gaff.

❧

Next day I was there but Old Peter was not.

"Good morning, Myron. I believe I can do it this time. I'll jolly well try. But, Old Peter is a might hard for me to understand with the dialect and no teeth and all. Can you understand him?" I did so want to make good.

"Oh aye. It is tough. I should have given you fair warning. The other day the damndest thing happened to Old Peter. He lives alone up near Keswick and he's sleeping with his window open. Well, don't you know a raven came flying along early one morning and stopped on the sill just long enough to snatch Pete's false teeth right off of his bed table. Flew away with them the sneaky thing did. So he's up to Penrith this morning to order new choppers."

Natty, you naughty bird.

"Well, that is unusual isn't it?" I couldn't snitch on the snatcher. Anyway what good would it do? Syd had done away with the teeth. "So can I sweep up or anything?"

Myron said, "No, we'll try again tomorrow. I'll see if I can get a chalkboard or something for Old Pete until his teeth come. There's plenty of meat cut until then. But Tom Cail is going quail hunting and he'll likely shoot himself a fat lot of the little beggars. He's bringing some first thing tomorrow for me to sell up

Chesterfield House way. So I figure you and Pete can start work on smaller game. How does that sound?"

I never thought I'd say that dressing out quail sounded quite like heaven, but life pulsed with relativity.

"It sounds fine. Closer to chickens. I'll see you in the morning then." I hated to add to my tab, but I had to ask for Claire's sake. "Myron, you don't know how I hate to ask, but I need some stomach powder. It's for Claire. She's caught a flu bug I guess."

"Sure thing, Glory. Anything for Claire. Hey, come to think on it, I saw her with the young Rand fellow yesterday, Eunice Quimby's nephew. They were down by bridge over River Cocker. Aren't they seeing quite a lot of one another these days? Could be we'll be hearing wedding bells before too long, eh?"

Albert, still here?

- 9 -

CLAIRE

Mum came in looking pasty as a half baked loaf and didn't waste a minute.

"Claire, I'd like to talk with you." She hung her jacket and hat.

I'd been careful not to let on that Albert and I were seeing one another since I knew she didn't approve. One of several Crossing busybodies must have ratted me out.

I sat at the kitchen table poring over the pastry section of our family cookery book. I'd planned to bait the hook with sweets when Albert and I met that afternoon. I tried to ignore the niggling worry that my period was overdue.

"Right here. What is it?" I stuffed loose pages back into the old standby, and hoped the coming discourse had nothing to do with Albert, though that look of parental concern was hard to mistake.

"Didn't you start work yesterday? Way to go, Mum. How was it?" There was a fancy lemon cookie I liked the looks of but doubted we had the ingredients. Probably would have to settle for shortbread. I had a way with it.

"Well, yes and no." Mum smiled wearily. "It's a sticky business. Not sure I'll last really. Myron Shiverson hired me on as a trainee to old Peter Holmes. Can you fancy it?"

Mum pulled up a chair and slumped down in it, hand resting on her tummy; now there was a warning signal.

"Trouble is I can't understand a word he says. First off, he's got the old dialect, and if that weren't enough, he's got nary a tooth in his head." She laughed.

"That would be a rough go. What will you do?" I checked the sugar bin. Good, there was enough for a small batch.

"Today Pete had gone to town to order a new set of teeth, so that should help. But I'm not sure I can handle all the blood and guts. Ringing a chicken's neck is unpleasant, but if you would have been there when he stuck that pig with the...running down..., oh it was too much. I passed out clean on the floor. Certainly never fancied myself a butcher. Not something I ever dreamed of as a girl, that's certain. Did you hear?"

"Are you all right? I mean did you hurt yourself when you fell?" I gave her a quick once over.

"Oh yeah, I'm fine. Myron said that tomorrow we'd be dressing out a few quail so I should be able to manage it." Mum's face looked drawn. Lately I'd noticed lines around her eyes and mouth and not a few gray hairs. Losing Dad had aged her.

Syd entered looking grim. No doubt, she had another excuse to weasel out of classes. She was forever trying to stay home with her precious animals.

"Mummie, I don't feel so good." Syd was an understudy for Eunice's look of agony.

Mum held her wrist to Syd's forehead as she had countless times.

"You feel a trifle warm. Why don't you hop into bed and I'll bring you a cup of mint tea directly. I have some things to discuss with Claire and I'll be in. Oh, that reminds me." She returned to me. "How's the tum? Myron allowed I could have this medicine on account. Said he'd do anything for you and Syd. Wasn't that kind?" She removed a small packet from her pocketbook and laid it on the table between us.

"Dear old Mr. S. That was kind. It was worse this morning, but thanks. Good to have, in case."

Mum went from light-hearted to grim. I didn't want to hear what she was about to say.

Syd hung around and whinged, "Can't I stay and listen?

"No. And that tone is irritating. This is between Claire and me. Go snuggle up with Jingles and Reggie. They've missed you something awful since school started." Mum patted her behind as she left, and I knew Syd had begun to resent bum love pats.

Before Mum could collect her intentions, I asked, "What did you dream of becoming when you were little? Was it always a wife and mother type? Not that I think there's anything wrong in that." I brought down the mixing bowl.

She chuckled. "I thought I'd told you. Maybe not. I used to think about becoming a train engineer, of all things. Isn't that a silly notion? But I'd fancy myself moving this great, iron beast down track and blowing the whistle by Jennie Brown's house. Even took a lesson from Dad's engineer chum, Alan Dover. He drove for the Cleator and Workington Railway. I climbed into the cab and he showed me the levers, how to start her up, forwards and backwards. An engineer, a man's position—that would make their jaws gape when they found out it was meek Gloria Compton at the helm. I think it would have impressed Dad."

Mum took a deep breath. "Going to bake? You haven't darkened the kitchen in awhile. I thought maybe you'd lost your love of cooking."

I looked at my poor Mum.

"Yes, I'm baking shortbread cookies; some are for Albert Rand." I waited while preparing a defense.

Mum frowned. "Now, that's what I needed to talk with you about when I came in—you and that Albert Rand."

"I knew it," I interrupted. "That Albert Rand, indeed."

"Have you been seeing him all these weeks? I didn't even know he was still in town. What's he doing? Living off of Eunice and Roger's generosity?"

The more worried she became, the more she trembled.

I stood and held her shoulders gently. "Mum, you may as well know and accept that Albert and I are in love. We see a lot of one another, and I don't get why you despise him so. He reminds me a lot of Dad." Mum huffed and shook her head at that observation.

I turned toward the door. "Guess you just can't remember what it was like to be young and in love." I regretted the words as I fired them. An awkward silence followed. "Sorry, Mum."

"I remember more than you know. And more each day," Mum said. "Why haven't I seen Albert? Why hasn't he gotten to know me if he loves you? I'm your mother. Why does he sneak around like a fox? Myron said he'd seen you down by the bridge over the River Cocker. I wouldn't have known he was still here otherwise."

A chill went through me. "Oh? What else did the prying Mr. Shiverson have to say?" I wondered how long he'd stuck around.

"Claire! That's not fair. Myron considers you and Syd as daughters. He was just making an innocent comment, probably thinking I knew all about it. It would be natural that I did, if the two of you were...on the up and up." Mum was so old fashioned. That dress after all.

I got up to leave but couldn't look her in the eye. Irritation erupted so quickly I couldn't stop it or the venom.

"You mean no love making? Is that what you mean when you say 'on the up and up'? I told you Albert loves me! He told me so and any day now, he's going to ask me to become Mrs. Albert

Rand. He's just waiting for the right time and place." I broke down and cried.

Mum came to comfort me but I'd have none of it. I wanted Albert to hold me, love me and tell me everything would be all right.

"Why did Dad have to go? He didn't have to. He would have made you understand."

The cookies would wait. I grabbed a sweater and left to find Albert.

⨏

These lakeside days with Albert were the culmination of a reoccurring dream. I'd been standing on the bank many nights, a silent onlooker as far back as I could recall. Sometimes years passed before the dream reappeared as vivid as ever, stripped of actors or dialogue until now. The stage was set for purpose, with thunderclouds building in the water and a bare tree over their special place like a monk praying. Mum was my age when Dad had proposed. Perhaps this was where fiction and reality became one.

Each time we met, I was surer of Albert. He cared deeply for me. He'd told me and convinced me it was so. It was easy, really.

"I've dreamed of this spot all my life," I told him as I lounged in the grass. "Only it was just a place in time, no people. I knew it had meaning. Except the scene always ended with a frightful storm that tore up trees and sent the water into fits and spirals. Where we're lying was flooded and strewn with black moss. It scared me when I was a little girl." I plucked up some grass. "I'd wake crying and Mum would come and comfort me." I lay back down in the grass and began unbuttoning my blouse to get Albert's attention.

Albert turned over on his stomach next to me, chewing on a grass stalk. He shaded his eyes against the setting sun to look at me.

"I'll bet you were a stunner of a little girl." Albert looked into my eyes as if heaven was behind them. He held the key that was sure. I returned the favor and saw a man after my father's own heart. How I wished Dad could have met him, and that Mum wasn't so cynical.

"I still have my dolls in the attic somewhere. Agnes was my favorite. She had long brown hair and a blue ribbon. Agnes had oodles of friends. She was the most popular girl in the county until one Christmas when the folks brought Betsy home wrapped in pink tissue paper." I laid my arms back over my head and looked at Albert who appeared to be listening and began kissing my hands.

"Agnes' hair eventually looked like a scouring pad from me washing it with bar soap then jerking through the tangles. At some point, I'd given her a bob out of frustration. Her legs had scrapes from so many trips up the climbing tree, then tumbling out, and one eye stuck so that she was perpetually winking." I demonstrated. "She looked like a floozy. I'm ashamed to say it, but I shunned her. Betsy took over the number one spot for my affections." I laughed. "See how fickle I can be?" Albert drew closer.

"I always wanted a tree house too, but Dad was so busy with Syd and their work. Farmers called on him all hours for a hard lambing or colic. It was never ending. And what about you, Bonnie Prince Albert? I'll bet you were a one with the small and big girls alike. I can see you stealing kisses behind a tree or wherever you could manage it and passing notes in class with the teacher's back turned." I threw a seedpod at him.

He took a deep breath and sat back. "You're not far wrong. But females haven't been my sole pastime. I was also a fair hand with a cricket bat. And I managed to keep my marks up so that Dad stayed off my backside." Albert began to run his fingers over my eyelet lace blouse. "Pretty soon I'll have to put those studies to use, you know. I can't continue mooching off Aunt Eunice much longer. She's starting with the hints. Like 'So, Albert love, 'I heard they was doing a bit of hiring over Carlisle way. Sounded like right good wages, benefits too.' Then she smiles that toothy smile. I get it." He looked up and I followed his gaze to the first evening star.

I wondered where we'd be living a year from now—not Rake-foot Crossing. Albert would make something of himself and I'd be beside him as Mrs. Rand. Claire Rand. Sounded rather flat, but our lives would be anything but.

"There now. That's enough talk." Albert kissed me as a husband should kiss a wife, like Mum and Dad must have kissed, and the wind rifled the trees and stirred up the natural things.

- 10 -

GLORY

"**M**orning, Myron?" My timid greeting ran into the cracks of the well stocked market and hid. But Myron heard and raised a lustrous head among the crooknecks.

"Aye, a good morning it is too, Glory Stone. With seven fat quail awaiting your delicate hand. Old Pete will try to be back with us tomorrow. Gave his knee a twist exiting the train yesterday, so he's sitting it out with a bag of ice and beef broth til his teeth come. Do you think you can give those dainty birds a dressing down?" Myron's pluck gave me the leverage to nod.

"I'd like to have a go at them. They're like small chickens, right, only more expensive?"

"Yeah. The birds is all the same. Pluck out the feathers, out with their guts, if you'll pardon my wordage, and what's left is what you got. Don't know why folks think they're such a delicacy. They bring a fine price at Chesterfield's but they're all covered over with rice or some such starch to hide how little meat there is. Give me a ruddy pork chop." Myron chuckled. "You'll find the birds in the icebox."

I approached the backroom to don a man-sized coat. Rolling up the stovepipe sleeves, I found my hands to wash them, then opened the icebox and went for my covey. Sure enough, there were seven birds lying like Snow White's dwarves asleep on their beds. I hated to disturb them. I lifted one out to begin with, and looked around for the tools of my new trade. A large cleaver hanging on the wall next to the cutting surface would more than do for the heads and feet but I'd need a sharp knife for the gutting. I found one in a wooden block on the counter. First things first though, to pluck. I began pulling on larger feathers that clung to their purpose. Perhaps Pete used tweezers or pliers for this part of the job. I looked but didn't find anything suitable so yanked away the best I knew. At this rate, I doubted I'd finish with them all before day's end.

The tiny pin feathers I scraped off with a paring knife. It took me thirty seven minutes to rid the first bird of its plumage. Times seven. This wouldn't do, and that's not counting the cutting up. It would be a long day. Once the feathers were off, it looked like a newly hatched chick, which pecked at my conscience. But Myron was paying me to dispatch the poor thing, and not to snivel about it.

Slam! I was afraid if I didn't give the cleaver my all, the head would be only half severed, a vision I sought to avoid. I needn't have concerned myself because not only did head cleanly separate from body; the blow actually sent the shooter rolling across the table and onto the floor. It traveled faster than when it had wings.

Was there a point to the wings? Surely not even a toothpick-sized sliver of meat clung to the tiny bones. I didn't know how they served these birds in those swell places, but these would be enjoyed flightless. Wham…Wham.

The remainder wasn't worth the work needed to separate

muscle from bone, but I slit its gullet, cleaned out the shot and removed the insides as I had many a chicken. This once free-roaming woodland creature yielded no more than two rounded tablespoons of sustenance. It would take a lot of starch to make this bird a meal.

"How are we coming in here?" Myron's head made an entry through the butchery door and glanced around. "Thought I heard a noise."

"One bird done. You need them all by today, right?" I asked as though it was the simplest request and I'd have a lot of time leftover for thumb twiddling.

"Right. Got to pack them in dry ice and have them off."

"Right. I forgot to ask, do you want the wings left on? They're so pitifully lacking, don't you think?" I worried as the wings lie positioned in disembodied flight on the cutting table.

He followed my gaze. "Normally we leave them on, if only for visual interest in the pre...sentation, they call it. Sometimes they're laid out on a bed of greens like they was flying with a plum or tomato where the head used to be. But no matter about this one." He picked up a wing and let it flop back down. He looked at the puddle of flesh remaining as I stood over it with a knife three times its size. "Might want to give that one a break. Believe he's had it." He was smiling, but less so as he retreated from the carnage.

What was I doing there? Gloria Stone was clearly out of place, like a child driving a locomotive. I had no talents beyond my garden wall and no chance beyond a fool's of being Rakefoot's butcher. I would complete the task even if I saw the sunrise, but then tell Myron and Old Peter to find a suitable trainee.

❧

Myron was gracious, allowing me to save face by staying at the birds until I'd dispatched them. After cleaning the butchery, it was nearly 1:00 a.m. I locked up and walked home in the cool, quiet night like a boxer hammered for fifteen rounds, knowing he'd lost the decision in the third.

I was whacked after only earning one day's wages. I looked to an autumn moon for sympathy—the same moon, John's and mine. It would have remembered us, as we often walked in its lesser light. I'd heard some people couldn't see the man in the moon. John not only saw him, but named him. He called him Morgan after Mergenthaler, his favorite cheese. Morgan Moon. Silly notion I guess, but that was just the kind of thing John did, named inanimate objects.

When Morgan was at full serving, we'd used him as a scapegoat for any crazy game we thought up. One June night we'd left the girls asleep in their beds, grabbed a bottle of stout and went to the river to swim in the buff.

John had toasted me that night, 'Glory, my radiant wife, after twenty years you still shine.' And then to the moon, 'I'm afraid you'll take a back seat, old boy.'

I never said a word after a sentiment like that. I didn't want to eclipse the sound of it with my voice. I stopped and stared into a sullen sky, clinging to the candy floss memory. It melted as I tasted it—splashing, laughing till our bellies hurt and kissing as the water dripped down.

A bat flapping blind overhead brought me back to earth, and the pain. I had to get home to the girls. Neither had been well.

The frogs had signed off for the year and gone to their hibernation beds. My thick shoes shuffling on the gravel roadway was the only regular sound. It was eerie-like being out alone so late. Something rattled the bushes across the road—skunk or possum likely. The air was so still I could have heard a cricket wipe its mouth.

I'd rung Claire to let them know I'd be late and didn't know how late, so hopefully they'd had supper and gone to bed. I kept walking but shortly I heard extra footsteps so I stopped. I wished I had Eunice's spike, although I'd have no more idea how to use it than she would. But I couldn't help thinking about that woman in Liverpool, which put my nerves on high alert. I took a few steps, and glanced over at what I thought was a tree shadow. It seemed closer and I clearly heard another footfall, and not that of a small animal. It was gaining on me. *Should I run?* My heart raced but my legs felt like tree trunks. I'd been on my feet all day and could not will them to move any faster. Then something clapped onto my shoulder.

"Glory Stone?"

"Who is it?" I turned, shielding my face with my pocketbook.

"In heaven's name, it's only me. What business has you about this time of night?" He looked worried.

"Oh, Axel, thank God it's you. You gave me a fright. I worked late at market and was on my way home." I felt ashamed to tell people what I was about.

"I think I heard something about that. Glory, dear, please let me know if there's anything I can do, will you? Do you need money? Food? Just ask." Biggs' hand slid from my shoulder down to the small of my back. The warmth felt reassuring, but I wished it were John's hand.

"Ah, you've done too much already, bless you. Paying for the funeral was far and away more than I could have asked." I breathed easier.

"It was pure pleasure. Let me walk you the rest of the way. You shouldn't be wondering about alone in the pitch dark you know."

"It's not too dark. Morgan is most full." I smiled at the memory. "Did John ever tell you we called the moon Morgan?"

He looked up. "I used to see that moon from my nursery window. We're old chums."

"Ah." I continued, "I was just thinking of John and remembering one of the many fun times we had. And what about you, my good man? What brings you out into deserted streets at this wee hour?"

"Oh, couldn't sleep so I was just walking, trying to tire my sorry self out." Axel looked ragged. "Guess I got in the habit when I was on patrol."

"I'm sorry. You've struggled like that ever since…"

"Since Trudy." He finished. "It's all right, you can say her name. Each time it gets easier." He looked away. "She wasn't the easiest person to live with, in all honesty. Trudy complained about plans I made. She was never very, shall we say, simpatico to our way of living—Mutti's and mine. And you might know that they never got on well. Nevertheless, one gets used to having someone around, and the first few weeks after she left I thought I'd go crazy. Made fool decisions that could have cost me my position. One day I was filling in for the signalman who'd taken ill. By dozing at the signal, I came that close to causing a head on collision between east and westbound Cauliflower engines, one pulling coal, the other, with passengers." Biggs rubbed his brow. "I could have killed everyone aboard. Neither was scheduled to stop." He kicked at a stone. "After that, I decided I had to take control and stop living in the past. Trudy was gone, and I knew she was never coming back. It was out of my hands."

"I never heard that story. It's hard to leave the past when it was so perfect." I looked up at him, realizing his former life was not as satisfying as mine had been.

Axel looked at me and rubbed his gloves together. "You, my dear, need to move forward as well. Stop dwelling on John and reliving shadows that are no more and can never be again. It will only make progress more difficult for the girls. They're watching their mum." He patted my shoulder.

"You know," I began. "Syd doesn't believe John's dead. She…"

Biggs stopped and frowned at me then resumed walking.

"Perfectly normal. A twelve-year-old child not wanting to believe her daddy's gone." He wiped his moustache with his finger and thumb. "Why does she feel that way? Does she have reason to doubt his death?"

Axel and Syd had formed a special bond since the news and had spent a lot of time together. I was surprised he didn't know, but I couldn't betray Syd's trust.

"Just doesn't believe it, she says. You're probably right; she's in a period of denial that will pass." The moon was there, looking down on us from a little higher than before. "I still have unanswered questions—no death certificate, for one."

"Really?" Biggs seemed surprised, too. "Well, it should come. Let me know if you don't receive it soon, will you? I'll see what I can do to hurry things up."

He'd shown some of us the letter Trudy had left on their dresser next to a portrait of the two of them on honeymoon in Krakow. In her delicate hand it said, 'Dear Axel, as you read this letter I shall be well on. It should come as no surprise to you that we have irreconcilable differences. I've had my fill of country life and want to experience firsthand what's available elsewhere. No need trying to locate me, as I've left the country and am adamant in my decision. Give my love to Donnie if you see him. Take care, Trudy.'

The village couldn't help itself and gossiped about whether they ever divorced. Possible scenarios had kept Eunice busy for weeks. But she never turned up anything more concrete than what she thought was Trudy's wedding band. She made a squawk of seeing it on his desk in the station shortly after he divulged the letter. But that didn't prove anything. If she'd left him, why not the ring? Axel still wore his. I finally convinced her to keep quiet about his experience.

"Well here we are. Thanks for the escort. Oh, by the way, Syd keeps pestering me to ask about the pups." The girls always locked the door. I hunted for my key.

"Pups?"

"The puppies John rescued. She seems to think they're our

responsibility, but so much time has passed, I suppose they've been disposed of or found homes by now. Of course, how would you know? I told her I'd ask anyway. She has a heart for animals, like her pop." I located my key at last, then dropped it in the gravel. Axel stooped to get it.

"Ah, yes, the pups. Dear Syd. She is very like her pop. She's become my chum of late. I'll do my best to find out for her and ring up Carlisle Station tomorrow. " Axel cleared his throat. "Yes, that'll be my first duty of the day. I'll inquire of Robert Pumfrey, station master there." He turned the lock.

"Well, no worries if you don't turn up anything. Syd will be all right. She has enough animals to fill a small ark. And that's another story. Any road, good night, Axel, and thanks again." I squeezed his arm and managed to squeeze a smile out of him in the bargain.

I went inside and quietly made my way to the girls' room to check on Syd.

"Mum? Why are you so late?" Syd sounded puny, different from her usual gripe.

"Didn't Claire tell you? I phoned saying I'd be late." I sat on the edge of her bed and felt Syd's clammy head.

"Yes, but I didn't think you'd be this late. I feel near to death. My throat hurts something awful and I ache all over. I'm so glad you're home." Syd closed her eyes and relaxed into her pillow.

Claire joined the conversation from her side of the room.

"Welcome home." The way she said it sounded more like an accusation than a greeting. "Syd's been setting up a fuss all night. Guess I should have rung you at work. I couldn't do anything to make her better. She wouldn't touch her supper. What have you been at anyway?" Claire was a nervy one when inconvenienced.

I sighed. "Mutilating birds." I turned back to Syd. "You are hot, my tea party princess. I'll bring some cool cloths and snug in with you tonight. We'll have to ring up Doc Farnaham tomorrow first thing. Oh, and I saw Axel Biggs on my way home. I asked after the puppies and he promised he'd ring up Carlisle Station in the morning and find out what he could.

"Axel Biggs?" Claire asked. "What was he doing out at 1:00 in the morning? Doesn't he know the war's over and he doesn't have to keep watch over us any longer?" Her chuckle was a disgusted one. Axel had taken his role as village Air Raid Patrol rather seriously. "Come to think on it, I saw the light quite late in station office last week. It was the night I was at Barbara's for her birthday get-together. What does he do all hours?"

"Said he had trouble sleeping. He gave me a proper fright, but afterward I was glad of him. And you'll do better to keep a respectful tone about a man who cares for his community. He even offered us money."

"Good. I hope you took it. We're in sorry need of some things around here." Claire's observations—always at the ready.

I closed my eyes and rubbed my forehead. "We haven't come to that yet. I'm going to start looking for a different position right off. I should have known butchering wouldn't cut it."

"Nice one, Mum." Claire laughed.

"What? Oh, yeah." I looked at Syd who had mercifully found sleep while I stroked her hair and thought back to when she was a wee one. Oh, for those simple days when these walls housed my purpose and I knew how to handle all that a day required.

I hadn't the guinea for a doctor visit and couldn't see myself asking Myron for an advance so soon, especially with what we owed. Myron knew I wouldn't be there much longer. He shook his head when leaving me to it last night. It was good of him to give me a go, but I would quit and so save him the discomfort of sacking me. What next, I wondered?

- 11 -

CLAIRE

"How did you find this place?" Albert clambered over a hay bale, bottle in hand and joined me in the castle keep.

"Isn't it fabulous? We can't stay long. Mum told me about it. It's Syd's fortress. I guess she spends hours up here talking to her animals and writing in a diary. I wonder...yeah, here it is. She'd never know if we read a couple pages. I'll bet she has a lot to say about her big sis. This could be good." I opened the small book. "Strange. Much of it's ripped out. Guess she's afraid of someone reading it." I closed and returned the journal.

"Syd and Mum had a tea party out here, so I got to thinking it might be cozy for us to have a private party." I spread a worn coverlet over the hay. "What have you there, Prince Albert? Doesn't look like tea." I chewed a hay straw.

"This stuff's good for what ails you and goes down easy, like strawberry soda. I brought glasses." When Albert leaned near, I caught an intoxicating whiff of his King's Men cologne.

"I don't know. What if someone should find us?"

"Your mum's at the butchery and Syd's sick in bed. What's the worry?"

"I can't leave Sis alone for long."

I didn't drink as a rule. Not because of any moral conviction, I'd just never thought it sounded pleasant to wake with a ruddy headache and my face in the loo. But Dad enjoyed his nightly ale and was no worse for wear, plus I didn't want to disappoint Albert and appear the backward country bumpkin, so I held the glass steady while he filled it.

"Whoa. I'm new at this you know. Are you trying to take advantage of me?" We laughed. Yeah, that was a good one.

Albert took a slug from his glass, and I guessed he'd learned to throw them back in the RAF. Maybe he was trying to work up courage to pop the question. I wanted him sober for that. The bittersweet taste reminded me of the awful so-called cherry flavored cough syrup of my youth. It tasted nothing like cherries, rather like the pits. I about gagged.

"What do you think? I got it special from a reliable source." Albert looked silly with some of the red stuff on his lip.

"Did Myron Shiverson sell it to you? Didn't know he carried liquors."

"Nope. All I had to do was wait until dear Uncle and Aunty took their afternoon snooze. I raided their liquor cabinet while they snored. Pretty fair supply, too." He drained his glass and poured another.

Albert assured her, "It's all right, Love. This isn't my first time." He reached for me, but I sat back.

"First I want to talk—to hear about your boyhood: toys you favored, veggies you hated and dumped in the flower pot, pets, daydreams—all the details." I felt fuzzy around the edges and set the glass aside. "I've talked about me and my problems, but you haven't said much."

"Yeah? I can't imagine why you'd care about that kid stuff."

"Just want to get to know you better."

He tipped his head and made a slow journey from my eyes down the length of my body and back. I felt every inch of it. He made me feel desirable and special, and I'd learned how to capture his heart. There would be time for talk later, after we were an old married couple. There would be long nights staring up at the stars with deep conversation flowing between us, and laughter, much laughter. He was too humble to talk about himself.

"Talk is for amateurs." Albert took me in his arms. "Come to Papa."

This time I didn't hold back. This was our present communication. It was passionate and brought us that much closer, like in the movies. As I reclined in the tower, Albert assumed his rightful place. It was good to feel someone strong in charge again.

I hoped he'd propose soon.

❦

"Albert. I heard someone drive up." He'd fallen asleep. "Albert!" I shoved at his shoulder. "Get up. I'm sure I heard something. No one must find us up here. C'mon! Get dressed!" I hurried to pull on my clothes, but Albert just lay there on his back with his mouth gaped open. One too many nips of the strawberry medicine had left him unresponsive. Prince Albert was canned.

I looked out the open loft. There was the doctor's black sedan in the driveway.

"It's Doc Farnaham with Mum! He's here to look in on Syd and she's going to wonder where I am. Albert, we have to get out of here while they're in the house and come up with an excuse. Now please get moving!" I pushed at him again and drew his response.

"Oh bloody hell!" He swiped awkwardly at me. "What difference does it make anyhow? They're all going to find out sooner or later, eh?" Albert yelled at me.

"Albert, please, for my sake, just get dressed and let's go. I think they've gone inside."

I saw a man I didn't recognize, or like. In fact, I hated to admit that Albert's character had diminished over the past weeks from the man I'd met, though I suppose he'd proper excuse. He still had healing to get through. I'd read about psychological trauma soldiers reported— recurring nightmares of watching their chums die hideous deaths. Albert hadn't faced that, but it would take time for him to feel like a civilian.

I looked at him—staggering, struggling to dress—and felt pity. Yeah, he'd never raised his voice to me like that before, but the drinks were to blame. I was glad he hadn't proposed in that state, as I would have had to refuse in hopes he'd ask again on a good day.

It was sad, but I doubted he'd remember this dreamy after-noon, or that I'd worn daisies in my hair. The party was over. I suddenly felt we were trespassing on sacred ground, a place watched over by an invisible guardian. We had no business in Syd's territory. I spotted a box wedged into a shelf scratched out of the hay. While Albert was still flummoxing around, I opened the lid, and there were Dad's toiletries. I smelled his after-shave, the famil-iar tobacco, and I cried.

"See here. Why the tears, Cupcake?" Albert noticed. "What's this, eh?" Before I could stop him, he grabbed the Meerschaum, stood up and stuck it between his teeth pretending to puff away. "Look. I'm bloody Sherlock Holmes!" he yelled. Clearly, drinking made him deaf as well as irritating.

"Stop it!" I stood and lunged for the pipe. Albert dodged, leav-ing nothing but air between the concrete floor and me.

❧

"Claire! Claire, can you hear me?"

It's Mum. And someone else. What's happened?

"Let me take a look."

Doc Farnaham's voice. Is Mum angry?
"We better not move her," Doc said.
Why can't I move? I'm scared, and cold.
"She could have broken bones or internal injuries. We need to summon an ambulance and get her to hospital where I can give her a thorough going over. The way she's lying here, it appears she's had a fall. Glory, you need to ring them up. I'll stay here with Claire and check her vitals." I could hear the click and clank of instruments as he pulled them from his leather bag. He began with a cold stethoscope on my chest.

"Monty," Mum recited a familiar line. "I have no money. As I've said, I don't even have enough for Syd's care and now this. I quit the market. I won't be getting but one day's wages, barely enough to pay for the ink on my bill there." Mum was near to a panic.

"Pull yourself together, old girl. I'm afraid it's got to be done. We'll need x-rays. The hospital won't be as costly if I'm the attending physician. Two of your stellar apple pies will do nicely for a starter. Now, no weaseling out." Doc's attention returned to me. "Hello. I think she's coming to."

I revived, somewhere between the conversation echoing around me and a dream about a disappearing clown on a train. I was frustrated because no one would believe I'd seen him, though I tried to convince anyone who would listen that he was real and dangerous. When I opened my eyes to find Mum and Doc Farnaham leaning over me with curious faces, I felt the impulse to laugh but didn't. Mum stroked my hair and smiled while her brows remained furrowed. What a lot of trouble I'd put her through of late. I closed my eyes to see how the dream ended.

"I'll go make the call and check on Syd." Mum said. Her shoes scuffed through the grass as she ran off. I wondered if Doc saw me smiling, or if I was just thinking about smiling. I wanted to see Mum running so I opened my eyes again but evidently Mum covered turf faster than I thought or maybe it had been longer than I thought. *What's happened to me?*

"Ah. Now we have you back," the doctor sounded relieved. "You had us rather worried, old chum. Are you able to give me the lowdown?"

I tried to tell him I didn't remember anything, but no sound came of the effort. I panicked and tried to sit up. My only communication was with tears.

"There, now." Doc Farnaham spoke gently and laid me back down. "You'll be all right presently. You rest. It's common for a person to lose her faculties temporarily over a nasty blow. Keep you from lippin' off to your mum for awhile." Doc shined a stream of blinding light into my eyes and felt my racing pulse while he stared at his pocket watch.

"Your pup, Jingles wouldn't leave off barking until he brought us to you lying here. Fine dog, that. You've a nasty bump on your head and hay in your hair. I'm no detective, but it doesn't require a professional to deduce you must have been inside the barn at some point. No matter, we'll worry with details later."

I craved sleep. I determined to find that clown and drag him before the magistrate.

"No. None of that now. Let's keep awake, shall we? There's a good girl," the doctor said cheerfully, giving my cheeks a soft patting. "It's important to stay with us."

Mum scuttled back.

"She's awake! Claire, darling." Mum kissed me and I smelled her sachet. The tender touch of her lips made me feel like crying again. "What happened, can't you tell us?" She turned to Doc. "Ambulance is on the way and Eunice can sit with Syd."

Isn't Albert here? He could tell them what happened.

"It's getting to be a ruddy emergency ward at your place, Mrs. Stone, what with two sick girls on my hands." He looked at me and smiled. Doc had always reminded me of a slim, more distinguished version of Father Christmas with his white, tailored beard and kind eyes that crinkled like skin on a pudding when he smiled.

"Best not try and force an explanation until she's ready. We may have to call in that Holmes fellow to solve the mystery. I could be Doctor Watson, what?" Doc chuckled, and I was glad he didn't mention to Mum I couldn't talk. I wondered how serious it was.

As Doc leaned over to study my eyes again, I noticed a pipe stem poking from his coat pocket and something clicked—Sherlock Holmes, yes.

- 12 -

GLORY

"I'll bet Claire was with Albert, the snake," Syd blurted. A ratty Dr. Doolittle book slipped off the bed. "Is she OK? Did she break something? I've got to talk to her!" Jingles and Reggie, her sick-bed watch, started when she flung back her covers. Jingles had done a good dog's work alerting us. I scratched his ears for the umpteenth time and he well might have said 'I love her too,' with four circular thumps of his tail.

"Get back in bed." I pulled the covers back over her bare legs and tried to keep the worry out of my voice. "She's conscious and Doc is with her. Eunice is coming to look after you while we go to hospital for x-rays."

I had filled Syd in on what little I knew of the happenings while we waited and waited for Eunice and for the blasted ambulance to arrive from Keswick.

"The thought had crossed my mind about Albert." Didn't mention other unholy notions that had played through. "He sure wasn't anywhere about when we found her. Wonder what she was doing in the barn?" My stomach churned and I needed to be with her. "Can you eat something now, little one? Eunice will be here presently and you might not like what she serves up." I needed to busy my hands.

"Yes, I'd prefer something you made. The last time she cooked for us it was liver and onions slopping about in gravy. Liver… and…onions." Her emphasis was not lost on me. "Pop never calls me little one. He makes me feel grown up. I'm nearly thirteen." Syd stroked the fat cat name of Blarney Bill, or BB for short, who'd also become bedridden with her in hopes of an easy snack. "Claire will be all right, won't she?"

"Yes, Doc will put her right I'm sure." I went to the window and glanced up road then returned to the familiar. Looking around our quarters, I realized how impossible it seemed for people not to take their situations for granted. I paced and went for a glass of water, partly to ward off another spell.

I took painful inventory of the way our furnishings reminded me of John and family times. How many hours had we spent around that wireless listening to BBC radio plays? For a few years now, our reception had been limited to war talk and *V for Victory Broadcasts*. John had fit his club chair so attractively. As he listened and looked at his periodicals, he puffed, the smoke signaling contentment about the room. I needed him badly, times like these.

There were the girls' places when they were small. I'd left them as they were. Claire's was an antique, child-sized high backed chair with two crude repairs to the understructure. It was one of many treasures Goby had left to me. I used it to set Claire down in the corner more than once for a sassy mouth. Just now, a little sass would be music to my ears.

Syd's red rocker had waggled the pups back and forth when she wasn't parked in it, pulled up next John. She was an early reader. At three, I recall John helping her sound out words from his veterinary magazines. It was the funniest thing her trying to pronounce words with an R in them. Guensey, Jewsey, Wode Island Wed Wooster.

I sat on the other side of John in the overstuffed chair. I'd mended so many holey trousers and socks sitting on that peony throne, there was nigh enough makings underneath the cushion to outfit a sewing basket.

A siren wail gave voice to my melancholy and pulled me back up through the years. The ambulance had finally arrived and Eunice came through the front door with her hair in pin curls, a vanity case in one hand and a deck of cards in the other.

"I came quick as I could, love. How's Claire?" Eunice came toward me crouched for a fit should it be bad news.

"We don't know yet. Doctor Farnaham thinks she's had a nasty fall. Wants her to have a proper look over to make sure all's right, that's it." I hesitated, "She hasn't spoken since we found her." I grabbed my coat from the peg and put on rubbers.

"Not a word?" I could almost hear the squeak and crunch, as she searched through memory scraps for a similar situation. "That very thing happened to an undertaker over Blencow way. A cussed old geezer name of Digger got beat about the head with a poker by his missus when he came home potted and shouting profanities at her and the brids. One time it was one blow too many and poof, no more lip from him. Didn't stop him from putting his fist to the mug though, the old fish." She cackled then waxed reverent. "Now that was a marriage that stood the test."

The thing about her was, even during a crisis, she did cheer the worst of it without trying. Her bent was to squeeze every breath of drama from a situation and leave it gasping. There was nothing left of despair once she'd had a hold.

I looked out the window then came over to give Syd a kiss and squeeze.

"Doc says that sort of thing is common with head trauma and

that it will likely be temporary. Um, before I go, have you seen Albert today by chance?"

"Well it was a funny thing about that boy. This afternoon he come tearing through the house like his trousers was afire. Said he'd a keen opportunity for work, packed his bags quick as you can say 'flat foot floogie', and he was gone on the 6:15. I didn't get to pack him a supper for the train or give him a hug or anything." Eunice watched me.

"Interesting." I felt my hackles rise and wondered if I should be calling the police.

"What do you make of young folk these days?" She went on. "Here he'd been with us for three whole months and all of a sudden he's off like buckshot." Eunice smiled widely at Syd who for once listened intently to their chatty neighbor. "And how are you, little one? How are you bearing up with all this catastrophe?" Eunice acted out her question as well as saying it, then looked down realizing she'd shuffled over in bedroom slippers.

"Better, thank you. Worried about my sister though." She turned toward me.

"Do you know where Albert was off to?" I asked while Eunice began unfurling her hair. The pins in her mouth made her sound some like Old Peter.

"You know, he was in such a hurry. I'll get in touch with his folks and find out more about it." She picked through her hair with her long nails.

The ambulance lights raced red around the kitchen walls. I grabbed my pocketbook. "I've got to go. Monty's following in his car and I'm riding with him. I was just about to fix something for Syd's supper. Would you mind? Just something simple like butter and jam on bread." I doubted Eunice would take my suggestion but I tried.

"Thanks, Mum," Syd said woefully. "Tell Claire I'm thinking

of her and that me and the animals will say prayers." She looked at Eunice as if this supper might be her last.

"All right, love, all right now," Eunice fussed. "Don't worry about this little chicken."

She yelled as I exited, "I brought over my Paulette Goddard Make-Up Kit and a deck of cards in case she'd rather play rummy." A flash of showmanship and she was off to perform in the kitchen.

ᘒ

I hadn't been in a hospital waiting room since Dad's illness. The smell of disinfectant nauseated me. The walls surely must have had a coat or two of paint since then, but they were still the same bilious green. Some slick painting contractor must have struck a perennial bargain with all the hospitals and old people's homes offering a smashing deal on Aphid Green.

I buried my head in an article about Tyrone Power's latest romance to avoid eye contact and conversation. I'd sized up the woman in the large print dress two chairs down for a talker. She smiled at everyone who walked by and I felt sure she had words of wisdom to impart. I was irritable just now and therefore disliked people, including myself. It was an escalating cycle of disgust.

Nurses came and went down the shiny, tiled hall next to me, squeaking by in their thick-soled oxfords, rattling carts with trays full of pill bottles and bland, aluminum-encased meals. I wouldn't want to work there and have to endure that wretched aroma and be around sick people incessantly.

For nearly three hours, I took out my frustrations by mentally beating up on Keswick Hospital personnel. Griping kept my mind off an attack. I dared not even entertain the idea of one. Sometimes that's all it took. I'd located the washroom when we first came inside in case I needed a dodge.

I helped myself to the drinking fountain for the fifth time, though water was a poor excuse for a meal. I collected a lint-covered five pence from the folds of my purse—enough for a cup of coffee.

Finally, Doctor Farnaham came through the double doors for Hospital Personnel Only. I tried to read his expression and saw melodrama.

"Well? How is she? Was she able to tell you anything?" Let the man speak, for God's sake, I reprimanded myself.

"Let's go to the cafeteria. I'll buy." He tossed my mangled paper cup into a waste bin.

"Just tell me about Claire." I looked at him as we walked so he would say something.

"Claire will be fine, Glory."

I relaxed some.

"She'll need proper rest and good food, but she'll come out of this fine." He looked concerned. "It will take time." There was more.

I chose random dishes from the food line and found a private booth.

"She has two broken ribs, which will heal on their own and miscellaneous bruising. She'll be very sore for several days. There are no internal injuries—at least not the kind an x-ray reveals. Claire is starting to remember, and that's good. She can also speak. But...she doesn't want to right now—not to me, not anybody. That's where time and patience are needed."

I looked at my tray to see what I was eating. "What else, Monty? Please say it." The macaroni cheese I'd swallowed refused to go down.

"This is hard. I've known your family. Hell, I birthed your girls. But sometimes there are wounds that medicine and doctors can't fix. Claire wouldn't tell me much about what happened in that barn, just that she fell from the hayloft. Sometimes even accidents like this one can be blessings in disguise." He took a drink of coffee and ran his large hand over his face then looked at his plate.

I was already playing it out in my head, the plausible scenario between Claire and Albert.

"I knew it. He did it, didn't he? I knew he was up to no good. I tried to warn her but she just wouldn't listen. She's too grown up to listen to her mum!" There I was again, helpless at my girl's pain.

"Who was up to no good?" he asked.

"That nephew of Eunice and Roger Quimby's, Albert Rand, that's who." I'd have spat if I could.

"Glory, listen to me. There's more and there's no easy way to say it." He took my hands. "Claire was early on with child. I doubt she knew for certain."

A man cleaning off tables rattled past us with a cart full of dirty dishes.

"What?" I watched the clean-up man go and pulled my hands away. "I mean, are you sure?" I felt my eyes welling up. My stomach hurt. I could hardly stand the sorrow I felt for Claire. I knew Albert was a fast mover but I'd never imagined this. I was growing old and forgetful like Claire said.

Monty continued, "I wanted to tell you first and let you decide."

"Decide? You said 'was with child.' I'm assuming she lost the...baby?" I said it.

"Yes, she did. But you, I, and one out-of-town nurse are the only ones who know. Nobody else would have to. Claire wouldn't have to."

- 13 -

GLORY

I was relieved Claire didn't have to stay the night in hospital. On the ride home, Monty and I tried to find something gay to talk about—something to take her mind off the reality of the situation as far as she knew it, but Claire only stared out the window, and I couldn't fake it for long. Albert had confirmed my thoughts. He wasn't just a user; he was a coward. If John were with us, there wouldn't be any confusion about how to handle Albert.

John wasn't a violent man, but it was a different matter where his girls were involved. He'd stepped outside the Brakeman's Tabby one night to punch a fellow in the nose for making a careless comment about my dress. When the girls were small, they begged me to tell the story of how their dad made the startled chap apologize while wiping blood from his face.

When Monty dropped us off back home, it was late. I thanked him for all he'd done and promised I'd get to work on the pies as soon as I could. He'd closed his eyes and smiled at the prospect, dear man.

I was the one helping Claire inside this time. No fire, but we noticed a strange odor. Then I remembered I'd left Eunice in charge of the kitchen. Squash casserole hadn't been her only diversion, no. Syd was shocking in her made-over glory. The make-up was so thickly applied she looked like the frosted clown cake we'd made for her eighth birthday. Eunice had pulled her hair onto the top of her head in a bun with a large plastic rose for an exclamation point. The fact that she wasn't smiling didn't help her look. Syd was mortified.

"Oh! So glad you both came home." Eunice said as she looked from me to Claire and back. "How did it go?" She yanked me off to the side. "Can she answer for herself?"

I removed Eunice's claw from my arm. "Yes, she's found her voice. But I'm afraid she's not up to visiting."

"Is Claire all right? Are you all right, Claire? Syd asked, concerned and eager to shed the limelight.

"I'll be fine. A bit sore." Claire didn't give her sis a second look.

My grown girl had survived a tough battle, yet she was with us and I was grateful. I couldn't think on the prospect of losing my firstborn too. I walked Claire to the bedroom, her form reminding me of a willowy ghost. When I helped her into a nightgown, I saw bruising coming on.

"Can I bring you anything? A glass of warm milk? You haven't had any supper, and Doc said you're to have rest and good food." She needed me again.

"I couldn't keep anything down. The pain pills make me sick. I'll eat something tomorrow."

"I'd like to know what happened. You know I'm ready to listen," I tried not to stare. "Whenever."

She looked at me, and some tears escaped her resolve. I held her lightly and stroked her hair with hospital smell clinging to it as fresh sorrow swamped me. For the first time, I entertained murder. I wanted Albert dead because that was the only way I could be sure he'd never bother Claire again.

"I will soon, Mum." She let me go.

I placed the pain relievers on her nightstand and went for a glass of water.

"You can take one every four hours or maybe cut one in two and take it with a cracker. Call me if you need me in the night. Maybe I should get the bell." I kissed her nose like in the old days and she didn't mind. "There'll be time for sorting out the what's what. Right now you just try and get some sleep." I left the door ajar and saw Claire turn over but I doubted sleep would come willingly. Where would she put this new loss? It came too soon.

I rejoined the world of glamour queens and went for Claire's bell in the cupboard.

"Welcome home, Claire," Eunice called into her bedroom. "You're looking right fine." She shook her head and gave a shudder to me, then in a voice she thought hushed said, "She looks like the deuce but I guess she's been through the ringer today, poor dear. Did you ever find out what happened? Was she able to tell you anything?" Eunice lit a fresh fag and blew smoke at the ceiling.

Syd sat, quiet and staring.

"It's been a hard day for all of us." I sank into the cushion. "She told the doc only that she'd fallen from the hay loft. Not sure why she was up there, but hopefully she'll feel like telling us more tomorrow." I couldn't look Eunice in the eye.

Syd spoke up, "The hay loft? I hope they didn't bugger up my things!"

I'd have to be careful. Eunice had a way of getting at things, like a badger. I couldn't divulge all. If she learned we suspected Albert of foul play she might tip him off, blood being thicker and all. This foul mess hadn't only ripped up another chapter in our family's life; it could bollix up my friendship with Eunice in the bargain.

"Well you just lie back and let me fix you a dish of tea," Eunice offered.

"No, it's too late. Might keep me awake, and I've had enough trouble sleeping." I chanced another look at Syd. "I guess I can see what the two of you have been up to." I tried to be perky about it.

"She chose the makeover to rummy." Eunice beamed. "Well, what do you think of your little starlet? Doesn't she look like a young Merle Oberon?"

"Where is she? I can't find her under all that grease paint." I looked at Eunice. "Honestly Eunice, don't you think this business is a bit silly for a twelve-year-old? Especially one who spends most of her time chasing pigs." Syd looked forlorn, like a washed-up trollop.

"Well any day now she'll get an invite to a school dance. Don't they have them in your year, Syd? Seems they did when my kids started secondary school. And you would say yes, wouldn't you if a nice young man asked?" Eunice's eyes bugged like Syd should accept right then.

"Not really." Syd's thick, red lips looked absurd when she moved them. "I'm not keen on dancing like some of the girls. Seems like a waste of time." She risked another look at herself in the hand mirror and stuck out her tongue. "This might work for Halloween. Do you think you could do it again, Aunt Eunice?" She threw Eunice a dry bone.

"You mean you want to dress up like a movie star? Why, sure we can do it again! Whenever you like. I could be your personal makeup artist." Syd smiled at me with red teeth, and Eunice was pacified. "Well I'd best get back to my hovel and make sure Roger hasn't poisoned the cat or anything, not that it's in him." She laughed. "I'll be over to check on Claire tomorrow and bring her a stout bowl of my tripe stew. Full of vitamins and vigor." She held onto the V's so that her teeth got to solo.

I was grateful for Eunice's help despite her eccentricities or perhaps because of them. Much as I didn't like to admit it, I needed her.

She was almost out the door when she turned and added, "Maybe Claire can tell us why Albert was in such a hurry to leave. I'm sure I've never seen the like, ungrateful squab."

I had another name for him just under my breath.

"What'd you say, love?" Eunice poked her head back inside.

"I said I'm almost out of mustard."

"Oh? Well." The door closed.

৵৲

It was Friday morning and I was in our bedroom dressing for town. I'd planned and dreaded a full day of job hunting for all the good it would do. I would inquire through Rakefoot Crossing proper where shopkeepers knew me and would at least be kind in their refusal. Wouldn't take but an hour or so, then, if I had strength, I'd hop the train for Penrith. There were more doors to hammer there, but employers could afford to be choosy, so why choose me?

I gave myself the once-over in the old cheval mirror and tried not to be overly smiley, appear confident-like and look taller like city women in papers. But my five four frame was no more convincing than Syd had been in her masquerade. If I smiled with my lips closed, I could at least hide that overbite. John had defended it, said it made me look young and innocent. There might be another who loved me in spite of my flaws, but never for them.

I kept suffering the what–ifs. What if I can't find a job? What if the neighbors find out about Claire and she has to leave or suffer their judgement? What if we had to move to Chicago and live with my sister, Ruby and her cigar-chewing husband, Beans? I wouldn't know how to act in a big city. I wondered if Beans smoked cigars while flipping burgers in his and sis's White Castle eatery. And if he still called people "honyocks," whatever that was.

Claire was still asleep. Leaving the girls in their condition went against the grain but it had to be. I'd leave a note on the kitchen table and ask Eunice to check in on them. Syd was well enough to fend for herself and would be back at school Monday, like it or not. An extra day of recuperating wouldn't hurt though, especially with yesterday's excitement. Maybe by then, her lips would return to their normal color.

I struggled to sort out the route to take regarding Albert. I couldn't just let it go, or could I? It might be best for Claire if I did. At least he was out of her life. Couldn't say for sure what part he'd played in her fall, if any. But there could be no denying his role in the other business. Claire would tell me more, but then I'd walk a tightrope of what to share and with whom. I needed sound advice and my two best sources were gone. Even before Dad died, John filled in nicely when it came to reason and solution. He could make straight my philandering notions.

Biggs. He was the logical choice. I'd ring him up when I got back and invite him to Sunday supper. I felt we owed him for all he'd done. We'd find a time to speak privately about Claire and Albert. I would not tell him about the baby.

The baby. It was odd to think there had been one even briefly. My grandchild sure, even if it was just a wee bit of mystery when it left us. Doc said it was only a few weeks along and doubted Claire would even notice. It would seem like a delayed monthly visit, and likely a great weight off. In my head, I knew our daughter was no longer a child. But my heart remembered otherwise and wouldn't go along.

Any road, Biggs it was. I had to trust someone. A meal was small payment but maybe someday it could be more.

✑

The wind shook out my skirt like a tablecloth at a picnic as I tottled to the commercial hub of our humble village. It was a good trick to look professional while taming the clothes that fought me. My feet hurt already and the pointy heels speared dried sycamore leaves collecting on the walk, forcing me to stop every so often to remove them.

Even before I started off, discouragement was part of my outfit. A fresh, autumn nip gave my cheeks a swat I needed—like Mum used to on winter nights when I cleaved to the melancholy. I was glad of my wool coat, old or no. Waterlogged clouds sagged so close, I felt like I could poke them with my bumbershoot. I knew their promise, but they hadn't broken yet. A whirling dervish beat up debris on the road, trying to change the world but it was all hullabaloo.

Hurrying past Myron's market, I couldn't help peek inside. I wondered if he'd found my replacement with Old Pete. "Good fortune to them with knobs on," I said. I'd never look at a cut of meat the same that's sure. Or quail.

Next stop down line was The Sunny Buns Bakery. I could fancy myself baking pies for a living and likely should have tried it first. Sally Ramsbottom owned and ran the tiny shop six days a week, all the day long. She had a good head for business and a consuming weakness for sweets.

I didn't know Sally well. She and husband, Scotty, had moved to the Crossing from Edinburgh last spring. Their present concern had formerly been a haberdashery. It had enjoyed but a brief run since the locals were partial to plain working clothes. They wore Wellies over old shoes most the year so there was little calling for dressy oxfords. The former owners had just begun their liquidation sale when in stepped Sally R. She bought a fine boiled linen shirt, a pair of penny loafers and the shop.

The only clue to the shop being anything but a bakery was a leftover male mannequin turned female. It dominated the front window holding a pan full of plaster muffins with oversized oven mitts. Their rude attempt at gender modification included a pair of tart tins, a flapper wig, and lip rouge that extended well beyond the mouth's perimeter. It looked like the female impersonator from The Fandango Music Hall. The calico dress hung in folds for it was extra large. Logic told me it had been Sally's. If their aim was to arrest the attention of passers-by, it worked the first time or two.

The painted exterior of the shop was cheery, rain or shine—white with yellow trim and hand painted daisies skipping over the lintel. I'd assumed this was another of Sally's talents. On the front window, she painted a sun with robust cheeks smiling in wide eyed delight upon a steaming pan of hot cross buns. Surely, it would be pleasant to work for anyone with this kind of glad tidings. I entered, a budding ray of hope within my chest. I was about to step up to the counter when the proprietress squeezed through the backroom doorway to greet me.

"What'll you have," she slurred without a smile. Sally had fuzz for hair like that left in a currying brush. As if useful, a sliver of white, scalloped headpiece floated atop. Sally was wide. If she ever questioned a loss of profits, she'd need look no further than the nearest mirror.

"Hello, Mrs. Ramsbottom…"

She interrupted at this point.

"Do I know ye?" She lifted her chin and cocked her head, waiting for the answer.

"No. That is I don't think so. You see…"

"Then why don't you introduce yourself before you go calling me by my name?" She chuckled and looked round like she had an audience, but it was just we two. She was abrupt and not akin to her surroundings. Possibly, it was her man with the creative hand.

"Are you here to make a purchase or just gawk at the wallpaper?" What an odd time for her to smile. I smiled back.

She wiped her fingers on a grimy apron. It was then that I noticed there were two blobs of berry preserves on her nose and upper lip as if she'd eaten a filled bun without use of her hands. I must have been overdue because I laughed openly at her face, yes, but mostly at the irony of this rude woman in such promising circumstances.

"I'll be in the back when you've finished amusing yourself. Yeast dough waits for no one." With that, she shoehorned herself through the opening and I heard mutterings in between pounding on the bread board.

I saw no point in asking for employment. Besides, she was no smiling sunshine, more like the hot cross buns and I doubted I would please her with my more winsome ways.

I pursued the gamut of Crossing establishments to no avail, from the Green Street Café to Farber's Feed and Grain. I even offered to wait tables at Brakeman's Tabby. No takers. One glance at my high heels and frowsy wool coat and they concluded that I was not a fit for their trade. From buns to bales to bottles, I didn't belong. With icy fingers deep in old pockets, I walked my sorry self home, leaving Penrith for another day.

Syd must have been hovering by the window. She met me at the door.

"Mummie, I must talk with you while Claire's napping." Syd had dressed. I was glad to see her strong again.

"How is she? Has she eaten anything?" I removed my hat and coat and went to boil water for tea.

"She's terrible sore, but yes, she ate. I made us some tomato and cucumber sandwiches. And we had some of Eunice's soup." She made a face and stepped upon the rung of the kitchen chair.

"Don't stand on that. You mean Eunice's tripe soup?" I was amazed. They must have been ravenous.

"It wasn't so bad as long as we drank the broth and didn't stir up chunks from the bottom. But that's not what I need to talk with you about." She kneeled in the chair with her arms over the back. "I went out to check on my animals today and visit my hay castle. I found this." She handed me a glass with a red drop or two of a liquid that smelled of alcohol. "And there was more red stuff that had spilled on the hay. And someone had gotten into my box of Pop's things. It was open and the pipe had fallen between a couple bales. I think Claire and Albert were up there…drinking." Syd's eyes were wide and she'd changed positions on the chair four times in the telling.

"You haven't mentioned this to anyone?"

"No. Well, just BB the cat but…"

"Thank you, Syd. I'll talk with Claire about it when she wakes up. Now, you change into your jams and into bed. You don't want a relapse." I hugged her to me.

"Don't you want me to show you?"

"It's getting dark. You can show me tomorrow. I'm going to call Biggs and invite him over for Sunday supper. What would you think of company for a change?" I asked.

"That's fine. Don't know what we're going to have though. There's nothing in the pantry." Syd knew it was a sore subject.

"I'll figure something out, now off with you." I swatted her and she quickly turned on me with a scowl. I'd forgotten her bum, bull's-eye for years of love pats, was now off limits.

I walked to the phone and asked Gladys to connect me with Biggs.

"Hello?"

"Hello, Biggs? Glory."

"Oh hello, Glory dear. How are you? Heard Claire had a little mishap. She's recovered?"

News travels like a shot by Euni-gram.

"Why yes, she's much better thanks. Mostly just a bump on the noggin'. What I called about was to see if you'd take supper with us on Sunday. I'd like a chance to thank you in a small way for all you've done for the girls and me. Plus…there's a matter I'd like to ask your advice about." I waited, not wanting to go into detail.

"That sounds wonderful! I haven't had one of your home cooked meals since…oh well I don't know when." He sounded embarrassed.

"It's all right, Axel. I know when it was. It was John's forty-third birthday, just before they called him for the Army. So that's been far too long. Will you come?" I tried to sound positive.

"I'd love nothing better. What time?"

"Would 4:00 be too early?"

"You may count on me." He said. "And I've a little surprise for Syd but don't tell."

"See you then." I hung the receiver feeling happy at the thought of entertaining a guest, even if it was just Biggs.

- 14 -

SYD

27 October, 1945

Dear Pop,

Any day now, I expect to turn round and find you standing there waiting for me to join you on a call. Can't wait to hear what you've been about.

Natty's speech is coming along splendidly and today he outdid himself. He brought home a gold ring! At least I think it's gold, and I think it's a wedding ring. I'm going to show it to Mum tomorrow. We could sure use the money from selling it. I'm afraid of being poor, but I know she'll make me turn it in to Biggs at station so's the owner can claim it.

The other night when Mum, Claire and I were listening to the wireless, there was an interesting story about the Germans. Not sure how our side found out, but their Special Operations is trying to teach dogs to communicate. I am not making this up. By using pedals and objects the dog can choose, they claim to be teaching certain of their canines to talk. One terrier supposedly asked a woman reporter if she could wag her tail! Ha!

It's not news to me. I've known all along we can talk to animals. I've been working with Jingles and Reggie on this. It can be as subtle as a look in their eyes. Most would take me for crazy. But maybe not the Germans. Ha.

Claire isn't seeing the Rand character any longer and am I glad. Mum has pretty much kept me in the dark. She doesn't realize I know about the birds and bees malarkey. I think Claire and Albert were up to some heavy petting in the barn. Claire took a nasty tumble out the loft but she's better now.

Biggs has taken me under his wing, as they say. He asks me if wouldn't I want another daddy. I confided in him that I don't have need of one since I don't believe you're dead, and he just sighed and patted my head. I feel sorry for him. Not sure why, but he puts me in mind of Dodger, that poor bloodhound that got kicked around by the night guard in the Cumberland pencil factory. Remember, we rescued him and gave him to that widow lady in York?

I think Biggs misses his job as Air Raid Captain. It made him feel important like. He keeps his helmet in a closet and takes it down for me along with a box of old British lead soldiers that belonged to his pop. Biggs said his Mutti, like he calls her, never would let him play with them. Sometimes he wants me to play with them so I sort of pretend but I'm not much for toy soldiers. I like Biggs but not when he stares at Mummie, which he does a lot.

Pop, I don't mean to worry you but you should come home, as soon as you're able.

Love,

Syd

- 15 -

GLORY

Desperation drove me to having the old girl done in. The milk cow, Greta, had been in our family since Syd was able to hold her baby cup. Greta was a sleek Jersey with soulful eyes and a gracious way. The girls had straddled her and woven dandelion wreaths for her soft ears. That's why I sat in the loo and cried with my head in my hands, so the girls wouldn't hear.

I wasn't sure I could get past Greta's eyes or the girls' wrath, but we needed meat, and not just for Sunday company. Even a smallish cow would fill the empty meat safe. And Eunice said I could use the stone cold room Roger built onto their house, since with rationing, it was never full. How in the wide world could I lead Greta down the road to Old Pete? I knew he was swift about the business and that he had a kind heart for animals away from duty, but Greta was family.

Claire was in her room yet recuperating and I'd put Syd to polishing silver. I wanted this supper special.

"I'll be back presently. Going to market," I said as casually as I could.

"Can I go too?" Syd asked. "I haven't been out the house in over a week."

"I know, but I need you to stay on the silver until I get back. I have other jobs for you to do." I hurried out, denying her time to grouse.

I held my stomach as I neared Jersey, Greta Stone lunching in her favored patch.

Her broad behind was to me. I felt the diabolical traitor. She'd heard my steps through the tall grass and looked over her back, flicking flies at both ends. She leveled her eyes at me, an effective defense, while her jaw rotated. I'd actually brought her a carrot—how low. Then she went and greeted me with a kindly '*maaaw*'. There were tears in my eyes as I slipped the rope over her head.

"I'm sorry, girl. I would never do this if I didn't have to feed the family. I'd live on eggs and turnip greens." I blubbered between sentences.

I led her round back to avoid Syd spying us through the kitchen window. Greta didn't fuss, just followed along sweet and unsuspecting—heaping coals on my head.

We were going along nice as you please when Greta kicked the bucket. Stepped into it more like, making an ungodly racket as she clomped along, *ka-clang*, like one of those one man bands. Next thing, I heard the front door's familiar bang, and there came Syd at a trot for us.

"I've told you a hundred times to put that milk bucket back in the shed where it belongs!" I was red-faced but not with anger as she might have thought. "Now look what's happened." I pointed at her ensnared hoof. It took Syd a minute but she caught up. I knew she would.

"Where are you going with her?" Syd asked.

"I was restless and decided to go for a walk."

"With Greta?" Syd began stroking Greta's smooth head and their eyes met.

"Yes, well she could use some exercise." I fed Greta the carrot. She had it coming. "She's been looking fat lately to me, and I just thought she'd like to see a bit of the countryside. There now, if you have to know." I was such a pitiful liar.

Syd hesitated. "Nobody takes a cow for a walk, a horse maybe but not a cow."

Syd hefted Greta's hoof on her knee and deftly removed the bucket.

"Oh well, forget about it. I'll just take her back." I steered Greta who belched and, I'm certain sure, smirked through her lashes. I called back, "Catch me a chicken!"

❧

Sunday was wet. I didn't have to go to market for anything, and the menu was simple. Biggs couldn't expect more than fried chicken, potatoes, greens and bread. Plus Syd and I had baked a squash pie that sent spice through the cottage reminding us of pleasanter holidays.

Claire was up, though slower moving and down in spirits.

"What time is company to arrive?" asked Claire as she lowered herself onto the divan. She spat out the word company like rotten meat.

"I told him 4:00. Aren't you glad of a visitor?"

"I guess, but why him? Why not Roger and Eunice?"

"I felt we needed to thank him. We'll have Roger and Eunice over; it's just that we're a little short on edibles at the moment." I grew doubly frustrated.

"All he ever wants to talk about is Axel Biggs." Claire continued. "Thinks he's ruddy king of Cumbria. I don't trust him."

"I like Biggs. We're friends." Syd chimed in. "He let me ride one of the trains to Keswick and back for free and bought tea and biscuits in the refreshment room after." Syd told us this as she set the table for four.

"He did? When?" I asked.

"Couple weeks ago. It was a short day at school so I came through town early. He saw me through his office window and motioned me in. It was jolly. He pointed out historical places along the way I'd never heard of."

"I wasn't aware you had a half day, young lady. You should have told me instead of traveling all over the country on your own. Cripe's sake."

"Sorry Mum, but it was Biggs after all." She thought I was overreacting.

"From now on I need to know about changes in your schedule. Do you understand? And you still need to ask my permission to go places. I don't care who it is." I turned toward the tray of buns.

"Ah, applesauce." Syd said under her breath. She folded linen napkins and slid them under the cutlery.

"No backtalk!"

So much had happened right under my nose that I wasn't a party to. How could it be in such a tiny household? I felt I was surviving in a cocoon in the midst of an overrun garden. If John were there, he would be savvy. I was more than half useless without him.

I dobbed a bit of lard on each of the buns, slid the rack into the oven and checked the clock.

"Syd, when you're done there, put the plum preserves in the crystal dish." I forked crispy chicken pieces onto the good Royal Ducal platter and my mouth set to watering.

"Knock, knock. Anyone home?" Biggs opened the door a crack and called to us, as he stood drenched under the porch covering.

"Welcome, Axel. You must be soaked through, and you'll ruin those good, leather gloves. Just hang your coat there, and leave your rubbers and bumbershoot on the mat, please." I checked my face in the cupboard glass. "Come warm yourself."

"Mmm. Something smells heavenly." He exclaimed inhaling deeply. He sheltered something beneath his overcoat.

Axel stooped to enter our doorway. I so rarely saw him without his cap. I forgot he was bald as a buzzard with a peaked head to match his nose. Even his teeth gave the impression of sharpness when we saw them, which was a lot lately. He wanted filing around his edges.

"Hope it's as good as it smells. Haven't made chicken in a while so if I haven't lost my touch it'll be passable." I'd eaten a stray nugget out of the pan earlier and knew it was delicious. "Have a seat and make yourself comfortable. We're just waiting on the buns now." My stomach fluttered as if this was my first meal. Must have been having a man to do for again.

"Take your time, Glory. It'll give me a chance to spring my little surprise on Syd."

At the mention of her name and surprise in the same sentence, Syd appeared, demure and smiling.

"Hello, Mr. Biggs. What was that you said?"

"You heard correctly. I brought you something." He held one hand under his coat. "Your mum told me you'd been asking after the puppies your poor daddy saved." Biggs wore a strange expression. "No one seemed to know anything about them, but I located this little girl who needs careful looking after." With that pronouncement, he withdrew a wiggling, spaniel mix pup and handed her to Syd's open arms.

"Oh, Biggs! She is a beauty. Thank you! I'm going to call her Kate. It's a name I've been saving. It fits her." Syd was ecstatic. "Thank you so much!"

I hadn't seen her that happy since the black day I'd spoiled the party. I could have kissed him for putting the smile back on her face, but wouldn't want to raise a false notion.

"Axel, how kind. John would be glad. I won't even complain that it's another mouth to feed." I laughed feebly.

"Yes, wouldn't John be delighted?" He mused.

I began finishing the last of the preparations and felt the familiar tingle and sweat begin to creep up. My cheeks flushed, my heart pounded. I grew nauseous and weak. The green chair was there to support my heaviness and help me recover.

"You all right?" Biggs asked, alarmed. He came and put his arm about my shoulders.

"I'll be fine. I may have overdone things a little. I divided bulbs at cemetery yesterday. My back and legs are sore."

The truth about the attacks was too scary to share. It was odd and didn't have a solution I knew of. I kept hoping time would work out the infirmity.

Biggs noticed Claire watching from the front room.

"Hello, Claire. I hope you're feeling better after your unfortunate incident. Took a tumble from the loft was it?" Axel came toward her.

She moved around the table to her place, "I'm doing quite well, thank you."

"Supper's ready, let's all sit," I called. "Axel, you may sit here at the head."

Claire narrowed her eyes at me.

As we gathered round our family table, a perverted melancholy reached out to choke me. I thought I would enjoy the meal now that the attack had passed, but I felt a sad fifth presence over our counterfeit group.

Conversation moved like a goods train, coupling and uncoupling its load in awkward jerks and starts. Biggs and I occupied most of the talk while Syd sat content, stuffing herself with Kate in her lap, who whined and yipped while the other dogs sniffed her over.

"Have you heard from Ronnie lately?" I ventured. Ronnie was

his and Trudy's only son. He'd had a troubled reputation. We rarely brought him up in surface conversation but if I was to confide in Biggs about Claire and Albert, I didn't feel out of place asking after his wayward son. "Is he about Claire's age?" I couldn't remember but no one had seen him in a while.

"Ronnie turned just sixteen on his last birthday. He's always tried acting older than his years, but he's still a mere boy." Axel smiled sadly. "He doesn't communicate with me, Glory. I thought you knew that. Ran off after his mother left—heard he joined up with a carnival as a roustabout."

"I am sorry to bring it up. I was hoping for good news." Wished I'd known a good joke about then.

Claire couldn't have melted a butter pat in her mouth. She rarely looked up and I was ashamed at her treatment of an old family friend. I could only lay the rudeness to her troubles of late. I didn't want to force too much on her in the way of manners, but I could tell Biggs noticed.

"So, Claire, what do you think you'll be doing now that Land Army work is through?" he asked.

I hadn't had the courage to ask, but I'd stewed some over it and was thankful he hadn't mentioned Albert.

"There aren't a lot of choices for women are there, if they choose not to marry and tie themselves up with apron strings that is?"

I tasted her bitterness in the greens.

"You'd once talked of hiring yourself out as nanny at the manor house," I reminded her.

"Dalemain, you mean?" Biggs asked. "You know, I happened to run into a former school chum who's working there for Special Ops. You remember Mavis Cartwright, Glory. John dated her quite a while, as I recall."

"Oh, yes. I remember Mavis. Who did she end up marrying? Anyone we know?"

"I guess her work has been her life. She's still single. Dalemain is such a lovely home. As you'll recall, Glory, that's where my mother worked as a kitchen maid after Father died. Quite the hub of activity once they set up operations there. Glory?"

"Yes, sorry, Dalemain, that's it." I wondered how near Mavis came to being Mrs. Stone instead of me. "I think Claire had a connection with one of the servants. Wasn't she to talk to the Missus about you?" I smiled at Claire, trying to will pleasantness from her.

"I doubt that will pan out. A lot of girls want that job and I've no further education or experience." She returned to pushing mashers around her plate like a petulant child. "Mother, may I be excused? I'm not feeling well." She was already on her way.

"Of course. Can I get you anything?"

"No, thank you. I just need some rest. Guess I'm not as well as I thought." She turned and glanced around. "Mr. Biggs."

"Mr.?" He chuckled. "Just Biggs. Do get some rest, Claire." He watched her go. "Seems like she's got more than bruises to deal with," he said to me, jabbing his knife her direction, then aiming for his fourth piece of chicken. Good thing Claire wasn't hungry. I'd have to come up with another plan for Syd's lunch.

"This is simply delicious, Glory. You've done a fine job of picking up where you left off in the kitchen." He looked self-conscious even though he couldn't have known about the lamb's quarters draping his tooth.

"Thank you. I must admit it was nice cooking for a full table again." I didn't want to put Biggs on the wrong track, but it was satisfying to feed a man again. It had always been a pleasure watching John enjoy his meal.

"And there's dessert." Syd added. "Mum and I made a stunner of a pie. I should think you could smell it." I hoped he didn't notice her staring at his nose.

"I think I detect a whiff of cinnamon and maybe a dash of nutmeg? I might have to let my supper settle before I can enjoy it to the full." Biggs stooped low and petted Kate who relieved herself on the rug. "Blast." Biggs shuffled his feet away.

"OK, me too." Syd ran for a rag. "I'm going to take Kate out to the back garden." She headed for the coat rack.

"Hold on. You're just getting over flu. I think you best stay in and have Kate get to know Reggie and Jingles. They're enough for her for one day don't you think?" I shouldn't have phrased it as a question.

"No. And I haven't been out much except when I found you walking Greta, and then when I went to check on my castle. Remember? That's when I found…"

"No arguments please. After you clean that up, take Kate into our room so Biggs and I can enjoy a private chat."

She looked at me strangely but did as I asked.

Axel and I moved into the front room. He chose John's chair, I suppose, by default. It was the only chair large enough to accommodate his stretch. He put his feet up on the ottoman and obliged me on making himself comfortable.

"It can't be easy raising two girls without a man. Do you mind if I smoke?" He pulled a fine Trighinopoli cigar from his coat pocket. I knew it by the band.

"Not at all." I moved the lighter and ash tray to the table next John's chair. The composition was complete.

Biggs continued, "He was the disciplinarian in your house was he not?" Biggs seemed curious but continued with his own memory. "Not so when I was growing up." It was meine Deutsche mutter who wielded the rod in our home, God rest her." He smiled sharply.

"Yes, I remember you once described her as a no-nonsense sort." One night at The Brakeman's Tabby, a few rounds had blurred the line of discretion and he'd shared hard stories about his mother—of strange punishments meant to suit the crime, but cruel and humiliating. Yet he'd held her in high esteem and loved her dearly, perhaps as much as Trudy.

"She knew best!" He slapped his thigh, which sent Reggie trotting over to me. "By Jove, she knew how to make us sit up and take notice. My father was a quiet, subservient man with many phobias and physical complaints. But Mutter was long-suffering and cared for him until his untimely end." Biggs gave his cigar a tap. "I wouldn't be the man I am today if it weren't for Mutti."

"That's admirable and right, that she should care for him," I said. "You're right about raising the girls," I spoke low. "And that brings me to something I wanted to ask. Not having someone to help sort things out has been rough. I realized you were the closest man in our lives now, so I thought to turn your direction for a little advice."

I was nervous. It felt odd confiding in Biggs sitting in John's chair smoking a cigar with his feet propped. I guarded my words. "Can I get you a cup of tea or chicory? We don't have coffee." I started for the kitchen.

"I think to wait and have some with my pie if it's all the same."

"Surely." I returned to the divan and lowered my voice again. "Well, my dilemma is with Claire and her relationship with Albert Rand, Eunice's nephew. They'd been seeing one another right along since he came for his welcome home party. You were there."

He nodded seriously. "Yes, I'm aware they were seeing one another."

"I thought they were moving too fast but Claire always became defensive when I tried to talk with her about it. Well, he may have been with her Thursday when she had her accident, assuming it was an accident. But she refuses to discuss what happened." My anger flared with thoughts of him and his slippery way.

"When Eunice came to watch Syd while we went to hospital, she said Albert had skipped. He high-tailed it out of Rakefoot Station saying he had some work offer. Wouldn't you think it's more than mere coincidence that these events happened together? Now I wonder what should be done about it." I skipped the details of

Claire's injuries and took a deep breath. "To further complicate the issue, he's my best friend's nephew. I could sever a long relationship simply by suspecting Albert. I don't want to embarrass Claire or make it harder on her. I don't even know where Albert is. Axel, I don't know what to do. If she were your daughter, how would you handle it?"

I felt better having laid it out, but Biggs wasn't John; my stomach was in knots because I knew I couldn't just leave it with him and be about my gardening.

He took a long draw from his cigar and squinted through the smoke pillow.

"You have to ask yourself the right question. It's not, 'Am I going to tick Eunice off or embarrass Claire?' The question is— what is the moral thing to do?" He studied me through a haze. "You must get at the truth. And if Claire refuses to tell you, you'll need to track down young Albert and extract the truth from him. A hard thing for a woman to do certainly." He shook his head and looked at the carpet while taking another puff.

Biggs hadn't lightened my load except to spotlight the challenge and eliminate the weaseling out option for which I'd hoped. *What am I thinking asking a man? Always up for a ruddy battle.*

"That's what I was afraid of. But I know you're right. I'm going to try and nail Claire down tomorrow and get at what happened." That still wouldn't address the issue of his taking advantage of a grieving young woman. That was a separate issue I wasn't ready to share with Biggs or anyone. Not even Claire.

Biggs added, "I'd like you to call me if there's anything I can do, Glory. You know I do have feelings for the girls and I'd go a long way to do right by them."

"Thank you, Axel, but I think I'm going to have to push through somehow."

"Just don't push yourself over the edge," he warned. "You've been through it over the past few months. You don't want to go working yourself into a nervous breakdown." He pointed the lit end of his cigar at me.

I hadn't considered that. Those attacks could be a prelude to the real thing. I could end up in a mental sanitarium, then where would the girls be?

Syd burst into the room and halted my spiral.

"Jingles is playing with the pup already and she's not afraid of him. Is anyone ready for pie besides me?" She carried Kate in an egg basket lined with a saddle blanket remnant—her version of playing dolls.

Biggs tamped out his cigar, stood, stretched to the ceiling where his fingers left eight evenly spaced grease marks and declared, "Biggs is willin'!"

- 16 -

CLAIRE

I woke midday on Halloween with emotions calling through me like hellish birds. Out my window, the sky crawled with restless clouds that shifted and writhed away from any recognizable shape. I turned over and stared at a cluster of water spots on the ceiling. When I stared and blurred my eyes, I saw that connecting them made a horse's head and bridle.

He'd deserted me.

I wouldn't contact Albert. He hadn't sought me out since skittering off like a scalded cat—rather cowardly, I thought, for someone who flew airplanes through enemy territory with a target on his bum. Was the prospect of a future with me so repulsive? He wasn't one to tie down with anyone, let alone a small town nobody with nothing going. Our relationship had been a farce of my own making, and I grieved my portrayal of a gullible female. Ingrid couldn't have played it better.

At least now I knew I wasn't with child, thank God. That would have put Mum over the edge sure. And I didn't want

Albert's baby, though it had seemed the most romantic notion. It was unfair that news of fresh life could be cause for rejoicing or the end of the world given the whims of those responsible. Loneliness was easier born than strife, if that's all love meant.

I propped myself on one elbow and looked over at Syd's made bed. *Oh yeah, school.* It was hard getting up these days. I rolled over where my eyes rested on the pill bottle. I pictured Albert's false face and told myself it wasn't worth chucking it all for a clown. *Anyone who paints a smile on.*

I'd had little appetite, but this morning something smelled good—griddle cakes. Mum must have made a fresh batch since she and Syd would have eaten hours ago.

I closed my eyes and inhaled. After twenty-five years of the real thing with Dad and three months without even the hope of his return, Mum was surviving. How long would the family last?

Mum shuffled near the door; her knock barely qualified as one. "Claire? You awake? I've got oatcakes and scrambled eggs." Mum always could chase the blues off with something tasty.

"Yeah, I'm getting up." Rising from bed took determination, but the pain eased as I moved and was less excruciating each day.

I pulled on the white chenille bathrobe Dad sent for my birthday last. Its deep pockets had snobby-looking poodle appliqués. Not my style, but he had tried, and it blocked the chill between the crisp autumn morning and me. I stepped into slippers and opened the door.

"Smells good, gotta say." I covered a yawn.

"Sounds like you'll be having your appetite back. That's good." Mum gave my frame a quick evaluation.

The quintessential Mum, scrambling up fresh eggs—something we had. She was pretty for an older woman—pretty for anybody. I'd always thought so and worried she'd remarry too soon. I wasn't ready for a substitute dad, and most particularly not Biggs. I didn't know why, but figured he was up to something, possibly illegal, definitely shady; and it was only a matter of time before they'd root him out.

"I'm sorry I didn't listen to you before about Albert. Guess I can be right pig-headed." I spooned preserves onto a cake and forked a bite. I lifted my glass and tasted Greta's beautiful, cold milk all the way down.

"Thank you for that, Claire. Yes, you can be. But there's something I need to talk with you about." Mum brought a smoking cup to the table and took her usual chair. I sure hoped she wasn't going to tell me she'd decided to allow Biggs to court her. I never could stomach greasy Axel Biggs calling for Mum all poshed up with a box of chocolates behind his back and ulterior motives up his sleeve.

Mum began, "You never told me anything about your accident other than you fell from the loft. Naturally, I have questions: what were you doing up there, how did you fall, who was with you? Was Albert with you? Because Syd found..." The questions came at me like mortar rounds.

"Whoa. How about one at a time?" I felt the old rub at Mum's interrogation.

"Sorry. It's just that I've been piecing together scenarios since it happened, but I knew you needed time." She smiled and sipped her tea. The cup rattled when she set it down.

"Yes, Albert was with me. It was one of many times we were... together." I couldn't break her heart with details. "It was stupid. All of it was supremely stupid and short-sighted. I never want to see him again. So you don't have to worry about Mr. Rand anymore. I'm glad he's gone, and glad I found out what he was before it was too late." It was too late for some things.

Mum looked at me with pity, as if she was about to say something and stopped herself. Then she said, "Well I'm, I'm relieved of that. He's jolly well trotted off but what I do want to know is; did he have anything to do with your fall? Syd found a glass with a bit of alcohol in the loft."

"No. It was purely accidental. Yes, Albert brought a bottle of something. I had a taste and didn't like the stuff, but he went and got himself potted. I found Syd's treasure of Dad's things and Albert nabbed the pipe and was messing about, playing the fool. I didn't like it, went to grab it away from him and fell. That's it. Can't blame him directly."

I was sick with the memory that replayed like an unabsolved confession. I pushed my plate away. Shame was the specter that dragged me back. I couldn't stay in the same room with Mum's eyes.

"I'm going for a walk. Need to give me muscles a stretch."

"Let me go with you."

"No. I need to think." I went to my room and eased into some trousers, a sweater, and walking shoes. I lifted my coat and headed out the door.

"Don't wait up for me," I called. "I'm going to stop by Helen's on the way back."

As I left the house, Natty, perched above the stoop, took me by surprise. "Merry CHRIST—mas!" I knew Dad and Syd had trained the crazy thing to talk but this was a new phrase.

"You're a tad early, bird." I was impressed, however, and a little unnerved. His voice reminded me of Dad's. In fact, as it came to me, that was exactly how Dad used to say it, with an exaggerated accent on the first syllable. *Poor Syd. She's trained a raven to sound like him.*

"Merry CHRIST—mas." It repeated.

Dad's vetting companion apparently missed him too, judging by his racketing whenever someone exited the house. Today I was his target. He cawed at me from an oak, dropped an acorn onto the path, and flew down plucking a few strands of my hair.

"Ouch! Stupid bird." I felt for blood.

Didn't they eat carcasses? I tossed the acorn back at him and he flew north squawking.

Chilly solitude suited me fine. I strode through stiffness to get somewhere fast. I couldn't separate from the desperate person I'd become. My self-assurance, instincts—traits I'd relied on had come to rubbish and left me struggling in the dark. A good stretch of the legs couldn't hurt—something the folks had taught me well.

Our village lay deserted this time of year, not that there'd been many tourists in recent times—mostly journalists and fewer of them now since they followed destruction. I needed to escape the sameness. Maybe a secretarial position in Manchester or Liverpool. I could work and save for a ticket to visit my aunt and uncle in The States. I couldn't tolerate this seed of a town. Here I shrunk with the years. Mum would be upset, but she left her family. And she'd have Syd for awhile yet.

Breath puffs blew back at me. I picked up a stout alder branch to help buoy my wobbly legs. Stabbing it into the damp earth, I moved on up a hill toward Grisedale and talked to the sky as the village and all within earshot receded.

"What if I had become a mum?" I was relieved but shook my head. I once dreamed of a family. Now I wasn't sure that road was anything but painful. Why was all this rot happening to us? I looked around to see if there was anybody and continued into the trees. "WHY US?" I yelled. The answer came in a wind playing past my ears—as cold a response as ever I'd come to expect.

I stopped, thinking I'd heard another voice. Had they heard me? I'd groused my way a good three kilometers from home. Not bad for a convalescent. Yes, there it was again—someone, louder this time. Talking to himself? I was coming toward him. Maybe it was a lunatic living off the land or a returned soldier with a mental disorder. That could be dangerous, but so could unresolved curiosity, according to Eunice. I crept forward. There, a man's voice rose and fell on the breeze, giving a speech or something. I crept closer.

Remaining stealthy was difficult with the blasted, crunching leaves underfoot. I left the pathway and started through the trees, timing my movement over the damp earth when the wind gusted.

"...sacrifice....for our sake......weight of glory.....impossible barricade ...." The words came and went until I received an entire sentence and with it, the perpetrator.

"If we were capable of being good enough, so-called, we would have no need of a savior." The chap smiled and rubbed his hands together, evidently pleased with his philosophy.

There, in a clearing where trees and shrubs had formed a sort of arboreal amphitheater, was a man, a teacher? He didn't look like any teacher I'd seen, with a tweed cap pulled over shaggy, red hair. A student maybe. I watched from behind the trees, enthralled as this odd young person waved his arms and paced, lecturing the trees. My lunatic suspicions returned.

Wanting to stay, I knew I should head back, but what a remarkable scene. It demanded satisfaction from a distance. I settled on a rocky berm and listened as his voice peaked when he meant to drive a point home and cracked when excitement overtook him. I felt the urge to laugh rumble up. The orator would often stop and check himself from a stack of papers on a stump, weighted with a rock.

When his hat blew off in a fit of determined expository, I couldn't stand it. Having held back too long, I let go a hearty belly-laugh.

"Who's there?" He whirled round, scanning for the eavesdropper.

I thought to continue hiding but felt sorry for the weird boy.

"I come in peace." I approached his court, leaving room to run. His face turned a shade of self-conscious russet.

"I'm afraid I've appeared the fool." He picked his cap up off the ground, slapping it against his trousers and introduced himself as Liam McClelland from Bailieborough, Ireland. His eyes were like flint and his frame looked like he'd been doing a lot more walking and talking than eating. His smile was friendly in an elfin way.

"Claire Stone. And I'm sorry for interrupting your class or

whatever you have here. What are you doing anyway?" The itch was about to be scratched.

"Oh I'm practicing before the audience." He gestured dramatically toward the trees. "My forest congregation. I'm a theology student at Ridley Hall, Cambridge and I'm to give a talk on the nature of grace come Friday." He looked at his notes.

"Do you think you've convinced them?" I laughed and looked at the trees, then added, "I didn't realize I'd come so far. I'd best start home." I was in no mood for small talk, though Liam's performance had distracted me from worry. I asked, "You're a long way from university. Did you walk all the way?"

"Ah, no. Took the train as far as Penrith, and then set about afoot. I'd heard about the natural beauty of this area and decided to see for myself." His prolonged eye on me made me self-conscious. "It's quiet. Nature puts a perspective to life when I take my studies or myself too seriously. You actually took care of the latter today, thank you, Miss Stone."

"I see. Well, I'm sure you'll do fine. You certainly have the enthusiasm for it. Best of luck." I turned to go.

"Uh, do you come this way often?" He asked.

"Yes." I continued walking but Liam kept talking. Something told me this was what he loved, hearing himself talk.

"Do you live around here?" His voice cracked.

"Rakefoot Crossing." I said over my shoulder then cursed myself for a fool. "Three or so kilometers." I thought the distance would discourage him.

"Mightn't I walk you home, then? It'll be dark. It's Halloween." He glanced around.

The sky had haunted me dimly all day, brightening little from noonday to dusk. I knew I wouldn't beat the night home.

"I say," I began. "It's nice of you to offer, but how would you get home?" Was he capable of taking a hint? "Besides, I'm stopping at a friend's to listen to a new record. May be there awhile, so…it'll be late when I'm through."

"Well, maybe I might like listening to the record, then you could put me up for the night and I could make my way back tomorrow on the train." His eyes positively sparkled. Theology student, huh.

I turned and looked him over. "My Mum will likely be okay with it. You could sack out on the divan. It's passable as a bed." I hoped I wouldn't regret it, but he came off harmless.

"Excellent." He fairly skipped to catch up.

- 17 -

GLORY

In the middle of night I stumbled over shoes on my way to the loo. It first slipped my notice they were men's loafers. On the return trip, my eyes had adapted and I could see the man to whose feet they belonged sacked out on our divan. I startled myself with a half-hearted squeal. "Who the blazes are you?" The stranger had been sleeping, but he woke and blinked at me. I grabbed an ashtray.

"Get out! Get out! Before I throw this as hard as I can straight at your buggered shaggy head!" Not too scary, but it was all I could come up with on short notice. I hoped the girls were all right and wanted to check but thought better of it.

The more I looked him over and saw his look of terrified confusion, the less intimidated I was, so I switched on the overhead light. He was a living scarecrow of a man.

"Oh, shh, oh! Calm your bustle, Mrs. Stone. Shh. Don't hit me with that weapon you got there." He was a smallish man, bouncing from one foot to the other with his arms flying upwards to cover his head.

"I mean you no harm at all. You see, it started when your fair daughter, Claire, walked farther than she thought, and...found me talking to the forest, when my hat fell off and she laughed, ha oh, glory, and she asked if I'd convinced them, the trees that is, haha, then it got dark, so I walked your lovely daughter with the willies home, and I live a long way from here."

He continued the bobbing. I didn't know but it was his way under duress.

As I lowered my pitching arm, he spread his arms as if the nonsense he'd spouted explained everything. Was I dreaming? Was he an overgrown leprechaun? With all I'd been through, I might have thought it was my due. So, where was the pot of treasure?

"AAAaaaeekk!" Syd was the first of the girls to emerge. She gave an encore of my performance and wasted no time on questions. Grabbing one of his scuffed shoes, she launched right in beating his shoulders.

"Stop!" Claire yelled with her eyes closed. "He's all right. This is my new friend, Liam...Liam..." A yawn garbled the rest.

"McClelland, Ma'am." He went to doff his cap but our lamp was wearing it. "From Bailieborough, Ireland, County Cavan."

Claire said, "He's a preacher."

"A teacher," He clarified. "I hope to be."

"Teacher!" Syd asked, "What time is it? It's dark out."

I squinted at the kitchen clock. "It's a little after five."

"Ohhh," Syd groaned. "I'm going back to bed. But I want a complete rundown later."

She obviously wasn't worried about a strange man in our home. And strange he was.

"I don't think I could go back to sleep." Claire headed for the water closet.

"I'm certain I won't," Liam was too cheery as he grabbed his shoes off the floor. "I'll just be on my way to station."

"Just hold up. Somewhere back there you mentioned walking

my daughter home after dark. I want to know whether I should thank you or go for a heavier weapon." I sighed and moved toward the kitchen to put on water for tea. "You may as well stay to breakfast. You've earned it."

Liam straddled a chair in the kitchen and explained himself as I cracked eggs. He wasn't shy though he claimed it as a weakness. That's why he practiced his speech making in the woods, he said, so he could get over his timidity. The logic of that escaped me and I thought he'd confused the word with temerity. He loved to talk.

"Where do you and your daughters attend services?" He asked as if the whole of Rakefoot Crossing were a congregation.

"We don't," I said. "Oh, we used to before the war, but I just couldn't see going through the motions any longer. If God is running things, why so much suffering and bloodshed? Excuse me, Reverend, but it doesn't make sense, know what I mean?" I lifted fried eggs onto a plate.

He looked thoughtful. "I do indeed, but I'm not a reverend anybody. It's a wonder to me he'll have anything to do with the lot of us."

"What?"

"It's been my observation that it's not God who has failed man, but rather the other way round."

Liam tucked a napkin down his shirtfront and looked hungry. "Do you believe in the invisible realm? Spiritual doings?" he asked. "Maybe we can't see all that's happening right now—here in your kitchen maybe." He looked at the ceiling—scouting for angels, I imagined.

I thought he was playing with me, yet he seemed sincere. Any road, he was giving me chills and I didn't want religion before tea.

"I haven't had time to consider such things. With John gone, he's my deceased husband, it got easier to stay home and putter in garden." I thought that would finish it.

"Ah, I got a glimpse at that garden in the dark. There's something in the sincerity of nature. It's proud ye must be. I was telling that to Claire."

"I've felt something while working the soil; like it was part of a larger effort, or I was. I don't know."

"Beautifully put, Mrs. Stone." Liam smiled out the window.

"Glory. Do you like fried potatoes?" I pulled a few from the pantry.

"Oh dear me, yes. My mother fries them in pork fat with bits of ham and scallions. I miss her cooking something awful." He rubbed his hands together.

Claire sauntered in and eased into a chair across from Liam. She must not have given a care for what he thought of her, way she looked.

"Has Liam saved your soul?" She chuckled.

"Claire, I don't think you should make fun of another's profession." I looked at Liam, embarrassed. "Really, you can be frightfully rude." Ho now, I braced for the backlash, but she laughed.

"Oh I joked about it with him on our way here. He knows how I feel about religious stuff. A lot of rubbish in finery I call it." She rose to get the milk and winced. "Oh, I think I pushed myself too far with yesterday's stroll. My apologies, Mr. M. I never realize how complete an arse I am until after the fact. Then it's too late." Claire dished food onto her plate.

"Miss Stone, apology accepted. It hasn't been long since I felt much the same." Liam didn't seem insulted in the least. "I'm just relieved I'm not a loaded down ass making my way to hell. Aside from that, I can make you no promises for my behavior on any given day." He loaded up his fork.

"Uh, would you like to say grace?" He was a guest in our home and I wanted to make him feel comfortable even if Claire didn't have the manners of a field hand.

"Surely." He looked right pleased, like he was overdue. He pushed back his chair and stood with eyes wide open as if he could see through the ceiling and up to Heaven's gate. "Father in Heaven, I'm surely grateful to you for allowing me to meet up with these fine, country folk." He smiled at us all. "Thank you too for seeing to it we got home safe last night." He winked at Claire.

Claire laughed and looked at me. Was he having me on after all?

On he went, "Thank you for these tasty eggs and taters and bless the hands that cooked them. And, come fill the empty places." He sat down and commenced taming a ravenous appetite.

"Well thank you, Liam. Never heard grace expressed quite that forthright before," I said.

"With the mister departed, how is it you can keep body and soul together, financially I'm meaning? Or is that too personal?" He looked around. Maybe he was a robber after all, sly one.

I answered warily. "It's not easy Mr. McClelland. We don't have much that's certain—no money hid nor nothing of the sort." I refilled his milk glass.

"Thank you, ma'am. I couldn't help noticing all the fine antiques you have about the place. I bet they'd bring a pretty penny in the marketplace." He scooted back his chair. "Take this fine china teapot here." He took hold of Gran's yellow rose pot.

"All right! I'm onto you, McClelland, or whoever you are. Put that teapot right where you found it and back out that door." This time a hot cast iron skillet was handy. "Preacher indeed. You probably are a preacher, filling folks full of hope one minute so's you can steal their hard earned coppers in the name of God. Well, I've been taken by pitchmen before."

"Mum!" It was Claire's turn to be horrified. "Now who's out of line?"

"Dear Mrs. Stone, again you have me at a disadvantage." His arms flew up over his mop. "I was merely going to make a suggestion. Claire shared a bit of the situation last night as we had the long walk. She said you'd looked for work with little success. She's been worried and you too I'm certain. It's obvious you love your girls. Can I tell you my idea?" He stood still this time, and I knew I'd allowed fear to make a fool of me.

"Forgive me, Liam. I've been through so much of late, I'm afraid I've become suspicious. Please, finish your breakfast and tell me your plan." I replaced the skillet and took my chair. I'd reminded myself of Eunice, dear God.

"Well. How about if you sell these fine antiques? I know your darlin' grandmother left them to you, but who can tell, it may have been for such a time as this. And wouldn't she be wanting you to make the best use of them? What good would they be just setting around if you end up with no place to set them?"

He had a point. "But where would I sell them? I couldn't bear to have all manner of strangers traipsing in and out of our home, disrupting our lives."

"No, Mum. Here's the best part." Claire explained. "I know Mr. Biggs looks favorably on you and while I do NOT mean to encourage anything there, you likely could use it to your advantage and get his permission to set up a booth in the corner of the station to sell your wares. Call it Glory's Treasures or something. Biggs could charge a small rent. Anything he gets would be extra coin in his pocket. Most of Great Gran's lovelies are just sitting in the attic collecting webs anyway. Wouldn't it be nice having them out for others to appreciate?" Claire looked at Liam who was beaming like the sun, as if he'd solved a giant riddle. It just could be that he had.

Syd joined us in the kitchen rubbing her eyes, squinted at Liam and asked, "Who are you, anyway?"

※

"Glory, dear. How nice to hear from you so soon. I'd just been saying, 'Biggs needs to go over, check on the Stone family and let them know how much he enjoyed supper.' You know, I couldn't stop thinking about you and your chicken. To what do I owe this delight?"

I'd rung Biggs up at work. And though he was spreading it on thick as Birds Custard, it could only help my cause. I'd decided to waste no time and set about pursuing the plan Liam and Claire had suggested.

"Thank you, Axel, for the compliments. It was our pleasure. I've something I'd like to discuss with you, a business proposition. Is there a chance I could meet with you at your office, like today?"

"Well now doesn't that sound official?" I heard his mouth crackle and pictured the sharp grin. "Biggs better make time for a matter as special as that." He sounded as if he was addressing a small child, and self doubt crept in. "Let's check the calendar. How about lunch? We could meet at the café about noon." Was that his breathing or a train?

"I have something on for lunch," I lied. "How about 1:30 in your station office?"

"I guess that will do. Wear something pretty, now. I grow weary of seeing little besides dark uniforms and bowlers."

Clearly, Biggs had an imagination. I'd never thought of him as anything more than a family friend. Considering a romance in my life was impossible, no matter what Eunice said.

The issue of what to wear now took on delicate proportions. I couldn't dress frowsy to gain his pity, especially after what he'd said. He might be insulted and refuse my request. On the other hand, I didn't want to fluff myself up like a carnival prize for fear of him jumping to conclusions. I took him for a jumper.

As 1:30 approached, I got the anxious spell out of the way before leaving home.

It was a wet day and I'd chosen something classy, yet modest. With my heavy wool coat and no-nonsense pumps there was no possible way he could mistake my look as an invitation to pursue.

The streets were quiet, normal for this time of day. Inside

the station house, a few travelers lounged about the oak benches, rubbed to a caramel sheen from years of waiting bums. One portly man perused a paper at the bookseller's, who looked as though he'd just as soon sell it to him. Through the refreshment room window, I noticed two or three heads imbibing. Should I set up a proper shop, I'd have to keep regular time. Hours may pass with few visitors. The station would become my second home.

Biggs' office was like a sales clerk's sample of a grand manor. It had pieces of elegance without proper spacing to appreciate them, as if he'd wedged them in wherever they fit.

I walked in, but Axel wasn't there so I took a seat in front of the mahogany desk, a behemoth of the furniture kingdom. The one visitor's chair was of spare cafe styling that trembled when I sat. Biggs' leather chair loomed vacant like my future. Centered in the wall between his chair and the station, was a glass about 25 centimeters square. I'd never noticed it before. It was dark but transparent and I could see figures moving through the room opposite. Claire had been right about the one-way glass. It made sense though, for keeping an eye out, especially during his Air Raid Patrol days. I noticed the picture of Trudy he usually kept next his typewriter had been relocated to a shelf of books. Probably decided to take a dose of his medicine about getting on with life. A pair of large, black leather gloves lay on his desk.

There was no doubt whose office I was in. If the furnishings didn't give it away, bold, block lettering on opaque glass in the door spelled out, Axel Biggs, esq.—station master.

The two-fold smack of his deliberate footstep and shadowed image preceded him and was visible through the glass. It distorted his features making his nose appear longer, villain-like. I took a deep breath and sat up straight, my pocketbook before me. This was Biggs for Nelly's sake, not some prison guard. Though I could view him as a one-man parole board, able to free me from debtor's prison should he take to my notion.

The doorknob turned and in strode Biggs, the Station Master, replete in his regulation black. He looked rather spiffy in his official finery, I thought. When he removed his cap, there was a halo imprint round his head. *Snug fit.* His smile seemed meatier than the words that followed.

"Good to see you, Glory dear." He placed a hand on my shoulder and looked straight down at me. "Can I get you a cup of water or maybe something from the refreshment room?"

Craning my neck to see him I said, "No, thank you."

He moved around the desk to his throne and I'm not sure how he could look taller sitting down but I began to feel like a tot who'd wandered off from home. I fingered the divots my nails left in my pocketbook and took a deep breath. I reminded myself this was just as much an opportunity for him.

"Well now, I've been racking my brain, but I have to confess I'm at a loss as to why you'd be coming to see me on...business, did you say?" He extracted a long cigar from an interior coat pocket and proceeded to light it, not asking if I minded this time. A series of long drags and a plume of smoke later, Biggs invited my query. "What can I do for you?"

I cleared my throat, wishing I'd taken him up on the water.

"Well, it's like this. I know you of all people realize the financial crisis I face with my family just now." I relaxed as I talked even though my voice sounded precocious. "Claire and a new friend of hers have come up with what I like to think is a possible solution to my pressing need, as well as a boon for you," I remembered to add. "As you know, my Grandmother Compton, or Goby as we call her, left an attic full of antiques to me. Well, they're not doing us a whole lot of good locked away out of sight now are they?" I chuckled.

Biggs caught me fiddling with my wedding ring.

I continued, "I thought—that is we wondered if you mightn't let out a small corner of the station, maybe four by four meters or so, for a booth to offer my goods to the public. I could pay rent plus a percentage of the sales and still likely profit something to help ends meet."

There, now it was up to him. I shifted in my chair and for the first time noticed how loud the tick was from a clock on the wall behind me.

He put his cigar to lips that were sticking straight out as if to kiss it rather than smoke it. He continued to squint at me as if he expected me to go on, like the plan was too naive.

"That's it. What do you think of the likelihood of such a venture?" I forced a smile.

After several more seconds of awkward silence, he placed his cigar in the ashtray and leaned forward over his desk.

"I'm for it." He frowned, "on a trial basis that is. And I'll have to gain permission from the board before we proceed, but I've been around long enough to have earned a level of liberty concerning station decisions. Provided they approve, shall we start out with say, just ten percent of sales?"

He took my hand to shake on it. Just like that, I was to be a shopkeeper.

- 18 -

GLORY

Eunice clucked plenty when I rang her up. She was against my idea from the start but reluctantly agreed to come over to help clean the merchandise and ready it for sale. I needed the help but could have done without the commentary. Eunice would never agree to a plan she hadn't concocted, and to her mind, the only reasonable solution was for me to remarry, preferably Finlay, 'so's we could be sissies.'

I went on the defensive. "I appreciate your concern, no mistake. But I can't marry anyone now. Maybe someday when the timing's right." I started up the attic stairs with Eunice a border collie at my heels.

"You're making a big mistake setting up shop in station. Why, you're opening yourself and your precious gewgaws to every robber in the county. How you going to protect them from thievery when you ain't around?" she asked.

Eunice was puffing by the time we reached the top. I was sure it was the most exercise for her since the barmaid encounter. Today she wore cotton gloves to protect her prized nails, and an orange kerchief surrounded her large hair. Even my attic was her stage.

"Station doors are locked at night. If I'm not there, someone else will be. I'll tuck most smalls that folks could walk off with inside a secured display cabinet. Axel found one that belonged to the old haberdashery. You know, the one that became Sunny Buns Bakery. Claire's going to help too and give me a break so I can spend time in garden and with cooking. I hope it will keep her from leaving the Crossing, for now anyway." Such an understatement. "I could really use some moral support from you just now, Eunice."

That gave Eunice an opening. "Who's the scruffy gentleman I saw Claire walking with to station? He sure hasn't got a thing on Albert in the looks department." She made a face, waved down some webs from the rafters, and scooted a couple boxes toward the center of the room.

She added, "We heard from Albert the other day. Sent us a note by post. Right apologetic it was. He asked after Claire. I know he disappeared strange enough, but she ought to forgive and have another go. They made such a handsome pair and he's landed him a good job in Liverpool booking acts in a music hall." Eunice began humming.

I literally bit my tongue to prevent World War III. Had I told her what I thought of deserter Albert, it would end with me having no best friend and no help.

"The 'scruffy gentleman' you referred to is Liam McClelland He's an Irishman she met while walking. He's a seminary student or some such, taking classes at Cambridge. Seems a nice young man, but they've just met and she doesn't seem too keen on him. All the same I'm sure her days with Albert are over. She's not looking for romance with anyone just now."

I hoped to change the subject before Eunice became defensive. Once she sank a tooth into an argument, especially involving a relative, she was a tiger like to suffocate all who disagreed before she'd turn loose.

"What's Roger up to these days?"

"Roger?"

"Your husband."

"Oh, him. When I left, he was getting ready to bake some Sally Lund bread. He's become a regular little housewifey. If I'm not careful I'll be looking for a job right alongside you." She laughed and got me laughing too.

Opening the flaps of the first box released an olfactory link to magic days in Goby's home. An eternal child, waiting in some unspoiled sanctum, took me there. I carefully unwrapped the first item, a white porcelain mouse. This gilded vermin had crouched on the small, mahogany table next Goby's reading chair as if it were waiting for a biscuit. She'd called him Nibbles and let me play with it if I was careful.

Goby had labeled everything, bless her. On mouse's bottom, she'd taped a bit of paper on which she'd handwritten Worcester 1825. The figure was without flaw and precious to me, but I hadn't a clue what price to attach or how to part with it.

Next item, wrapped in soft cloth, was a white cat that except for being feline could have been Nibbles' brother. Made by the same company; this was Perkins. He and Nibbles were civilized chums because conversation was safer amusement for those of fragile make up. They had taunted the Staffordshire dogs, powerless to pursue from the mantelpiece. I played for hours, my legs curled on the rug taking them through their day's journey. A whiff of leather-bound volumes in their built-in bookcases and the tinkle of the musical box Goby wound, and all was right and without a care.

There was fine jewelry, clothing and hats past their style, even dolls from her childhood and Mum's; some were crude but all were special. I loved Grandmum's hand–fashioned corn cob dolls more than the bisque Jumeau beauties of Mother's. The old cob lasses smacked of earth and strong character. I imagined myself quite like Goby as a girl.

A lifetime of collected luxury was at my command. The shiny Bateman silver that had graced Irish linen cloths and stuffed the mouths of influential Londoners would provide tucker for the Stone family table. I'd called up British porcelain jugs and tea things into service. I would not enjoy them for their original purpose but someone would. And the same providence that enabled my grandparents to flourish would come full circle, I hoped.

I had enough to fill a small shop to overflowing. Each box was like buried treasure. These wonderful items had sat for years above a life that went forward without them. Farm life hadn't suited them and Liam was right—Goby would discourage sentimentality, especially at the cost of our livelihood, but want them put to practical use.

Grandmum and Granddad Compton had money but no pretense. They were the exception in those days because of their country roots. Oh, they hobnobbed within the social elite but maintained their authenticity, never looking with scorn at the less fortunate, rather, feeling akin to them—perhaps missing their simple company.

We visited from time to time from our Lakeland farm. Usually we went for Christmas holiday. They had the grandest tree I'd seen outside of one in Hyde Park. I spent hours lying underneath, searching a cottony forest for pine cones, paper angels and candy baskets. Those ornaments waited in pasteboard somewhere. Could I pack them off with strangers? I knew I'd be asking that question often in coming weeks, but our survival was in the answer.

"Eunice, how would you like to take the train to Manchester and do a little antique sniffing? I need an education if I'm to do this right." I glanced round at my trumpery.

"I'm always up for an escape from the ho hum. When shall we go?" Eunice sneezed.

"How about this weekend?"

"All righty. Finlay might like to join us. He could be our body-guard." She grinned like Alice's cat.

I laughed at the notion of Finlay being anyone's bodyguard. "Syd would make a better bodyguard than Finlay." She knew I was right but would be bound to defend him.

"Don't kid yourself. He's small but wiry. You got to watch out for them wiry fellows. They slink up on you." She said it in a sing song way that made me nervous and looked at me out the corners of her heavily lined lids.

"No Eunice, no. Let's go to station and see where I'm to set up shop." I brushed dust from my hands and backside.

◈

The station was busy. One train on the up platform had just emptied itself of passengers, while a second on the down took on lumber and cases of lead pencils. There had been special trains running through-out the war. A body never knew if a troop train or one loaded with military equipment would take priority and put a passenger train off its time. That was just the way.

The tandem might of the engines commanded respect and drew me near their strength. I was afraid to touch them, though I wanted to. What would folks think of a grown woman stroking a train? I closed my eyes so that the heat and smell from stilled wheels and grease-blackened iron parts filled my head. I stood next the giants, loyal monsters, while they chuffed and pulsed and took on water and coal, then exhaled onto the waiting travelers. Their hearts beat strength inside my chest, and the promissory hiss of releasing steam did not disappoint. Trains provided strange comfort over me.

We went inside where I viewed the old haunt with fresh eyes. The high walls were deepened Cumbrian oak. The reward for eighty years of village service was a warm patina that reached around to embrace us on sills and door posts. Wood well tended improved with age. Long brass rods with green glass shades hung from the ceiling like well behaved spiders.

I thought about how many people shuffled through this humble building and began to feel the old panic heat up. The steam sound and passenger voices mingled, built to a roar and crowded my head. Having to run even a simple business suddenly seemed beyond me. I saw them watching, expectant. What made me think I could do this? I chose a bench nearby while Eunice studied me.

"What's wrong?" she asked. "Do you think it be more than you can handle? Because if it is…"

I stopped her before she got a head up. "No. I'll be fine. Just a mite warmish in here." I made myself stand before I was ready and laid a hand on the back of the bench. "Let's find Axel."

We walked to his office and I rapped on the glass.

"Come in." Biggs was big. Everything about him loomed large within his maximized office space — his frame, his feet propped on the desk and a cigar he puffed. All grand sized.

"Hello, Axel." I tried to sound business-friendly but the next thing he did was to grin. Why always with the infernal grin and why did I let it dig at me so?

"Eunice and I are here to discuss where the shop is to be. Do you have the time now to take a look?" I worried for a moment that Biggs had changed his mind about the shop — he'd thought it over and decided it wouldn't work for his station, or the board had nixed it. I felt relief at seeing his feet come down and his jacket go on.

"Hello, ladies. As a matter of fact I think I have the perfect location for your little endeavor." He strode through, parting what few travelers there were, and we kept up.

He kept walking to the extreme opposite side of the entrance and away from any feature that would assure regular foot traffic. I didn't wish to complain fresh out of the gate, but I questioned his choice.

"What the hell?" Eunice eloquently beat me to the punch. She looked at me to see if didn't I agree with her assessment.

"Eunice, just a minute please. Axel, isn't this corner a bit out of the way? It's rather dark. I'm not sure folks will see there's a shop here."

His lips barely moved when he replied, "It's the only area with an electrical plug not in use. I figured you'd want to plug in lamps and clocks or such. Yes?"

I couldn't chance him thinking I was a troublesome female and give him cause to back out. "Oh. Well, the lamps I have to sell are oil and kerosene, and clocks run by manual wind, but all right then. I might need the outlet."

Eunice heaved an audible sigh and I gave her a look that shut her up short term.

"Maybe I can brighten it up with a large sign or ribbons, tasteful of course, but something to catch the patrons' eye." Imagining the cupboards and cabinetry birthed the merchant in me, and the promise of commerce made me forget my nerves. "I lay awake last night trying to think up a name, and think I'll call my corner, Stone Revival Antiques. What do you think?" I looked at each of them without finding the encouragement I sought.

"Well I'm open to suggestions, but I like it. Stone Revival Antiques."

"Sounds like a church meeting," Eunice said. "Will you have hymns playing on the Victrola?" Her teeth and face busted out while Biggs stared into space.

He broke free of his thoughts. "I'll have two workers carry the case over. Face it toward the entrance." Biggs instructed.

"Yes. That will do for the jewelry and small items. I can work from behind," I stood behind the invisible case like a child playing store.

Off he went and I was relieved that the venture appeared to be underway and so thankful to Axel for his part in making this possible.

"What about S and Q Enterprises?" Eunice inquired.

"Sounds like a stone quarry," I answered. "Q for Quimby I assume? No, Eunice."

"Anyway S was first," she asserted. She extracted an emery board from her bag and began fiddling and filing at her nails.

༒

The trip we made to Manchester proved educational. I'd scribbled pages of notes concerning the asking prices of goods similar to mine. I came away both encouraged and dumbfounded that I could clear a fat profit if the tags I'd seen were realistic. We'd soon find out. Eunice came away with an old vaudevillian make-up kit, which thrilled her no end since they were still rationing lipstick, and ingredients for cosmetics were in short supply.

I also learned that many of my antiques were in a rare class. Hubert, one of the Manchester shop owners, was a regular magpie in a bowler. Hubert shelled out advice and experience liberally, with colorful provenance concerning his goods. His volumes of "free" information preceded a solid wink. I didn't know but to thank him for his time and leave post haste.

The girls were excited and Syd planned to curry Ollie for a grand opening. She thought free rides to the kiddies with an advertisement on the pony's flanks would bring in trade. I wasn't sure I wanted a circus atmosphere but a rather more elegant look, like the uptown establishments. Class was to be my new middle name, now I was a proprietress.

Axel was helpful in certain ways but laid down the law with strict guidelines concerning signage and its prominence. He said it was the board's doing. They didn't want a show of frivolity in the station and I assured him we were in agreement. Axel helped move shelving units and cabinetry I'd borrowed from my front room. When all was ready, I began positioning my carefully washed and tagged merchandise on the shelves with museum putty and mixed feelings.

Claire had offered her artistic talent to paint a large sign—a velvety red rose on a green background because of my love for roses, with the words Stone Revival Antiques in gold, old style lettering with black trim. This could be on a board no larger than one meter by two, which would hang on the wall behind. The gold paint had a metallic sheen that reflected station lights from a good distance. I had to catch eyes somehow without raising board eyebrows.

Curiosity drew onlookers as I worked. I smiled until my cheeks ached and told them to be sure to come check out the fine goods once we were open official. I recognized most as local farmers. Nosing about with stories of their own family goods was all they'd be doing. I counted largely on city people escaping the grit and rubble to take the country air of Rakefoot Crossing, which now included the high class offerings of Stone Revival Antiques.

- 19 -

GLORY

Four weeks passed like a snap with my shop flowing smartly and me running things. Business was good and building as word went forth. It didn't take long for me to feel at home behind the counter. With a little practice, math skills reappeared, and I learned to count back change proper.

The flirtatious Manchester merchant had suggested that spending money was necessary to making same, and that some type of sales gimmick was useful. So I took what remained after paying the market bill and sunk it, as it were, into my first attempt at drumming up trade.

Today marked my first month in business and I was celebrating. The first customer of the day would stand to receive two dozen of Claire's shortbread dream cookies—all done up in a neat package lined with pink sateen. The box had previously held gift soaps from Eunice for my birthday last. I'd set it on the back stoop to air and covered the fabric over with parchment in hopes the cookies wouldn't taste of rose petals. I wondered what sort of response I could expect from fliers I'd tacked up on the station bulletin board and Myron's store.

I kept an eye on the station clock. At 10 AM, I would open. There was no throng straining the gate. In fact, there was no one, but I waited, cookies at the ready and money box stocked like always.

I straightened necklaces in the jewelry case and added two ruby rings that had sparkled like strawberries in the desert on Aunt V's aged fingers.

I stood to a customer waiting—two in fact. They were elderly men, probably nearing seventy-five or eighty judging by their bark textured faces, but I could tell they were still in the game. Impressive in three piece suits, one a pinstripe, they'd detoured to Rakefoot Crossing in high style. With canes over their arms, they lifted fedoras and addressed me. I was instantly fond of them and glad to see their like had survived the many changes.

"How d'you do, Madam." This from the larger and more stooped of the pair and evidently the spokesman. "Fine shop you have here." He peered up sideways at me through heavy rimmed glasses by way of a bowed neck. His hair, though thin, shone smooth with a crimp like Christmas tinsel. His smile was like a warming fire from the caverns of his cheeks. "Allow me to introduce myself and my friend. My name is General Milton W. Pickering and this is my amiable companion, Fenwick Smyth, call him Wicky." They bowed slightly. Mr. Smyth murmured something and added a smile ember of his own.

General Pickering had once filled out his frame. I could wager by the size of his wingtips and circumference of his belt that, in his prime, he had made quick work of a porterhouse steak. Though his ears, feet and middle held their ground, all else had retreated.

Wicky Smyth had a Cyrano nose, without the dash. It looked as though it had ended reluctantly, with enough material leftover for a decisive drop. Unlike Milton's, Wicky's hair whispered brown gone by among the gray and lay dutifully to one side save for a central spray.

"I'm pleased to meet you both, I'm sure." Instantly charmed, I held out my hand to Milton who brushed my knuckles with respectful lips. I might have blushed.

The General spoke as to be heard over the roar of a train engine, only there was no train. The apparatus flanking his right ear was either ineffective or in need of a tune-up. Any road, he shouted pleasantries at me and even though I saw heads turning across station, I accepted them in good spirit.

"General Pickering..." I began.

"No, no now I'll not have that!" He held up his hand and seriously roared, "Milton or nothing at all!" Witnesses within a hundred yards learned his name. I hoped they didn't suspect me of mistreatment. He continued, "My war was over a long time ago." But two highly polished medals—the Military and Victoria Crosses, reposed just shy of concealed on his vest. He continued. "It was The Great War, you realize. I had the honor to serve Britain in the Navy under Sir Reginald Bacon." He drew a deep breath and a pipe and pouch from his jacket pocket. I waited for the story to break.

He poked his pipe with Granger Tobacco, one of John's brands. I inhaled as he cupped his hand and lowered a match to the bowl. The milky curls tickled my memory and I hoped he and his pipe would linger.

His friend leaned an elbow on the counter and settled in. He appeared wistful, as if all that could have ruffled him in life already had.

"Something in your case, Missus, reminded me of a time on the coast at Dover. It was me and my men's job to keep them German U-boats from crossing over the Channel, which was a main target. Dover Patrol our mission was called." He stopped and held his pipe in his teeth. He was journeying back to a particular day in 1915, and that could take a minute or two. But it was as if he changed his mind and thought better of going on. "Boys like guns," was all that followed as he looked into the case. He made his best attempt at standing tall and reached for his coin purse to purchase a toy Howitzer. He said it was for his great grandchap. "We lost his father, my grandson, at Normandy—a little over a year now. The filthy bastards, excuse me, madam. But their hell-driven machine guns did their worst that day. And we gave our best." The general pulled out a handkerchief.

"Here now. I am sorry, Milton." I squeezed his arm. "Sometimes I forget I'm not the only one. My husband of nearly twenty-five years is gone as well, I think. Rail accident, they said." We were quiet.

"Excuse me but, you said you 'think.' There's doubt?"

I'd said too much. "Well, no, I mean I don't know. I never saw him at the funeral. Closed casket. And…our daughter, Sydney…" My heart began to thud. I turned round and located the stool.

Then he looked at me with all the sincerity of his religious conviction and said, "I can almost guarantee you'll see your man again one day, Glory Stone." He patted my shoulder as a sympathetic comrade.

I saw the cookies and wiped my eyes. "Say, you know that makes you my first customer of the day." I caught myself talking loudly, partly for him to hear but also for the bystanders. "That makes you winner of this special box of cookies baked for the occasion by my daughter, Claire. She's won ribbons for these gems at county fair I'll have you know." With great flourish and pomp, I lifted the box far higher over the counter than needed and handed it to a surprised General Pickering.

"Well, just look at that," he said in staccato fashion. He looked as pleased as if I'd handed him the Versailles Treaty. He addressed Wicky, "These'll go down good with a hot glass of rum punch later, eh?" To which his amiable friend flashed a hearty thumbs up and mumbled something to the affirmative behind the nose tip.

The onlookers strolled over to see what the excitement was about and the general turned promoter.

"Just see, ladies and gents, what you could have had if you'd had the foresight to trade at uh…" He stalled, realizing he didn't know my name or the name of the shop. "What's the name, Missus?"

"Glory Stone and Stone Revival Antiques," I beamed.

He held his hand high in the air and proclaimed, "Dory Sloan and Stone Reminder Antiques!" He whipped his arm around and I readied to catch him should he go off balance. "How'd you come to a name like that?" he asked.

Wicky's eyes fixed on his shoes. Neither of us corrected the general. I figured I'd squeezed about all the notoriety I deserved from one box of cookies anyhow.

"Thank you, General, I mean Milton. You haven't told me what you gents are doing here in Rakefoot Crossing. Not much on this time of year." I wrapped the tin gun in tissue paper and wrote out his receipt.

The two exchanged glances but again it was Milton who piped up.

"Wicky here was born and raised in these vales. It'd been awhile since he'd visited so one Sunday after services I says, 'How's about a train trip up to your old stomping grounds, Wick? We could look up your cousin…Pearl.' He was game so here we are on holiday."

Smyth licked his lips and stuck his hands in his pockets.

"Oh? I don't believe I know anybody named Pearl around. Who is she?" I asked.

Wicky Smyth spoke evenly. "She's my Aunt Rosie's middle girl. Two years younger than I." He looked nervous. Was he just shy? "Two years younger. That makes her seventy smack on doesn't it, Milton?"

"Hmm? Hard to believe." He couldn't have heard the soft spoken Wicky, but Milton shook his head and the subject of Pearl changed to commerce. "How long have you had your business here, Missus?" Milton smiled and took a turn about the rest of the booth, testing the widths of the two aisles. "You've got some fine antiques. Reminds me of when I was a boy. How'd you come by it all?" I wished I had chairs to offer them. I was saving the furniture for last, hoping I wouldn't have to part with it.

"I've only been open a month. These were mostly my Grand-mother Compton's things from London. I hate to sell them, but with John gone we needed money."

"You needed honey, eh?" He looked down ruefully shaking his head. "Love it on scones. Impossible to come by with all the rationing, but I shouldn't think it would require selling all this." Milton perused the shop but the station too. He appeared to be taking it all in like a child on an untried playground. "A fine look-ing station, this. Must have a capable station master at the helm?" He turned stiffly toward me.

"Yes. Axel Biggs is a man devoted to duty and this station. He cares about the village and the people in it I think." I spoke loudly toward him. "Don't know where my girls and me would be if it hadn't been for his kindness when John passed. And then he saw that I got my shop here. He spoke to the Board of Directors and put a word in for me."

"Oh, good fellow." He nodded then recollected something. "Old Marshall Bickerstaff used to be on the board of the C.K. and P. line. We served together. Would you know if he's still around?"

"I don't know who's on the board. I've never met them. Always let Mr. Biggs do the talking for me since I wouldn't know what to say. But I could find out for you," I offered. My throat grew tired from the strain of being heard. Onlookers had figured out that we had a deaf person there, that the shouting held no sensational purpose, and had long since wandered off.

"Don't bother yourself, Missus. I may drop round to his office one of these days while we're here." Milton found an ash bin against the wall and tapped his pipe remains into the metal dish. Mr. Smyth examined a brass seaman's sextant.

"Were you in the Navy too, Mr. Smyth?" I sought to draw him out.

"Ah, no Madam," was all he said and laid the instrument down like a scolded child. "Hinfantry."

"We best be pushing on eh, my friend? Don't want to miss our noon meal at the inn. And we'll enjoy these tasties a bit later." He held up his prize.

Seeing them made me lonely for another time—for Dad.

"Please do come see us again," I urged.

Milton looked back over his shoulder as he repositioned his hat and pressed the mahogany cane into service. "Don't worry, Missus. We'll be back to check on you, make sure you're being treated right." He winked.

-20-

CLAIRE

"Tell me we'll have roast again when Pop comes home." Syd and a pale sausage stared at one another. "I don't even remember what beef tastes like."

I answered with a question of my own. "When are you going to have a talk with her?" I turned to Mum who gave a pleading look. "Don't you think her fantasy has run its course? It's embarrassing when my friends are around."

Mum shook a fresh loaf from the pan.

"Doesn't she think *what's* run its course?" Syd asked.

"Please let's not go into this at Sunday dinner." Mum tried to slice the warm bread with a dull knife. "Have you heard anything more of Liam? I rather liked him."

Dear Mum, artful dodger of painful topics.

Syd piped up, "You needn't change the subject on my account. I know what Claire's talking about. She doesn't believe me about Pop coming home. It's because she has no faith. She hates God. I heard her say so, after Albert." Syd's smile had a wicked edge.

"I was upset." I responded. "Anyway I'm pretty sure nobody heard me but you, snitcher."

"Great grief. Why can't we just have a peaceful meal together?" Mum walked around to Syd and knelt by her chair. She ran her fingers over Syd's hair, and I'd an idea of what would follow.

"I'll admit to still having doubts I thought I'd come to grips with, but perhaps it's best if we...if you keep your special thoughts about Pop to your diary for the time being." I thought of Syd's diary with the missing pages. Mum looked in her eyes but Syd remained quiet with her fingers resting on her chin—looking from me to Mum and back again. She reached for her milk.

"All right, let's talk shop," I said. "Stone Revival Antiques. Has a nice ring to it. Sounds like a stone circle might jump up and shout hallelujahs or something."

I timed the comment for Syd to bust up and blow milk out her nose. It worked.

"Oh girls. Syd, I will want to talk with you later." Mum went for a towel.

"Stone Revival is a play on words, Claire, as I'm sure you're aware. You're just trying to be clever. It's supposed to stand for our revival: yours, Syd's and mine, along with restoring objects to their usefulness. You can poke fun but I took in three pounds ten last week. I was able to pay off Shiverson's bill, and use coupons I've saved to pick up extras for holiday sweets." She smiled Mum's pre-war smile—with teeth. "There's going to be some baking going on around here or I'll know the reason. I want to give a few sweets to neighbors to thank them for their support during our calamity. Oh, Claire, I gave your cookies away to the kindest old men at shop. One of them bought a toy gun."

"That's nice. Not sure how it'll help business. I would have enjoyed one or two."

"Before I forget, has anyone seen Cassidy? He's missing again." Syd asked.

"I haven't. You shouldn't mother your animals so," I said.

"Cassidy's special. He needs extra looking after since he's crippled. Plus, he loves me most of all the cats." Syd answered. "He wakes me from nightmares with his paw on my lips."

"I'll help you look for him later," I offered, feeling slightly the heel.

The phone rang and Mum went to answer it, returning to the table with a pained look.

"Who was that?" I asked.

"Biggs has called a meeting with me for tomorrow. Something about new regulations or some such foolishness. Men of position need to find a way to complicate, just about the time plans get rolling along smooth like. I'm not saying it's his idea, mind, probably the board." She rolled her eyes like Syd and I.

"Well, keep your guard up." I warned. "And to answer your earlier question, no I haven't heard from Liam. Why would I? I expect he's at school and wish him the best."

"Did I ask after Liam? Oh yeah, I guess I did." Mum could be annoying.

I took the rag from her and swiped up Syd's explosion, checking the potatoes. "As long as we're celebrating, I have good news as well. I now have, or soon will anyway, a position at Dalemain Manor as a proper tour guide to the gawking public. In hopes for an increase in tourism hereabouts, they're going to open the old place. I'm to point with proper decorum toward the whiskered faces on the walls and tell about their storied lives." I sniffed. "The new tour will include aspects of the Special Operations training that recently took place there; and how they transformed a portion of the family home into a giant bivouac, disturbing the family ghosts."

"Oh Claire, that's marvelous!" Mum was ecstatic. She looked beautiful, in fact. I knew she'd be pleased, and I was glad to deliver the news. My thoughts had changed about leaving the Crossing, for a while anyway. Albert's memory gouged at me, but he'd gone and the angry restlessness had lost its punch. I didn't want to be the reason Mum rushed into a premature marriage.

"Of course it won't start right off—not until spring, but they'll pay me during training. Meanwhile I'll be able to help in shop, and when I'm at the manor, good old Eunice can take over my shift. She's one eager beaver that one. She strolled by when I was working the counter the other day and a man came up while I was occupied. She bustled right in and grabbed the key to the case before I said, 'Excuse me, Eunice, but I can take care of it.' I said it real polite but she seemed put out." I laughed. "By the way, jewelry is selling. Is there more?"

"Yes, I have more of Goby's and Aunt Verla's. Aunt V loved shiny things." Mother hummed and reached for the teapot. For one bright moment, I thought maybe life had only hiccupped, that nothing as bleak as death had happened.

"Just like Natty," said Syd

"Yes," Mum laughed. "That silly bird. Did I tell you those were Old Pete's teeth he stole? When Myron told me, I barely kept from laughing and giving the old thief away."

"That is rich. Reminds me I haven't checked his stash today. Maybe he'll find me a necklace to wear to the Christmas dance," Syd looked at Mum.

"You want to go?" Mum asked.

"I think Pop would like it if I did," I saw that Syd remembered I was there and braced for a retort.

"You and Natty are a couple of lowdown thieves!" I said. "You can't have that bird pinching jewelry for you."

"I can't help what he finds. And anyway, if folks leave stuff lying about careless they deserve to lose them I say. And yes, I think it might be fun to go to the dance, though I don't know how." I saw Syd hang a bit of meat under the table for the quickest dog.

"What a little judge we have." I continued. "Next time you leave your clothes strewn about the floor I'll remember what you said and donate them to the charity bazaar." I spooned into a parsnip stew.

"Girls. Syd, I'm with Claire on Natty's findings. You should try to locate the rightful owner should Natty snatch something of value. You could take it to station and let Biggs post a notice on the bulletin board."

Syd fidgeted in her chair. "I told Pop, I mean, I knew you'd say that."

"Why? What did Natty bring you?" Mum asked. "You told Pop?"

Syd sighed, and I scooted closer thinking this should be good.

"First, don't make fun, Claire, or I won't tell either of you a thing ever again.

"Very good, little sis. Spill." Mum shot me her angry brow.

"Instead of writing in my diary like before, I've been writing to…Pop. That's all." Syd looked at me. The missing pages flashed to mind but I sat still so she'd go on. "It makes me feel like we're having our old talks. So, I wrote him about Natty's latest find." Syd got up and walked to their room. I heard a drawer slide open and she came out with something in her fist.

"He found this ring—who knows where. It's a gold wedding band, I think."

"Blimey. If you take that to Biggs, he'll likely sell it at the Penrith hock shop." I was in rare form and enjoying myself.

"Claire," Mum said. She was too touchy about Biggs. "There you go again picking on Biggs. Don't forget if it wasn't for his willingness about the business we'd be up a creek, no mistake." I looked down and mouthed the last line with her.

Syd handed the ring to Mum. She stared at it for a long time then scooted her chair and used the table to stand. She looked a bit wobbly as she walked to the front room and returned with her readers on, clutching the ring and holding it directly under the kitchen globe. She made a thorough examination of the inside of the band, then removed her glasses and sat.

"What is it?" I asked. "An inscription?"

"What do you see?" Syd came around behind to look over her shoulder.

Mum asked Syd, "When did you say you found this?"

"I'm not sure. Maybe a couple weeks ago. Why?"

"Yes, what is it? I pressed her.

"A couple weeks ago." Mum repeated. She stared at the floor then slowly turned toward us.

"Girls." She took a deep breath. "This is your father's ring."

"Get...out. Are you sure?" I asked, taking it from her and looking it over.

"Positive. There's the Celtic cross he had the jeweler etch on the inside when we wed." She worked to remove her own ring. "Remember? I have an identical cross on mine. Have a look." She handed it over and I saw where twenty-five years had left a chaste replica around Mum's finger.

"Of course he would!" Syd exclaimed and began clapping and skipping around the room.

"Oh, here we go," I moaned.

Syd continued. "Don't you get it? Pop gave his ring to Natty knowing he'd bring it to the stash I showed him. He wanted to tell us he's alive, and he must be close. Natty knows where he is!" She resumed twirling and banged into the icebox.

I laughed and tried to stem the tide of boundless optimism. "Little sis, why would Dad use a bird to deliver a message like that when there are any number of other, more conventional ways? Better yet, why doesn't he just come home? Sorry to say, it's silly."

Syd answered, "Oh, Claire. Stop being such a Naysay Nellie. Maybe Natty was the only one he could trust to deliver a message like that. It may be that no one is supposed to know he's alive— not even us. OR..." Her smile faded. "Perhaps he's in trouble." She looked to Mum.

Mum still seemed to be thinking or numb. I couldn't tell which.

I said, "There's a logical explanation for this if we keep our heads. Somehow, the Army misplaced Dad's ring when they returned his things. You both know Natty takes stuff from open windows; that's proven." I looked from one to the other—Syd with her Pollyanna eyebrows and Mum, poor Mum. "Well, for cripe's sake. You're not going along with this, are you, Mum? You've come such a long way to rise above your grief and now, to begin entertaining ideas of Dad being alive could throw you right back." I wasn't sure of my statement and began to sense a crumbling of resolve. Syd said she'd been writing in her diary to Pop. Was she mailing the pages somewhere? I would find a time to ask her in private and suffer the wrath of her knowing I peeked.

Syd chimed in, "And I suppose Natty flew all the way to the Army office in Carlisle to retrieve Pop's ring. We've never received Pop's other things, have we, Mum?"

Mum stirred. "No, we haven't. I would be inclined to agree with you, Claire, but for five things."

I handed back her wedding ring.

"Your father carved notches beside the cross, one for every five years we celebrated together. There were four when he left for duty—two on either side. And I could understand if he'd added the fifth while he was away—for our twenty-fifth. But, why would he carve in five more? Have another look." Mum held her stomach. "There are ten notches—fifty years' worth."

Syd and I fought to see. I looked at her, and she nodded.

- 21 -

GLORY

Our meeting was for nine o'clock. Through the window, I saw Biggs check himself in the mirror and strain breakfast from his moustache with a tiny comb that looked as if it was made special for the duty. I wondered what kind of news he planned to deliver, though my thoughts were preoccupied, no mistake. I'd tied John's ring to my brassiere strap so I could feel it against my chest, a talisman.

I knocked softly and heard a *cush* sound as he eased into his leather chair.

"Come in," he said charitably.

"Hello, Biggs. You didn't say what this was about. I suppose it has something to do with the shop?" I took the chair of fragile make-up opposite his. As he studied me, my palms began to sweat.

"Glory, you're like a golden ray on this gloomy day." He chuckled at his rhyme. "Would you care for some tea?" He reached for the pot. "I was just going to help myself to a second cup." Biggs was on his best behavior.

"No, thank you. I've had mine." I removed my gloves. "I don't mean to seem in a rush but I will need to open by ten. I didn't think to have anyone take over this morning." I half declared it, as I looked up at him sitting large.

"No, no, I won't keep you, Glory. There are just a couple of unfortunate mandates the higher powers have handed down; how bored they must get." He shook his head and looked at my legs. "But, having gotten your selling legs so to speak, you should recoup in no time, dear." He took a long slurp of steaming black tea.

The poor excuse for a chair squeaked as I shifted. "What sort of mandates, Axel?"

"Well, they're upping the rent. Sorry to say, they see how well you're doing and frankly, greed comes to mind. But alas, they hold the cards, don't they?" He lit a cigar. "They want to increase their share to twenty percent beginning next week, the blaggards."

"Twenty percent? That's double what I'm paying! Who's in charge? Maybe I could go and...explain, tell them how bl...bleak my situation is without this income. And they did agree to the terms."

Biggs' eyebrows rose. "Uh, yes, Glory dear, but unfortunately you don't have anything in writing, an oversight on my part to be sure and my deepest apologies for that. But I'm afraid it wouldn't do for you to try to speak with them. They're just a graying herd of pipe tokers who lost their souls to capitalism long ago. Your pleading would do nothing to move them and might even cause them to eliminate the mess altogether and give you the rout. No, I tried reasoning with them already and no dice. I know it will be harder temporarily, but I believe you'll bounce back."

Biggs tried to enter my eyes. He'd tried before. He shook out a handkerchief and handed it to me. I looked past it and him, out the window to a train. "Well you said there were a couple of mandates. Is there more?"

"A decrease in the size of your space." He plunged right in. "Right now you're at four by four, is that so?" He frowned.

"Yes."

"It's just that they feel it impedes traffic in that corner by the rear doors. They'd prefer you to limit your shop to no more than a three and a half by three concern." Biggs picked some lint off his sleeve and appeared to fix on my overbite.

"So, let's see. They want twice the rent with less retail space." I bit my lip but instead of crying as he likely expected, I added, "They sound like poor businessmen indeed. They want a bigger piece of a smaller pie. I should think they'd want to expand a business they were sharing in so richly. How in the world they ever built a railroad is beyond me." I laughed. "I just may have to go in search of more astute landlords if that's the direction their bound to take." I looked Biggs square in the eyes and rose from the failing perch.

He put down his cigar and popped out of his chair. "Don't be too hasty. You get far more traffic through the station on any given day than anyplace else."

Indisputable. "Right you are. We'll see how it goes for now, I suppose. But they best not keep digging or their gold mine will cave in and the old goats will find their proceeds in someone else's vault."

With that, I bid him good day and started for the door. But Biggs stopped me and shifted gears.

"Before you go, Glory dear, I'd like to ask if you would accompany me to a concert of classical music at Liberty Hall in Keswick Saturday next?"

He leaned forward to take my hand but I resisted. His timing was way off. I hesitated and smiled, but the answer was no. "I'm not ready to date, Axel. But thank you for asking. I appreciate being asked." I turned.

"Oh, but is that what you think? Because no, it wouldn't be a date. We're old friends." Biggs tried to reassure me.

"It sounds like a date to me. Anyway it's time I opened the

shop so I can start making some coin for the railroad tycoons."
I left shaking my head but nearly ran into my two old friends as
they headed for Biggs' office. "Why, hello. Going for that jaw-wag
with Biggs you mentioned?"

"Jabbing at pigs?" General Pickering's hearing device hadn't
improved. "Not today. We want to have a chat with your station
master. Have a few things we'd like to talk over with him." He
looked at Mr. Smyth who remained solemn then straightened
himself up enough to speak.

"You said he might know that Bickerstaff fellow—friend of
yours, right?" Wicky said and looked from the general to me.

"Quite right. Quite right. Yes. Well, good day, Glory." They entered.

I found their demeanor changed and my curiosity piqued. I
stood near the office door, out of sight and eavesdropped, peeking
over the window ledge. Eunice would have been proud.

"Good to finally meet you, Mr. Biggs. Glory's told us many
good things about you, and said you might be keen to hear some
firsthand tales about The Great War."

I did not recall telling him any such thing. Quite the contrary,
I'd perceived that the old men irritated Axel beyond reason.

"I recall one time with Bickerstaff; it was in the autumn of 1914.
Me and Bicky was on guard...," the general launched into a scene.

"I say, General, as much as I enjoy the vivid history lesson,
I simply have piles of work to do." Biggs gave a pained look and
gestured toward a hill of paper.

"Yes, of course. Sitting all day. Painful situation. There's good
salve for that now. See your druggist; he'll put you right!"

I chuckled as Milton, oblivious to his error, toked away on his
pipe and dreamed out the window.

"We were on guard duty and the enemy was known to be biv-
ouacked in the immediate vicinity. Well, Bicky heard a rustling in
the bushes and raised his bayonet..." He set down the smoldering
pipe and poised an invisible weapon at Biggs' freshly shaved head.

I knew the general's brand of tobacco was particularly offensive to Biggs, who waved off the smoke meandering toward him and put on his cap.

"General Pickering we've established on another occasion that I don't know your Bickerstaff fellow!" Biggs spoke loudly. I had no problem hearing them. "I need to do some work here! It's been a pleasure meeting with you and Wicky, I mean Smyth!" Mr. Smyth smiled as Biggs nodded his head up and down vigorously as though the general was blind as well as deaf and extended the right hand of a farewell to arms.

The General glanced stiff necked and sideways about Biggs' office, visibly impressed with everything but Biggs' hand hanging there, then noticed a picture frame faced down on a shelf. "Oh dear. Looks as if a picture of a loved one has toppled here." He rose heavily and plucked it from under a stack of books that went sprawling to the floor.

Biggs sighed, took it from him and laid it on the corner of his desk. "Thank you. I'll take care of that if you don't mind. Do come again, General. Won't you?" Biggs placed his hand on the general's broad, stooped back and aimed him vaguely toward the door.

"Another comely woman. Is that your missus, Mr. Biggs? She's a delicate little thing. Don't you agree, Wick? Must be a fireball with the red hair. Hoo boy, them redheads." He chuckled.

"Oh yes, lovely," Fenwick agreed.

"She was my wife, yes."

Axel positioned the portrait back on the shelf and I leaned in.

"Was, ye say?" General Pickering and Fenwick Smyth turned round having whiffed fresh subject. "She passed on then," Pickering shook his head. "She appears so full of pluck in this image. What took her from you, Mr. Biggs?" From where I crouched, I could see the general look straight into Bigg's eyes with his gray ones without blinking.

"She didn't die, she ran off, if you must know." Biggs looked nearly helpless in his frustration. I thought possibly to rescue him, but this was too good.

"Ran away? What from? Or was it another man? A thieving fox in the henhouse, eh?" Pickering drew his invisible piece again, this time drawing a bead on his friend. Mr. Smyth chuckled and held up his hands in mock surrender. They waited for an answer.

"Just left one day! Wasn't happy I guess! Anything else you'd like to know? A questionnaire I could fill out?" Axel's face turned red as he massaged his forehead.

"Sorry old chum." Pickering quieted down. "Didn't mean to stir the pot. Losing the missus can be tough no matter how it come to be."

The general looked at the chair, threatening to sit again. Biggs actually kicked it out of reach. This was rich. I'd never seen him behave so rudely.

"Well! I guess us two old retreads need to be moving along and let this man get to it!" Pickering bellowed. "And you never heard of First Sergeant Marshall Bickerstaff? He's on the C.K. and P. Railroad Board of Directors." Pickering bent low.

"For the last time, no. I never heard of the gent. Maybe he's since retired."

Axel wiped his forehead with a handkerchief and made a show of reading a notice on his desk.

"Fired? I doubt it. Was always a good man of business. And you do regular business with the board, right? Glory Stone, your lovely proprietress of the antique shop in the corner says you're her spokesman. Must have a lot of faith in your negotiating skills." Was Pickering asking him? "She's a lovely thing. She and her daughter, what's her name?"

They were discussing the girls and me. The shop would wait.

"Claire, Milton. I think it's Claire, isn't it?" Smyth looked to Axel.

"Yes, her daughter is Claire. And yes, I do a bit of business with the board from time to time." Biggs sat behind his desk purposing to work and looking quite determined to ignore them.

"Seems like to me you might get an idea about Mrs. Stone. She without a man, you without a cook." The general allowed a wry smile and looked sideways through his glasses. "Excuse me if I speak too bold, Mr. Biggs, but if I was you..."

Why the old matchmaker.

Axel, exasperated beyond any concern for etiquette evidently, fired on the poor general.

"If you were me," he rose slowly from behind his grand desk, "you'd likely take a hint that your company wasn't required any longer and let a working man pursue his calling in peace!"

The two men assessed the situation with a startled glance toward one another then turned to go. As they exited, Biggs couldn't resist one final admission.

"And here's something to chew on with tea. Mrs. Stone and I are keeping regular company and I intend to woo and wed her!" He flipped the switch on a small, electric fan atop his file cabinets so that the whirling brass blades threw their smoke out with them.

I dropped my pocketbook and all heads except the general's turned toward me. I ducked and scrambled straightaway for my shop but I must have been a spectacle with my cheeks rosy hot. I didn't know if Axel was in earnest or just trying to impress the men-folk, but one thing sure, if he was serious, we were not within one hundred miles of the same neighborhood as far as our relationship was concerned.

- 22 -

SYD

27 November 1945

Dear Pop,

Brilliant! That's all I can say. I found your ring in Natty's stash, so you must be close by. I didn't know it was yours until I showed Mum. You should have seen her face. I thought she would faint. I danced around the room, but Claire laughed when I hit the icebox. I didn't much care. What a fabulous notion to add the extra marks. At least now Mum has real reason to question. Not sure what she'll do about it. Not sure we should do anything but hope.

Claire is still trying to squash our hopes. Maybe she's afraid to believe in such a miracle. I could understand that I guess. Adults seem to give up quicker. She confessed to finding my diary in the loft and asked me where all the pages went. I was so peeved at her for peeking; I had a fit and refused to tell her anything. I couldn't tell her anything.

I just wish I knew you were all right. You must not be a prisoner if you're that near. I pray for you every day and night, as I know you do for us.

I haven't said much to Biggs because I didn't know if I should. I'm thinking you're in some sort of secret service and I wouldn't want to make a bollocks of it by spilling the beans.

Biggs and I spend time together. We had fun when he took me to Keswick to see the sights. I forgot to tell Mum and she got after me. I didn't mean to keep it from her; I just didn't think she'd care. Biggs said he wants to show me Whitehaven on the coast next. I was too little to remember the last time we went to the beach as a family. He wants to show me the ships and historical places. I'll be sure to ask Mum this time, though. Perhaps she'll join us.

I guess I'm going to the school Christmas dance. I would never hear the end of it from Eunice Quimby if I didn't, and anyway, I guess I should at least try looking like a girl once in awhile. Claire said she would teach me how to dance and fix my hair. It was the nicest she's been to me in a while, so I took it as a sign I should go.

Claire seems happier now Albert's gone. She's friends with a funny Irish chappy named Liam. Mum and I like him, especially Mum. I know you will too. We could all be a solid bunch.

Pop, I think Biggs is lonely. He's never said so, but I don't think he feels as if anyone cares for him, except maybe me. Since Trudy left and his mum died, he's like a grown-up orphan, isn't he? He spends a lot of time in that old, dark basement, fiddling with the telegraph and oiling his Mutti's gloves.

I'm not sure his childhood was all that jolly, either. He told me she used to wear a different pair of gloves each time she spanked him. She said it was because she didn't want to soil her hands on him. Isn't that a horrid thing to say to your child? He defends his mum and says she knew best, but I don't know.

He taught me an old German lullaby called Guter Mond. It means 'good moon.' But his mum didn't sing it to him. He used to look out the window of his nursery as a boy and sing himself sleepy with it.

I should remind him that God loves him.

Hope to see your mug soon.

Love and hugs,

Syd

- 23 -

CLAIRE

I grabbed my slicker, gloves and scarf. "Time for a walk. Do the boys want to come?" I rough-housed the dogs into a yapping frenzy. "Come on, lads." Reggie and Jingles trotted close by, nosing through the sleeping garden and out to the road along the same well-worn path. It was a walk that never got old. I had to try and process this news about Dad's ring turning up.

Winter's arrival stirred the wings of the southbound birds, and the trees, like bare chorus girls, waited. Were trees like foxes— their vitals slowing so they were numb to the teeth of the wind and storms? Hard to imagine how anything survived such brutal punishment then appeared better for it in spring.

I'd gone but a short distance when I noticed the dogs had discovered something lying half on the path and partly under a bush. I came closer and was saddened to discover it was Cassidy, Syd's cat. It didn't look as though anything had got him just that he'd lain down and died.

"Poor fellow." I knew Syd put a lot of store by him. She told us he woke her from nightmares. She'd been through so much of late, like all of us. I reckoned I could spare her this grief, and that it might be easier if Syd thought he just disappeared. I lifted Cassidy and took him off the path to a large drift of leaves in a draw. There I covered him over where Syd wouldn't see. "Come on, lads. Leave him in peace."

I didn't mean to, but I thought of Liam again. He was entertaining if not attractive. "You fellows liked him, didn't you, huh?" The dogs looked at me and one another, tongues and tails wagging. They were agreeable to anything now that they were on a lark.

I crossed the bridge over the River Greta, the one Syd had named our cow after, and headed toward Grisedale Forest, my favorite refuge. I sang softly at first. It was a silly piece I'd learned in grammar school about a lady who had too many cats. Finding Cassidy must have sparked the memory, but I walked in rhythm with the lyrics.

"Oh the woman of Eads had a few cats too many,

She couldn't turn round without tumbling o'er.

Her husband grew vexed, said she couldn't have any,

So she laid him out soundly right there on the floor.

CHORUS:

The woman of Eads, the woman of Eads,

Her cats produced kittens as a garden does weeds.

The six-month-old kitten litters with ease. The jolly old woman of Eads."

I opened my mouth to begin the second of twelve verses, only with more gusto, but another voice rang out.

"Oh the woman of Eads had a cat for a doorstop,

A cat for a pillow and one for her feet.

She couldn't fix grub, out the kettle one would hop,

A flavor of feline in all she did eat.

Ohhh, the woman of Eads, the wom…"

"Liam?" I was astounded to find him there.

"A fun song, eh, m'lady?" It was Liam sure enough.

"What in the wide world?" To say I was surprised would have been a grave understatement, but I couldn't say I was disheartened.

"Do you think if we keep meeting like this, there will be talk?" He bounced and smiled thinly. "I'm OK with it, by the way, if there is."

Weren't those the same clothes he had on before?

"Did you flunk out?" I asked.

"No, lass. Can't get my fill of the scenery up this way that's all." He made a show of looking around.

Jingles and Reggie romped around him as if he was their long lost littermate.

"Hello, boys. How's it going there?" He knelt and welcomed their approval, then, out of the cloudy blue, stood and said, "How about a row on the lake?"

"In a boat, now? With the dogs?" I noticed the sky.

"Yes, a boat would be helpful on the water." He held out his hand but I didn't take it though I followed, staring at his unconventional hair.

We visited as we walked and in no time, stole upon Derwentwater, largest lake in the area where dinghies for the renting bobbed and waited, ready for a crew. I had no idea how Liam paid the man at the kiosk but evidently he gave him something because Liam next ushered me to a chosen craft and helped me in. I accepted his hand this time and stepped into the rocking boat. I sat with the dogs at one end. They seemed delightfully confused and wagged with a will. Liam shoved the boat free of the gravel, bid farewell to the meandering waterfowl onlookers and leapt aboard.

"There are two sets of oars, lass." He nodded toward the starboard side.

"So there are." I made no move to retrieve them. "I have the dogs. They're not used to water," I lied. "Not sure the weather's going to bless our voyage," I forecasted. "This seems like a proper daft idea to me." I felt keenly alive and recognized the stomach flutter as a welcome sensation from childhood adventures.

"It's not the weather I'm worried about." By then, he'd rowed out a good distance. "It's this leak here."

Liam removed his shoe to get at his sock in order to stuff a small hole. I refused to panic and wondered if he'd seen the hole before. Skepticism had become my default position, and generally beat out the more charitable benefit of the doubt.

"Don't think you're going to use anything of mine for leak stoppage." I wrapped my coat close around me as the wind picked up.

Liam eyed the clouds. "It is looking a bit nasty. You may be right about my idea. But I think we can make it to St. Herbert's." He laid into the oars.

St. Herbert's was one of four islands on the sprawling lake, situated near center. Locals supposedly had Herb to thank for bringing Christianity to The Lake District. I wondered if he'd also given Liam this notion.

Liam McClelland exhibited surprising finesse with the oars. There were muscles hiding under that derelict coat. He'd earned a measure of respect, and I was eager to make the island, so I picked up the other set of oars to lend a hand. Never let it be said I was a piker.

Our small craft felt like a matchstick afloat in the choppy drink. As the gale took hold, we blew off course and had trouble communicating. I'd heard stories of those caught in sudden high waves on the lakes. A few hadn't ended well. It helped if one knew what sort of clouds to watch for. Evidently, Mr. McClelland was not expert in Cumbrian weather patterns. I was upset at myself again for listening to a man I barely knew. If I could have kicked myself square in the bum without falling overboard, I'd have tried it just then.

"Give it your all and pull to your right. We're going to make the island." At least he sounded sure of himself. But I'd known other men like that.

I pulled as hard as I could. I was strong from the physical Land Army experience, and had recovered from my fall. Between the two of us, it looked as if we would buck the wind. Water was coming in fast, not only from the sock-stopped hole, but also from blowing sprays over the sides. I turned to look behind me. The island still looked a long way off, and then came drenching rain.

"Can you swim?" I yelled, trying not to betray a dread of having to save us both.

"Yes. And I won't let anything happen to you!" I thought he smiled, but maybe it was a grimace against the rain. I chose to believe him but the dogs were not convinced.

"Jingles! Reggie!" I tucked them under my legs and covered them with my coat.

Three inches and rising, cold lake water challenged us from the hull.

"Should I begin bailing out?" I shouted.

"No! You stay put!" Liam thought I meant I was going to try to swim for it.

"No, I mean the water!" I scooped up a pitiful amount with my hands.

"No use. I think we should keep pulling! We're making headway." Liam looked to the troublesome sky. He was soaked and looked exhausted. So was I. My shoulders burned with each pull of the oars.

We stroked in unison but remained stationery. Neither of us could keep up the effort much longer. I heard Liam mutter something.

The wind began to change direction. It tucked down around

us as a blanket spread over the waves, propelling us toward the island. It was odd; however, the winds of The Lakes were unpredictable. The island trees loomed closer. We would make it, sodden but alive.

The dinghy rammed onto the sandy shore. Liam jumped out and grabbed the rope to heave it up as far as he could out of the waves. I grabbed Reggie and coaxed Jingles to follow me out of the swamping craft. We ran together under the protection of a tree canopy to the moss-covered stone remains of St. Herbert's hermitage.

"Whew! That was a close one, eh? If only there was a pot of tea and biscuits waiting we'd be all set," Liam declared.

"How about dry clothes and a thick, down comforter...make that two, while we're at the wishing," I added, shivering.

Then reality, like fog, began to settle. We were the only ones on this island and it was getting dark. The temperature would drop. There was no way for us to reach shore before nightfall and no way of contacting Mum. What in Rob Roy was the proprietor thinking to rent out a rowing boat under those conditions? How well did I know this crazy Irishman who had rowed me smack into near doom? One thing, if a certain situation arose between us, I felt certain I could take him. Whatever the night held in its fist, I would never view St. Herbert's Hideaway the same.

Liam reached in his vest pocket and held out a soggy sweet. "Care for a peppermint?"

∽

We four sat huddled in the resurrected chapel. We were out of the rain and wind at least, but the stones made for chilly conductors and the persistent wind found a way inside. It was then that Liam chose to recite a poem.

"Blest be that hand Divine, which gently laid

My heart at rest beneath this humble shade;

The world's a stately bark, on dangerous seas,

With pleasure seen, but boarded at our peril;

Here on a single plank, thrown safe on shore,

I hear the tumult of the distant throng,

As that of seas remote or dying storms;

And meditate on scenes more silent still,

Pursue my theme, and fight the fear of death.'"

"Thank you, Mr. John Richardson," Liam finished.

I stared at him for several seconds before I could speak, wondering if it was his way to turn poet under pressure. "That was a beautiful and appropriate selection, but we're in a fix here," I reminded.

The dogs whined for food and my stomach mimicked them. Liam was obviously used to going without. I wondered if I outweighed him.

"I was afraid I might not see you again," Liam wrung his cap. "That's why I came up with this sorry notion of the island and all. It's a beautiful place. I wanted to share it with you." He shook his head and stared out at the jeering storm.

"Now don't be getting melodramatic on top of our other worries." He'd caught me off guard, which wasn't easy these days. This trying little man made it near impossible to keep a good mad on. "I had a choice, didn't I? I could have said no, and then neither of us would be in this mess. It was exciting; I'll have to say that. We just need to keep our wits and go with the plan." I turned toward him. "So what is your plan?" I hoped there was one. "What would Herbert do if he lived here alone?"

"I would suppose he'd have firewood put by. There's a fireplace. Maybe there's wood somewhere." Liam suggested.

"There could be," I said. "They still use this place for celebrations." Liam and I hunted corners and alcoves in the twilight.

"Here! A box with a few logs anyway and a lighter!" I yelled over to him.

"I'll just gather a little sparking material, here." Liam collected a small heap of dry branches and twigs from under the eave. It wasn't long before he'd built a respectable fire, even though we'd have to ration the wood.

We draped our coats on the rock mantle and stood to the flames, drying the remainder. Jingles circled a few times then plopped on the floor in front of the fire having given up on dinner. Reggie conformed to his middle.

"We can't stand here all night," Liam announced.

"No? What did you have in mind, or should I ask?"

"Don't go thinking too highly of yourself, miss." Liam shot back. "I'll not be taking advantage of you, have no fear. There will be time enough for that after I find the one who knows my thoughts, shares my dreams and we settle down to a proper marriage. I'll not be rushing." Liam spoke his mind and I stood accused, his words a prosecution.

"Well, all right!" I sat down on a bench, stunned by his candor; then stared at the fire to hide my emotion. "Then we understand one another." I also understood at that point I was disqualified for breaking the rules had I been interested, which I was not.

He added, "But like it or not, we'll have to stick close together through the long night. There's not enough wood to warm the place adequately so we need to follow the dogs' example to keep from getting hypothermia. So…" Liam looked awkward. "… once our clothes are dry we can lie next one another and the pups and use our coats for bedcovers. A happy little family." He chuckled as if he'd gone soft.

"What do you know about this Herbert fellow, anything?" I

asked to have something to say, plus it couldn't hurt to bring up religion about then.

"I don't know much. He was close friends with St. Cuthbert, considered the patron saint of Northern England. St. Herbert was a bit of a hermit once he came here but supposedly performed miracles during his childhood and ministry. One was to find the ring of a Scottish queen in a fish's belly and save her from execution for infidelity."

"But how did that...? Never mind." I curled up next the dogs.

Liam lay down next to us and pulled his coat over. "We were made to live forever."

He felt warm against me, and his words caravanned into a soothing hum as I drifted off and dreamed. The room became an ice maze with my abstract reflection at every turn, but a fireball led me through.

- 24 -

GLORY

I ate dinner uninterrupted. It was quiet that afternoon, and I regretted having asked Claire to take over at 1:00. She was out late. Never did hear her come in, but I was beat.

"Those two old duffers are fast becoming burrs on my backside." Biggs had appeared. "I saw them talking to you the other day. Where did they come from anyway?"

I felt awkward around Axel since overhearing his conversation with Milton and Wicky, but I played ignorant. "Oh? They're just a couple of playboys, one retired Navy, here on holiday. He bought a toy gun, sweet old man. Deaf as a post but what a talker."

"Don't I know."

"The other, Fenwick Smyth, has family hereabouts. Do you know anyone named Pearl?" I slid the case door closed and locked it.

Biggs seemed distracted. "Pearl who? They were here a long time that first visit." He removed his cap and rubbed a palm over his perspiring head.

"I didn't get her last name. I can't think of who she is, but I suppose there could be a few people around I haven't met. General Pickering, the Navy man, said he thought he knew one of the board members from the line. Marshall somebody...started with a B I think. He said he might stop by and see you while they're here and ask after him." I watched for a reaction and wasn't disappointed.

"Well, they did STOP by. Dropped anchor in my office more like. Thought they'd never leave. He rambled on for an hour about the old war and this Bickerstaff fellow I don't know. Do notify me if they become bothersome, won't you?" Biggs asked.

I chuckled at his irritation. *Woo and wed, my foot.* "They didn't bother me in the least. I enjoyed their company." I'm sure I didn't know why Axel was in a stew. He surely wasn't jealous. My stomach began to hurt. I reached for my pocketbook and an antacid.

"Oh don't give it another thought." In a wink, he changed, leaning his frame on my counter with his face so close I could smell his pickled egg lunch. "I'm not sure what's come over me lately. Too much work and not enough play no doubt. When will you consent to allow me to wine and dine you? A little frolic would do you good as well. You're looking downright peaked. No strings attached, of course."

Couldn't argue with that, though I didn't care for the frolicking reference. I'd noticed my drawn reflection recent days. Teatime with Eunice and the trip to Manchester had been my only amusements in months.

Biggs always seemed to be there when I needed him most, almost as if he knew ahead of time. Claire wouldn't approve, but I couldn't wind my life to her timetable.

"It might be nice at that, Axel, as friends."

I stepped back and offered my hand.

He enveloped it in his gloves, stood tall and sighed. "Certainly, Glory dear. You know I only have your best interest at heart. Yours and the girls'. Speaking of the girls, wasn't Claire supposed to come on at 1:00? It's nearly half past. You'll have to get after her."

I looked at the station clock. It wasn't like her to be late.

"She was late getting home last night. Took the dogs for a long walk and planned to stop at a friend's place. You know young people, living in the moment, never thinking of consequences so long as they're having a good time." Glad I'd taken the antacid, maybe another one too. Come to think on it, I hadn't seen the dogs that morning.

"I'm sure she's fine," Biggs assured. "I must get back. I'll call you with details about our lark. Would Friday evening be soon enough?"

"Yes, good bye." *Had Claire said anything about being late?* "Biggs?"

"Yes, Glory?"

"Would you ring up my house? She's probably forgotten the schedule."

"Right. Be back shortly." He strode off.

I never could decide whether children were more of a worry when they were little or after they were out of grasp. A mum really didn't have much say once they were grown. She was more of a fixture—available for advice if they asked and so wanting them to ask.

Biggs wasn't smiling as he approached.

"No answer at home. I'll have a drive round. Any idea where she might be?"

I found the stool and settled as heat rose up my neck.

"Well, she has a chum near Appleby she visits now and again, but it's odd she wouldn't call. You might try the lake. She takes the dogs there." My voice quivered from a fear I couldn't say aloud.

"Don't worry, Glory dear. We'll find the old girl. Biggs is on the trail—one step ahead." He seemed positively illuminated.

A couple of customers distracted me for a time. One of them was Lavinia Brown. Lavinia pumped the organ for events at Crosthwaite, including John's and my wedding. I hadn't seen her for quite some time, but knew she collected old mystery books. It happened I had two volumes by Doyle she needed. I looked past Mrs. Brown to a frantic Sydney coming toward me.

"Mummie. Excuse me, Missus." She glanced at Lavinia who looked on keenly. "Mum, the dogs are gone and Claire never slept in her bed last night. I noticed Jingles and Reggie weren't around for their feed this morning before school, but I just thought they were fagged out. What are you going to do?"

"Now don't fret. Biggs is out looking for her. She was to take over at 1:00. If he's not back soon I'll close up shop and inform the authorities." I tried not to look horrified, but knew I was no good at fooling her.

"Do you think HE had anything to do with it?" Syd asked me looking at Mrs. Brown. I knew the he to whom she referred was Albert and hoped I wouldn't be sorry for not pursuing him into an early grave.

"I doubt he'd have the brass to show up here again, love. Don't want you to worry now. These things usually turn out fine and worry comes to rubbish."

- 25 -

CLAIRE

It was a quiet row back the next morning. Liam had stopped the hole with a wooden dowel he'd carved with his pocketknife. Lake Derwent had calmed, with loons and moorhens bobbing and trying not to stare. They would glance away and move off as soon as the bedraggled couple with dogs floated near. I glanced round to see if anyone else was on the water. I worried that Mum would be in a state of hysteria since I'd no way of notifying anyone of our situation.

Liam seemed to have lost his voice, and I was glad of it. To my relief, I didn't have to get tough. True to his word, he'd minded his hands. No surprises. He didn't snore. I thought it was him, but turned out to be Reggie.

"I said I was sorry, Lass." Liam broke the calm.

"I know. There's no need to bring it up. I just want to get home and relieve my mum and sister." I was so hungry a coot looked tempting.

"I'll be reconciling myself with your dear mother for a good long while," Liam added. "I think she fancies me a bit." He rubbed Jingles' neck. Jingles held no grudges.

I doubted he'd get the chance. A second out–of–town bloke bringing me home after hours would not play well.

"We could sing '*Row, Row, Row Your Boat*.'" Liam seemed bent on turning the tide that had gone against him. "Or I could recite the next oration I'm to be giving in class. It's about... sweet forgiveness."

"Row, row, row your boat gently down the stream..." I commenced.

"A-row, row, row your boat gently down the stream. Merrily, merrily, merrily, merrily, life is but a dream." Liam picked right up.

He was oblivious that I had stopped singing. I watched him. He threw his head back, and his pipes rang over the water.

He stopped suddenly. "It's not, you know."

"Not?"

"Not a dream. Life isn't a dream."

If I didn't change the subject, I knew a sermon lurked just below the surface.

"I dreamed last night that you had two heads. One was always singing and the other was preaching." I laughed. "Oh wait. It wasn't a dream."

Liam stared at me. I wondered if I'd crossed the line or if he had one.

"You may think you're well above the likes of me with your Ingrid Bergmire face and high-toned ways, but I know girls back in Lancashire who'd simply leap to be right there where you're sitting. Right there." He tossed the oars down. "It's your turn to row."

"I'm high-toned?" I picked up the gauntlet. "You're the one who made it clear last night that I wasn't good enough for the likes of you, and that I needn't bother my head about tempting you to sin because that was impossible." I kicked at an oar. "And it's not Bergmire, it's Berg–MAN. Many, many people have told me

I'm the spitting image of her. I've had folks stop me in midstride and ask for my autograph, so there!" I grabbed the oars and began stroking like one of the Oxford Eight.

"They got the spitting part right anyway. Like a cat with its back humped up," Liam tried for a mad cat imitation. "Excuse me, miss, for wasting your time sharing my ideals and dreams. I mistook you for someone who might care. I won't make the same mistake twice." Evidently, he didn't know what to do with his hands, so he began rubbing the dogs with vigor. I was appalled as the traitorous beasts actually began licking his face. They'd chosen sides as far as I was concerned. Sydney could jolly well walk them from now on.

Shore was coming up fast but not fast enough to suit me. I could see the boat house plus a crowd. Some had rented boats, but rowed back. Liam turned round, saw the people and took the oars from me. As we grew closer, the voices intermingled, sounding much like a henhouse at egg-laying time. Then a chorus of shouts and hoorays floated out to greet us. I saw Mum with a hanky. Biggs had his nasty arm round her shoulders. Syd waved. Eunice's hair was in motion. They were a relieved lot. Was there an officer in uniform there? I felt the utter fool, but felt for Liam too and what he was about to face from the shoreline mob—sorry, but a little glad too. Cat indeed.

The boat rammed onto the shore at the legs of our greeting party. Liam stood and offered his hand to me, but I side–stepped him and called for the fickle dogs to follow. They looked confused, looking from me to Liam until I shouted their names, and they jerked and came with me.

Mum ran over and hugged me while Biggs hovered in the background, giving Liam a good stare down. Syd tried to hug her big sis without looking too excited.

Mum looked at Liam. "Liam. What in the world…"

It was impossible for Liam to get a word in with all the confusion. A breeze plucked at his hair.

Axel Biggs broke in, "Young man. I hope you understand there will be consequences for what you've done. Dire consequences." Gulls flapped over our group, hopeful for eats with such an animated crowd.

I wished Biggs would clam up and that a bird would lob digested fish waste square on his head. This wasn't his jurisdiction.

The boathouse keeper looked to be planning his response to the tumult and weighing his potential liability. He had sounded the alarm when he arrived at the boathouse and found their dinghy still out. At least he'd done that much. He added heartily, "I knowed there'd be trouble when storm blew in. I tried to warn them but the' would na' listen. Squalls come up sudden–like on the lakes, thou all know. That's why I called police in the early morning when I noticed the boat wasn't back." He twisted his cap around in calloused mitts, then donning it, examined the rowing boat.

I figured the truth was more like—he took Liam's money, handed him the oars and trotted off to douse his moustache in froth at the pub, never giving the couple or the weather a blinking thought.

The large-gutted policeman waded in like a mother duck, "Hold on now just a minute! We mean to ascertain the truth of this situation, but it won't do no good all a you trying to talk at once. Let's go to station and use your living quarters to sort it all out, Mr. Biggs, if you're willing." He pushed back at the crowd with meaty hands and by the affirmative nods and murmurs; they all accepted this as his invitation.

"Not all of ye, now!" He announced. "You'll get the dope on them soon enough. Go on about your business. Go on now. Be off." For a small man, he commanded the situation admirably.

The villagers weren't happy about being shooed off the plumiest tidbit to come down the pikes in awhile; but they retreated, many of them calling out to Mum to ring them up if there was anything they could do and that she had a friend in them. One man, eyes downcast, dropped his club.

"I'm her best friend. I go," Eunice stated.

"Thank you, Eunice, but I think the fewer people the better." Mum said. "I'll fill you in on details tomorrow over tea." Mum looked the worse. I'd done it again.

❧

Back at Biggs' for black tea and judgment, the interrogators leveled their best shots at Liam between gulps. First Biggs, then Mum, then police and back to Biggs. He always nabbed the last word. They were all accusing Liam of immoral motives, though at least Mum was phrasing her assumptions as questions. I must have become invisible at some point, as they weren't even looking in my direction. After all, I did represent fifty percent of the missing equation.

I could answer all their questions; 'Young man, what were your real intentions when you decided to try a fool trick like taking a helpless young woman out on the water with a storm coming?' Answer: His only motive was to spend time with Claire, get to know her better, and to share a special place of his discovery. 'Young man, didn't you know there was a real likelihood of a storm on the lake given the look of the clouds and that your boat could capsize?' Answer: Truth was Mr. McClelland was wholly unfamiliar with the threat of Lakeland skies or the danger posed to one on the water when storm breaks. But I wasn't.

The more they spewed questions the more time I had to analyze the situation. The findings were enlightening. Whatever I thought of his looks or beliefs, I'd been unfair. The verdict was not guilty—perhaps by reason of insanity—but definitely innocent of wrongful intent. Finally, I'd had it with the clamor.

"Hold on just one ruddy minute!" I shouted and stood.

The room was silent but for my gurgling stomach. I moved

beside the fireplace and took the hearth for a soapbox. "You're all talking as if I'd checked my brain while all this was happening—as if I never had a choice in the proceedings. Well I did. And like a knotty-headed goose, I agreed to go rowing with Mr. McClelland of my own will. If it's anyone's fault, it's mine. I saw the clouds coming. Mr. McClelland is not from these parts and therefore unfamiliar with Lakeland weather." I began to sense that I'd missed my calling as a barrister. "Furthermore, he was nothing if not a complete…monk the entire night. These dogs didn't see anything you all couldn't have seen." Jingles smiled up at me. "So put away your bobby sticks and tacky suppositions, and leave the lad alone."

I looked right at Biggs, who seemed to bare his teeth. "I'm famished. Can we please just go home?" I turned to Mum. "Sorry again, Mum, for putting you through it. You know I'd have let you know had there been any way possible."

Mum held me close and said, "I'm glad you're safe. I feel like locking you in your room." She smiled with one hand on her stomach, the other extended to Liam and said, "Thank you, young man, for taking care of my reckless girl."

He took her hand but drew her in and hugged her. I watched the spectacle. From now on there would be no living with her. Liam was her boy.

- 26 -

GLORY

Mud and manure sucked at the Wellington boots John gave me shortly after proposing. I'd thought it an odd sort of engagement present, and perhaps I should reconsider, but he assured me his intentions were practical and that a country vet's spouse would have need of them. He'd kept a straight face when explaining, 'She may at any time of day or blinking night be called upon to join him at a calving.' His prophecy had come true many times, but he was far too magnetic for me to worry over minor inconveniences.

John was an unpredictable romantic, the best kind. He'd stuffed gifts inside each boot that my feet discovered when trying them on. The right boot held a red silk shawl with apple green and yellow curlicues running through like vines and with fringe all around. It was beautiful, but I hadn't worn it in a while. The left boot was chock full of candy to the ankle — wrapped praline candy and a silver bracelet with two heart shaped garnets, my birthstone. He ate the candy seeing as how it was his favorite. I wished he were with me now. I'd wrap myself in his shawl—a love offering.

Home and garden had suffered since my plunge into the business world. The garden was dormant but wanted cleaning. The girls didn't know first thing about tending garden except Claire had helped with weeding and seemed to enjoy the flowers right enough. Neither one would pester me for the hoe.

The girls and I had begun this day in the barn early. I wanted Syd there for a family meeting before school. So there we were — three kerchief-headed Stone women mucking stalls and coops, milking Greta and imitating farmhands. Better late than never. Only Syd felt at home. She'd brought to my attention that since her pop had gone, we'd left her alone to tend the animals. Claire had reminded her more than once that she was the one who kept adding to the zoo and planned to run a veterinary practice. It was still a lot to ask. Judging from the depth and smell of the nasty task, we'd waited too long to lend a hand.

"Are you going on a date with Biggs?" Syd asked unexpectedly. She heaved a shovelful into the barrow. "I'm okay with it if you're just friends like he and I are, but if it's a date…"

"It's not a date," I assured her. "I wouldn't remember how to date, nor do I wish to. We're just two old chums taking supper together." It felt as strange saying it as it was to be shoveling chicken manure.

"Because Pop wouldn't like it," Syd added.

Claire shot milk frothing into the pail and asked, "Did Biggs ask you? Did he pick the spot? Is he paying?" She didn't wait for answers. "It's a date." Greta turned and looked at her.

"I made it perfectly clear to him when I accepted that we go as friends. If he misunderstood, that's his worry." I was eager to change the subject. Talking about it made me wish I'd not agreed. "This rich manure will make grand tea for the gardens but it's much too hot to put on the soils straight. You must dilute it. Something you girls need to know."

"I hope my hubby's a gardener," Syd said. "I'll be too busy

making animal rounds." Then she added, "Come to think on it, I hope he can cook and raise the kiddies too." She giggled.

Claire laughed, "Next thing, you'll be wanting him to have the kiddies."

I couldn't think now about where the money for schooling would come from. The morning was flying along so I got to the point of our rare reunion.

"Women, I've called you here this morning not just for chores but to discuss something I've drawn up as a household plan. I think it's pretty obvious that your mum can't manage house, barn, garden and shop without cooperation from the two of you." I looked at their faces and was relieved that up to this point they only eyed one another.

"I've made a sort of a schedule dividing up the various jobs. That's not to say you're stuck, necessarily, with your assignment, because there are after all some jobs none of us would likely choose." I looked at the stall floor for emphasis and Syd chuckled. "We'll divide disagreeable tasks like these among the three of us, but you girls are old enough to see and tend to chores as needs be, whether or not it's on your schedule. So I'm just asking that we pitch in and work together instead of being off in our own worlds somewhere. The three of us should form a union—Stone Women United or something. We're still a family, and I need the both of you to help as much as you need me to provide. How's it sounding so far?"

"Great, Mum." Syd was the first to throw in. "I like to help. It makes me feel more mature. I'm not a little kid. I can do some of the cooking if…"

"I'll pick up slack in the galley," Claire interjected. "But you can help, little sister. I'd also like to worm your gardening secrets out of you, Mum. You don't intend to take them to the grave, surely?"

I laughed. "You and Mary Thompkins. I know what my flowers like, that's all. They thrive on understanding."

Claire stared into the milk bucket then said, "Mary Thompkins and I have an understanding. Whoever uncovers the secret formula first will share it with the other. I'm not kidding, that's what she's holding me to." Claire's laughter was like a vitamin shot. She was back. I was afraid to break the run, but wondered if she pined for Albert. For right now, we were content beyond happiness — joy maybe.

∽

I hoped I'd scrubbed long enough to remove all evidence of my earlier task. That smell could find a hold and linger. But I dabbed some of Claire's lilac water in my hair for good measure and not because this was a date.

Axel showed at the front door with a fistful of flowers. I'd said goodbye to the girls and scooted out the door so they couldn't witness the spectacle. He ushered me to his car and opened the door. Darned if this didn't feel like a date.

It felt strange riding in a car again. What had it been, close to five years? Axel was treating me to one of the nicest supper houses in England, so I made an effort to enjoy the scenery. I'd worn the one good dress, which didn't reveal any more than my taste in fashion ten years hence, and a surviving string of Aunt Verla's pearls. John's shawl was the crowning touch.

We passed the flicker of Coniston and continued into the night over moon-bright trees and hills, through a larch wood, then up. When we rose atop the last crest, Biggs declared, "There she sits." Our destination was still a ways off but Chesterfield's substantial glow made for a cheering target in the dark. We rolled down a dirt road and pulled up to a vibrant 18th-century country manor.

I heard violins when Axel came round to my door and extended his hand. As we entered, I located the musicians on a corner stage. A brunette with a feather bird in her hair played the cello with her eyes closed, while a young Italian-looking man cradled a violin, and another gent with no hair gave his flute what for. The room was over-warm from the fire growling inside a massive fireplace. People sitting near it appeared to be melting and enjoying it. Chandeliers reflected the gaiety around the room like Goby's crystal goblets on her holiday table. The diners wore understated smiles as if they were above such things as delight and seemed to move in slow motion. I overheard a man order quail amandine and smiled.

So this was Chesterfield's on the inside — a dinner house so fine there was no danger of seeing anyone I knew and no embarrassing questions. It would take time to digest every opulent detail and I looked forward to not being rushed.

John and I, through twenty-five years of marriage, hadn't been able to spring for its grand style. Given my dated chiffon drape, I was relieved they allowed us past the entry hall. At least the shawl was timeless.

Axel showed a different side of himself, addressing the maitre d' like a gentleman. He coolly removed his hat, coat, and gloves — handing them over to the hatcheck as if he'd done it a hundred times, when I knew blamed well he hadn't. He pulled my chair out at table.

Axel looked striking in a black suit, white shirt, black tie and shiny oxfords. Predictable, classic. He reminded me a little of a film noir mobster, though he wasn't half bad looking really, by candlelight.

I admired how the wait staff responded to him, attentive and respectful in their diffidence. Axel lit his cigar, tossing the match without watching it land spot on the silver tray. He was more obvious about his gender than John had been. John hadn't needed to prove his manhood.

With no one peering over my shoulder, I fully intended to enjoy the evening in, what had Eunice labeled it — 'sublime comfort' — and to savor exceptional dishes with good company. I couldn't say for sure I deserved it but I hoped I did.

The waiter handed me a menu without prices. The first entree I saw was Duck a l'Orange with chestnut stuffing. I'd just begun to salivate, when someone lifted the banquet from my hands.

"Glory, please, if I may? I shall order for the both of us." Axel smiled and placed my menu on the table. Maybe he was worried I'd pick something beyond his pocketbook, but I doubted it. He simply took pleasure in making my decision for me. Romantic, in an old fashioned sort of way.

"I think we'll begin with a nice Dom Perignon '28." The words strolled off his tongue as if wearing a topper and tails.

"Very good, sir," the snappy dressed waiter looked impressed too.

"Axel, are you sure? Isn't that Champagne?" I asked.

"Tut, Glory dear; the best Champagne. Now that I've got you out with me I want to show you a little of what you've been missing." He dabbed at his upper lip with the mint green napkin though he'd neither eaten nor drunk anything.

I had an idea of a station master's salary. Though they made a respectable living for themselves and their families, this brand of high class entertainment would be rich indeed and never a regular go.

The waiter glided back with a white towel folded over one arm and a cart bearing a silver bucket of ice and a bottle. He maneuvered the cork, which did not go flying across the room as Eunice had once described when she and Roger had returned to London. He set two elegant stemware pieces in front of us, though they were not as fine as the Stevens & Williams goblets I'd recently sold. He poured a generous amount of bubbles, leaving the remainder swaddled like a royal infant. Axel lifted his glass high toward me and I knew enough to do likewise as a toast was forthcoming. John and I had toasted with stout over fool things like, 'to not being awakened in the middle of the night by Dunder's Hereford bull.' Or, 'to your Uncle Bob', neither of us having an Uncle Bob.

"What a beautiful smile…" Biggs' voice came at me. "…and charming overbite. Have you considered having it fixed, provided money was available?" The way he stared at my mouth, I became self conscious.

He was still holding his glass aloft. I forgot, were we toasting my teeth?

"No matter," he continued. "Here's to the Glory of a glorious evening. May tonight serve as a mere precursor of many special times together throughout the coming years."

We clinked, and I wondered was a toast binding? I took a sip and it was The Folies Bergere on my tongue. As evening moved into night and soup and salad came and went, an effervescent chorus line danced and kicked its way into my head. I was not a drinker by reputation and the room transformed into a fairyland with vague characters at each table. Axel, who now appeared as Arthur Treacher, classic butler in film, emptied the last of the bottle into my glass.

"Drink up, Glory my dear. You're only young once and the night is but a pup."

I found it impudent that a servant should speak thusly to me.

☙

The ride home gave me a chance to collect my thoughts and by the time Axel pulled up to the house I was back in form and hoping like anything I hadn't incriminated myself.

"Thank you, Axel, for a truly, truly lovely time. Without a doubt the grandest meal I've had. I'll remember this evening for a long time." He walked me to the door and now stood. I hoped he didn't feel I owed him something, like a...kiss or anything. "Well, good night. I'd ask you in for tea, but I have to rise early with Syd." I looked disappointed and turned toward the door.

"Very well. I'll release you for now and see you tomorrow." He patted my face. "I shall dream about our evening. Will you?"

"Yes, indeed. And it's time to decorate the shop for Christmas. Hoping for brisk holiday trade."

Not a romance.

I went inside a house that was deathly quiet. The girls were asleep, thankfully. I still had visions of Chesterfield's whirling through my head, and the taste of garlic vinaigrette on my tongue. Why was I suddenly so blue?

I hung my coat and opened the girls' bedroom door. All was well, but I stepped inside. Claire still slept on her back with one leg out of the coverings and the opposite arm over her head. How was it possible she could be even more beautiful asleep? I turned toward the soft blow of Syd's open-mouth breathing. I walked over and bent to stroke her bangs. Sorrow caught me by the throat and a choking sound escaped. I left their room, hurried to my own, and closed the door where I fell sobbing, my face buried in our bed.

"I'm sorry! I'm sorry, John. Sorry." I pulled myself up and climbed inside our closet so the girls wouldn't hear, but I had to let go. I found John's flannel shirts, breathed them in between moaning sobs that frightened me with their intensity, and wrapped the empty shirtsleeves close. I could only imagine him, and it scared me that it had become harder to picture his face. His photograph sat on my nightstand, but I couldn't feel his arms anymore. The flesh and blood man, my counterpart, was gone.

"It was not a date. I could never love anyone but you!" I confessed between reckless tears and needing to breathe. "I love you, John! I miss you! Life is terrifying and lonely without you. I can't do it anymore." I cried until my stomach felt rock-like. My head throbbed though I barely noticed. "And what am I to do with your ring? Why ever don't you come home if you're alive?" Slumped on a pile of his work shoes in the corner of the closet floor, I cried on—with each thought of him, fresh tears gushed over some pent bank. A parade of recollections scrolled past, and I made myself look.

Maybe a couple of hours passed, and then I slept.

- 27 -

CLAIRE

Liam sent a stone hurtling seven skips. "C.S. Lewis said, 'God gives His gifts where He finds the vessel empty enough to receive them.' I've heard Lewis at Magdalen College. His reason plays in my head like a familiar song I've never heard." He sat on a boulder next to me and looked into the bare hemlock over us.

I loved Bassenthwaite Lake — Bass Lake, the locals called it. There was a peace about winter by the water. Dad had taken us fishing and picnicking there on many a bank holiday. Now it was a harbor from the head clamor. I wasn't sure why Liam still hung around, but I didn't have the heart to pack him off. Besides, I felt comfortable with him and free to share my opinion without fear of ridicule, and he did like to talk.

I said, "It just seems to me that Christians are no better then anyone else and actually less generous sometimes — except with judgment. Always willing to stick their noses in and call the kettle black, as the saying goes. My grandparents put love where their beliefs were." I watched a trout surface for a fly.

"I see your point. Without Jesus, they are no better. I think human judgment might be the unholy offspring of fear and legalism, or maybe they think they've outgrown the need for grace." Liam looked at me with that crooked smile. "Or, maybe they're out and out frauds. There's plenty of bubbly calling itself Champagne, when the genuine nectar comes only from France." Liam slipped on a rock and his left foot sank into the muddy shallows.

"And I think you're a loony. Just as sure as them bobbing on the water." I didn't know how else to answer.

While wringing out his sock he looked at me and replied, "And you — are a beautiful woman. Strong too, a frightening combination for some."

He saw me as strong and beautiful? I'd never been attracted to his type. Why did he have to knock me off guard with that sort of talk?

"Not for you though, I suppose." I flirted.

"No. I don't think so." He stared at me but I didn't feel threatened, just flattered. "You're not what one would call safe; but safety all the time is a bore, wouldn't you agree? And it's not the same as being true." He spent time in my eyes without release.

I did not want to go there again. I moved to the water's edge. "Now why didn't we bring a pole? They're breaking all around us." I laughed, reminding myself of Mum.

"Don't be afraid of me, Lassie." He reached out his hand. "I'll go the long way round not to hurt you." He came to me.

"Liam, you don't know me; if you did, you wouldn't talk so. Let's just admit we're too different and save ourselves a lot of grief."

"I care about you, Claire." Liam gently turned my shoulders to face him. "I want to know your ins and outs, comings and goings." He came closer.

I wanted to believe him, and wanted him to kiss me, and the scoundrel did.

I enjoyed the kiss all by itself. It held a lifetime of promise without desperation. We'd turned a corner onto a road I hadn't seen coming. In fact, we were way up the path and the subject of Albert had never come up.

"There now." Liam sounded like he was gentling a skittish mare. "I know you're not one to be giving your kisses away willy-nilly." He smoothed my hair. "Ye must have some feeling for me? A little?" He looked into my eyes.

I turned and tried to regain my senses. I had feeling right enough.

"No, Mr. McClelland, I do not give my kisses away willy or nilly!" I strode toward town feeling slightly off balance. "Coming?"

When I looked back, Liam stood gaping. I'd have to tell him sure enough, but dreaded it. At least it would end the foolishness.

"You're an unsafe woman!" He yelled against the wind. "What did I say?"

∽

I burst into the station late for my post and sure that I wore my encounter blazing like the neon signs in Brakeman's Tabby.

"There you are. I was about to call out Bert, the squatty cop again." Mum looked too closely. "You look flushed. What are you up to?"

"Just come from the lake. I had to run part way when I realized I might be past my time. Sorry." I untied my kerchief and hung my coat. I stooped to check my face in the antique mirror and saw my smeared lips.

"Uh, was Liam with you?" Mum had noticed too. That's not what I wanted; yet I was tired of hiding things from her. I was too old to be dodging issues.

"Yes, he was. We skipped rocks. Business been any good?" I repainted my lips.

Mum grinned. "Business? You mean monkey business? Because I'd say it looks pretty good, yes."

"Whatever are you talking so ridiculously about?"

"Never mind." Mum chuckled, handed over the smock we wore to protect our clothing and fluffed at her hair. "Axel is taking me to lunch at the café. Do you want me to bring you something?"

When had Biggs become Axel? "No, thank you."

"All right. I'll see you at home unless you have a date?" There was that smirk again.

"A date? With whom? No, I'll be home for supper, will you?"

Mum headed for Biggs' office, and I dropped the lip rouge into my bag. I held the sales book as a prop while reliving that kiss.

శా

"How d'ya do, Miss? This shop certainly can boast some of the fairest proprietresses I've heard tell of. You're as lovely as the other maid we met here a few days back. In fact, do I notice a resemblance betwixt the two of you?"

These had to be the men Mum told me about, but I waited for the official introduction.

"Allow us to introduce ourselves. I'm General Milton Pickering and this here's my comrade, Fenwick Smyth." They bowed.

"Pleased to meet you, sirs. The name's Claire Stone and that was my fair mum you met before. She's told me so much about you I feel as if we're already acquainted." I put out my hand and received the general's spare kiss. "What may I show you today?"

The general looked a little sheepish then bellowed, "Don't happen to have any of those cookies lying about?" He winked with an open gob as if he hoped I might lay one on his waiting taste buds. He added, "Tasted of roses."

Travelers waiting for a train were startled from their naps and magazines. Wicky chuckled and checked his shoes.

"Ah, no. Sorry, General; but I'm glad you found them satisfactory; I enjoy baking." I felt quite charitable now. I spoke loud and slow. "I believe Mum told me you bought a toy gun, was that it?"

The General shouted an enthusiastic yes and leaned his torso over the offerings in the counter. "What do you have I can't live without today?" He straightened somewhat and hobbled among the knickknacks and books picking up one or two and reading their titles. "I've read these." He shuffled back up to me while Wicky took out a pipe and pouch. Leaning an elbow on the glass Milton declared, "A fine young woman like yourself should be out with her young man enjoying the sights and sounds of the holiday season, not clerking in shop." He sniffed Fenwick's smoke and remembered his own pipe.

That was loud enough for the vicar to have heard at Crosthwaite. If they were to talk romance, it would have to be one sided. I didn't need the entire village hearing about my love life, if I had one of those. But Milton hadn't achieved the rank of general for nothing. He advanced.

"Who is your young man, Miss? Maybe we know him. We don't live here abouts, but we come down every so often to visit Wick's Cousin Beryl. She's all alone now, poor homely woman." He thought he'd whispered it. They both drew on their pipes, resembling two odd-sized chimneys.

"It's Pearl, Milton," Fenwick was quick to correct him, but he didn't hear.

"Now we don't need to go into that, do we?" I tried to chuckle it off, but Milton would have none of it.

"Give us his name or we'll wait for your mum and bother it out of her."

No, not that.

"We just want to know who he is so we can decide if he's good enough for you. We learned of your poor father and we're right sorry. A girl needs a father. Well, we know we ain't kin, but we've taken a shine to the two of you damsels in distress, isn't that what we said, Wicky?"

"Aye, General. That's what we calls them." Fenwick smiled a broad one and wiped his shoe on his pants leg.

"Well, I don't have a young man," I wasn't sure it was a lie since it wasn't readily established. Yes, it was a lie of sorts, but it wasn't their business anyhow, even though their concern was endearing.

"I think I'll put out some new stock, if you gents will excuse me." My red face and I ducked behind the counter, but not before I saw Biggs striding toward us.

"New frock you said? I've no use for a frock." The general refused.

Biggs intervened, "Just what is all the hollering about over in this corner, Miss Stone?"

Milton turned toward Biggs, straightening as much as his situation would grant. "Hello, Mr. Biggs! Good to see you looking smart. How is that certain, um, medical situation we discussed? " He glanced toward me briefly and extended his hand. Biggs obliged a dead mackerel sort of response with his.

"See here, I don't know if you're aware but you're creating quite a scene. My passengers think there's something foul afoot when they hear you cry out like that."

"Really? Like what?" The General inquired innocently.

A flustered Biggs looked at Fenwick who smiled and lifted his pipe in greeting.

"Mr. Biggs." I motioned him over. "The general is quite deaf."

"See here!" The general blasted again. "How goes the piles situation?" He turned toward his quiet friend and mumbled, "I think I asked him that before."

"There is no such situation!" Now without realizing, he was shouting every bit as loud as the general. Milton had a way of drawing people within his decibels.

"Wicky and I have wanted to come and have another talk with you. I'm in acquaintance with a member of the C.K. and P. Railroad board. Do you know Marshall Bickerstaff?"

Biggs looked all at sea. It was shaping up to be a memorable afternoon. He pulled out a hanky and wiped his sweat streaked nose and forehead. Biggs was rarely out of form. This was better than a matinee; plus he had taken the attention completely off my supposed beau. All I needed was for Liam to walk in about now; I wasn't sure where he'd gone.

I looked out at the swell of people who'd gathered to gawk. Then, by the newsstand, peering over a copy of *Tales of Wonder*, I thought I recognized a familiar figure.

Wicky trailed along after The General who had a firm hold on Biggs' elbow with one hand, cane stabbing along the floor in the other and was ushering him toward the station office. As the trio moved off, Albert snaked in.

My breath grew short and my stomach contracted. I wanted to run for the loo. I never imagined he'd have nerve to come round, and didn't know whether to act indifferent or lob a paperweight at his head.

"Hello, love!" Albert's smile could melt the polar ice cap. The creep was still so blasted good looking. Seeing him put me right back to our meeting times. I'd just come from their location. "Long time no... see. I've missed your lovely face." That's not where he was looking. "But I don't suppose you want to have anything to do with me." He pouted and looked up through his enviable lashes.

"You're right. I don't." I'd no trouble agreeing, but couldn't stop there. "But since you've decided to pop by, I have some questions for you." I paced, the counter a barrier between us.

"All right, shoot—provided you don't have an old firearm back there." Albert stood straight, cap in hand.

"Well the first one is fairly blinking obvious. How is it you left me lying on the ground, maybe dead, for Mum and the doc to find? You didn't even tell anyone! And you, nowhere to be found. When I think of that day, I want to tie a rope around your neck and drag you through the village!" I tried not to yell, but the memory was like coal oil on flame.

"I can explain if you'll let me," Albert put up his hands in surrender.

"Go ahead, can't wait to hear it."

"First off, I knew you weren't dead. I made sure of that. I was frightfully scared because if your mum found me with you and drinking, I knew she wouldn't let me see you, and I didn't want that. So I ran but not too far, just off in some nearby bushes. Jingles ran after me and I sent him to the house. Smart dog you have there. I saw him run for the house and heard him barking. I waited until I saw them coming, then I hightailed it to Aunt Eunice's and started packing. Just like a scared rabbit, I ran but I didn't know what to do. And Claire, believe me when I tell you I am sorry. I don't expect you to speak to me again, but my conscience got to hounding me and I had to come. I'm sorry and I'd like to try and make it up with you." I smelled his cologne.

"So, you do have a conscience then? Apology accepted, but that doesn't change anything as far as I'm concerned. I'll never forget that awful night in hospital. I can't look at you without thinking of the whole episode and how I... So, I'm working now and I have a customer. Excuse me, Albert, but I don't think we should see one another." I'd have to hold on and release the tears later. How I wished he'd stayed away.

"I'll wait till you're through there." Albert circled like a hyena, smelling potential and looking over the finery for which, I knew, he had no regard.

I finished with the flustered customer and was about to ask Albert to leave again when someone else walked up, humming.

"How's it going, Lass?"

- 28 -

CLAIRE

"**L**iam. Where did you come from?" I only imagined that I was nervous before. I hadn't discussed Albert with Liam because I'd never imagined it would be necessary. A week ago, Liam was a friend; now I'd memorized his kiss.

"From Bailieborough. I told you," he said.

"No, I mean just now." I looked around at Albert who stared at the two of us from beside a shelf of French porcelain.

"I was able to keep up with you for a ways, but then when you pulled away, decided to stop off at the refreshment room for something salty and a pint to wash it down." He'd noticed Albert. "Is that a friend of yours staring a hole in us big enough to drive a lorry through?"

Sighing, I said, "He used to be. Liam, this is Albert Rand. Albert, Liam McClelland." I felt trapped and sick.

The two men nodded at one another, then Albert moved in for the kill.

"Is this your new chap, then?" Albert asked.

Liam looked at me, but my tongue was in a double knot.

"You might say that," offered Liam. "We've been keeping regular company." Liam's jaw became assertive.

"Well, are you promised to this man?" Albert drew a line with his question not lost on Liam by the way he straightened himself.

Where was Biggs when he could have proved useful? I took a breath and said, "It's none of your business, Mr. Rand. I asked you to leave."

Albert's grin dissolved into malice.

"Have you happened to mention to Mr. McClelland that you were once promised to me?"

"I do not recall any such arrangement." My neck grew hot.

"See here now," Liam stepped between us; he was no coward. Albert was nearly twice his size and still in good form from the military. "I don't like the way you're upsetting my friend. You'd best move along."

I hoped there was first aid in Biggs' office.

Albert looked him in the eyes for what seemed like eternity, but slowly backed away, "I don't wish to embarrass Miss Stone by causing a scene at her place of business and splattering blood on her pretty things, so I'll go for now." He turned to me. "I'll be around, Love." He snickered and walked off cock-sure. "Friend. Ha."

"Former romance, I take it?" Liam inquired. "Whatever did you see in him?"

"Yes." I lowered my eyes. "I've looked for the chance to tell you about Albert."

"Oh don't get me wrong, Lass. I'm not angry. I realize we've had other relationships, swell lookers like us. I haven't told you about the gal friends, either. I reckon that was a part of the getting to know I referred to before." He was all tenderness when he asked, "Oh now, did that blowhard make you cry?"

⤫

I closed shop at five. Liam and I boarded a train bound for Keswick and the hospital of my nightmares. Liam knew a little of that night and had invited me to go with him on hospital visits. It was for kindness' sake he went. He enjoyed sharing some jollies with those who were stuck in a sick bed for Christmas.

"It's been a pure delight chatting with folks in hospital during break," Liam said. "Some little shavers need a visit from himself the Elf. The hospital keeps a suit tucked away for the occasion. Oh, I don't fill out the britches like some St. Nicks; but what I lack in girth I make up for in enthusiasm. HO! HO! and HO!" Liam earned the immediate attention of fellow travelers; a cluster of schoolgirls laughed and whispered with their heads together.

The gentle rocking loosed memories of family train trips and Mum's cold sausage sandwiches with Colman's mustard. Visiting any other city, even one as near as Keswick, reminded me that there was a world of possibilities, and as the track zipped closed behind us, problems flew past with neighboring farms.

Conversation flowed like becks through the fells. I'd never been with anyone I could talk with so easily, but the topic of Albert was conspicuous by its absence. I wondered at Liam's not asking, but maybe he was waiting for me. He was the waiting type. I didn't care to think about those days with Albert.

It was a quick trip; Liam offered his hand when we exited by box steps the porter set down. Liam had a regular schedule with certain of the patients. He toted a satchel that held a Bible, deck of cards and some funny books for children. We had a few minutes before visiting hours.

The December afternoon had offered a rare combination of rain and sun, normally the kind of weather we enjoyed in spring. But it was chilly and snow clouds threatened if I didn't miss my forecast. Liam put his arm around me with no argument. Light from a cast iron platoon of street lamps ignited puddles as an invitation to walk. This Christmas, the shops worked for their share of fewer shoppers. Since war, competition had been keen among vendors, and we had morale to keep up so window dressings were especially festive.

My choice was The Squire's Bakery, mostly because of the intoxicating smell of hot bread. Iced ginger men with currant eyes held hands and circled a red platter. White frosted layer cakes draped with glacé fruit made my mouth water and enticed us inside where we succumbed to sharing a warm mince tart.

With his nose against the glass, Liam made his mark on the window of Toading's Toys, child that he was. He could have watched the model railroad for hours. It was an exceptional train, puffing smoke balls as it moved over felt hills and under block bridges—past farms with pigs and a woman feeding chickens and stations with clanging signals that lit. Liam recounted the poignant lives of the tiny passengers, and as they neared their destination, a small but rapt crowd had gathered behind him. I observed their expressions in the glass. He had transported them to that special dimension of childlike wonder. I knew Liam was a man, a story-teller to whom folks would listen.

The Keswick Station tower clock reminded us there was a timetable to keep.

As we entered the drama that was Keswick Memorial Hospital, I started at the medicinal smells and sanitizers—a world apart from the bakery. Bright lighting reflected off the polished linoleum floor and was strangely depressing. I took Liam's arm.

We stopped at the nurse's station. "Hello, Nurse Audrey," Liam announced himself. "How are you this chill winter evening? This is my friend, Claire. She'll be going along with me, if it's all right." He laid his arm around my shoulders and gave me a squeeze.

"Hello, Mr. McClelland. I'm jolly. Always a pleasure to have you. Your friend is welcome, just don't forget that visiting hours end at 8:00, Mr. M., 8:00. Last time one of the cleaning women heard you telling jokes in Mr. Stokes' room past 10:30."

"Heard me? She brought the cake! The dirty snitcher."

The nurse laughed, looked at me with hesitation, and then handed Liam two badges marked Visitor. "Liam has started something. I just don't know what's to become of us when he heads south after holiday." Another look my way. Perhaps she'd set her nurse's cap for him. He pinned a badge on me, then his.

"Let's see what's doing in the geriatric ward. Some great stories there. I haven't yet come away without a grain or two of wisdom, a story and a pack of Beemans blackjack gum."

"Maybe I should wait out here." I started for a cluster of black chairs.

"Nonsense," Liam said. "These old dears would be cheered to lay their peepers on a young thing. You're not going to deny them the opportunity?" He didn't wait for an answer just took me gently by the waist and ushered me to the first door.

We stopped outside room 150. The nurse who'd accompanied us, knocked and entered to see if the occupant felt up to visitors.

"Come right in," she said. "This is Mrs. Lavinia Brown, aka Winnie. When she's not playing the organ at Crosthwaite Church, she adores mystery stories and is well up on multiple methods of murder. She's recently done in her gall bladder."

"Very good," said Liam. "We shall avoid her wrong side." He winked at her.

The nurse added, "Do try at serious conversation tonight, Mr. McClelland. Mrs. B. is trying hard not to laugh and risk undoing the doctor's lovely stitchery work. She doesn't know yet, but he embroidered two of the duckiest rosebuds on her middle." She exited.

The prostrate Mrs. Brown was near bursting her literal seams while not making a sound.

"I think Mum knows this woman," I was surprised to see a familiar face.

Lavinia caught her breath and broke in, "Yes, I've known your mum and dad longer than you have, miss. In fact, I played the wedding song that brought a radiant Gloria Compton down the aisle. I remember that bonnie day well." I could see the day in her eyes.

"Fantastic," I exclaimed. "I should have recalled you, Mrs. Brown, from when I was a girl. Fancy not seeing you since then."

Call me Winnie." She chuckled and grimaced. "I visited your mum's shop the day you disappeared. I learned later that it was Liam with whom you decided to play at Captain's Courageous."

"Yes, we definitely hit the news chain about town that day and probably for months to come." I rolled my eyes Liam's direction.

"I'm so glad to see the two of you together and getting on famously. So, when were you married? Liam hasn't divulged word one."

"Oh, well, you see …," Liam began.

"Oh no!" I jumped in. "I mean we're only just getting acquainted. There's still such a lot to learn."

"Pish. Discovery comes once vows are said. Don't waste time; it's precious, young people. I know." Winnie nodded toward a picture of a handsome officer on her nightstand. "That is my Mr. Brown—killed in the last war. We have no children. Always thought there'd be plenty of time for that. Now I wish we'd had offspring for solace in my later years."

Just then, the plastic curtain serving as a barrier betwixt Winnie and her roommate was thrown back, startling us.

"Winnie! Are you going to keep those unrelated visitors all to yourself? How about me? I want visiting." This petition came from a squat woman whose bare legs and wiggling toes dangled over the side of her bed. Her chestnut hair, cut straight across at the bangs, hung in a pyramid around her ripe face. "My name's Mary. She doesn't share chocolates either." Mary used her hand to shield her words from Winnie and added, "She's selfish. Lived alone too long, I reckon." Mary hadn't a full set of teeth.

"Pay no attention to her. She doesn't need another chocolate, for pity sake." Winnie reached for the precious cache. "Would you like a chocolate, Claire? Liam?" She waved the box in Mary's direction so she could get a good sniff.

"See here," I spoke on Mary's behalf. "That seems a bit cruel."

Liam smiled and took my hand.

Mary cackled, "It's a game we play. She knows I'll be into them two shakes after she's out. I've eaten half the box!" She laughed and nearly fell off the bed. "Lavinia and I've known one another since we was little ones. We've never shared anything, except Bobby Shorter, eh, Winn?" Another howl and I felt sure it would bring the nurse, and it did.

"Another party in 150." Nurse Audrey arrived on the scene. "I'm glad you're all having such a high time but you'll have to keep it down. Folks are trying to rest." She looked at me, so I apologized for the group.

"Well send 'em over!" Mary let go. "And see if they got a bottle hid while you're at it."

"Back in bed, Typhoid Mary, instigator of mayhem." The nurse tucked her in bed like a naughty girl.

I couldn't imagine Mary and Lavinia as friends; the two were so different. Apparently, it sometimes worked that way, like with Mum and Eunice.

"What'll it be tonight, Winnie, my sweet? A game of rummy, a run-down of your latest caper?" Liam asked.

Her pale eyes looked up at him and she said, "Me lad, tonight how about a read from the good book?"

"Right. Any particular passage?" Liam sat in a metal folding chair and began flipping wispy pages. He'd marked them all up so that I didn't know how he could make out the words.

"You choose." Lavinia closed her eyes and reclined on the pillow.

I broke in. "Liam, if you'll excuse me, I'm going to find a water fountain. I'll be back presently." I didn't care to listen to Bible verses; it made me feel lonesome. I thought I'd passed the water near the nurse's station. On my way back, I looked over the magazines and glanced through a couple movie tabloids. No one was really happy—not the rich and famous, that's sure.

I saw Nurse Audrey return to the room rolling a cart with hospital gadgetry aboard. Quarters were tight already, so I remained in the waiting room and pondered my fate with Liam. We had little in common. I wished I could be content with that.

I breezed through three articles about better homemaking, and headed back to the room to see what was taking so long. My hand barely touched the door handle, when I heard the nurse say my name. I waited.

"My audience has dozed off," Liam said. "Not a good sign."

"What's your lady friend's last name?" The nurse asked.

"Stone. Why?"

"Claire Stone. Oh now I recall. I was on duty in emergency the night of her accident. I knew I'd seen her somewhere."

I put my ear next the door.

"Yes, Claire did mention something about taking a tumble from her barn," Liam replied. "That must have been a rough one. Lucky she escaped with a few bruises and a couple of cracked ribs."

"Yes. But sad about the baby." The nurse added.

"Baby?" Liam asked.

"The wee one she lost." Nurse Audrey caught herself too late. "Oh, maybe I shouldn't have mentioned anything. Please forget I said it." The cart began to rattle.

"You...you've got her confused with someone else." Liam added. "Claire's not married."

"Yes. That's it. I must have her confused with another Stone. Many stones in the Lakes! Ha. Excuse me, Mr. McClelland. I have to get back to station." The nurse came toward the door.

Audrey had been looking at me strangely all evening—now I knew why. What was that about a baby? I pushed open the door as Audrey tried to exit.

"Just a moment, if you please. What sort of business did I hear out there? Why are you discussing my medical records behind my back?" I stood firm, not allowing the nurse past. "And what's that nonsense about, a baby, was it?"

She appeared frightened near tears. "Please, Miss, I could lose my job. I'm sorry. I thought Liam knew about it. I never was good at keeping my mouth shut. Please don't report me to Nurse Mansfield."

Liam appeared as shocked as I. I didn't know if Winnie and Mary were feigning sleep, or if sleeping pills had knocked them out, but they remained mute.

"I've no idea what the twit is yammering about," I said. "Let's please go."

Liam didn't move. Just stared at his lap. Finally he slowly stood and said, "Claire, darlin', perhaps you should check your records with the desk. You're entitled to see what's there." He spoke softly, and he didn't look at me.

- 29 -

GLORY

John's and my bedroom hadn't changed except that there were no more mud-caked pants and shoes smelling of barnyard to lift with a stick, and no ashes in the feed store ashtray on his nightstand. There still was a 'his' side. I kept to established territory from routine. I'd left the walls papered over in dark green English ivy. Now, as I looked about, I couldn't bear the thought of changing one blessed thing. I wished there were smelly clothes and ashes and a reason to clean. The ghost camped there was welcome along with his mess.

I was relieved Eunice agreed to go with me to Carlisle. I meant to face my fears and get answers left unsatisfied by numerous calls and letters to the Army office of records. I had written to a London office and addressed it to the name on the telegram; but messages left with secretaries and letters returned marked, 'no such person,' achieved nothing but deeper frustration. If John lost his life in Carlisle, maybe I would see the train that took him. Would it carry his blood stains? Would someone be willing to show me where they found him?

Axel was right to push me on, though it didn't come natural. I was glad of Axel's patience. He hadn't tried to kiss me, thank heaven, but I'd seen the look. He'd been such a major force in our lives since John's death. I felt I owed him a reprieve, so I was taking care of business on my own. I didn't want to bother him with what was actually my personal affair.

While dressing, the same dread fell as before I saw Syd's teacher. I'd written out my requests for the men who made up the Cockermouth, Keswick, and Penrith Railroad Board. The first might be a reach. It was to have them purchase an advert in the *London Times* for northbound travelers. They could combine an ad for hotels and such in the area if it suited. I asked them to return Stone Revival to its original dimensions and for a neon sign on wall behind. We'd scurried about under cover of darkness—mice long enough. I checked myself in the full length mirror. I wanted them to see me.

The reflection nodded and said I looked a bit of all right. I topped her off with a straw pancake hat. John allowed I could buy it before the family boarded a train to Edinburgh for a sheep show. I knew there'd be fancy women there and wanted to represent the Lakes in style.

I heard Eunice knock then come without invite, the custom. "Glory?"

She found me. "Lord love a fricasseed duck, look at you! Why, if Finlay saw you looking like that he'd overcome his shy ways but quick." She was a party in the making and made up head to varnished toenails that peered at the world through open-toed pumps. "Do you think we'll have time to stop at druggist, the one that carries them little figurines? I'd like to get the Chinese pair for the shelf over the loo. I swore if I ever got back there I'd buy that set no matter what Roger thinks." She bobbed in the bedroom mirror and rubbed her teeth.

"Oh, I suppose so but remember, Eunice, the reasons we're going."

"I know, I know. To rise above your debilitating fear of seeing where our dear John was killed and talk to the railroad board." She recited the words as if studying for an examination. "Not sure what I can do, but I'm happy to be of service and get out the house. Roger smelled up the place awful polishing his wingtips. Not sure why. He never goes anywhere." One more check in the mirror. "By the by, guess who's back in town?"

I thought of a handful of people. "Your Randy?" Her son from Edinburgh sometimes visited.

"No. But you're on the right track. It is a relation."

"Finlay. He's come to spend Christmas holiday with you and Roger. I think you said he might do that." I gathered my gloves and pocketbook.

"Well he still might come and I hope he does to give old Biggs a run for his money, but that's not the someone I'm thinking of." Her smile loomed and she twisted like a child with an all-day sucker.

"You'll have to tell me or I'm afraid we'll be late for the train." Then the horror hit me just before she named it.

"Nephew Albert is back. And he wants to make it up with Claire." I sat on the bed.

"What's the matter? Aren't you glad? It's about time Claire was getting herself engaged, and unless I miss my guess, that's exactly what young Albert has on his brain. Likely a spring wedding." Her mouth went into overdrive. "Ho, maybe a double wedding! Mother and daughter. Wouldn't that be fun? I'd be your matron of honor, in tangerine."

"No!" I practically screamed, taking her by surprise. "Eunice, I'm sorry but I never felt that Albert and Claire were right for one another." Prizewinner of an understatement, that. "After he disappeared, Claire was devastated but she's healing now and seeing someone else."

"You mean that weasel peeler of an Irishman?" She snorted

her disapproval. "He's no match for a beauty like Claire. She and Albert look like a real smart couple. I'm surprised you didn't notice." She sounded put out.

"Well looks aren't everything and I like Liam, even if he is smallish."

"Smallish? Don't you worry about him blowing off in a stiff wind? And what about that hair?" She added. "And grand kiddies! Crikey, what if they took after him?" She made a hideous face.

"I'm sure I'd love them all the same. He treats Claire like royalty, and I want her to be happy. That's what matters." I started for the door still determined to catch the train, but worry was back in town.

∾

On the ride to Carlisle, I employed my old method of keeping Eunice preoccupied with other topics to avoid discussing Albert. Besides, the car was fairly full up with villagers I knew, and I didn't care to share Claire's personal life with the nosey lot.

"Axel and I had a right nice time at Chesterfield's the other night. Posh. Our ARP General Biggs seems to know his way around the gentry. He ordered champagne--" I looked out the window as we passed Bass Lake and noticed a couple beneath a tree on the opposite bank. "--from France."

The train slowed and I saw the sign for Carlisle Station. I wondered if I could stand.

"Up you go, dear." She tugged at my arm.

"Let's wait for the others to get off," I said. "I need a minute." My stomach sure needed time and bicarbonate.

June Shiverson, Myron's wife, passed and spoke. Also Sally Ramsbottom. She didn't speak and found the aisle maddeningly narrow. But the aroma of fresh baked buns trailed after her like a savory toilette.

As I looked out the window at the tracks and train cars,

I pictured the scene and invited pain. Did a man die there? He wasn't just any man. He was mine. It was a busy station, and no one saw him in time to shout a warning.

I heard Eunice sharing her secret to younger looking skin using egg whites with a toothless woman who looked 103. I stood to go, though my legs felt inadequate for the job. My stomach insisted that I was asking too much. But I'd come to do battle.

"All right then." I took a deep breath. The toothless one eyed me as I stood. "Think I'll stop at the ticket window first."

Eunice had on her serious, friend-in-need face. I loved that face. Clearly, I should get her something extra plummy this Christmas.

There was a steady drizzle and a short queue under the awning at window. I might have coaxed the knot in my stomach loose with a dish of tea but I stood. Eunice had me by the arm, which made it worse, but I wouldn't say anything for the world. Finally, I was next.

"Hello. My name is Gloria Stone. About four months back, my husband, John Stone, was involved in an accident in this rail yard, on these tracks and...was killed. Perhaps you heard about it?" Poor thing, wasn't expecting that.

The young redhead, Emily, according to her name badge, looked at me and said, "I'm sorry, mum, no I haven't. But I was just put on here four weeks hence, since Land Army was through." She looked at the man behind me.

"Oh well that explains it. Could you tell me, where would I go if I should like more information, or perhaps to talk with someone who was here at the time?" Eunice hung close and squeezed my arm so tightly I began losing circulation from the elbow down. I patted her hand and she relaxed.

"Well, I should surely think the station master, Mr. Pumfrey, would be able to answer your questions." She smiled sadly. "He's right in there." She pointed to a station office.

"Thank you, Love," said Eunice and steered me around and into the small confines.

There was a man behind the desk with his head buried in a ledger and wearing after shave that could curl boards. I cleared my throat.

"Oh, hello, ladies. Sorry, trying like the dickens to figure where the error is with the books. My, they can be a clunking great pain." He slammed the book closed and stood. "I welcome a diversion. What may I do for you?"

"My name is Gloria Stone." I waited, hoping he'd recognize the name so I wouldn't have to voice my request again. He didn't, evidently, so I continued. "My husband, John Stone, had a fatal accident here at your station about four months ago while returning from his post. I came for more information and to talk with someone who was there." I looked around and found a chair.

His eyes were green. I noticed because he stared at me wide-eyed—as if I'd asked for directions to Jupiter.

He broke free of the confusion that held him and said, "Do excuse my lack of manners, ladies. Please have a chair." He pulled out another for Eunice. "These books you know," he said with a hand to his forehead. Surely, his station couldn't have hosted so many deaths that he would forget one in four months. There would have been reports to file. It would have been big news in town. The seconds stretched out.

"I'm frightfully sorry, Mrs. Stone, but I just don't recall any such incident here. Strange thing is, you're not the first to ask. The station master from Rakefoot Crossing, Axel Biggs, asked about that very incident several weeks ago and inquired about a bag of puppies. Authorities must have given the two of you wrong information, is all I can guess. Perhaps a different station? I am deeply sorry for your loss." His flimsy excuse made him grin inappropriately.

"Is there anyone else I could ask?" My head began to throb and heat made the route up my neck, warming my ears. The sooty windows closed toward me. This hadn't been a good day. I knew I was passing out.

❧

"Here, she's back with us." Mr. Pumfrey sounded relieved.

I heard Eunice clucking then saw her earnest face. She dobbed at my cheeks and forehead with a cold, wet cloth that felt reviving. Someone had moved me to a leather sofa in Mr. Pumfrey's office. Maybe I'd landed on the floor like a splayed insect with my dress hiked up. I was a spectacle again. How I hated being a spectacle.

"So sorry," I tried to sit but felt sick. "Oh, dear."

"Now just relax. Take some deep breaths," said the dutiful station master. "You'll soon be right again. Vickers, go fetch a glass of water for the lady." A boy named Vickers rushed off.

I resumed a mental search for how the station master could be oblivious at his watch and why Biggs hadn't mentioned it, but had only spoken of the puppies before. The dead end hit me unexpectedly. I didn't know what to do.

Mr. Pumfrey offered, "It's quite possible that with an accident involving any form of neglect or engineer error, the board members would try to keep it on the QT, if you know what I mean. May have been fretting over a possible lawsuit." He eyed me. "I'm not sure."

I rose to a seated position and began to recoup as Vickers handed me a glass of tepid water.

"It so happens I plan to see the board today. I have an appointment with them at 2:00. Good gosh, what time is it?" I asked Eunice.

"Don't fret. Only 12:00. I think we should have us something to eat and give you a chance to come round." She nodded at Mr. Pumfrey who agreed. "Can you show us to your refreshment room?" Eunice took my elbow.

"Vickers, please escort the ladies to the refreshment room and while you're at it, point the way to the board room. There's a good lad." He reached for the ledger and resumed a pained look.

"Thank you," I said. "It was a difficult decision for me to come here."

"I'm sure of that, Mrs. Stone. And I do hope you find what you're looking for," Mr. Pumfrey said.

Unless they had John alive somewhere, that would be impossible. The boy, dressed in blue uniform, showed us the way to a spacious eatery with crowded tables and more lined up at bar.

I couldn't stop thinking of what Mr. Pumfrey had said about the board covering up John's death. I suppose it made sense; but was it ethical or legal?

"I want cheese sandwich and chips," Eunice said, closing her eyes and inhaling our neighbor's lunch. "Will you be able to eat something, Love?"

"Yes, I think so. Let's have a look at the menu."

❧

"I now call this meeting to order." One of the blue suits rapped the gavel atop an impressive carved desk.

Eunice and I sat at the far end of a lengthy rectangle with twelve matching chairs, half of them occupied. I sat up tall, and the table still strafed my chest. One large wall had two multi-paned windows that looked out on the fair town of Carlisle, largest in Cumbria. Maps papered the wall behind the men, illustrating the entire rail structure of the U. K. The tiny tracks looked like an ant trail marching through England, Wales and Scotland. My pocketbook and I faced two gray and two bald members. The ceiling fans also neared retirement as they swirled tobacco smoke and laid it back over us.

Eunice whispered. "I feel like we was in one of them courtroom dramas, don't you, Glory?" Eunice's brain was a card catalog of movies, where she was always a character.

Eunice checked her face in a gold-toned compact, swiped the post-lunch lipstick application from her teeth, and prepared to be entertained.

"This isn't a courtroom, Eunice. It's a boardroom and those men are not actors. They hold a dear slice of my livelihood in their hands." I glanced over and she still had that far away look—lost in a scene somewhere. "Look, this might get pretty dull. Did you bring a magazine?"

I'd insulted her. "I am an adult you know. I'll be fine." She straightened herself, pulled at her collar, and added, "Do you smell Ben-Gay?"

The head suit continued, "Today we have two visitors from our neighboring village of Rakefoot Crossing. Mr. Axel Biggs is the station master there. Am I correct, Mrs. uh..." He checked his paper. "...Stone?" He looked at both of us and I nodded.

"In light of the fact that we have onlookers at today's meeting I should like to make the motion we postpone the reading of the minutes and discussion of future business until the ladies have stated their purpose here. Do I hear a second?"

"Scnd." One of the bald ones spoke.

"Those in favor?"

"Aye." They were a bland chorus.

"Excuse me, Mr. Chairman, but I've got something to say." I interrupted the proceedings.

"What's that?" He opened his eyes. "Yes, Mrs. Stone?"

"Concerning future business..." I began.

"Speak up if you please, Mrs. Stone. Some of us don't hear as well as we used to." He looked at his comrades whose blank expressions verified his statement.

"Sorry. Concerning future business, I have something to discuss with you that would be appropriate for that portion of the meeting." I'd stood at some point. "It's concerning my antique shop located inside your station at Rakefoot Crossing."

They cleared musty throats, peered at one another through smoke fogged glasses, and the chairman swigged something amber colored.

"Well, perhaps it would be best if you were to explain to those of us present the full reason for your visit." It was clear visitors inside these hallowed walls were rare. They certainly acted queer, studying us as if we were museum pieces rather than plain country women.

I looked at Eunice who nodded me on.

"First off, let me introduce my friend here, Mrs. Quimby." Eunice nodded. "You know I'm Mrs. Stone, but we don't know who you are. Don't you think it would be nice if you introduced yourselves?" My hands were sweating but my legs were locked in the upright position. "And you might offer my friend and me a drop of whatever's in your glasses." I turned around to Eunice whose mouth was open.

"Of course, of course. Right you are, Mrs. Stone. Gentlemen, where are our manners? To my right is Mr. T. Percival Mandrake. Next to him with the cigar is Edward Maloney. On my left, Orville Smith and I am Marshall Bickerstaff at your service." He bowed his head slightly.

I'd heard that name before. Mr. Bickerstaff jangled a small bell and a servant entered.

"Drinks for the ladies, Hamilton. We're drinking Scotch. Perhaps you'd care for a glass of sherry or...tea?"

"Scotch suits us, thank you," I replied.

"She fainted earlier," Eunice threw in.

Hamilton reappeared moments later carrying a tray with an ice bucket, crystal decanter and two matching glasses. He poured them over the rocks in front of us and scurried off. I'd never drunk Scotch in my life but I tipped the glass and stifled a gag.

"Thank you ever so, sir," Eunice said from behind me. "Hits the spot after the train ride and all we been through." I looked at her and smiled. She winked at me and shut up.

I took a deep breath. "Four months ago at this station, my husband, John Stone, was on his way home after being discharged from the Army, but he was backed over by one of your trains." A couple of heads jerked and moved but they refrained from looking at one another. "They pronounced him dead at the scene once they discovered him. I'm not sure how much time had passed." I took another sip. "The two employees I've questioned, one being your station master, know nothing of the incident. I find that odd. What can you tell me about that day, 17 July last?" I took my seat and waited.

While the other three men looked awkward, Mr. Bickerstaff proceeded, as was the custom.

"Mrs. Stone, first off please allow us to extend our deepest sympathies. No amount of explanation can account for yours and your daughters' loss; but I'm afraid we've no idea what you're talking about."

"What's that? I assure you, gentlemen, I have no intention whatever of bringing a suit against the line. I simply need more information. Mr. Pumfrey suggested that you might keep such an accident from the public because of the negative publicity it would invite." I hoped that would loosen their tongues.

He left his chair, lit a cigar and began pacing behind the table. "It's true that each year it seems another concern, which required service by the line, goes under. Ironworks, coal mines, woolen mills; all suffering from imported competition. Why, if we hadn't had the war to keep us rolling, we may have gone belly up alto-gether," he actually chuckled.

"We've protected the good name of our railroad at all costs and frankly, we do not need this kind of negative report. If there was a careless accident such as you described, we would be in further jeopardy, as would the livelihoods of all those under our employ. I don't know whether to apologize for that; but we must ask that you contact the Army for details concerning your husband's death and leave the railroad out of it altogether." Mr. Bickerstaff appeared sincere if not a bit sloshed.

The subject and the day's course had worn me down—my

spirit flagged. I accepted his statement without a fight and even more frustrated than when I'd arrived. My numbness had nothing to do with the whiskey.

After a brief but much needed recess, the business meeting went well for me, likely out of pity. The board unanimously agreed I could have whatever I asked with regard to the shop as long as Axel approved. It was as if my shop was another surprise. They stopped short of agreeing to the advertisement. Given the former speech, I understood; however, had I been on the board, I would have suggested that tourism was their future.

He signed off with, "Oh. And be sure to give Milton my best. Tell the old general to come round for a game of chess one of these days."

That was it. Bickerstaff was Milton's old chum and he was on the board. But Axel said he never heard of him. How did Bickerstaff know I knew Milton? And how did he know I had daughters? I had not intended to leave with more questions than when I arrived.

- 30 -

CLAIRE

*C*laire *Ellen Stone (20) female patient, multiple hematomas and abrasions following a ten plus foot fall. X-rays positive for fractures of numbers two and three ribs on right side, circulation, movement and sensation normal. Pt had substantial vaginal bleeding. Pt believed to be early in first trimester of pregnancy at time of fall. Probable miscarriage.*

That last entry explained a lot. They'd listed it among the minor injuries. If I skimmed over the words, it might go unnoticed that for six or eight weeks I was with child. Words would not clear me in Liam's world, so I kept my mouth shut.

The train ride home from Keswick was a forlorn version of the ride there. I scanned for a seat apart from Liam to avoid breathing his disdain but there were only two together. I stared out the window--watching the scenes pass by, pigs and bridges, and a woman feeding chickens, and wishing I was aboard the toy shop train, bound for obscurity.

Liam hid behind his King James all the way back to Rakefoot Crossing.

☙

Days passed and I did not hear from Mr. McClelland since he'd had the bum luck of being present at the airing of my indiscretion. My sin. I'd planned to tell all. The news obliterated us as a match like I reckoned it would. And why not? Those two weeks with him had been like a silent comedy with life moving at thrice normal speed. Now, shame was a back-alley dog hanging around for scraps to make me forget what might have been.

Mum's signature was on the hospital report. That fact threatened to overwhelm me. The one person to whom I could run in troubled times had joined the growing ranks of deserters: Dad, then Albert, Liam, and now my own Mum.

First time back at shop, who had greeted me but jolly old Albert. He said he'd be around and he wasn't always a liar. At least he took me as I was. Liam was a good sort for somebody else, not a girl like me who craved excitement and wanted to experience all life had to offer. He belonged with a subservient, object of perfection without spot or wrinkle—some heavenly vision from Magdalen.

"Claire, you home?" Mum called from the entry.

She knocked. "Yes," I said.

"What a day!" Mum continued to talk through the door. I heard the pot go on. "Thanks for filling in at shop. Are you trying for a lie-down?"

"Yes." I couldn't say more.

"Oh. Well I guess I can tell you about it later if you're interested. You know I told you that Eunice and I were going to Carlisle today?"

The issue at hand sat on me like a market hog. I had to have it out or suffocate. I jerked open the door.

"Claire, love, you look as though you've been…"

"Crying. No kidding."

Mum came near. "What's wrong? Doesn't have anything to do with Albert, does it? I heard he was back."

"Indirectly." I paced around the kitchen. "Sometimes it's those we're nearest who hurt us most." I looked at her. "Those you would least suspect in all the world."

Mum began twisting her apron ties. "Tell me what's wrong, Claire. Maybe I can help."

I hated to scrape open the wound; but anger overcame humiliation.

"How could you possibly rationalize not telling me the truth about that night in hospital?" Tears came fresh as I yelled the difficult question—an unfair question no daughter should have to ask. "About the baby, Mum. The baby?" I screamed through the tears. "My baby!"

Mum found the chair and sat heavily. Obviously, she was shocked that I would find her out.

"Oh, Claire. Please don't be angry. I can handle anything but that." Now Mum turned on the waterworks. "Doc Farnaham put the idea in my head that no one would have to know about the child except him and me. How in heaven's name did you come to find out?"

"So I have the good doctor to thank as well. How unprofessional, if not illegal. I rode with Liam to Keswick Hospital so's he could do his good works. The nurse, Mum, the nurse who assisted the good doctor was there. She recognized my name and said 'what a shame about the...baby.'" My face felt hot as I patrolled the confines of our small kitchen. "'What a shame about the baby.' Then she caught herself after the damage. It wasn't her fault. It was yours!"

"Can you even look at me? Liam couldn't look at me once he found out. I wanted to run and keep running, to get clear away, but didn't know where to go. Damn it, Mum! I can't believe you would keep something like that from me. I had a right to know! As despicable as Albert's cowardice was, he had a right to know. Who do you think you are, God?" I picked up a chair and felt like throwing it through the window.

Mum shook her head and started, "Please, please listen to me, Claire."

"But what could you possibly say?" I yelled.

She closed her eyes and spoke over me. "I wanted to spare you the hurt and humiliation. That was the point. I reasoned, what was the good of telling you? The baby was gone, and I thought things would go even harder if you knew about it." She cried but kept talking. "Someday when you're a mum..." She stopped. "Maybe you'll understand that it was because I loved you more than my own life that I kept quiet. I knew things would be impossible here if anyone got wind of yours and Albert's affair." Mum looked exhausted but she had hit on it.

I interrupted. "It was your standing in community you were thinking of."

"No! I..."

"All the sidelong glances you'd have to endure. Face it, Mum, you're a coward! You're first instinct has always been to avoid confrontation. Even with Syd! She still believes Dad is alive because you can't bear to set her straight. Another thing, you don't love Biggs but you can't tell him to bug off because you're afraid of hurting his feelings. He's 'done so much'." I mocked her often repeated words.

Mum took a shaky breath and looked at me. Tears streaked her face. "I've long admired your strength, Claire. How I've wished I had your fire—your resolve to push beyond hard times, whatever the cost. The damping will happen, later. But I must defend my cowardice and remind you that I've gone through these past months too—only as a mother—the one responsible for her family. I've challenged dragons the likes of which you have not yet seen, and I've beat them back, somehow."

Mum looked out her window to the gray. "I wish you'd sheath your sword, Claire. I'm on your side, and though I may not approve of every decision you make, my love for you carries no conditions. We can't know all that's going on in a person. Sometimes what appears as weakness is another rung on the ladder for the one we condemn, but we cut off their feet with our judgment." Mum glanced at me. "And there are many degrees of love. I've enjoyed time with Axel. Life can be lonely; and even though he nor anyone will ever come near replacing your dad, Axel Biggs is a good friend and may become more at some point. I thought you should know." She kept looking out the window.

I couldn't deal with that nightmare just then and sought to return to the subject at hand. "That's a quarrel for another day. Sorry I brought it up. What you did was wrong, Mother. And I'm never going to forgive you for it." Conversation was going nowhere. I grabbed my waterproofs and left.

"Morning glory!" Natty squawked and racketed overhead, depositing a rusty screw at my feet. I stood—deciding whether to meet Albert by the lake again as we'd planned or go off by myself. Mum's attempted defense was a surprise. I didn't want to hear the truth of her argument, if there was any.

Seeing Albert had lost its shine, but I headed toward the lake for lack of a better plan. Funny how I'd never noticed the annoying way he adds an h to all his s's. Like shcones instead of scones or yesh for yes. Did he think it was sexy? Did he always talk like that or just with women? Claire imagined him saluting his C.O. 'Yesh, shir.'

I thought it would help but I felt worse after dumping on Mum. I lifted my collar against a cold rain and pulled on my hat brim. I'd never venture out if I couldn't brave the downpours in these parts. Though lately I'd been eyeing Dad's Austin wasting away in the garage. I started her up now and again to keep the battery going, but never went further than Keswick. Surely, gasoline rationing would end by the time I began work at Dalemain. For now, it was foot power since there was no money for petrol anyhow.

Christmas was a couple weeks off. Maybe I could drag Albert to the Keswick shops. I'd like to get Syd a book about dog breeds I saw at Powell's. I'd have to get something for Mum too.

The rain let up. I approached the infamous tree, and shook a few drops over Albert. I laughed, but he didn't find it amusing.

"Why can't we go to your barn cashle?" He had the cheek to ask.

"Why? You're asking me?" I rolled my eyes in disgust. Our relationship certainly had changed course. I wasn't eager to comply with Albert's baser instincts any longer but dangled the promise like a carrot. The realization that he was no longer my white knight depressed me.

I'd grown accustomed to Liam hanging around. He and Albert had nothing in common besides gender, but if Mum could use a creep like Biggs as a substitute for Dad, I could use Albert.

"I need to do some Christmas shopping. Want to drive me?" I asked half heartedly.

"Where to?" asked Albert

"Keswick. I saw a book for Syd in one of the shops." I swiped the rain from the front of his hair. He grabbed my hand and began kissing my arm. "Are you coming?" I pulled back.

"Oh, well I guess. They do have a lively pub there. I can wet my whistle while you're puttering about." He pulled out his keys.

We started for his new car. I opened the passenger door and Liam's lopsided smile appeared in my head from when he helped me down the train steps.

"Hope you're not thinking of buying me anything." Albert's voice intervened. "I'd feel the lout if you got me something and I'd nothing for you. This little baby is taking most of my ready cash nowadays and for the next few years." He patted the steering wheel.

His choice of vocabulary struck a nerve. "Don't worry," I assured him. "I wouldn't dream of making you feel the lout." He could manage that on his own. I did not intend to give him a blessed thing.

- 31 -

SYD

15 December 1945

Dear Pop,

I'm feeling blue today. Sometimes I wonder if I really am making all this up in my head, about your being alive I mean. It has been so long. If so, then strangers are reading my letters—a thought I can't bear. Who taught Natty those new phrases, if not you? I thought I knew where you were. I won't write it here. And what about the ring?

I'm sad too because Claire and Liam had a row and he hasn't been round. Not sure Mum knows, but that bum, Albert is back in town. Claire has mentioned him and that he has a job and a car—big deal. He's still a first class J-E-R-K! I don't get how she can't see what a clown he is. Now, Claire and Mum seem on the outs about something or another. He must have everything to do with it.

As if all that weren't enough, Cassidy, my bosom cat, the large gray one with the gimp leg, is still missing and I'm afraid something's got him. I miss him terribly, especially at night, but I've about given up hope of seeing him again.

Remember when I said I didn't want to grow up? Well, it's happening anyway, like it or not. The monthly monster has struck. Now I have cramps and all that business to deal with on top of everything. I can see no good that can come of it. I wish I were a boy. I'm no beauty like Claire. I'm chubby and plain. And I have large, knobby knees. Claire and I had some good talks until recently. She was kinder when Liam was around.

A week ago, we danced in our room to swing music on the wireless. She's teaching me how for the school Christmas dance. She said to let the boy lead, that way he can take the blame when we look like country clods. Ha. I'm no Ginger Rogers, that's for sure, but I am getting the hang of it. At the first, I trod on her feet and we fell on the bed laughing and could barely stop. I do want her to think well of me. I wish I had her Ingrid B. nose.

Pop, maybe I shouldn't tell you this, but I think you ought to know. Claire thinks you love me more than her. She told me so. I said it wasn't true—that you love us the same. But I guess she feels that way because we spend so much time together on account of the animals and my wanting to be a vet.

Isn't it strange? We're each one of us jealous of something the other has. I never dreamed that Claire could envy me since she seems so strong. You have to spend time alone with people to know who they are behind their talk. Like Biggs, for example; he and I are quite chummy. I do hope you don't mind. I don't need to tell you that no one could take your place.

He asked me along to go crow shooting with him! I was horrified at the prospect and he must have seen it on my face because he quickly apologized and called himself a thoughtless lout. I said I didn't think him a lout. Lots of people shoot crows, especially farmers, but knowing he's capable of killing for the sake of sport makes me feel less close with him.

Now, Pop, what I'm going to tell you next may poke a little. That's what the doc says just before the needle jab. Mum went to a fancy restaurant with Biggs—Chesterfield's. She kept telling us it wasn't a date but she is the only one who believed it. We were asleep when she got home, but I woke and pretend slept when she checked on us. She ran to your room where I heard her crying. I think she felt bad because of you. Sure, Mum will always love you.

Would adore seeing you at Christmas. Meanwhile, keep a stiff upper and we shall do same.

Love and kisses,

Syd

- 32 -

GLORY

Christmas was supposed to gladden hearts. This year was hard. If it hadn't been for the girls, I wouldn't have celebrated at all, though Claire still wasn't speaking to me. John was keen on Christmas with all the trimmings. I couldn't look at a wreath or hear *God Rest Ye Merry Gentlemen* without feeling the hollow his absence left behind. Lighted trees reminded me of a song he'd taught Syd about Jesus being the light of the world; only she said it like 'wold.' She was three, so that made it nine years ago.

"Am I silly to set out mince pie and brandy for Father Christmas this year and carrots for the reindeer?" Syd asked. "I mean, he might not be real. It could have been Pop before. We haven't heard reindeer noises on the roof since Pop went into the Army, but maybe if I leave…it, he'll come." She began clearing space for her offerings. John was our Father Christmas all the year. Optimism had disappeared with him and the war until recently.

A fire snapped in the grate as Syd hung up her stocking with 'Sydney or Syd' written in black grease pen on the rolled cuff. She wanted no identity confusion between her and her sister, since that could prove calamitous in her judgment. Syd was expectant like all kids on Christmas Eve. They may have lost a loved one during war, but when the stockings went up, hope was the bait inside them to lure goodies from gloom.

Slowly we'd begun to gather our legs under us and try life as an appetizer again. Yet without John, we would never see the like of the former Noel. And I didn't know how to set things right with my daughter. I couldn't change the circumstances surrounding our rift. I could only wait and hope.

A chaste snow drifted over fields and rooftops during the night—first of the season. Several centimeters had fallen, assuring a white Christmas and at least one dirt freckled snowman. I knew it meant as much to Claire as Syd and I, though she'd been preoccupied and aloof since our run-in. I hurt every day for Claire and carried the weight of guilt. I loved her. I reckoned she missed the believing too.

Claire asked Syd, "Who is it you think will come for the treats?" She pushed a holly berry onto her needle and the string grew redder along with her irritation.

"Pop, of course," she answered. "Father Christmas is make-believe, I think. Is he?"

"One is as likely to show as the other, little sis. If we do glimpse someone in a red suit and beard, you can bet it will be Biggs trying to play the part of a jolly old daddy. Something I don't reckon he'd be good at if his past performance is any indication." She shook her head in disgust and stabbed her finger. "Oh!"

I started to scold Claire again for criticizing Axel but didn't want to make things worse. Ironically, he had mentioned a couple days ago that he wanted to don the venerable costume for the girls and me. Said it would 'make him feel jolly to oblige.' I wasn't so sure, being as this was our first Christmas without their dad in the title role, but he'd insisted we all needed to keep herding forward while making the best of the present. I was glad he wanted to take part.

"Of course you should leave the treats," I said. "It's a good plan. I didn't realize you doubted Father Christmas." This year marked the loss of innocence.

Poor Syd stared into the flames, her arms wrapped around her shoulders, but she wasn't downcast. Fire danced in her eyes. I hoped the disappointment wouldn't prove too great. It's as I thought, this holiday had folks looking up, except maybe Claire. Real conversation had been non existent between us most recently. I'd felt the chasm widening again as it had after news of John. *It could be a long winter.*

"Will Biggs join us, Mum? He'll be alone otherwise, won't he?" Syd asked. "Maybe he'll bring presents!" At least she'd thought of his welfare first.

"He did say he'd join us for the day, yes, and the Quimbys. Finlay may come. We'll play games and sing. Roger may take off dancing, who knows?" Because of the restrictions I'd suffered at shop earlier, I hoped Axel did bring gifts, for the girls anyway. Eunice would be good for something suitably gaudy for them. I wasn't able to do much except a special meal.

"Guess Albert will be with them then. Cause he's back and been hanging about." Claire said casually.

My stomach tightened. "What a nerve to come skulking around here again. What does he take you for? He will never be welcome in this house. I hope you know that." I got up and started fussing aimlessly in the kitchen. "You haven't encouraged him, surely?" I looked at Syd, afraid Claire might let slip about the baby.

"I've seen him. Why not? Albert accepts me for who and what I am, which is more than I can say for the absent Mr. McClelland."

That explained Claire's cynical attitude toward Christmas. She did miss Liam. But have Albert here? How could I tell Eunice and Roger he wasn't welcome?

"You didn't forget the crackers? We must pull crackers," Syd said, in a world apart. "Then each person will read their fortune aloud."

I tied a green ribbon around a box of chocolates for Eunice and Roger. I had also bought the Chinese figurines from the Carlisle drug store. It was either that or suffer having them thrown into conversations where they had no business.

There was a lot to be thankful for. No more night raids and blackouts, though Northern England hadn't had as much to fear as the port towns and sad London. One bomb did hit a Lakes farm I knew of, killing the entire family instantly. That was the exception besides Knowley's. The family went together.

Syd and I hummed as carols floated in over the wireless from The Music Box hall in London. A large crowd had gathered and their collective voices made Silent Night especially bittersweet. This was a happy time for some, with their loved ones home and Hitler finally where he belonged.

"Where's Liam spending his Christmas?" I took a chance.

"With his family in Bailieborough I should think. He has three brothers and two younger sisters. Large family." Claire sucked at her sore finger and we were talking.

She rattled off the information as if it was of no concern, but I'd seen a card addressed to him on her dressing table only two days before. I hadn't read it, but Liam's name was on the envelope with a sketch of a rainbow. She had marked over the pot of gold and made it a scuttle of coal more like. I loved Liam. He seemed the genuine article. But we hadn't seen him now since the showdown at Keswick, and I wondered if maybe he wasn't the gracious man he'd seemed. Guess I couldn't blame him entirely.

"It would have been nice having him join us. He's a barrel of fun." I had to say it but not without cringing. Claire responded as if she'd declined a cup of tea after thinking it over.

"Yeah, that would have been nice." She turned her back to me and moved to drape the tree with her string of berries and cones.

"Your garlands look festive, Claire. I appreciate them more than shiny, store bought baubles," I said.

"German children call their trees tannenbaums," Syd informed us.

"We don't care what German brats call it. They've a lot of nerve celebrating Christmas." Claire snapped. "They're the ones trying to kill us, in case you hadn't heard."

"You don't believe and you decorate a tree," Syd objected. "Anyway, the kids aren't the ones."

"Well their big brothers and fathers have done in plenty of sheep and doggies and kitties with their plan to dominate the world. Did you even think of that?" Claire leveled a strategic volley of her own. "And I never said I didn't believe." She glanced toward me.

"I've never heard you say you did." Syd didn't shrink from her sister.

"Well come to that, I've never heard you confess your undying faith to a supreme being. Who's teaching you about Germans anyway?"

"My schoolteacher, that's who. And I'm not the one judging them, you are." Syd bit both wings off a butter cookie angel. "You don't know everything about me."

"Mrs. Vinson?" I asked, attempting to stem the tide.

"Miss Vinson, yes. She said we shouldn't hate all the Germans because of the bad ones." She dipped the grounded angel headfirst into her milk glass. "She said there were a lot of good German people who've gone to prison and even been killed for not cooperating with The Third Reich, as they call it."

"I admire Miss Vinson. She's a good woman," I said. "Axel is half German."

Syd looked alarmed. "But he's on our side."

"There's another reason not to like them." Claire laughed.

"What do you have against Axel, really? Let's have this out," I blurted.

Did I want to know? He and I had gotten closer. I'd hoped

her scorn of him was because nobody could replace her dad rather than hatred for the man. "He's done a lot for us," I reminded.

"I've heard that. With what motive, I wonder?" Claire sneered. "Oh Mum, if you like Biggs, though I can't imagine how, I won't stand in your way. Just don't expect me to think of him as a father figure because I could never do that. And, for crimeny sake, don't ask me to be your bridesmaid. I'd sooner stand up with you and a baboon than Biggs."

"That's unkind. You've gone on a mental rampage if you think I'm close to marrying anyone." The notion shouldn't have shaken me. I had wondered about my future in the cold middle of night. Surely, Claire had wondered as well. Nothing would proceed there until we had definitive closure about John, no matter how long it took.

"If you believe I'm the only one thinking of wedlock, oh, Mum, how can you be so daft?" At least she smiled when she said it.

Jingles came into the room dragging something. I thought he'd gotten into a box of Christmas decorations.

"What's that you've got there, boy?" Syd sat next to him on the floor to have a closer look. "It's Cassidy's collar!" She jumped up, bounded outside letting the screen door slam, and began calling for her favorite animal as she had for weeks now.

"Oh, good gosh, no," Claire said shaking her head. "Syd! I've got to talk with you," she called as she went out after her little sis. When they came back inside, Claire had her arm around Syd's shoulders.

"What is it?" Syd asked, still clutching the worn collar.

Claire began, "I know what happened to Cassidy."

"You do?" I asked. "But, why..."

Syd looked worried. "Is he alive?"

"I found him when I was out for a walk one day. It looked as if he just died where he was. I...buried him under a mound of leaves where you wouldn't see him. I'm sorry, sis." Claire looked sick.

"When was this?" Tears formed in Syd's eyes as she looked at Claire for an answer.

"It's been several weeks."

"Why didn't you tell me?" Syd began to cry. "You know I've been looking for him all this time and you didn't say anything?"

"I thought what you didn't know wouldn't hurt you." Claire looked at me.

"But I had a right to know! He was the best cat. I would have given him a proper burial." Syd ran to their room and slammed the door.

Claire and I stood there, the irony not lost on either of us. Claire came to me with tears in her eyes. "Oh, Mum. I'm sorry."

ℭ

Later that night, Claire joined Syd in their room where they discussed Cassidy's many noble qualities over cups of cocoa. We planned to hold a proper funeral for him after the holidays when Syd would read special words over a grave that would contain only one ratty collar. It was the thought that counted, Syd said. She planned to mark his resting place with a cross made from the stems of red rose cuttings. And though Claire had assured Syd she knew she could never replace Cassidy, she offered to help find another cat when she felt ready.

- 33 -

GLORY

At 1:00 A.M. the three of us woke to a frightening clamor on the roof. I grabbed a club I'd taken to keeping under my bed and crept toward the front of the house for a look. The girls met me, mussed and cat-eyed.

"What the hell?" Claire voiced her concern.

"Claire, please don't curse in front of Syd,"

"The roof is caving in and you're worried about my blinking language?"

Had she not opened her mouth, Claire would have appeared almost angelic standing there in her chenille robe, a shaft of full moon stroking the length of her hair. But, she spoke so the effect wasn't all it might have been.

Syd chimed in, "I'm not a baby, Mother. I've heard bad words. Much worse ones. Like..."

"Never mind." I waylaid a grammar school barrage. "I don't need a recitation. Now you girls stay out of sight while I try to get to the bottom of this."

I moved toward the edge of the large picture window in front, with shuffling and breathing at my back.

"I told you girls to stay out of sight."

"Oh, Mum." Syd giggled.

Trying to describe the noise above us, I'd say it sounded like a gathering of heavy-set people, walking on stilts over the roof, while occasionally sliding and falling.

"Did you hear a moo just then? Claire asked.

"Yes!" Syd hesitated then said, "Don't reindeer make a noise like that?"

"Shhh!" I tried to silence them but we were undone. "Maybe I best just ring for the police."

"Wait, Mum. It is Christmas after all," Syd advised.

"What does that have to do with the price of bananas?" Claire asked.

Syd answered, "What? Oh, maybe it's...I don't know but maybe it's someone we weren't expecting."

"Well that's brilliant," Claire agreed.

"HO! HO! HO! Whoa!" Santa had found the Stone home.

Syd looked at Claire and me wide eyed. "I told you so."

An object rattled down the chimney. We ran in blind because I'd kept the lights off to cloak our movement. Whatever it was, it landed in a smoldering pile of ashes and half burnt logs. It looked like a bag of some sort. Claire and Syd rushed to rescue it from flaming up.

"Wait! Don't touch that! You don't know what it is," I said, in homage to mums the world over.

"Mum, it's Christmas—noise on the roof, ho ho ho, bag down chimney." Syd stood amazed at my ignorance.

They snatched the smoking pouch from destruction as I watched, still as a vertical corpse in plaid pyjamas.

"What's inside?" Being cowardly, I waited for the girls to tell me.

"Presents!" Syd yelled. "One for each of us!"

Meanwhile, the noise carried on above only with more sliding nonsense. Another distinct moo, more frantic this time I thought. I hoped my roof would survive a visit from this St. Nick. And who the blazes was it? Axel?

"Do not open any of those gifts until we find out what the hell is going on," I shouted.

"You said hell!" Syd was on it like Natty on a grub.

"All right. Just leave them be until we know they're safe."

I looked out the front window again and as my eyes had adjusted, could now see that there was a long, wooden plank forming a ramp from yard to roofline. It may have been what John used to load livestock into the lorry. I could almost have been convinced this was all within the realm of sanity, until another bang and one bovine hoof and foreleg plunged straight through the porch roof and hung there. More mooing.

Tossing caution out the window, I exited the house with club poised cricket fashion and avoiding said hoof. By moonlight, I could just make out our Greta in a compromised position atop our roof. There was also a person up there muttering to himself and crawling on all fours, apparently trying to come to poor Greta's aid. He was dressed all in red from his head to his foot. If it was Father Christmas, he'd been off his feed because he was a right smallish old elf.

"Ho, ho and...heh heh... ho, Mrs. Stone, uh, Glory. Sorry to be making such racket." It was Liam. "I wanted to make a little authentic patter up on the roof like old Father Christmas you know—give the girls a thrill. But..." He gestured nervously toward our cow. "Greta here is no flying reindeer." He collapsed into a fit of laughter and I wondered was he tight?

I stood and waited for him to finish, weighing my reaction. I could have joined him easy enough, but my cow was on the roof. When he finally chuckled himself out, his eyes roved everywhere but where Greta lay, chewing her cud, obviously not in pain. Liam had settled her with his shushing and cooing and now provided her entertainment.

"No, Liam, she isn't. She's a cow," I basked in the comfort of hard facts. "But we best get her down, eh? You'll need help."

The girls were miles ahead of me because out the door they came with coats thrown over nightgowns and muck-stained Wellies.

Syd was a giggling mess. That was all she could bring herself to do seemingly, so I left her to it. Of all of us, she would know how to coax Greta back down the plank. Likely, it would involve cow candy, which she ran to the barn to fetch, while Liam pulled on the dangling appendage from above.

Claire and I shared a priceless glance. She wasn't about to show her delight at having Liam appear, dressed as he was. The situation presented a hopeful package but we would revel silently meanwhile.

Greta had bestowed a holiday pie on his boots. I discovered this when the wind shifted. A snowy beard, while still hanging below his face, had slipped so that his nose protruded from where the mouth should have been. It looked like his nostrils were doing the talking.

He clung to his britches with one hand and said, "The hospital allowed I could borrow the suit just for tonight after the children were tucked snugly in and I'd placed the donated gifts beneath their tree." He looked more bumfoosled than usual. "All the patients got one. Oh, except for Mrs. Brown, Winnie. Nothing for her, poor soul."

Liam had Claire pegged. He knew if he rambled long enough she'd join in no matter how miffed, especially if there was mention of an injustice.

"Why not Winnie?" she asked.

"Did somebody say something?" Liam cocked his head and listened. "Oh, Claire, why not Winnie? Well, you see they discharged the fine woman several days ago. She's home for the holiday. And she wants us to come see her at first opportunity." With that, Liam sliced into Greta's pie with one shoe and took a jolly slide down the livestock ramp.

- 34 -

GLORY

"MERRY CHRISTMAS! Merry Christmas, duckys! In we come, ready or else!"

Eunice wore a bonnet colorful as Sunday funnies and her arms were full of food. I'd asked her not to bother cooking for our sakes but she mistook my meaning. She entered our room in cannonball fashion. I should have realized she'd go all out to put a jolly face on this Christmas.

"Merry Christmas, Eunice," I said, relieving her of a hot dish of something that smelled strongly of horseradish. "Roger, Merry Christmas, and Finlay. Glad you could make it." The girls joined us in a round of hugs and pecks. Roger and Finlay laid packages under the tree then Roger dropped into his visiting chair.

Eunice said, "I hate to be the bearer of bad news right now, but someone's gone and made a ruddy muck-hole of your roof and porch. Looks as if the Shinnett lads have been up to skullduggery again. On Christmas Day too." She shook her head and looked at me to catch if it was fresh news.

I looked at Liam, beaming like a choirboy and safe with Claire wrapped up like a prize pumpkin in his arms. "Yes, it is a mess, isn't it?" I said.

"We can help you get that cleaned up, ah, Mrs. Stone." Liam looked at Claire who'd raised eyebrows at the 'we.' "And I'll fix that hole in your roof straight off."

"Not today you won't. Today we're celebrating." For once, I wasn't faking it. I felt like a party. "And stop calling me Mrs. Stone or I'll call you Father McClelland."

It was then I saw Albert's silhouette in the doorway. At least he had the decency to hesitate. Yesterday I hadn't a clue what I would say to Eunice and Roger. I could not have allowed their nephew to cross our threshold even if it cost our friendship. But a grand visitor landed above us who'd changed the outlook. Father Christmas had come, and I wanted Albert there to greet him. Oh, I wanted him there. I never said I was above a good gloat, mind, especially when the planning was clean out of my hands.

"Come in, Albert. No sense standing in the cold on Christmas morning," I said with no cheer. It was the best I could do.

He cleared his throat and lowered his head. "Thank you, Mrs. Stone. It's right gracious of you." He left mud and transgressions on the mat and entered the Stone home.

"I believe you've met Liam?" I gestured to the man who held my daughter like the prize she was.

Liam extended one hand while the other arm held fast to Claire's shoulder. "Mr. Rand and I have met, yes." Liam looked him in the eye. I thought he might wring the blood from Albert's hand and breath out of Claire, but she didn't seem to mind.

Eunice held a prolonged look of disdain throughout the drama. Unless Albert confided in her, which I doubted or I'd have heard, she would never know that our friendship had dangled over a precipice. She would not understand that substance trumped superficial every day of the year.

Syd and Claire had arranged a sumptuous plate of holiday sweets to set on the coffee table. Syd and I were alone in the kitchen as the others found their places. I said to her, "What say we get this party started?" I glanced out the window. "I can't imagine where Axel is. Must have got tied up at station. I didn't think trains ran on Christmas."

"Wouldn't it be grand if he and Pop showed together?" Syd's face answered that one as she poured out cups of punch.

I combed her tangles with my fingers. "You mustn't count on that." Right or wrong, by now, I'd grown used to and privately fond of Syd's keeping John alive. Remarks she made did no harm as far as I could see. Claire became increasingly annoyed so Syd had learned not to speak of it in her presence. I never encouraged it or agreed that he had survived, and I was far from convinced otherwise.

I entered with the tray of sweets and saw Eunice digging at poor Finlay's ribs with her elbow so that she nearly upset his drink. She whispered something urgent in his ear. His nose and chin matched the berry garland. I tried not to stare, but when a sense of the festive seized me, it generally grabbed me by impulse and so I inquired.

"What's going on you two?" I chuckled at the siblings.

"Go on, before Axel gets here," Eunice whispered loud enough for us all to hear. She'd taken up Finlay's situation as well as my own in hopes the twain would meet.

Now all eyes were on a poor man who was not accustomed to the spotlight. He stood and approached me. He looked at the rug then at my chin. "I wonder if...I should like the chance to sit next to you at table, Mrs. Stone, uh, Glory." He'd nowhere to retreat so he flopped back onto a chair behind him, forgetting that Roger reposed there. Roger lost his breath at the lapful of surprise. Finlay was instantly up and at a loss as to where to go.

Eunice took over. "Brother of mine, it's Rufus for your life's companion, no mistake."

"You're welcome to sit next to me, Finlay. I should be delighted," I suppressed the laughter. Claire wasn't the only one with a heart for the underdog. "Here, have one of Claire's shortbread cookies." I offered him the plate and a dodge.

"I think Liam should have the honors of being Father Christmas," Syd said. "After all, he has the costume for it."

Liam didn't hesitate. "I should be happy to oblige, however, the venerable uniform is worse for wear after my scuttling over the globe last night, including several neighboring pastures. It wants a scrub. But in keeping with tradition I'll wear the hat and beard." He gave Albert a look before getting up to find the items. Albert remained in the straight backed chair requiring nothing but spiced nog and anonymity.

Liam reappeared as a combination of Father Christmas from the neck up and one of his elf helpers from beard down. He reached for the first package in ceremonious fashion.

"Attention all, attention. This one says, 'to Glory with love like a sis from Eunice.' Ho ho ho." His voice had lowered a couple octaves as he handed it over to my waiting arms. As a rule, I knew what my surprise was long before this as Eunice struggled with secrets, but this year she had remained mum on the subject. I opened the box and lifted back tissue paper to find a white, lace-edged peignoir set with delicate pink rosebuds dotting the bodice. It looked suspiciously like what one would wear on a honeymoon.

"How do you like it, love? Finlay helped pick it out." Eunice had no tact, and Finlay laid into a fistful of cookies.

"Well it's lovely," I said as I covered it back with the tissue.

"We'd like to see what Eunice got you." It was Syd, blasted curious kid.

No secrets with that crowd. I lifted it lilting from its confines.

The nighty floated out like a gossamer waft of midsummer night's dream.

Oohs and ahhs spilled from the women, even Eunice who'd bought and wrapped it—especially her. Well it was quite fine and likely cost a pretty penny. Maybe I would have need of such alluring fluff one day. I was thankful Axel wasn't there to see it and wondered a second time what could have kept him.

"To Mum, with love from Claire." He handed me another.

"Should I stand back?" I joked. When I lifted the lid from the box, there was a gorgeous, shining Bassett-Lowke model train engine. I cherished it right off. "Oh, Claire. How perfect." I admired the fine detailing.

"To remind you to dream. It blows real smoke too," she said with a grin.

"Thank you so much." I went over and hugged her. "I'm going to put it on my night table." I couldn't stop fondling the meticulously crafted toy. "Maybe my dreams will revive."

Liam dashed for the next one. It was small. With fewer gifts, we enjoyed the luxury of taking our time, watching each person's delight, genuine or otherwise.

"Ho, ho, ho! For the beauteous Claire Stone from a smitten Liam McClelland." Father Christmas carried it over then knelt beside her. "I know for a fact he's been good all year."

"Oh I don't doubt that for a second," Claire agreed. I wondered if she knew how much her joy showed. It was as if she had grown a new heart.

Liam was purpose driven. He lifted the small, but weighty box. The room and all souls within it held their breath as he laid out his plan for our daughter's future.

"From the day you stole upon me in the forest and I heard the laugh that charged my soul, I knew you were queen of my life— the beautiful and strong match to my needs. And even though I know I don't measure up in the looks department, although me mam says I clean up fairly well and lasses have said I have a queer sort of a, never mind. No one in the world could love you more than I do." A quick glance toward Albert. "If you'll have me, Claire Stone, I promise to respect the fire God used to fashion you, earn your respect and no less in return, and work ever so hard at making you happy enough to go on laughing with me." He presented the open box.

My stalwart Claire didn't need to restrain her tears. She was free indeed.

"I love you, you crazy leprechaun," was all she could manage as he removed the timeless gold symbol from the box and placed it on her finger. My hand went to my chest. John's ring went with me everywhere. She was free but I was not, and that was fine by me.

His eyes were wet when he asked her, "Can I be taking that for a yes then?"

"Yes, Liam. Definitely yes!"

They hugged, restoring Christmas to its former luster. Even the dogs reaffirmed their choice, wagging and looking around as if to say 'we knew it all along.'

Eunice was next up, swallowing Claire and Liam in her embrace like a surrogate hen. I knew she wouldn't hold a grudge that Claire had dodged her nephew. No doubt, she already had someone else floating in on the horizon for him. Now, it might be a different story with brother, Finlay. Eunice would continue to ram him at me until I yelled uncle or diverted her attention.

Albert ambled over, stuck his hand out to Liam and said, "Congratulations, old man. You're getting a real peach there you know." He flashed his tried and true dazzler her way and Claire pulled Liam close as a pit to the peach. Albert excused himself for a smoke.

"Thanks, Albert, you old herring gut. Better luck next time," Liam called after him. His chest puffed out like a blowfish.

"Well that was supposed to be the grand finale." Liam said. "I couldn't wait." He clapped—one single, decisive slap.

"That's all right, Liam, son." Liam was my boy now. Was it too early to call him the man of the house? How I wished John could have known him.

"Let's open the presents that came down the chimney!" Syd had each gift memorized. She had reported several times that the sack held three gifts—one for each Stone female.

"Very good," I said. "Liam, you didn't have to do that. I imagine that sparkler on Claire's finger set you back some." I hoped I hadn't embarrassed him.

He looked at me for a few seconds. "Oh, but they're not from me, no. I saw them sitting just outside the door and, on a whim, flung them down the chimney. I thought they were from Mr. Biggs." He looked around for Axel. "Was there no note?"

A spark of mystery ignited Syd as she examined the tags fastened carefully to each gift once more. It wasn't likely she'd missed anything the other forty-seven times.

She took the first one in hand announcing, "'For Claire.'" She delivered it to Claire's lap. "'For Syd.'" She tucked hers close. "'For Glory, my one and only true love.' Oh my." I reached for mine. "I don't like the tune of that," Syd muttered.

The wording embarrassed me. "Well, I think you must be right, Liam. They must be from Axel, though I think he went a bit overboard with the tag. Has anyone seen him today?" I looked at Eunice and Roger who shook their heads.

"Open 'em!" It was Eunice. "Or I will."

"You go first, Claire," Syd volunteered.

All eyes were on Claire as she undid the ribbon, since we felt the mystery that surrounded these tokens.

She lifted a dazzling thing from the box. As she examined it, shafts of rainbow lights sprayed over the walls, the ceiling, and us.

"It's a tiara," Claire said.

"How lovely," I said. It put me in mind of a cardboard version she'd worn as a child. She used to pretend she was a famous singer wearing that and my old dance dress with wedge heels.

"That's an odd gift, I say," Eunice chimed. "Biggs don't know Claire very well evidently. She wouldn't wear that, would you, Claire? Not the type."

Claire looked at the stunning headpiece—turning it over. "No. I mean, I might. I'm not sure it's from Biggs." She looked up and checked everyone in the room but no one claimed any knowledge.

Eunice reached for it. "Now, I would wear it on occasion."

She would wear it to burn rubbish or pluck a duck but I wouldn't say so.

"No!" Claire seemed to overreact as she drew the tiara out of reach. She eyed Albert who looked nothing but awkward. "It has special meaning, that's all." She was unsettled. Her hands shook as she placed it carefully back in its wrapping and closed the lid.

"Sorry, deary, I'm sure." Eunice was hurt.

"I'd like to know who it's from," Liam said. "A fine headpiece like that." He watched Albert.

Albert finally threw up his hands and exclaimed, "It's not from me. OK?"

"Me next." Syd's package was the largest and she couldn't wait and made quick work of the wrappings. "I think it's a...it is! It's my very own veterinarian satchel! See, it has my initials in gold lettering—SCS. Like Pop's." She unlatched the brass fastener. "Instruments too!"

While Syd pulled out and caressed half a dozen vetting instruments, I wondered where Axel was getting the extra money of late. Who else could have sent such extravagances?

I was aware of my beating childish heart as I undid the wrapping on my box in record time. The mood had turned. It wasn't much like a raucous Christmas gathering at all. Deep inside hills of white tissue paper rested a tin. I pulled it out.

I felt Eunice's breath on my right ear.

"Camp Coffee? Someone is having you on, old girl," Eunice busted out and into the same ear. "You sure got the short end of the presents, love. I'm extra glad I sprung for that nighty now." She grabbed a napkin to wipe her eyes. I wiped my ear and read the label.

Camp Coffee with chicory essence. There was a yellow lithograph of a small child carrying a sloshing cup with the words, "Daddy likes it full" below them. I realized about then that I might have the same look on my face Claire had as she contemplated her tiara. The tin was light so I assumed it was empty but I opened it. It wasn't empty. I stuck my hand inside and felt something soft. I pulled out a silk neckerchief. It was lovely, like many neckerchiefs I'd admired. But this one was red with apple green and yellow curly cues throughout—the same pattern as the shawl John had bought me twenty-five years ago. I got up and headed for the kitchen to think—to be away.

"I'm going to get the goose cooking," I said.

Eunice saw something wasn't right with me. She had trouble getting off the divan so Roger pushed on her bum with his foot. She swayed as she stood and followed me to the kitchen.

"Now, what's going on with you and them strange gifts?" She was a ravenous beast when there was news to be got. "I saw your lips go white and Claire—staring like a dress shop dummy."

"I don't have time to go into the whole conversation with you just now but this…is a part of it." I untied Syd's discovery from my strap. "It's John's wedding ring; Syd found it in Natty's stump. It has the Celtic cross inside. No one would have one like it. Plus…"

"Holy mother a pearl," Eunice breathed in as she gazed at it.

"There's something else, and don't yell out or anything." I handed her the ring. "Look real close where the cross is. Do you recall John had it engraved that way and cut a new mark for every five years we were wed? Well now, there are six extra slashes. I could understand if it was one more than when he left since our twenty-fifth would have been this past August, the day of your party, but there are five additional marks—fifty years worth. It has to be a message. Don't you think so?"

Eunice squinted and turned the ring at various angles. "I don't make anything of them. They're just gouges. Maybe Natty made them with his claws. You've been listening to too many Yard stories." She handed it back.

"You're blind. It means something, I tell you. Natty doesn't carry stuff with his feet. He carries them in his bill. Maybe John was trying to let me know he was alive. He could be in danger." I looked toward the others. "But where to turn next?" My whispering came in raspy bursts. "I've already tried everything I know. And too much digging in the wrong places might be dangerous for John…or England. I don't know." I stuck the ring in my pocket, opened the drawer with aprons and tossed her a splashy floral.

"Listen," I warned her. "I know it'll be a challenge, but you're my best mate and I'm counting on you. You have to promise me you'll keep what I tell you cinched tight under your gas mask. Do you understand?"

"There's more?" Eunice barely nodded and poised for incoming. "All righty. But I still don't see nothing."

"Never mind then. You might as well know I'm starting to believe Syd's right about his being alive. I have questions."

"Now you're having me on. What questions?" she asked. "Are you sure you're not just taking up with Syd because it's what you want to believe?" Eunice went to the pantry, opened the meat safe and pulled out the goose for which we'd pooled our coupons and money.

"I did at first. But too many things don't add up. And as Syd observed, we never saw John after the supposed accident." I went for the butter on the cold shelf.

"I'm not sure you would have wanted to, love," Eunice said quietly. She picked up the bowl of chestnut stuffing I'd made ahead and began cramming it into the bird's cavity. She hefted the pan into the Aga and closed the door, checking the temperature and the clock. She cleaned her hands and rubbed them together.

Eunice took the plates I'd gotten from the cupboard and set them on the dining table. "Look, the girls can do that. We've got time yet. Let's go upstairs and study that telegram together." Then she added, "And get out the death certificate."

"Eunice?" I said.

"What, love?"

"That's question number one. I've never received a death certificate. And when I visited the Army office after it, they had me file an official inquiry, but I haven't heard a word."

Eunice looked at me and I was afraid I knew the direction we were headed. I spoke first.

"Eunice, are you thinking what I'm thinking?"

"Ohhh." She moaned and shook her hands. "You have to know if it's John in that coffin." She jumped and knocked the table.

"Shhh! The girls must not find out."

"OK, OK," Eunice whispered loudly. "Well, what if John is inside? It's been a while." She placed her hands on my shoulders and looked into my eyes. "Are you ready for that?"

"Yes, I know. That's where you come in, my dear, intrepid Eunice." I leaned on her shoulder and looked back. "He, it might be wrapped. I've heard that sometimes that's what they do when a body is badly disfigured." I found my chair and tried to calm myself. Talking about this brought on the hints of a panic. "We may have to...unwrap it."

"I'm not sure what intrepid means but I'm thinking you want me to be the one to open the casket and look inside." Eunice's eyes bugged.

"Then, depending what you find, you could help me decide whether I should look for myself," I said. "I honestly don't know if I can, but at least you could prepare me and say what you see."

"Oh, love. I don't know. But I guess it's the only way you'll ever be at peace, dear girl." Eunice closed her eyes and bit her lip. "But, isn't there a law against digging up graves?"

"Of course there is. More reason to do it under cover of darkness. I think the sooner the better. Let's go later tonight."

"Tonight!" Eunice yelled.

"Shh!"

"Tonight?" Eunice whispered.

"We mustn't put it off or I won't be able to do it at all. We'll wait until the girls are asleep. Wear dark clothing. Do you have a shovel and a crowbar?"

- 35 -

GLORY

"**E**unice."

"Yes, love."

"What have you got on?"

We met at midnight--shovels, torches and pry bar in hand, also with knots in our throats and badgers in our tums. I felt as if all I'd attempted at finding out about John had led to this desperate moment.

"These are Roger's overalls. He uses them to clean out the septic. Why?"

"They smell poorly."

"Well, I doused them with an old bottle of lilac water." Eunice sounded hurt.

"It reeks like a perfumed outhouse. Was that your only dark clothing at hand?"

"I thought I needed something I wasn't afraid to get grubby. Are we going to stand here and flap over my wardrobe or get this done with? I'm about ready to turn back around and crawl into bed." Eunice took off toward the churchyard looking like someone from the wastewater treatment works, and I followed several paces behind.

Holly sprigs I'd left at John's grave as a Christmas remembrance still looked fresh. I'd visited every Friday after closing up shop. Often I'd sit and talk to him, tell him about the girls and me and what's doing in town. Laying out our problems--needing his answers and comforting way proved frustrating. Not sure what I expected, maybe sublime assurance that he was, in fact, alive somewhere. Mostly I'd stare down at his name on the stone with the dates and wonder if I could believe it. Now arrived the moment of truth, as they say in the novelettes. Out of everything I'd been through, this was by far the most trying challenge. I tried to prepare myself by imagining various scenarios, including the probability that the body may not be recognizable. I had to imagine the worst to prepare myself. Was that possible? I had never seen a decomposed human. But I felt sure that if John's remains rested there, no matter the condition, I would know. Never had I appreciated Eunice as I did just then.

"Should one of us keep a lookout whilst the other digs?" Eunice asked, assuming a guardian stance.

"I'm not sure we can afford the time. This will demand a lot from the both of us. Let's first check how hard the ground is."

Eunice stood at one end and I near the foot as we each sunk a shovel into the earth. Recent rain had made for pliable digging and for a while we made good progress.

"Eunice, do you have one of your stories you could tell about now? I need something to distract me from what it is I'm doing here."

"Not sure I can tell a proper story and shovel dirt simultaneous, but for your sake, I'll try, my girl." She leaned on her shovel handle, and I could hear her heavier breathing. She looked toward the dark night sky and what came out surprised me. "You know,

Roger and I was in love once. Did I never tell you how it was we met?"

"I don't recall your mentioning it."

"When I first saw Roger he was twelve feet tall."

Eunice could be one for extravagant tales, but this was a stretch even for her.

"I was in Kent visiting a friend whose family owned a hop farm. When my friend and I went for a stroll one gorgeous spring afternoon, we happened by the hop-stringers working on stilts. Roger looked down and whistled at me, nearly losing his balance in the bargain. He was slim and handsome and I liked his mouth right off even from so far down."

"A hop-stringer. How about that. No, you never told me." Our dirt piles grew as we talked and I tried to not think of the inevitable, but rather tried picturing Eunice and Roger as young lovers. It was surprisingly easy.

"He took me to the pictures. He enjoyed them then like I always did. But it were those lips of his that done me in. We kissed the whole matinee long. I couldn't keep off 'em."

She laughed and I wondered what all had transpired to alter their relationship so drastically. Did every old married couple turn down that route? I certainly hadn't seen John and I headed in that direction. I wondered if John had dissatisfied thoughts he didn't share with me. She had Roger and his lips to kiss whenever she chose, and I was digging up what was reported as my John's lifeless body.

As if reading my mind, Eunice added, "I guess I should try and appreciate Roger. But he doesn't bring much to the table these days, except the appetite of a elephant. He doesn't bring much to the bedroom, that's a fact."

"Stop, Eunice. I don't need to hear more." I rubbed my back which felt the strain low down. "Except, do you miss that part of your marriage much?" I took a breath and the rich scent of roses in the churchyard met me where I stood.

"Not like I used to. But I miss cuddling of a cold night. And holding hands on a walk to town." I couldn't think when I'd seen Eunice tear up. She wiped her eyes and said, "I'm feeling my muscles, that's a certainty."

"Here, have a chug of water," I handed off the jug across the widening hole. "I hope we're getting close; I need a breather. What time do you have?"

Eunice shined the torch at her wristwatch. "I make it to be about 2:00. We been at this for two hours? No wonder my arms feel like worm meat."

"Worm meat? Too bad we don't have Claire here to help. She grew strong working for Land Army, digging potatoes and post holes and what not."

"Go wake that chicken up!"

"Believe me, I thought to. But if I wake her, I'd have to get through a lecture from her first, then Syd will pop up and be all excited to see what's inside. She will not believe it's her pop. She could be damaged for life if it is. With four of us out here chattering and floundering around, we're sure to attract attention."

"Well I'm about beat." Eunice stretched out on the grass next another gravesite and read the name. "Minna Lina Gehlen Biggs Born 8-15-1875 Died 9-3-1944. Biggs' mum. I never knew they put John next to Minna Biggs. What did she die of?"

"Axel said her heart gave out one day after washing windows. A hard worker, seems she was always scrubbing at something." I looked around to check for anyone watching. "That vacant plot next John is for me."

"What if you was to remarry?" Eunice sat up and looked at me.

I could almost see Finlay floating around her head. "We need to stay at this. C'mon. Let's get it done and over. We only need to uncover the top enough to pry the lid." My stomach began to hurt so I pulled out a packet of antacid tablets and popped two in my mouth.

About a half hour later, I took a shovel full and hit on something hard. "Well, there it is." I felt weak in the legs.

Eunice finished off the dig on her side. We brushed the top clear.

"The casket still looks new," Eunice remarked. "Biggs sure was generous to spring for such a fine one. Glory? You alright?"

"Yeah. Okay. Let's get the crow bars. I don't think the lid is sealed, so hopefully we can find out quickly and be on with things." I began to cry. There was no way around it. "Okay, so Eunice, we'll pry the lid just open, then you lift it the rest of the way and I'll turn away and wait for you to tell me what or who you find. Are you ready?"

"Hell, no." Eunice seemed understandably reluctant. I don't think either of us realized how hard it would be to follow through on our plan when it came right down to the opening part. I just knew it couldn't be me.

"What about the smell?" Eunice had a point.

"Why don't we cover our faces with our jackets? Wrap them around like," I offered.

Eunice removed her jacket which stirred up the stink from Roger's overalls. At that point I wasn't sure I could make the call which smell might be the worse. I hoped silently she'd win out by default.

"Okay, oh lordy, here we go." She sounded like a woman with a mouth full of cotton balls, with the jacket over. "Glory, if I live through this, I don't want you ever giving me guff for anything ever again. Do you hear?"

"I hear." I sat poised to turn away as we opened the lid.

Eunice shook herself maybe to rid the heebie-jeebies, then, to my surprise, started to sing. She might have chosen a nice hymn, but no, it was a rendition of Jack Buchanan's ditty, *Everything Stops for Tea*. She sang softly.

"Oh the fact'ries may be roaring

With a boom-a-lacka, zooma-lacka-wee

But there isn't any roar when the clock strikes four

Everything stops for tea."

"Eunice, what are you thinking?" I inquired looking into her confused face.

Eunice continued being silly.

"It's a very good English custom, though the weather be cold or hot.

When they need a little pickup, you'll find a little teacup

Will always hit the spot.

"I'm thinking old Jack had a good notion when he come up with that song. Didn't you bring a jug of tea? I thought I saw you tuck something like it under your arm as we exited."

"No, Eunice. I did not think to bring tea. For cripe's sake. Did you bring the biscuits? What on earth?"

"Okay, alright." She looked at the object of her mission and continued to hum the perky tune under her breath. We slowly poised the edges of the bars into the crevice separating lid from bottom of John's casket. She took a deep breath and pulled down on the bar with me. I could see it gave way easily. I turned my face away and waited with eyes closed and heart thumping. My hand went to John's ring against my chest, and I rubbed it like a magic lamp. I could hear Eunice lift the lid the rest of the way. I waited.

"Oh, good God above! My stars of love," was all she said.

"Eunice!" I yelled out, then looked to make sure nobody was around. "Tell me what you see, for heaven's sake!" I whispered loudly. "Tell me! Should I look?"

She turned and clapped her hands on my arm. With the jacket still muffling her speech, all I could make out was, "Stone."

"Oh, Eunice, you can't mean it, it is John? I can't look. You've got to tell me plain." I thought I was going to be sick.

She yanked the jacket off her face and flung it into the bushes. She had a sort of a glazed smile on her face and her eyes were big and shiny. "No, Glory. I mean, stone! Stone. Stone is all that is inside this here coffin. As in two hunks of quarry granite and no body at home. Come here, old girl and feast your lovin' eyes!"

I crawled over and dared to "feast" as she suggested, but held my breath just the same.

I touched the stone slabs for myself. It was confirmed. "John's alive. Somewhere he is alive. He must be."

"Well he isn't here, that's a certainty! But, what now?"

I sat down hard on the dampness as I felt dizzy and weak. "I've no idea. I was sure tonight would end the questions. I couldn't have imagined a thing like this. Obviously John or someone wants us to believe he is deceased, but who and why?" I stared at the granite trying to wrap my brain around a new reality and another complication. "What should I tell the girls?" I didn't know whether to bawl or celebrate. "Would they replace a body with stone if it was too disfigured? Maybe to weight the coffin?"

"Oh, love, I think you can eliminate that possibility. They would let you know...but, they didn't, did they?"

- 36 -

SYD

Boxing Day

Dear Pop,

Christmas Day was splendid. Going over facts again and thinking about the Christ child being born in a feeding trough restored my faith you're alive, but I was terribly disappointed you didn't show. Since Natty reported in a few weeks ago chatting up 'Merry CHRIST-mas' the way you say it, I thought he was telling us you'd be here to celebrate. Such a party it would have been. Sweeter even than the one we planned before the telegram.

Oh, Pop! The vet satchel and instruments are everything I ever wanted! Mum and Claire were stunned with their gifts too. Brilliant clues, Pops, brilliant. Really got them thinking. Maybe soon, huh?

Natty appears to have narrowly dodged a bullet meant to do him in. Some of his pin feathers are missing and the message capsule was coming loose from his leg this last flight. He seems to be having a jolly time as a spy bird, though it may have become more dangerous for him. I do hope you got my letter. Anyhow, I suppose you did. The capsule was empty. Wish I knew who took a crack at him. It could have been fire from anyone, even Biggs. I'll be glad when this business is over with. I think it best I write less often; no sense putting Natty on the line more than necessary.

I understand you can't write back as Natty visits others at times. Are you working with secret codes? I'm dying to hear about it.

Meanwhile, big news is, hold onto your helmet—Claire and Liam are engaged! He appeared as Father Christmas after having been away a long time. They made it up and he popped the question and a ring on her finger yesterday during present opening. For once, she's shown good sense. I'm sure you'll like him as much as the lot of us.

Claire, Liam and I will be delivering Boxing Day goods to a few friends today. Since Sis and her beau can't seem to separate, they're taking a couple, and I'm delivering some of Mum's seeds to Mrs. Thompkins. She'll flip.

We'll meet at station for tea. After that, Mr. Biggs has arranged a grand surprise for Mum and the rest of us. He's providing rail passage to White-haven! Then down to visit St. Bees Head and Ravenglass. He hasn't told me all, but I suspect we may even spend the night at Barrow in Furness and ferry to the Isle of Man. I think Biggs has a chum on the island, someone with a foreign sounding name. I happened to see a note he'd taken from the telegraph with directions once we arrive there. It was nice of Biggs and will be a jolly trip, but I wish you could be here by then. He even bought me a ducky suitcase with a secret compartment. I haven't told a soul but you. Maybe I can be a spy too. I'm good at keeping secrets, aren't I? Think the MI5 could use a girl like me?

I smell apples cooking just now. Mum was moving around extra early in the kitchen this morning, fixing us a fancy breakfast. I'll bet you miss her pies something awful.

Love,

Syd

- 37 -

CLAIRE

*I*s Dad alive?

Privately, I'd removed the tiara from its wrappings four times—once just to admire it, and three times to look at myself wearing it. The list of possible givers was short. I'd eliminated everyone, and admitted to Liam that I'd begun to entertain doubts. He didn't say much.

My salvation had come in the nick. No telling where I'd have ended up with Albert circling. Would I have married him if he'd asked, a long shot in itself? Not likely. After stumbling on a pot of gold, one doesn't settle for silver plate. Liam was my rescuer. He'd landed on our housetop in baggy red britches and helped set my heart straight. Now, looking into his boyish face asleep, with spittle on my arm, I didn't want to move and risk waking the darling man.

I lay with my heavy end falling off the divan and Liam snoring softly. My arm went numb as I rolled over the events of yesterday and sucked their flavor like a piece of salted toffee. I think I heard

Mum come in from outside in the wee hours. She and the Quimby woman surely acted queer yesterday.

Once Liam and Greta were off the roof, Liam shed his reeking boots and we found a quiet place behind the Christmas tree. He explained that he hadn't needed much time in my absence to grieve the loss of the truest friend he'd ever had. His disappointment in not having met me sooner was genuine, and I wondered at the timing too, but who could say there wasn't an unseen purpose? He told me his best gift was the one he allowed himself in reclaiming me for his own.

I welcomed his gift of grace and forgave his disappearing act, inviting him in to a storehouse of lifelong dreams and doubts. Liam listened without fogging eyes, changing the subject, or offering more of a solution than a shoulder.

I confided Dad's seeming lack of enthusiasm for his firstborn. I told Liam about a nine-year-old girl—behind the wall of the room next to him, singing and believing she sounded rather good. She hoped her dad would drop his newspaper and come find the soloing angel. Had he come, Dad would have found her sitting cross legged on the bed, singing her heart out with a cardboard tiara and a hairbrush microphone. Maybe he did see me.

Liam suggested that Dad couldn't hear me with the wireless playing. Otherwise, given what he'd heard about John, he surely would have come. I chose to believe it. Liam said I was making up for lost time. I wondered what he meant.

Then Santa tossed a gift down the chimney that landed deep inside. The tiara cracked open a door of possibility, even though I was too afraid to throw my arms clean around it the way Syd had done. Yes, I, Claire, the bold talker, was afraid. In many ways, Syd was more the brave heart.

Christmas had been the best in years. Even the Christmases Dad had been with us during war cast a shadow because we knew he'd leave next day. At least he hadn't been overseas. His visits ceased as the war dragged on. We wrote but never heard back after his last letter that said they'd reassigned him, but we didn't know where. This holiday had gone a long way toward filling the empty places.

I was relieved Biggs hadn't shown, but hated the way Mum fussed on about him. That was a specter that lurked like a ghost signalman in the tunnel. Mum and Biggs. It was a dread I couldn't define, worse than one you could name. Best not to think on it until necessary. I wondered why Biggs didn't make himself useful elsewhere with post war duties. With his knowing German, they could surely use him in the British underground. Oddly, Syd had become his best and only chum it seemed. Just another example where little sis and I lived worlds apart.

I enjoyed teaching her to dance. Time spent on one another's toes seemed to heal a widening rift that began with Dad's enlistment. I wanted to be an example for Syd. We'd been close as girls. Now we laughed again. It felt relaxed and right.

I smelled something heavenly from the kitchen. Liam stirred.

જજ

It was Boxing Day. Liam, Syd and I made up an assembly line on the dining table with Mum popping in with tired eyes, a flushed face and nervous manner to check our capabilities. The Stone family ritual was to do up a few gift boxes for elderly friends and deliver a surprise of cheer. Mum said we were on the fence, meaning the Stone family could have been the ones on the receiving end since losing a loved one. But the business had done well, and she felt like doing the bestowing.

Following gift opening yesterday, Mum and Eunice seemed shrouded in mystery. Anytime someone inquired after it, they'd look at one another stone faced and change subject or ignore it altogether. Mum was in a fret over closed offices as if she had some official business that wouldn't wait. It was blasted frustrating to be sure and I figured it must have something to do with Dad. Twenty was old enough to be included in important family business and I had renewed interest. I suspected Biggs lurked somewhere in the mix since he'd never shown or rung up.

With Mum and Eunice busy with secrets, Mum allocated the deliveries to us three. Since we'd all made rather merry the night before, the work crew slept late. We didn't get boxes together until eleven o'clock so decided among us that it would be best to divide the routes. Liam and I were like Siamese twins and liked it that way. That left Syd, but she never seemed to mind playing the lone wolf. Since our chimney gifts, she too had acted all the more like a bubble at bursting.

One gift box held seeds from Mum's magical flower garden. She'd tied several packets in ribbon with Mary Thompkins as the lucky recipient. Mum had decided to extend the laurel out of respect for Mary's age and desperation. Syd looked forward to seeing her face when she delivered them, with compliments, from her mum.

Syd started for one end of town and Mary's cottage. Liam and I took biscuits and jams toward the opposite edge of Rakefoot where Tom Mayor lived with his spinster daughter, Spivey, the woman with the glass eye. Syd and I learned that Spivey removed the eye at night — placing it in a dish on her night table. Syd wasn't a squeamish person, but she'd recently confided she hoped Natty never toted that eyeball home. I heartily agreed.

"Meet you back at station for tea and biscuits at 3:00, right?" I called after her. Syd brought to mind Little Red Riding Hood in her red corduroy jacket.

"Right!" Syd called back. We heard but were preoccupied.

- 38 -

GLORY

wo hunks of granite lay reposed inside John's fancy casket. I'd seen it with my own eyes, but kept reminding myself it was not imagination at work. Eunice would back me up. John was alive. I never made it to bed.

Between trying to come to grips with our discovery and act normal for the kids' sake, I worried attacks would reclaim my days. By the time Eunice and I reburied the coffin, and cleaned ourselves up as much as could be, it was nigh to four in the a.m. I was shaking and Eunice wouldn't shut up and kept singing the tea song claiming it was four o'clock, after all. She went on like a henhouse at egg-laying until I thought she'd wake the neighborhood.

I needed someone to help clear my head. In fact, there seemed so many ways I could turn with the little I had to go on, I froze like an opossum caught in a garden raid. Facing the possible danger for John with a wrong move, and sure Eunice would over dramatize, I wished for a reliable source. I needed wisdom, and it couldn't come from Biggs this time. He was partial and admonished me whenever I so much as mentioned John's name. Sound heads were in blasted short supply.

So, I gathered my thoughts and resorted to what John had referred to as his primary offense—prayer. The word sounded strange. I planned to petition a God from whom I'd become estranged, for the first time since seeing John off at station—him smiling unnaturally and me blubbering requests for safety and a speedy return into his mac collar.

I was the nervy one with my fickle attitude, but before trying to fix a Boxing Day breakfast, I went outside and met the winter nip again, now with a chill in my heart. My bum met a cold bench beside the sleeping garden—the same bench where I'd delivered on our youngster the worst news of all. I remember feeling the diabolical liar as I said it and wondering why. I asked aloud, though it felt strange like I'd gone dotty, and maybe I had and didn't give a care.

"Dear God, before I beg favors, I should apologize for the sorry lack of communication. I guess I knew you were there, I just figured you didn't need me pestering, and oh, that's not right. Forget that." Now there I was after all this time asking after his help, and me trying to pull the wool over his eyes, all pious and shuffling up. I reckoned that if God was listening, he sensed mendacity right enough so I might as well have it out straight. "Truth is I didn't believe you were there. Not sure I do now." I listened for, I don't know—thunder maybe. But the air around me was so thick with quiet it was as if there was an eavesdropper holding his breath, waiting. "Somebody there?" I scanned the garden.

I saw the stick cross that John made after burying Jack, our first pup. It was thirteen years ago we buried Jack. Through all thirteen, I'd faithfully replaced the sticks when the wind and storms knocked them about. John was a believer in supernatural things, that's why I did it. There was substance behind the cross to him. I thought about the one that started it all and the fact of it standing vacant all this time. The story seemed too good to be true that we could live forever in a paradise, without war or pestilence. Maybe if it seemed that way, it must be so. I wanted to believe, yet knew I couldn't force God's hand if he was listening, and if he wasn't, well then, it didn't matter. I chose to believe in his capabilities. The result was in his court.

"I can't put this thing right on my own. And now, with the rocks in the coffin, message in the ring and those mystifying gifts, I must know what's happened to John. Is there something I should be doing?" I allowed the tears. I looked to the clouds, and blinked to clear my vision as salty drops mixed with cold ones on my tongue. "Please help me. I have got to put the matter to rest. A woman can only take so much, dear God, though apparently, it's a lot more than she thinks. And please keep our girls and Liam safe while I figure it out." The heavier rain came, pelting my head. "I'm…obliged and amen." I got up, dusting off my backside and wiped my cheeks against my shoulders. Anyway, I felt better. We'd see if anything came of it.

Returning to the comfort of my kitchen, it felt like a solid hug from Aunt Nancy. Only yesterday, I'd spent most of the day cooking for the loved ones within its familiarity. But today it was a smiling aunty with a hug. Very well, I could use one.

There were activities to fill this, a day of reflection and planning. A Boxing Day breakfast wasn't like most and neither were the new circumstances surrounding John's absence. Youngsters stayed up carousing night before so I knew I'd have time to make a dazzler even though I was exhausted and my thoughts were not on it. If I did nothing special, the children would be onto me right enough, asking more questions. Any road, without sleep, I was able to push through the morning.

I'd invited Eunice over and made her promise three times not to blurt out anything or act stranger than usual. County offices closed on holidays so we couldn't visit a records clerk again until tomorrow. Even after the ring, I'd ground under foot any hope of

278

John's being alive, that is until Christmas. Who but John would have known to give those gifts? I had only Biggs' word for John's accident and the telegram, which I now knew to be phony. I was beginning to doubt Biggs' too, about a lot of things. When I questioned Collins, he was a perfect clam.

I'd worked to convince myself John was gone; the concept of his reappearance seemed farfetched in the extreme. One thing of which I was certain, he would have come to us if he was able—crawling if need be.

We'd start the morning with coffee. Real coffee. None of that powdery muck. We were still using coupons for most everything; tea, sugar, butter and flour, coffee too, but I'd saved up. I dug out the coffee pot, hoping it would remember its job. Then I began to peel and slice some nice Bramley apples for Mum's Apple Charlotte.

Peelings spiraled away with thoughts of recent events. Axel had never shown yesterday; naturally, I wondered why. If he didn't ring soon, I would see him at station. He owed me some explanation. I sensed very definitely that he wanted forward progress where we were concerned--out of the question for now. Biggs wanted John's death and Trudy's disappearance put behind us and squelched any fond memory talk. It had been too soon for me to eliminate John from my life, let alone my vocabulary. And why had Axel become so agitated with the two old men? I didn't like that about him. They were harmless as could be.

Claire had never trusted Biggs. Now I think on it, Claire was blind to Albert's fakery I saw right along. Maybe I had blinders on with Axel. I've heard it said that a woman desperate in need of love would make a man out who she wanted him to be. Later she'd complain of how he changed. Women's hearts had big imaginations.

The apples were ready so I turned them into a stewing pot with a small amount of water and set about making a sugar puree. I turned the oven to 200 and began cutting bread slices into wedges to line the buttered mold. It felt fine using my hands for baking again. Patting up a satisfying pasty or loaf helped gather life into a familiar shape. Also, I knew from years of practice that the aroma of apples cooking down was a sure way to draw loafers out of their sacks. Thought will out.

"Mmm. There's nothing like sweet goodness from the oven to bring a man to his senses." Liam was up. "What is that heavenly concoction, Mrs. Stone?" He straddled one of the green chairs and watched with his wild Irish hair splayed like a worn broom.

I pretended not to hear.

"Mrs. Stone?"

I looked around. "I don't see a Mrs. Stone here but I can tell you it's Apple Charlotte you're drooling over."

Liam laughed and I liked the sound of it. "Right you are, Glory." He tipped forward against the table, and I hoped he didn't fall and skin his chin. "I'll get used to it."

"That's an improvement, but Mum will do even better." I looked forward to that. "Sorry about you having a lazy woman. Nothing to be done about it now. Any fool can see you're hooked solid. Has she stirred so much as a big toe?"

"I don't know, but I can examine her lovely feet if you like," Liam offered. "I know right where to find them."

"That's all right. I saw you two mighty snuggly on the divan this morning." I poured the apple concoction into the mould and began covering it with more buttered bread.

"You must have got up early this morning. If you'll excuse the observation, you're looking a little tired around the eyes. Did you sleep okay?" Liam asked me point blank. He helped himself to a mug of tea. "Thought I heard voices in the garden."

"I was up quite late. Voices? That was likely Syd talking to her pets. She gets up early to tend the animals then goes back to bed weekends and holidays. I felt ashamed, but I didn't want Liam to know I'd been out. He'd ask why and if I told him and it came to naught but cloudy breath, I didn't want to bring embarrassment on him.

"What's all the yakking about out here? Hi, Liam." Syd emerged petting Kate and looking as if she'd hibernated with a den of foxes. "Something smells good."

Our family was lifting the shade on life. Though the girls would never leap, flying into our bed on a Sunday morning and snuggle under the covers with the funnies and a torch, grandkids might. They said that time healed wounds, but Liam provided the balm to get rifts knitting together, no mistake. He'd appeared alone in the forest one gray day when Claire couldn't resist, and she blamed curiosity instead of providence for the draw.

"Eunice will be here soon. Why don't you get your sis up and make yourselves presentable. Plus I could use a little help here." I knew happiness by its long absence, and I was curious of its timing, as if the tide were about to turn for us.

"When do we eat?" Syd asked. "I'm famished."

"With a little help…" I repeated. "Perhaps forty five minutes."

"I'll lend a hand!" Liam was up and dipping a finger into the mold.

"All right. Let's see, what can a man do in the kitchen?"

"Anything a woman can do, and better," he shot back. "Most of the world's finest chefs are of the male persuasion."

"Yeah, but they learned to cook from their mums and grannies." I took bacon from the icebox. "Here, if I get you an apron and a pan do you think you can fry this pork without burning it?" I pushed away a shock of his hair with the back of my buttery hand.

"My dear Mum, as a matter of fact I can." Liam elbowed me lightly on his way to the sink to wash up. I couldn't help think how he and John would get on, given the chance.

❧

The youngsters went off powered by goodwill, coffee and apple pastry. Tomorrow, Liam would head south to finish his schooling, which would be hard on Claire, especially since her job at Dalemain didn't begin for another few months. Stone Revival Antiques would have to occupy her. I hoped my clientele would oblige.

With time to fill, Eunice and I settled ourselves on the divan and looked at one another unable to speak right off, unbelieving what we had unearthed just hours before.

"Did you sleep?" I asked.

"Not a blasted wink, are you kidding?" Eunice shoved in another bite of breakfast.

"I know what let's do." I was out of my seat. "Let's make a list of everything that's happened thus far and follow with possible explanations as to who might be at back of it and why." I retrieved a sheet of paper from the desk and laid it on the table before us. I handed Eunice the pencil since my nerves were high.

"This isn't something you can put to a vote, you know," Eunice said. "Either he's coming home or he's not."

"I know that. Wait, why wouldn't he come home? We know he's not dead."

"We only know he's not in coffin. He could still be dead elsewhere. Another thing, husbands have been known to do outlandish things in the name of duty or country or, another woman." Eunice looked nervously out the window.

"Another woman? What put that crazy idea in your head?" I felt for John's ring. I thought about Mavis, and how I once envied her long, golden hair and crystal blue eyes.

Eunice talked at the window. "Didn't Biggs say he saw Mavis Cartwright and she was working at Dalemain?"

"Yes, he said that, but ..."

"And your bird has been croaking out Dalemain to everybody like it's been spending time there."

"Oh, Eunice how farfetched can you be!" I was relieved the kids were gone.

"All I'm saying is if we're writing down all possibilities, we should include Mavis, that's all. Just a name on a list."

"They dated in high school. There is no connection. Do not put her name on that list." I hated to admit her picture had entered my brain more than once. She and John were very close, and Axel said she was still single after all these years. "Now, let's start writing down facts, not suppositions. Let's accomplish something here before it's time to join the youngsters." I checked the clock.

"Okay, all right, you mean like the fact that John went missing from his coffin?"

"Yes. Who would want everyone to believe John was dead if he isn't and why?"

"And if he is dead somewhere, why would they fool us with the granite and what happened to his body?" Eunice went off into her stage persona, using her hands to describe a scene. "Was it too mangled up and they needed weight in the coffin to make sure it stayed down under in a flood? Maybe that's why Biggs called for a closed casket. Cause he knew they wouldn't put a body smashed over by a train in there."

"Eunice, please. There's the ring. Write it down."

"You think it contains some message."

"I don't THINK it contains a message. I know it for fact. What else, who else…"

"Don't fly off. I'm trying to be, what's it called? Objective, yeah. So, if he didn't make those notches, who would and why? And we know Natty's been seen flying north of station. And that it was him what found it." Eunice wet the pencil and looked pleased. "That's about three things for the "alive" column, but one's a question. Does that count?"

"Well, yes. They're all questions at this point. That's a good start. And don't forget the gifts." I got up and retrieved the chicory tin from the kitchen counter.

"Didn't you reckon those were from Biggs?" Eunice asked.

"I didn't want to let on until I could mull it over, but no, I don't think that for a minute. And I don't believe Claire thought so either. I know Syd didn't, so who am I trying to fool? Syd's certain John's alive and that he knew exactly what she wanted—her own vet case, initialed just like his." My stomach began to ache. "Axel might have guessed at her wanting a case, but wouldn't have known the instruments to buy or had access to them."

"You think a ghost brought 'em? Just stepped out of the grave for a smoke and left them by your door?" She shook her head then caught herself. "I'm sorry, love, but why on God's blue planet wouldn't he just show himself if he was that close? It don't make a peck of sense." She took my hand and patted it between hers. "I don't want to see you fret yourself into the loony bin."

"Well where do you think John is then?" I pulled my hand away. How could Eunice not see the overwhelming evidence? I began fiddling with John's ring still fastened on my strap. "The fact there's no body in the grave is fairly blasted obvious to me! And those gifts represented things about us that Axel couldn't possibly have known or cared about. Like Claire's tiara, she had one similar when she was small. She wore it all the time, prancing about to get her Dad's attention. And this tin." I held it about an inch from her nose. "Who would give me something like this for Christmas?" I set it down hard on the table. "I called him chicory, remember?"

"The neckerchief was nice," she replied. "Maybe old Biggs didn't have a box to wrap it up in." Eunice still wanted to argue.

"Eunice. Don't you recognize the material?" I pulled out the fabric. "It's the same as the shawl John bought me twenty-five years ago." I stroked the piece, wondering if John's hands had recently touched it. I buried my face in it, trying for the smell of him. "He must have had the shawl made up special, kept some of the leftover material and took it with him when he left for Army work. I don't know, but the coincidence is too much."

Eunice was embarrassed. "Well how should I remember?

284

You've only worn it the once, haven't you?" She hefted herself off the chair and looked in the icebox. "Don't you ever buy beer?" She slammed the door and rattled the empty cookie jar on top. "Last time I saw the shawl was when you were dressing for your date with Mr. Biggs." She couldn't look at me when she said that.

Neither of us spoke for a bit.

"Anyway, I just don't want you to get your hopes too high," Eunice broke the silence.

I stood up and we hugged. She patted my back.

I picked at the edges of the Apple Charlotte remains. "Let's move forward. OK, we could go down to station and join the rest for tea and biscuits," I said, feeling more enthused than hungry. "The children are meeting there at 3:00."

Eunice got up and looked out the window. "Storm coming. Looks nasty. Hope the young'ns wore their waterproofs."

"They did. They don't have but a couple deliveries." I was uneasy and wished they hadn't gone.

A Nor 'ester had blown in from Highlands—first big storm of the season. The force prodded holly bushes to knocking and scratching against window panes. Uncommon darkness settled on the house and us. Trees over the house pelted the roof with twigs that clattered and sounded like small fists rapping. I thought I heard noise from John's work shed, like someone knocking things about.

"Did you hear that?" I looked at Eunice. "It can't be Syd."

"Yeah, I heard." Eunice's eyes grew large and she seemed to be holding her breath. "Could be the wind?"

She looked beyond me to the window. She let out with a beastly howl that sent me under the kitchen table. "What? What?" I shouted. "What is it?"

"Face." She looked under the table at me then closed her eyes. "A face in the window."

"Who is it, for cripe's sake?" A soft rap at the door and Eunice joined me under the table. "A fine pair of detectives we make." I started to climb out after peeking at the door from behind the tablecloth. "I can't see."

In an instant, our lights went out. I emerged from the table, knocking my head against the edge in the dimness and called out, "Hold on! I'm coming." Eunice remained submerged.

I looked toward the door window and could make out someone in a dark raincoat and hat. Axel maybe. My eyes had adjusted enough to make my way to the cupboard drawer and retrieve the torch. Not wanting to blind whoever it was, I held it away as I walked toward them.

"Who is it?" Eunice squeaked from below.

"I can't tell," I said. "Are you coming out?" I shot a beam of light under the table.

"Well, now I'm blinded," she said. "Be careful, Glory. It could be a prowler, what with that noise we just heard."

The visitor sounded again and tried the knob this time. He cupped his face with his hands and tried to see through the window. By then, the rain was torrential, and there was a waterfall pouring off the roof just beyond my stoop. He saw me and remained still, staring.

I pulled back the lock and turned the knob. "Axel?" The door opened to a sodden figure I yet did not recognize. Whoever it was, they had a queer way—a slow, eerie movement that made me want to shove them back and ring for police.

"Hello?" I peered into the face with my torch as a hand shot up to guard his eyes. He went to remove his hat and moved inside. "Tell me who you are or get out!" I raised the torch.

"Just hold on, Glory. One minute." It was a man and he knew me, but I didn't make a connection. He reached over and pulled a chair from the table, setting it behind me. Then his hands were up as if to take hold of my shoulders or fend me off should I start swinging. I backed away and scooted the chair so that it squawked against the linoleum.

"Don't blind me, Glory. I want to see your beautiful face." He stood there. "Everything's going to be fine. I'm sorry to do this to you."

- 39 -

GLORY

The voice was a weary example of one I recognized.

The dogs knew the stranger as they came at a gallop from the rear of the house.

"Wait." I looked and felt unsteady, but he held me. I peered at him trying to get a clear eyeful, afraid that I'd gone over the brink as Biggs warned I might. But Jingles and Reggie bore out my suspicions, jumping and yipping and slobbering, celebrating in joyous fashion the return of their master.

"You're not John." I shook my head and turned away. "John's dead, or missing. For five months."

He scooted the dogs back and faced me. "I'm right here, Glory. To stay." He kissed my cheek but I didn't feel it.

A solid thud came from under the table. "Bloody hell! What now? What did you say?" Eunice came out rubbing her head. "Did I hear you say...?" She stood with her mouth gaped open wide enough for the last train to London. "John Stone? My God, man! Where have you been? Have we got a lot to tell you! Right, Glory?"

"Eunice. Please get Glory a cold cloth and some brandy if we have it. She looks like she's headed for one of her fainting spells, poor darling."

I knew both voices; one of them I'd heard in dreams that seemed impossibly real, but my mind retreated to find sanctuary; somewhere safe that might give me the time, strength, and guts needed to throw the throttle into a sudden reverse. I was a heap on the kitchen chair again trying to understand. There was no cake, no smoke, no telegram this time.

"Don't touch me. Nobody touch me," I heard myself say.

Eunice shuffled up. "Here you go. Oh my God! Glory, you got to come round for this, love." She handed me a glass but saw I couldn't hold it, so she fed me the drink. "There's a girl." I coughed as the liquor caught in my throat. She laid a cool bit of terrycloth on my neck, and I began to revive, then cry.

"Dear God, you're back," I managed, while still gazing at the floor. I was afraid to move, to look up, or do anything that might shatter the vision. "Syd was right."

He moved closer and lifted my chin. I met John's loving eyes. He helped me off the chair and cupped my face in his hands. "I'm back, Glory. For good and all."

I looked into the dearest face that had started to lapse into shadow. I'd pictured those adoring eyes watching me sleep, and had seen them in every crowd. "You're back for good," I affirmed.

"I'm frightfully sorry we had to put you and the girls through this. We're nearly through."

"Hold me, John."

He tore off his dripping raincoat, took me in his arms and kissed me full on. I went and grew faint again. Only this time it was a welcome, intoxicating kind of a faint and I remained awake, because I wouldn't have missed this reunion for the world. "I can't believe it." I poked and prodded at him. I buried my face in his shirt and inhaled. And cried some more.

"I was afraid we might lose her from shock there for a minute," Eunice said, her teeth celebrating wholeheartedly.

"Come here, Eunice." John didn't release me but opened up another side for Eunice.

She began blubbering and wailing so loud she put me to shame. He was my returned husband after all.

"Welcome home, lad!" She said between breaths. "Welcome home." She found his handkerchief and blew her nose then put it back. She kept patting his back. "W…We dug you up last night." She laughed uproariously. She got us to laughing too. That was the thing about her. "Why the granite in yonder grave?" She held her shoulders.

"Good heavens! You know about that? Ladies, I wish I could explain now, but…where is everyone? Where's Syd?"

"She's delivering seed packets to Mary Thompkins. The girls are meeting at station for tea at 3:00. What's wrong?" I knew that look.

"Well, likely everything is just fine. Don't start worrying, Glory." He kissed me again. "But, I'll feel better once I find Syd." He reached for his coat.

"Is she in danger? Oh, John. What about Syd?" I struggled to form a coherent thought. "She knows more than she's told me, isn't that right?"

He held my shoulders. "I need your help."

He looked at his watch and talked as we pulled on our coats. "We have some time. She's likely on her way to station. Our dear old station master, Biggs has been up to some post-war shenanigans. It's because of him I had to play possum—to help the Army and Scotland Yard trace his communications with a certain Klaus Fuchs—deliverer of H-bomb secrets to the Soviets." He opened the door for us.

We stepped off into the rain and when John moved, I noticed how loose his clothes hung on him. "Axel Biggs?" This would be a

Boxing Day for the books, no mistake. "What does that have to do with Syd?" My stomach hurt and I felt the old panic commence. I didn't know how to handle the conflicting emotions of John's return with a frightening report about Syd's safety.

"I can't go into it right now. He and Syd have become quite chummy, you know."

We started for John's car. "Yes, I know. She felt rather sorry for him. But I wouldn't believe that he was dangerous." Claire had been right too. "Oh, John! What if Syd isn't at station?"

John's sedan was out from the garage and waiting. Good thing Claire had driven it to Keswick now and again. "Eunice, you head over to Mary's in case she hasn't left or is en route. If you see her, don't let her go. Glory and I will drive over to station and try to intercept her before she gets to Biggs. Hopefully, we won't need to go beyond Rakefoot."

"OK, John. You can count on me," Eunice agreed. "I'll sit on her if needs be."

ॐ

The station hummed with holiday traffic as we stepped inside. Several villagers stopped and stared at John as if they'd seen a ghost and therefore, didn't speak. I found it challenging not to stare at him myself, but Syd could be in danger and I scoured the crowd for her.

There, before us lounged my mannerly old chums. General Milton Pickering and Fenwick Smyth appeared to be holding up one side of the bookstall, though only one made an appearance of reading. They certainly had visited Smyth's cousin often and spent a lot of time in station as well.

"Good afternoon and how are you this holiday, Mrs. Stone?" Milton held John's arm and shook his hand solemnly. "Nice little surprise, what?" He turned sideways toward me with a devilish grin.

"Yes...indeed. You two know one another?" I asked.

John answered, "Milton and Fenwick are Yard men. They've been keeping a watch on you and the girls, my dear—making certain Biggs didn't take things too far in a personal direction; we know he had plans. Am I right, General?" He snugged me next to him and I felt the fool for the second time that afternoon. Milton was, at least, a real general.

"Wick and I have been busy, that's for sure. Now we wait." He gave the station a look over and out the door. "Rest of the boys should be here any moment, but we've lost track of our man Biggs, temporarily. He can't be far. No worries. They're bringing the dogs."

"Well. I have been solidly in the dark, haven't I?" Annoyance crowded fear. Yard men, huh.

"Have either of you seen Syd?" John looked at Wicky who had his frightful nose stuck between some pages.

"No, sir. Not a sign of her. Where's she supposed to be?" The general snapped-to.

"She's delivering a box just up road by herself, and then she's to come here for tea. It's nearly time. Have you seen Claire and Liam?"

"No. Not them either," replied the general as he checked his timepiece.

The general asked John, "What was in Syd's last letter?"

"Letter?" I regretted asking as soon as the word popped out and suspected at this point that I may as well keep quiet since I was a complete ignoramus where their secret society was concerned. "I do wish someone would tell me what the devil is going on."

"Natty hasn't shown for a couple weeks now. I reasoned that Biggs might take advantage of the extra holiday commotion at station." He glanced at me. "Based on things Syd had written, I knew it was time to break cover," John replied. "I received the order yesterday afternoon. Good thing too. Wasn't sure how much longer I could wait."

I began to say 'Natty?', but kept my gob shut and continued looking frantically for Syd's red jacket.

I looked out the door again and saw Claire and Liam headed our way, but Syd wasn't with them.

"Oh, John." I took his arm. "Claire's coming!" We looked at one another and I burst into tears again. I wanted to hold this moment in time, but I so wanted Syd here with the rest of us.

I watched as they entered the station and looked round. They nearly headed for the refreshment room, then Claire turned our direction. She lowered her head and stared.

"Claire," John said to himself. "Claire!" He yelled and waved, watching her come toward us until she stopped dead in her tracks.

"Dad?" Claire spoke. She looked at us.

"My angel girl." He held out his arms and she ran to him. "I'm so sorry, so sorry dear Claire." He stroked her hair as she buried her head in his chest and let go. "For many things."

I vaguely noticed folks staring, but it mattered not being the spectacle. In the midst of the marvel, I worried for our fifth portion and kept a lookout.

"Syd was right after all." Claire looked up at him, perhaps to make sure she wasn't dreaming, as had I. She held on. John looked into her teary face and wiped her cheeks with the back of his hand. "Is she here? Has she seen you?"

"Not yet. Oh, my girl. I dreamed of this moment. I'll be able to explain everything, but right now, we've got to find her. Have you seen Biggs?"

Claire couldn't stop staring and touching. Now we both fairly hung, one on each arm. We weren't letting him get far—or even walk with proper balance.

"Syd? Why, she was to visit Mary Thompkins. What's wrong?" The way she asked, I knew Biggs was already standing in the dock in her mind.

The rumble and hiss of a train stole our attention when it

pulled up to the platform. The doors opened and out came the porter to set the steps. A few passengers made their way toward the refreshment room. It was the 4:15 on its way to Carlisle and on to the beaches at Workington.

Milton and Fenwick hurried over and joined several policemen who spread out down the train. They would keep a close watch on any new boarders. I heard dogs yelping behind station. *Bloodhounds?* I couldn't wait much longer without doing something.

About then, Liam became conspicuous as the odd man out. We'd forgotten the poor fellow in all the chaos. His hand shot out toward John.

"Mr. Stone, I presume?"

John looked at him and allowed his hand to be shaken.

"Oh, golly. I clean forgot about Liam!" Claire turned. "Dad, this is a heck of a time to be introducing you to my fiancé, but here he is in the flesh—Liam McClelland, from Bailieborough, Ireland. Liam—John Stone, my dad." Claire began to cry again.

"Well now, I didn't know if I'd have the chance to meet the infamous Mr. Stone this side of the hereafter. Such a pleasure it is too." He pumped away. "Such a grand pleasure."

"It's good to finally meet you too, Liam. Welcome to the family. I know more about you than you might think." He checked his watch again. "It's 3:30. Not like Syd to be late."

"Mrs. Thompkins might be talking her head off about our garden, "Claire suggested.

"I can't just stand here. I'm going to start for Mary's," I said.

As I headed for the door, I heard John say, "Wait, Glory."

"I've got to find her, John!" I shouted. It felt odd calling him by name.

"Listen! Eunice is already checking with Mary. I think I know where Syd is. And Biggs."

"Even so, shouldn't we separate and begin looking different directions, in case?"

"Yes, we will if necessary." He looked at me with concern that started my stomach churning again. "But you alone must be the one to try where I'm thinking." He took me to him. "Anyone else finding them could prove dangerous for Syd."

Of course, I knew. It's where he spent most of his free time. Syd spoke of it often. "Biggs' basement."

- 40 -

GLORY

Basements did not rank highly among my favorite places. Granny had a roomy one in their centuries-old cottage. She used it for cold storage and home-canned wares. When called on to retrieve a jar of pears or blackberry jam, I imagined fat, leggy spiders ready to drop on my neck and rank-smelling bogey men waiting at the base of the funneling stairwell.

Just when my heart had stopped palpitating after grave digging, up cropped this assignment. But I was ready to do whatever seemed necessary to secure Syd's safety. I felt like I was walking in blind, and maybe that's how John wanted things. If I had the full story, I mightn't have enough nerve. My worrisome imagination did the job well enough. Axel was apparently a traitor to Britain—a shocking discovery in itself. How that could involve Syd was beyond me, but a potent mixture of ignorance and adrenalin had me on my way.

I wasn't alone. John, the Yard men, and two officers followed off apace. If Biggs didn't know authorities were on to him, he was deaf, blind and stupid. If he was aware, then he was not only the abused man Syd described; it made him a cornered and dangerous criminal. I took no weapon save my relationship with him and what power that bore. Words could alter the outcome for good or ill. I begged God for the right ones, hoping I hadn't used up my quota on John.

I slipped out the back of the station and heard those dogs moving through the woods behind, doing what they loved best. Frenzied yelping made me wonder what they'd found. The grass was tall and sloppy as it slapped my legs. His door was locked. I turned to the group behind, and John pointed to the closest window. I moved over and lifted the sash slowly as it gave way to an eerie vacancy. I glanced back at John. He nodded and gave the V for victory sign.

Sidestepping a mud puddle and sliding one leg over the sill, I hung onto the top of the window casing and pulled myself through. I stood to gain bearings despite legs that threatened to buckle. It was strange being in Biggs' house then. The room looked as it had when I'd been over for drinks. We'd listened to records and talked. I sat right there on his tan sofa—above whatever I was about to discover. But the atmosphere had become thick, like something malignant daring me to the challenge.

Syd had told me where the trap door to the basement was located. Someone, likely Biggs, had pushed aside the carpet that covered it. There was the door sure enough. My heart pounded as I took hold of the handle. I took a deep breath and lifted slowly to avoid any creaking. The gaping maw of a musty unknown opened as if to suck me down whole. Daylight brightened the first couple of steps as if there were no others, but just a drop beyond. Apparently, power was out over the village, and I had no torch.

The two officers slid through the window at the ready, while others remained outside.

John was right. I had to be the one to go down and try to

disarm Biggs if he was there with Syd. John sounded sure. *What if I'd waited too long?* Surprising Biggs would not be a good plan. My breathing came quicker so I sucked in acrid air, set foot on the first step and strained to see.

I called out to the dark, "Axel? Are you there?" I hoped he couldn't hear my heartbeat against the silence that followed. "It's Glory." *He knows that, stupid.* I took a couple more steps and one creaked, nearly sending me off the edge. "I...I wanted to talk with you."

"Come down, Glory," Biggs called calmly, firmly.

Adrenalin flushed throughout my body at the resonance in his voice.

"Al...All right. I've never seen your basement. It's rather dark with no power." I descended, holding to the one-sided stair rail. "Syd's told me some...about it. Is she with you?" Trying to sound cheery didn't work for me.

"Yes," he answered.

"I'm here, Mum. Come on down." She sounded small and far away.

"Syd." I sucked in a hard breath at the sound of her voice and tried keeping the panic out of mine. At least she was alive, not that I would make Axel out a murderer. He had no motive to hurt Syd, surely. "I'm trying, lamb."

I stopped at the bottom to get my bearings. "We...we missed you for Christmas, Axel." There was a tiny window up top allowing a small rectangle of light, but it took a while for my eyes to adjust. Now would have been his invitation to jump me if that's what he planned. As shapes appeared, I saw a finished basement like others. There was no sign of foul play. "Where were you yesterday?"

Something moved. I hoped it wasn't a rat. If it was a rat, I'd never had one rub against my leg before. It was a cat; the poor beast shied away when I reached to pat it.

"I didn't know you had a cat," I said.

"That's Grimalken, Mum. I've told you about him."

"Come join us, Glory," Biggs coaxed. "We're preparing for a big surprise."

"Oh? What kind of surprise?" I braced myself at the bottom as the two figures began to form against the stone wall; they sat next one another on straight chairs. *I'll pass on another surprise just now, thank you.*

"Can I tell her, Biggs?" Syd asked. She sounded happy—excited actually. But the silence between sentences was grim.

He looked at his pocket watch. "Now would be good." Biggs stood. In the dim light and beneath low ceilings, he appeared seven feet tall. He walked toward a desk.

I stepped down on the hard basement floor. I wanted to run to Syd but held back. As light came to me, I made out more details. There was the strange glove line-up she'd described. A disciplined row representing Biggs' anxious history. One set of bobbins was empty. Then I saw he wore a pair. His grip lay open on a small table. He'd been packing. Syd sat in her good winter coat and hat, a small case at her feet.

Syd piped up, "Biggs is taking us all on a trip! To Whitehaven at the coast and maybe on to the Isle of Man! Isn't that exciting?" She stood in her exuberance. Biggs watched her. "I wrote Pop about it just this morning but I didn't expect he'd make it."

"She wrote her pop. Isn't that dear?" Biggs opened the desk drawer. "Since he's supposed to be dead?"

"Yes, but he isn't," Syd reminded. "He'll be coming any day now."

I had to keep pretending. I couldn't even tell her about John. "Why, a trip. How wonderful." I looked at Biggs who appeared to be fingering something. "But, who will mind shop if I go away?" I wanted to keep myself between Biggs and the stairway but eased toward Syd.

The floorboards creaked overhead. Biggs' attention went to the ceiling.

"Are you expecting someone else?" I asked.

"No. We're leaving on that train so I don't have time for chit chat." He closed the grip and reached for his coat and hat.

"But Mum's not packed," Syd was alarmed. "I thought we weren't to leave until the 6:10. That's what you said." She looked at me.

"It's okay, lamb. We'll work things out," I replied calmly.

He put down his coat. "I didn't count on you showing up just now. Your presence here complicates things." Biggs paced in the dank confines. He rubbed his head and seemed confused. "But, since the fates aligned things this way, I won't contradict them. I strongly suggest you come with me now. Should you cooperate, I'll let Syd go and you can deliver the case instead." I saw fear in his eyes.

"What?" Syd protested. "That wasn't our plan. What do you mean? Deliver what case?"

"It was my plan, Syd dear." He withdrew a German handgun from the drawer and looked at it. He stroked the barrel. "This was Uncle Gustav's." He looked at me. "It shoots. Just missed a raven with it a few days ago. Blasted a few feathers." He chuckled. "The bugger got off." Syd couldn't see that he aimed the barrel at her head.

"Natty?" Syd looked as though she would cry, and I stifled a scream.

"I'll go with you!" I told him quickly. "Only, please don't… don't do anything for which you'll be sorry, Axel." I tried to calm Syd while hiding my own panic. "Biggs wouldn't shoot Natty, love." I looked in his eyes. "You wouldn't hurt something so helpless and innocent. Would you?"

He moved over and put an arm around Syd's shoulders, still holding the gun. "But this bird had a little message in a tube on his leg. I was able to retrieve it," Biggs said. He rubbed her shoulder. "Wonder how long that bit of mischief had been going on?"

"It was Natty!" Syd became angry. "Did you take Pop's letter too?"

"Be quiet, Syd!" I urged her. "Please, be quiet. As Axel and I work this out."

Biggs answered, "Pop's letter? Why, Syd you nearly ruined our surprise."

Grimalken leaped to a high bookcase and made me start. Biggs whipped the gun round as if to shoot it, but held off.

I spoke slowly, deliberately. "All right. Well, I know nothing about a letter, but if we're going to make that train, it's time." My heart shook my chest. I hoped to follow them out where the officers would be waiting, but I had no way of alerting them to the gun. I saw Axel bury it in his coat pocket. We were hostages. Unless, I could convince him otherwise.

"But, I don't want Mum to go without Claire and me," Syd said. She took off her hat and sat back down. "Not if everyone isn't coming."

"But it isn't up to you!" Biggs yelled, pulling the firearm once more, and my little girl saw that she was the target.

Syd let out a scream. "Mr. Biggs, what's wrong?"

"Syd, darling, be still! Axel, please, it was a good idea you had about letting her go and taking me instead. I'll go with you now, but give me the gun." I held out my hand that shook.

"Your mummy loves you, Sydney. Sometimes it wasn't easy for me to love my Mutti. She's gone, you know. But this is my chance to do something important for Germany to make her proud. Then, she will approve of me and love me." His dark eyes glistened. "Maybe she'll see what a strong and useful man I have become." He sat. He held the pistol carelessly. "She might see me. Do you think so?"

I couldn't explain what happened next—if it was just happening to me or if the others sensed it, but calm entered the room. I was not afraid of the spirit, if that's what it was, or of Axel any longer. Playing low and sweet in my head, I heard the strains of the bedtime song Axel had taught Syd; I began to hum it. Then I sang the words softly. I knew it was odd of me just then, but it came natural to sing the haunting refrain, first in German, then English.

"Guter mond du ghest stille durch sterben abendwolken hin. Dear moon, you go so quietly through the evening clouds…"

Biggs had been staring at the floor. He slowly turned to me. "You know that lullaby?"

"Syd taught me. It's lovely. *…deines schopfers wiser wille hieb auf jene bahn dich zieh'n. The wise will of your Creator directs you in your course."* Syd looked at me as if I'd gone off. I smiled and motioned for her to join me. Her clear, sweet voice chastened the dark, joining mine as she kept a wary eye on Biggs.

He stood and placed the gun in the drawer. Holding his head, he gazed out the tiny window.

"They know, Mutti," he said.

The train pulled out as I sang the last bit in English.

"Kindly shine for the weary one in the quiet little room. And your light will shine peace into the oppressed heart."

We didn't hear the officers come down. They looked at one another and at me with their weapons drawn. But they wouldn't need them. Syd ran to me, and I closed my eyes, holding her tightly while they put handcuffs on Axel Biggs, who went quietly.

- 41 -

GLORY

Syd did not know her pop had returned. She seemed blue since our return home. In fact, we had each lost a close friend--traitor or crazy man, he was no longer the man we thought we knew. But I had John, and she would have him soon.

John hatched a plan for their reunion that required an audience. We were all wise, except dear Syd. Claire and Liam, Eunice and Roger, and I became spectators for the Stone reunion stage.

We'd discussed Axel Biggs, and doubtless, the conversation would continue for as long as Eunice's tonsils held out. She commented, "You know his mum was a odd bird. He must've taken after her. The Mr. was a right nice fellow as far as I could tell, quiet and mannerly." We agreed.

A loud knock at the door and we all took notice by varying degrees. No one moved, though eyes darted to one another and some stifled a smile.

Syd looked around and when nobody went, said, "I'll go."

"Wonder who would be out on a night like this?" Liam asked a bit louder than normal.

Claire answered, "Only farmers and vets I know of." They glanced at each other.

Syd looked out the door window. "It's Mr. Pickering and Mr. Smyth, Mum." Syd had met them after Biggs' arrest but John had been absent by design. He didn't want their reunion to happen amid the chaos of a sad situation as it had with Claire and me.

"Well, let them in," I said.

She opened the door. They stood dripping in waterproofs. "Milton." I greeted them. "And Fenwick. How good of you to join us." I went for two more glasses. "I hope you're up for some brandy and interrogation, in that order." Syd had widened the opening but they stood.

"Glory, love, we met this farmer in such a pitiful state up road, we thought we'd direct the poor blighter here to you. He's looking for a vetnery." Milton wore his half smirk as he motioned stiffly toward a shadowy figure in dark rain gear. "Says he has a, what was it old chap, a...a...heifer with blocked teat?"

Fenwick turned round and faked a cough to hide his sniggering.

"Aye. That's it," the farmer answered in a gravelly voice, his hat pulled down.

"Come on in. It's cold." Syd shivered and motioned to them.

The three fakers entered, dripping over my entryway.

"I'm afraid my husband was the veterinarian in these parts. But my daughter, Syd here, can unblock a teat right enough. She learned a lot from him."

"I know how though I'm not yet licensed to do such work." She sounded so grown up. "I'd like to help if I can. Here now, let me take your coats and things and you can answer a few questions." They began removing their outerwear. "After you've had some refreshment, I'll follow you back and have a look at her, if you like."

"It's the old cow. She's lonesome," the imitation farmer muttered.

Syd looked at him with fresh interest.

"Lonesome? Well, an animal certainly can react queer-like when they miss someone. I've heard tell of cows withholding their milk in such times."

"This old girl sings Melancholy Baby."

Syd laughed. "Melancholy Baby, huh? I'm not sure I can do aught about that." She peered up at him, trying to get a better look.

"Not even join in a chorus?"

She giggled. "No. Say, what is this?"

"Then I guess the team of Stone and Stone best be back on job!" John threw off his hat.

"Pop!" Syd screamed. "Oh, Pop!" She buried her head into the man she'd believed in and waited for. "I knew it! Oh, Pop. Welcome home."

John scooped her up, and there were no words for the weeping. Then it was I, followed with sniffing and moans from every corner of the living room. Everyone rushed chattering to my door except Roger who just smiled with his attractive lips. I made use of our green kitchen chair and watched, sopping up the joy, which felt golden given all we'd suffered, and I recollected my prayer.

Eunice's eye liner had joined her lip rouge at the corners of her mouth but that didn't keep her from asking between gasps, "Would anyone like some spinach nips about now?"

At least two of us said no.

⸙

Once the team of Stone & Stone had wiped off the first wave of tears and prior to the next, John sat, hub of attention while the lot of us filled the living room trying to gain reason over the darkness that had laid siege to our home. Some of us held hands, some sat on top of another, others leaned their heads on nearby shoulders, and we were a completed jigsaw puzzle. Everyone had questions, so we let John tell his story and poked in our thoughts where able.

"About seven months back, the decoding branch of the Army got the notion I was of best use to them dead. They had intercepted some strange coded messages leaving Rakefoot Station and landing on the Isle of Man. Do you remember Mavis Cartwright, Glory, from secondary school? I dated her a while before we met."

"Yes. I remember. Eunice thought maybe the two of you had run off together since Axel told us she was working at Dalemain." I fingered John's ring, making a mental note to place it right back where it belonged, when we were alone.

Eunice clucked at me. "I did not say I thought they'd run off. I simply mentioned it as one of several possibilities when we was writing things down, is all." She lowered her eye crescents at me.

"So, Biggs knew she was there?" John resumed. "Anyway, turns out Mavis was a top notch decoder at Bletchley Park and transferred closer to home at Dalemain after war ended. The commander there had her take a look at the odd messages and sure enough, she recognized that old code Axel and I made up." He filled his pipe with a fresh poke. "Glory, you might recall back at school how we had fun with it at parties—impressing the girls and frustrating everyone else." He winked at me. "Biggs was able to send and receive simple telegraph messages about track conditions and car goods and lace them with logistical information concerning the escape they planned for Klaus Fuchs, friend of Biggs who was suspected of selling secrets to the Russians. Fuchs had been placed in an internment camp in Peel. They asked if I was willing to help nail down old Biggs for his part. After a fair amount of coercion, I finally agreed. So, I left the coal mines and joined the Special Operations Executive at Dalemain."

"I knew it!" Syd announced. "Were there other reasons why the Army picked on Mr. Biggs?"

"That was more than enough. Syd girl, try to understand. They had reasons for suspecting him of espionage for some time, and I was one of the few people around who knew him well—his habits and mannerisms. He doesn't have any friends I know of, except you. Axel Biggs and Klaus Fuchs have been chums since boyhood when Biggs' mum worked as a servant at Dalemain House before it was converted for war purposes. The Army also uncovered Minna Biggs, when she was still Minna Gehleg, working underground for Abwher, the German spy organization.

Mavis told the commander we were schoolmates and about the code she recognized. Biggs taught our code to Fuchs for future subversive plans, and I was able to decode Biggs' plan to free Fuchs from the Peveril internment camp on the Isle of Man." John looked satisfied with himself. It made him feel of greater use to his country to be used, for us all to be used, in this fashion by the Army. "I believe his plan for our Syd girl was simply one of hostage and to appear less suspicious in his dealings once he arrived there."

"Simply?" I couldn't help say. They'd asked, and he'd agreed. I looked at the familiar way his upper lip curled to the left when he grinned. I'd forgotten that. *Had his eyes lost their shine?* Simply.

John patted my arm and continued. "The only way the Army felt I could go undercover effectively was for everyone to believe I was dead, especially Biggs. If he were to know I was around, he'd know I was too close for comfort as I was the only other one who knew the code. Unfortunately, it was necessary for my family to believe I'd passed on to my reward as well. We couldn't risk anyone letting it slip in any way that they'd seen me or that I was still alive. Only then would Biggs feel at liberty to carry on." John reached out and stroked my hair and chin, then pulled on his pipe. I closed my eyes and inhaled.

"I nearly made a bollocks of it then," Syd said. "I told him you were still alive."

"Yes, but by the time he began doubting, we had all the evidence we needed, and that's when I knew you might be in danger and had to break cover."

Eunice zoomed in as soon as John took a breath. "Glory and

I dug up your coffin yesterday. We found the granite hunks they used." She shoved at Roger who had begun snoring.

John looked at the rug and shook his head. "I'm still amazed you two did that. Digging up that coffin had to have been hard work. I suppose my clues led you to that end eventually."

"Yes, the clues," I said, "and also the fact that Army never did issue a death certificate, and when Eunice and I visited Carlisle and came before the train board to find out more about it, no one knew a blasted thing." I covered my face and John put his arm around me.

"The train board? Obviously, I have a lot to learn as well. My poor Glory." John hugged my shoulders.

I didn't want to go casting gloom on the evening, but all I'd been through began heating up my insides like a boiling vat of lye about to spill over. I thought it might come roaring out in one major anger burst. My breathing came faster and so did tears as I looked around at everyone's faces who were all fixed on John, but I managed somehow to keep a lid on the pot.

"It was clever of them to use granite, wasn't it?" I spoke. "It took everything I had to go that far."

"Yes, I'm sure." he continued. "Authorities used the granite to replicate the heft of my body when it was carried. The coffin Biggs ordered arrived with the granite (me) already inside. Since they chose a train as the cause of death, the remains would have been unrecognizable and therefore, wrapped so there was little concern anyone would ask to see the body."

"Vicar Cavendish has a surprise coming, unless he's in on it as well," I said.

"Yes." John stirred up a nice blaze in the fireplace. It snapped and sparked as he held his pipe and watched the flames. "I'll go to them soon. We'll have to nullify the gravesite and remove the so-called remains." He chuckled but I couldn't share the humor.

John had made a choice. Ironically, he said, "I want you all to know, especially you, Glory, that I argued against fooling everyone with the lie, but Army Intelligence always commands the last word."

Claire added, "With Syd being so sure you were alive. I wanted to believe and was afraid; wondering pretty nigh drove me to the brink more than once." She looked at Liam. "But, Syd, what I want to know is how you were so certain, and what about this letter business between you and Dad using Natty? Why didn't you tell Mum and me everything?"

Syd walked over and sat next me. "I couldn't tell you everything because I didn't know everything. When Natty flew in and croaked, 'Dalemain,' that started me thinking. Only Pop and I trained him to talk and I knew I didn't teach him that. I thought possibly Pop was involved with something top secret close by. Other times I thought I was going balmy because I just wanted him alive. But mostly, I believed and wanted to give you and Claire hopes. Then later, Natty said 'Merry CHRIST-mas!' just like Pop said it, and I thought Pop was coming for Christmas." She leaned over on John and took his hand. "When you didn't show, I began doubting again."

Claire interjected, "Oh, so you didn't teach him that? He said that to me one afternoon. It was eerie."

"No. I didn't," Syd answered.

"I taught Natty that over time," John picked up. That was another clue meant to encourage without giving the game away. Any road, I knew the Army used carrier pigeons and other birds during wartime and they were reliable message carriers. I got the idea of using Natty same way since he often flew to see me at Dalemain, only I couldn't chance sending messages—only receive them. I procured a message capsule, fastened it to Natty's leg and sent him off. I knew Syd was bright enough and would put something in that capsule, though perhaps not getting the connection to whom it was going, at the first. Imagine my surprise first time he showed up with a full-on letter from home." He ruffled her hair.

"But, Syd, you told me in the loft that an angel or God had told you Pop was alive," I reminded her.

She looked sheepish. "Well, I didn't feel as if I could say that a bird told me. I couldn't risk what were just guesses at that point and possibly give Pop away in the bargain. I figured that if it was all from him, he was lying low for good reason. And too, I wanted to give you real hope and thought it would carry more clout that way. Sorry, Mum, but you and Claire seemed to lose faith. I thought that would give it a boost."

Liam asked, "Who was it that laid the bag of gifts by the door?"

"Oh, that was tricky, John explained. "I'd bought the gifts early for Christmas while working in Liverpool and kept them with me all that time. I bribed a fellow SOE to come round late Christmas Eve. He must have just left when you showed, Liam." He continued, "Natty brought snippets of your hair for me, Claire. I knew it was yours by the gold highlights. It brought me great comfort." He pulled out his billfold. "Here it is. I kept it with me."

Claire teared up. "I wanted to throttle that blasted bird when he did that." She laughed. "Just shows sometimes there's deeper meaning in trouble. I can look back over the past months and see a peck of good that come from these hard times." She admired her engagement ring and kissed Liam's cheek with a resounding smack.

"Likely they'll hang ex-Station Master Biggs," Liam blurted.

"No!" Syd cried out.

"I mean, then again, maybe not so long as he turns over evidence, that is," Liam added to pacify.

I realized Syd was possibly the truest friend Biggs ever had yet he never realized it. She likely knew him best and cared for him best, and I doubted he appreciated her loyalty except to use for his own purpose. He would have time for insights to dawn.

"He's only been hurt by those who should have loved him," Syd added.

For a few moments we were silent, to curse or give grace. We owed Syd that much.

The fire snapped and the pups yawned. It grew late, and later. Time sat on a back burner at a simmer. We talked, joked to relieve the weightier subjects and questions that hung in the air like smoke from a gunshot. We got a steady eyeful of one another so that no one would slip out of grasp. At least, that's how it felt to me.

In the weeks and months to follow, I was to have a hard time accepting the way the military had used our family in their game, but I kept mum. After learning the reasons, they fell flimsy on my hearing, considering the risks involved and how little they'd gained. I wondered if they'd used others in the same cruel way. If so, I would be curious as to how those families had coped. It didn't help when we found out later that Fuchs' uranium formulas were incomplete anyhow and, therefore, harmless.

- 42 -
GLORY

John would be the star witness for the smuggling conspiracy since he was the one responsible for nearly all evidence collected over wire between Biggs and his chum, Fuchs. Other persons from Dalemain would offer information concerning Minna Gehlen and her former affiliations with the German Secret Service organization, Abwehr.

I looked forward to a trip to Old Bailey in London to witness justice in action, something that would have scared the daylights out of me before. Eunice told me they'd taken Biggs' belongings from his house, including his glove alignment to obtain forensic evidence. I was adding to my vocabulary daily but did puzzle over why they would need that type of evidence. I found it ironic that the detectives also wore gloves in doing so and that theirs were white.

At Eunice's dogged insistence, the prosecutor had the note from Trudy analyzed. A handwriting expert from Liverpool studied it. Never knew they had such jobs. He said conclusively that

Biggs wrote it. He said he could tell by the dots on the i's, extra large loops of the l's and f's—among other things. I figured he'd tried to save face. It would all be in the court record.

Eunice reasoned that she and Roger would go along to help 'restore hope to London.' In other words, they planned to go on holiday and bother their children however long the trial took.

Winnie Brown, organist and mystery maven, was right about her suspicion of Biggs keeping a diary. They found it while cleaning out that hole of his, and there were several incriminating entries concerning his secret sharing and ties to Fuchs. He'd implicated himself, Milton said. We'd learned two pages were absent.

As disturbed a man as Biggs was, I would never tell anyone, except Syd maybe, that my heart pitied him. I knew folks made their choices, but he'd suffered a miserable childhood with that sick mother of his and him being the only child to bully.

No one, not even John, seemed to understand the serious reality that I had been Biggs' dangling carrot for nearly six months and there never had been any communications twixt him and the railroad board concerning my shop. He'd made that part up. The Army used me and so did Axel Biggs. One in the name of freedom, but both for control.

I was grateful to the bird, Natty, but thought John and Syd had gone a mite far in conspiring to promote him to house pet. And so it was. We soon learned where to look first for missing items. Syd, lover of puns, dubbed him the Nat Burglar. He was still a free creature and often chose the out of doors. Syd reckoned she'd have to chance bullets for liberty's sake.

When I finally got John to myself under cover—not above a good pun myself—we had catching up to do. We laughed like old times and made regular use of the scarf and the nighty Eunice gave me. Some pleasures are like riding a bicycle—it all comes back. I caught him up on news about my antique shop, and laughed over how old Pete tried to teach me butchering. I was relieved when

John agreed that keeping shop would give us the extra funds we'd need to pack Syd off to university one day. I'd become a woman of commerce with big ideas for Stone Revival. It would be interesting to see how the new station master would take to it. We hadn't met him. I'd heard he was a young man from Bath.

I broke the news as gently as possible to John about Claire and Albert Rand. Judging from John's reaction, I thought it best Albert stay clean away for his health.

We heard voices from the girls' room well past midnight. I thought after such a trying day, they would have dropped off quick-like. Instead, the day's excitement had served to energize Milton and Wicky. It was late following all the talk, and what with the nasty weather and brandy consumption, John and I insisted the two stay on. Claire, Syd and Liam were happy to sack out in the front room with our pets wedged like mortar between them.

❧

Life to the Stones became more relevant for a stretch. We'd learned each moment was a treasure, but we couldn't maintain our gratefulness. That's when we appreciated grace most.

June came. Claire and Liam wed in the garden at Crosthwaite. I cut white roses and John gave the bride away, but not without a qualifier. He'd turned to her and said, 'I'll never completely give you away, with respect to Liam. Whenever you need to talk, I'm here. Claire, you are the beautiful angel girl I love.'

- 43 -

SYD

23 January 1946

Dear Diary,

Today I'm thirteen. I feel older with this one. Mum's going to take me to Carlisle for a new dress. I will wear it to the St. Valentine's dance at school that Benjamin Eisenberg asked me to.

He's one of the poor Jewish boys who lost his parents in one of Hitler's hateful camps. Benjamin and his sister, Minia, came to live with Myron and June Shiverson. They're a jolly lot now. Ben loves animals too. He and Minia do not eat pork—a fact over which Old Pete regularly shakes his head.

It's more than grand to be back on calls with Pop. And I bring my own valise, just in case Pop forgets an instrument. It has happened.

The most exciting news is that my beautiful sis has asked me to be the Maid of Honor at her and Liam's wedding in June. I shall be proud to stand next her as witness to the happy event. I'm just hoping like anything Aunt Eunice doesn't try to finagle her way into doing my hair and make-up. Surely, Claire will not allow a calamity such as that to mar the day.

Lately, Aunt Eunice is busying herself writing jingles why she should be the next Lux soap girl. It's a contest they're having. The prize is a complete forty-two piece Googie Withers make-up kit and trip for two via a flight aboard the BOAC to the States—New York City then to Las Vegas is the name of the town, I think. It's in the wild west. She wants that trip more than anything, as she wants to meet up with Randolph Scott, the movie star, and is working daily toward the goal.

Dear diary, I have a grave confession. And that will serve as a dark pun when you read the rest. It's about Biggs. I hardly know where to begin but I know I must or I shall burst. I have no right to this information since I obtained same by being a dirty reader of another's diary, a low-down trick, as I well know.

I was feeding Grimalkin and by myself in his basement quarters as Biggs had gone upstairs to fetch us a snack. I noticed the journal when I was looking over his book selections. It was way on the bottom with no title on the spine so I got curious and pulled it out. The fact that a grown man kept one was irresistible.

By now, the authorities have read it because Mum said they found Biggs' diary with his things even though I put it back carefully, minus two pages, just where I found it.

The entry to which I refer is from 2 September from two autumns hence. It seems that poor Mr. Biggs had it much worse off than I thought with his mum. She is gone now and one cannot arrest a corpse.

Biggs' wife, Trudy, did not run off. She is most certainly dead. I'm not sure how Biggs' mum would have been strong enough to kill her since Mutti was quite frail for some time before she went. The facts were unclear. Some things I had to reason together by taking into account Mutti's violent way toward her only son.

Biggs wrote how he "dug a deep hole in woods behind station." That line gave me shivers. I neatly tore out two pages describing his feelings about

Trudi and his mum and put them in a safe place. I know Biggs would do anything to protect his Mutti. He loved her beyond all reason.

Nobody knows the whereabouts of their son, and Trudy is at rest in a shady setting. That Axel Biggs is a son of a deceased murderess no one need know. Hasn't he had trouble enough? I don't think he's well. In the head, I mean.

I have become quite reliable at keeping secrets.

Signing off for now,

Syd

THE END

Acknowledgements

Every author who writes acknowledgements realizes that the gratitude means infinitely more to her than the reader. But we must include them, the many dear souls who lent a heart or hand in some way, because they live throughout the pages. Writing would be an even lonelier road without them. They're an invisible audience, cheering us on late at night. Though there are many friends and family members who encouraged me from the start and remained steadfast in their belief in me, the following served active duty.

First is editor and writer, Lynn Leissler, who read *Stone Revival* in all its iterations so many times she must have it about memorized by now. Not only is Lynn a tireless editor, but a trusted and valued friend who poked and prodded at all the right times and places.

Award-winning fine artist, Lane Hall, is always there for me. His unflagging friendship, tireless support and cheerleading from the sidelines has meant the world. Hall is the logo artist for Aunt Sophie's Press.

Readers include Denise Fleming, Susan Gmur, Charlotte

Kline, my daughter--Emily Overstreet, author--Ann Shorey, and Barbara Young, who was raised in the Lake District and claimed she could not put *Stone Revival* down, bless her. Barbara also added priceless bits of authenticity to details in the lifestyle of Lakes families.

A special thank-you to Janis Rubus, whose tireless and practical encouragement always seemed to come at the right time, whether by note in the mail or catching me at church to praise my latest column. Her teacher's heart helps me see the larger purpose in everything I write. She told me it was time.

My thanks to artist, musician, and graphic designer, Ted Killian, for my fabulous cover design. His professionalism and attention to detail helped me understand how valuable the cover is as a marketing tool.

Thank you to Chrissy Hobbs of Indie Publishing Group for her professionalism in formatting *Stone Revival*. Her prompt communications and easy-to-understand instructions made the process pleasant and worry-free.

Thank you to my sister, Nancy Wolkis, who helped teach me to read before I started school. I remember sitting with her as she helped me sound out the hard words.

Most of all, I thank Mom and Dad, Wilma and Myron Dover. Mama instilled in me the value of books, a deep love of reading, and the power of words. She read to me every day and walked with me to gather armloads of books from the library. Dad worked hard for our family and made her staying home possible. I look forward to the reunion.

Made in the USA
Monee, IL
24 July 2021